W9-BNT-378

A TIME TO STAND

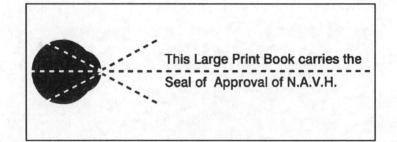

A TIME TO STAND

ROBERT WHITLOW

THORNDIKE PRESS
A part of Gale, a Cengage Company

Farmington Hills, Mich • San Francisco • New York • Waterville, Maine
Meriden, Conn • Mason, Ohio • Chicago

Thorndike Press, a part of Gale, a Cengage Company.

Thorndike Press® Large Print Christian Mystery.
The text of this Large Print edition is unabridged.
Other aspects of the book may vary from the original edition.
Set in 16 pt. Plantin.

LIBRARY OF CONGRESS CIP DATA ON FILE.
CATALOGUING IN PUBLICATION FOR THIS BOOK
IS AVAILABLE FROM THE LIBRARY OF CONGRESS

ISBN-13: 978-1-4328-4455-4 (hardcover)
ISBN-10: 1-4328-4455-5 (hardcover)

Published in 2017 by arrangement with Thomas Nelson, Inc., a division of HarperCollins Christian Publishing, Inc.

Printed in the United States of America
1 2 3 4 5 6 7 21 20 19 18 17

To everyone willing to take a stand for racial reconciliation and unity founded on the love of God and the power of the gospel of Jesus Christ

"There is neither Jew nor Gentile, neither slave nor free, nor is there male and female, for you are all one in Christ Jesus."

— GALATIANS 3:28

PROLOGUE

The cornstalks were waist high, poised for the explosion of growth that would bring them to head-high maturity under the smiling Georgia sun. Six men, hoes in hand, reached the end of their rows with choreographed efficiency. The corn stretched out over three hundred yards in every direction. Rooting out the weeds that competed for nutrients was the work of several days.

"Dinnertime!" called out the tall, angular man who served as informal field boss, a carryover from his role in the days before a man named Lincoln in a faraway place called Washington, DC, declared they were free.

The men placed their hoes on their shoulders and made their way to the cluster of shade trees surrounding the freshwater spring at the edge of the field. The land had once been part of the large farm where several of them worked without wages. The soldiers in blue uniforms who occupied the center of Campbellton for over a year after the fighting stopped had put an end to that arrangement. Now the men labored as sharecroppers. The landowner, Harold Grayson III, provided the mules, plows, seed, and guano fertilizer necessary to farm the land in return for a healthy percentage of the profits when the crop made it to market. Accustomed to working together for decades, the men banded together for the common good. The arrangement had worked well three out of the past five years. The other two years had put them in debt. Mr. Grayson cut the debt in half.

Raphael, wearing a homespun shirt and loose-fitting trousers secured with a piece of cotton twine, removed the straw hat from his head and wiped his dark brow with a red kerchief. The men sat down on the grass and shared a battered tin cup to drink cool water from a small spring that had been marked and protected by a ring of stones. Nash County had many natural springs that were created when subterranean rivers bubbled to the surface.

"Mr. Rafe," said the youngest of the black men, a broad-shouldered nineteen-year-old. "Has the Lord told you if it's gonna rain? If it does in the next week or so, this corn will be shooting up to the moon."

"I'm still praying on that one, James," their leader replied.

"While you're talkin' to the Lord, tell him to make it rain on our land and not on Master Benfield's farm," said Lanny, another one of the laborers.

Francis Benfield had earned the reputation of being the cruelest slave owner within fifty miles of Campbellton. Lanny bore scars on his back from a whipping he'd received when he was fifteen years old.

"The rain falls on the just and the unjust, Lanny," Rafe replied. "In his mercy, God doesn't give any of us what we deserve. And he's told me to be a-praying for all of Nash County, black or white, rich or poor."

"Here comes dinner," said one of the other men.

Above a slight rise at the edge of the field came two teenage girls and a young boy. The girls carried straw baskets, and the boy had an earthen jug in his right hand with his left hand beneath it for added support.

"Don't be droppin' that!" called out Lanny.

"No, sir," replied the boy as he came closer.

Rafe was father to the boy and the older of the two girls. The young people reached

11

the men reclining on the grass beside the spring. The boy handed the jug to his father, who tipped it back and took a long drink.

"Still cool," Rafe announced, wiping the white line of buttermilk from his upper lip.

He passed the jug to the man beside him. Each man took a long drink while the girls laid sticks of baked cornpone in a pile on a ground cloth. Beside the cornmeal dinner, they dished out a large mound of soft, salty butter onto an earthenware plate. The men dipped the cornpone into the butter and then washed it down with the rest of the buttermilk and more freshwater from the spring.

"Eat, young'uns," said Rafe.

"Mama and Missus Kate fed us before we left the house," said Sally Ann, who was Rafe's slender, bright-eyed daughter.

"But I'm still hungry," said Moses. "That jug was extra heavy today."

James dipped a stick of cornpone into the butter and handed it to Moses, who quickly took a big bite. James was sitting as close to Sally Ann as Rafe would allow.

"What do you say?" Rafe asked his son.

"Thank you, Lord Jesus," Moses mumbled, his mouth full. "And you, James."

After he finished eating his corn bread, Moses began to pick tiny yellow honeysuckle blossoms and squeeze out drops of juice. Sally Ann sat with her bare feet beneath her and her hands folded on her faded yellow dress. James dipped the tin cup into the spring and held it out to her. Their fingers touched slightly when she took it from his hand. Rafe saw it and smiled.

"James, did you hear what the preacher said on Sunday about the sins of the fathers landing on their children to the third and fourth generations of people?" he asked.

Wide-eyed, James cleared his throat. "Yes, sir. I did hear him say that."

Lanny spoke up. "Mr. Benfield's younger son, Frederick, died of pox when he was ten years old, and his older boy, Morgan, got hisself shot and killed somewhere up north during the war. And his daughter got left at the altar and is sitting there alone without a husband in that big house."

"That's all in God's hands for his choosing," Rafe said, keeping his eyes on James. "But do you remember what the preacher said about the children of the righteous?"

"I think so," James said, cutting his eyes toward Sally Ann. "But I can't recollect it just this minute."

"He said the Lord's blessing will run for a thousand generations on them that love him and obey his commandments," Sally Ann said.

"That's a long time, ain't it?" Rafe asked.

"Yes, Mr. Rafe, it sure is."

The air around the spring grew extra still. The men and the young people, even Moses, fixed their eyes on Rafe. And something bubbled up inside Rafe as real as the water in the nearby pool.

"Everything we do, and believe, and pray doesn't stop when the breath leaves out of our bodies and they lay us in the ground," he said. "It travels down through time until everybody but the Lord loses sight of it."

ONE

Stanley Jackson watched the six young men milling around in front of the drink coolers at the Westside Quik Mart. The convenience store clerk often worked the third shift alone. At six foot three and 245 pounds, he was only ten pounds heavier than when he'd wreaked havoc as a defensive lineman for the Campbellton High Colonels. Stan had received scholarship offers from a handful of small colleges, but he'd injured his right knee in a motorcycle wreck the summer after graduating from high school, and the opportunity to play football in return for a free education evaporated like the mist on a May morning in Georgia.

The store clerk glanced up at the surveillance camera that was aimed at the back of the store. The video feed linked directly to the security company headquarters in Atlanta. The unblinking eyes of the cameras recorded a twenty-four-hour-a-day reality

15

show boring enough to cure insomnia. There were two cameras inside the store and one outside. The camera that was supposed to cover the cash register hadn't worked in over a month.

Stan recognized two of the teenagers: Deshaun Hamlin, a quick and agile point guard on the high school basketball team; and Greg Ott, a regular customer who often came into the store with his stepmother. The other young men were strangers. One of the strangers opened the door of the cooler and took out a thirty-ounce bottle of malt liquor.

"You have to be twenty-one to buy beer!" Stan called out. "And that means a valid ID!"

Deshaun left the group and placed a plastic bottle filled with orange sports drink on the counter in front of the cash register.

"What you up to, Deshaun?" Stan asked. "I haven't seen you down at the rec center recently."

"I'm trying out for a summer league AAU team next month if my left shoulder is healed up by then," he said.

"What happened to your shoulder?" Stan asked.

"Dislocated it going up for a rebound a couple of weeks ago. Worst injury I've had since I broke my arm when I was a kid."

"You're still a kid," Stan answered with a smile. "And I can dunk on you anytime I want to."

"Only if I didn't steal the ball first," Deshaun replied. "Wait a second. I need to pick up a snack for my grandmother."

Deshaun stepped over to the nut rack. The other four young men had scattered, making it impossible for Stan to keep an eye on what they were doing. The oldest of the strangers approached with the bottle of malt liquor. Tall and lanky with a small goatee, he appeared to be in his midtwenties. He placed the alcohol on the counter with a five-dollar bill beside it.

"Ring it up," he said in a slow, deep voice. "You can keep the change."

"That's not how it works," Stan replied. "You show me an ID, and you keep the change."

Stan glanced past the man as two of the other teenagers came together in front of the meat snacks. Petty shoplifting was a constant problem at the store, and the expensive meat products were a popular item to steal. The man at the cash register took a battered wallet from the rear pocket of his jeans and fumbled through it. Stan could see a thick stack of twenty-dollar bills.

17

"Dude, I must have left it at Greg's house," he said. "We walked over here together. That's where my car is parked."

Greg Ott came over to the counter. "He's cool, Stan," Greg said. "He works for a trucking company hauling freight to Birmingham. He's got his CDL license. You know I wouldn't lie to you."

"Maybe so," Stan replied. "But I still need to see his license if he wants to buy this bottle."

Deshaun returned to pay for his sports drink and a bag of pistachios.

"Let me know when the season starts," Stan said as Deshaun gave him a ten-dollar bill. "I'd like to come watch a game."

"We'll be playing our home games at the Franklin Gym."

"Cool. Did you walk over here?"

"Yeah."

"You'd better get going. A storm is coming."

"Remember, I'm fast," Deshaun replied with a grin. "I can outrun lightning."

"Get outta here," Stan said.

When Deshaun moved out of Stan's line of sight, the clerk saw one of the unfamiliar teenagers slip a pack of premium beef jerky into a pocket of his baggy black pants.

"You have to pay for that!" Stan called out.

"Calm down," the man with the goatee said, raising his hand. "Bring that up here, son. I'll pay for it even if this clown isn't going to sell me anything to drink."

"Watch your mouth," Stan said.

"Listen, brother," the lanky man said with a smile. "Customer service is important."

The teenager placed the beef jerky on the counter and backed away. Deshaun moved toward the door.

"I'm taking off," Deshaun said to Greg. "Will I see you later at my grandma's house?"

"Swing by my place first," Greg replied. "There's something I want to show you."

"Okay."

Stan scanned the package of beef jerky. "That will be $8.29," he said.

"What a rip-off," the stranger replied as he reopened his wallet and placed a crumpled ten-dollar bill on the counter. He picked up the jerky and tossed it to the boy.

"Get, before I make jerky out of you!" he said to the teenager.

Greg and the other three young men left. Stan could see them standing in front of the store, where they huddled on the sidewalk before moving away. Stan touched the bottle of malt liquor.

"Put that back in the cooler where you found it," he said to the man with the goatee.

"That's your job, boss. And make sure you do it soon. It's no good if it isn't ice cold. I'll come back later to pick it up."

"With an ID. And leave your attitude in the parking lot," Stan responded, his temper rising.

Stan opened the cash register so he could count out the change from the purchase of the beef jerky. He picked up a quarter and reached for the smaller coins he needed.

"Don't stop," the man said. "I want it all."

Stan glanced up as the stranger shattered the malt liquor bottle. Amber-colored liquid spewed all over the counter. The man leaned over the counter and slashed the right side of Stan's neck with the jagged remains of the bottle. Blood spurted from the wound.

His eyes wide, Stan reached forward to grab the robber with his left arm, but the man slammed the remains of the bottle into the top of the clerk's hand. Stan cried out in pain and staggered backward. The stranger leaned over the counter and snatched all the twenties, tens, and fives from the drawer. Stan pressed his bleeding hand against the wound on his neck. The room began to spin, and he passed out. As he fell, Stan knocked over a rack of cigarettes behind the counter.

Officer Luke Nelson slowed to a stop as the traffic light turned red. He glanced down at the picture of Jane that he kept on the console when he patrolled alone. The photograph had been taken on a breezy evening at Hilton Head during their honeymoon. Wearing a peach-colored sundress, Jane stood barefoot in the sand. Her blond hair swirled away from her face, and her blue eyes shone with new love and the promise of future joy. When Luke glanced at the picture it also reminded him that Jane would be praying for him.

Luke moved the seat of the new police cruiser so that his feet comfortably rested on the gas and brake pedals. The vehicle still had a new-car smell, and Luke took in a deep breath. He was surprised when the chief offered to let him use the car for the night. As the city of Campbellton's newest officer, Luke usually drove a car whose next destination was the auto auction barn on Highway 29 south of town.

The state-of-the-art vehicle was equipped with an onboard computer and a dash camera, but Luke hadn't received the password for the computer, which controlled the camera. When he radioed the third-shift dispatcher for the code, she curtly informed him that she didn't know it, and he'd have to call the chief at home. Disturbing Chief Lockhart on a Saturday night wasn't on Luke's agenda for the evening.

Five feet ten inches tall and in good physical condition, Luke adjusted the rearview mirror slightly to the right. As he did, he saw the reflection of his closely cut brown hair, brown eyes, and square jaw softened by a dimple to the left side of his mouth. After high school, Luke had attended a community college where he majored in criminal justice. He paid the rent and bought groceries by driving a forklift on third shift at a warehouse. Upon graduation, he worked three years as a private security guard at a shopping mall before landing a job with the Atlanta Police Department. Initially thrilled with a real job in law enforcement, Luke was thrown into a high-stress environment that quickly became an emotionally draining grind. He began looking for a job in a suburban area. Campbellton was a small town, not suburbia, but when a position opened up, Jane encouraged him to accept it. The salary was much less than what Luke had earned in downtown Atlanta, but with their first child on the way, Luke gave in to his pregnant wife's wishes. Now, after a year and a half on the job, he was glad he'd listened to her.

Settling in with the Campbellton Police Department, Luke began to thrive. He loved his job. Over the past eighteen months, he'd written more traffic tickets than any other officer on the force. He was never late for work, and before baby Ashley's arrival, he was always the first man to volunteer for extra duty. His long-term goal was to become a sergeant, and Chief Lockhart had recently authorized Luke's attendance at a three-week law enforcement management program in Orlando. The voice of the third-shift dispatcher came over the radio, interrupting Luke's thoughts.

"All units respond to a possible 211 at the Westside Quik Mart. Fire and medic are in transit."

A 211 meant an armed robbery. Armed robberies were an every-week occurrence in Atlanta, but this was the first 211 call Luke had received since moving to Campbellton. His mind flashed back to tense situations he'd experienced in the inner city, and he transitioned into high-alert mode. His heart started beating faster.

There were three patrol cars on duty. Luke

was the farthest away from the convenience store. He turned on his siren and blue lights and pressed down on the accelerator. At this time of night, the few cars in his path pulled over as he sped past. The female dispatcher's voice again came over the radio.

"Be advised, primary suspects in the 211 are two young black males, Gregory Ott and Deshaun Hamlin; both live on East Nixon Street."

In addition to the city police, two Nash County Sheriff's Department vehicles were en route to the convenience store location. Luke entered the east part of town. The wind was blowing hard, causing the overhead traffic lights to sway from side to side.

"This is city police car 304," Luke said. "Unless needed at the scene of the 211, I'm requesting permission to go to East Nixon Street."

The dispatcher was silent for a moment. Luke slowed to normal speed as he approached the best place to turn off the highway if given permission to do so.

"10–4, car 304," the dispatcher said. "Proceed to East Nixon Street. Suspects potentially armed and dangerous. Hamlin, age sixteen, is six feet tall and weighs one hundred and sixty-five pounds. No physical description for Ott."

"10–4," Luke replied as his heart rate kicked up even more.

He hoped both the suspects were teenagers. Luke could wrestle to the ground men who outweighed him by seventy-five to a hundred pounds. With youngsters, words often did the job.

He turned onto a side street and debated whether to turn off his flashing blue lights to avoid letting Hamlin or Ott know that an officer was in the area. He chose to keep them on. Reaching the intersection for East Nixon Street, he made a right-hand turn. As he did, Luke flipped off the siren but kept the blue lights flashing. He drove slowly for two blocks. Then, just beyond the glow of a distant streetlight, he saw a figure run across the street. Luke pressed down hard on the accelerator, and the car shot forward another three hundred feet. He slammed on the brakes and pulled close to the curb.

"Dispatch, this is car 304," he said, keeping his voice calm and professional. "I'm in the 400 block of East Nixon Street with a possible sighting of one of the suspects. Request assistance."

"10–4. Will advise."

The dispatcher radioed Bruce Alverez, an officer with fifteen years' prior experience

25

serving on the Miami Police Department. Gruff and prickly, the older officer had moved to Campbellton after going through a nasty divorce. Because he was fluent in Spanish, Alverez was a huge asset in working with the growing Latino community in the area. Luke left his blue lights flashing and stared intently down the street at the spot where the person had crossed the road.

Suddenly, a figure wearing dark clothes appeared in the light of a streetlamp. He was wearing a loose-fitting shirt that was pressed against his body by the stiff breeze. Luke turned on the loudspeaker.

"You! Under the streetlight! Walk forward slowly!"

The figure beneath the light fit the description of the tall, slender suspect. The young man glanced to his right and began jogging toward the police car. Luke pressed the button for the transmitter.

"Slower!" he called out. "Put your hands over your head!"

The teenager put his hands on top of his head but didn't slow down. Luke tensed. The young man glanced again to the side where several houses were closely packed together. Luke couldn't see anyone else in the glow cast by the streetlight or the headlamps of the police car. He opened the door

26

of his vehicle and got out. The gusty wind was blowing directly into his face, and he had to squint. He placed one hand on his service weapon, a Glock 17. A flash of light far to the east signaled the approach of a storm.

"Deshaun Hamlin?" Luke called out when the young man was about 150 feet away.

"Yeah! I'm Deshaun!" the young man replied.

"Where's Ott?" Luke called out.

The young man slowed and turned sideways for a moment. Then he faced Luke and ran faster toward him.

"Don't shoot!" Deshaun cried out.

"Stop!" Luke commanded.

Instead of slowing down, Deshaun ran even faster. Adrenaline coursing through his veins, Luke pulled his weapon from his holster and held it in front of him as he'd done hundreds of times at the firing range. When the young man was about a hundred feet away, he passed through a deep shadow caused by a large tree that blocked the streetlight. Luke saw the teenager stick his right hand in the front pocket of his pants. Hearing a loud *pop,* Luke fired four shots in rapid succession. As the sound shattered the silence of the night, the young man fell to the ground in the middle of the roadway.

Luke began to shake uncontrollably. He managed to return his weapon to his holster. Even patrolling a beat in downtown Atlanta, he'd never had to fire his weapon. The threat of lethal force or the skillful use of his physical skills had always been enough. Hearing the sound of a siren, he turned as a police car, its blue lights flashing, sped around the corner and down the street. Luke's whole torso was now quivering. The car screeched to a halt, and Officer Alverez jumped out of the vehicle and ran past him. Alverez knelt by the body on the pavement and placed his hand on the man's neck, feeling for a carotid artery.

"Did you call for an ambulance?" Alverez yelled.

"No."

"Do it! Now!"

Luke reached through the door of his car and pressed the button on his radio. "We need an ambulance on East Nixon Street!" he shouted.

"What's your status?" the dispatcher demanded.

"Suspect is wounded."

"10–4."

Luke dropped the radio transmitter on the seat of the car. "Ambulance on the way!" he called out to Alverez. "Did you cuff him?"

"Where's the gun?" Alverez called out, turning his head toward Luke.

"Check underneath him! He took it from the front pocket of his pants and fired at me," Luke replied shakily.

A closer lightning strike released a clap of thunder that made Luke jump. He approached Alverez and the robbery suspect. The young man's face was turned away from him. The trembling that had threatened to take over Luke's chest lessened. The teenager made an odd sound. Alverez was applying pressure to a wound on the young man's chest. Luke took out his flashlight and shined it around on the pavement.

"He fired at least one shot," Luke said.

Something glistened on the pavement on the other side of the wounded man. Luke walked around Alverez and squatted down. It was metal. He started to pick it up.

"Leave that for later," Alverez said. "Help me here."

Before Luke could join Alverez, an ambulance came careening onto the street. Within seconds, the paramedics were on their knees beside the unconscious young man. Alverez stood and faced Luke.

"How many shots did you fire?" Alverez asked.

"Uh, I'm not exactly sure. It happened so

fast. Three, four."

Luke checked the chamber of his gun. "Four rounds."

"You hit him with two of them. Get Detective Maxwell on the radio."

Luke returned to the car. "Request the presence of Detective Maxwell on East Nixon Street. Priority one."

"10–4. Will reroute him from the convenience store."

Luke and Alverez stood beside the stretcher as the medics secured Hamlin. A few angry drops of rain began to fall. Luke caught a glimpse of the right side of the young man's head and shuddered. Alverez faced him. In the older officer's hands were a pocketknife, a folded piece of paper, a cell phone, and a half-empty package of beef jerky.

"Is this what you saw?" Alverez asked, holding up the knife. "It was in the front pocket of his pants."

"No, no." Luke shook his head. "He had a gun. I heard a shot."

The medics loaded Hamlin into the ambulance and slammed the doors shut. There was another lightning strike, this one even closer.

"There isn't a gun," Alverez replied over the sound of the approaching storm. He

30

pointed his flashlight at the area on the street where Hamlin had fallen. "The suspect was unarmed."

Luke swallowed. Siren blaring and lights flashing, the ambulance sped away.

"Where's Detective Maxwell?" Alverez asked.

"On his way."

Two

"Call *State v. Larimore,*" Judge Sidney Boswell said, peering over the top of his half-frame glasses. "The Court will now hear the defendant's extraordinary motion for new trial."

Adisa Johnson stood as her client, wearing an orange jumpsuit and bound with arm and leg shackles, shuffled into the courtroom. Leroy Larimore was forty-eight years old; he had slightly greasy black hair, piercing blue eyes, and rock-hard muscles that had been crafted by fourteen years of pumping iron at the Georgia State Prison in Reidsville. Larimore nodded nervously to Adisa, who leaned over to him.

"Remember what we went over last night at the jail," she said in a low voice. "Keep cool. The DNA expert will testify first. When it's your turn, keep your answers short and to the point. Don't add what you think might help. It won't."

"Yeah," Larimore replied and nodded as his eyes darted around the room. "I ain't gonna make the same mistake twice."

Despite multiple coaching sessions, Adisa seriously doubted her client, who had received only an eighth-grade education, would perform well on the witness stand. He looked guilty: refusing to make eye contact when he talked, mumbling instead of speaking clearly, exaggerating when he did speak, and exhibiting a very limited ability to control his temper. If being a poor witness was a crime in the state of Georgia, Leroy Larimore would be sleeping on a cot and washing his hands in a steel sink the size of a mixing bowl for another fifteen years.

Adisa glanced sideways at Mark Kildare, a senior staff attorney with the Fulton County district attorney's office. The small courtroom in downtown Atlanta was Kildare's home turf, not hers.

As a former prosecutor, Adisa was familiar with criminal law, but postconviction relief cases were a niche within a niche. In representing Larimore, she had drawn on experience obtained in law school when she worked on a special postconviction relief project. During the class, she unraveled the intricacies of the ancient doctrine of habeas corpus and federal court oversight of state court criminal proceedings. A brief she helped write resulted in the reversal of a conviction by the Eleventh Circuit Court of Appeals.

The constant confrontations with the dark side of society took a toll on Adisa, and when the opportunity came to land a position as an associate at Dixon and White, a national law firm with a branch office in Atlanta, she immediately left the Cobb County DA's office. One key to her receiving the job offer with a big firm was Adisa's educational background in accounting. She'd also received a stellar recommendation from a law school professor whom she'd assisted in writing a law review article about forensic accounting for mergers and acquisitions. Adisa gladly stopped focusing on violent criminals and shifted to advising corporate executives on multimillion-dollar deals.

When the Georgia Innocence Project sent out a plea for a private attorney to represent Leroy Larimore pro bono in an appeal based on newly evaluated DNA evidence, Adisa's prosecutorial and postconviction relief experience caused her name to shoot to the top of the list at Dixon and White. Large law firms welcomed the free positive publicity that came with pro bono work, and the only acceptable answer for Adisa to give when asked to volunteer was yes.

Adisa's curly dark hair was uniformly cut about two inches from her head, and she wore a navy-blue skirt, a crisp white blouse, and a simple gold chain around her neck. She'd recently blown up her clothes budget and purchased black leather heels that cost over five hundred dollars. The shoes added three inches to her five-foot-two-inch frame, and even though her feet might be killing her at the end of the day, it was a small price to pay to look her professional best.

The judge, an overweight man in his late fifties with a thick shock of white hair, was a former major felony prosecutor in the DeKalb County district attorney's office. His selection to hear the motion was an unlucky draw, but Adisa pushed any negative thoughts from her mind. The judge shuffled some papers on the bench and cleared his throat.

"I've read your prehearing brief, Ms. Johnson," the judge said. "It was quite lengthy."

"I wanted to be as comprehensive as possible."

"Did my office let you know that your request to submit expert testimony via deposition was denied?" the judge asked.

"Yes, Your Honor," Adisa replied. "Dr. McHenry is present in the courtroom. I believe the State is willing to stipulate the chain of custody for both the hair and the saliva residue delivered from the GBI evidence lab to Dr. McHenry's facility in Sandy Springs along with the DNA samples obtained from my client at the Reidsville penitentiary."

"Mr. Kildare," the judge said. "Your response?"

"Chain of custody is stipulated, Judge."

"Very well," the judge said to Adisa. "Proceed."

Dr. Joseph McHenry walked up to the witness stand and raised his right hand. Adisa administered the oath, and the forensic pathologist sat down.

"Please state your name and tell the Court your professional qualifications," she said.

Dr. McHenry was an autopilot witness. He'd testified over three hundred times in criminal cases, mostly for the prosecution, but also for the defense if the results of his testing supported the innocence of the accused. Adisa knew the doctor could talk without interruption for thirty minutes unless she reined him in.

"Most of my testimony has involved

homicides or suspected homicides," the witness said. "I'm often asked to analyze a corpse and determine the likely cause of death within a reasonable degree of medical certainty."

"But in this case, your inquiry was limited to DNA comparison."

"Yes."

"Using what technique?"

"There are several DNA analysis methods: automated short tandem repeats, or STRs; single nucleotide polymorphisms, or SNPs; mitochondrial DNA, or mtDNA; Y-chromosome DNA; and the restriction fragment length polymorphism, or RFLP, technique. Advances are coming online at a rapid clip. There is some interesting research going on at Stanford —"

"Which protocol did you use for the DNA samples delivered to you from the GBI lab and provided by Mr. Larimore in this case?" Adisa asked, interrupting.

"RFLP for both the saliva and the hair samples. It was the most appropriate methodology."

"Did the GBI provide enough material to perform the analysis and reach a conclusion?"

"Yes, as to hair. No, as to saliva. The passage of time had degraded any saliva left on the cigarette butt, rendering the sample nonproductive."

This wasn't news to Adisa, and she took it in stride. She heard Larimore grunt behind her and motioned with her hand for him to stay calm. The inmate was still fuming over the original prosecutor's use of the remains of a hand-rolled cigarette to link him to the victim, a seventy-three-year-old man who was sitting on the back porch of his residence when a robber surprised him, tied him up, burglarized his house, and stole his car.

"Please tell the Court the results of your testing on the hair samples," Adisa said.

"They did not match."

"Within what probability?"

"That's an odd question," the witness replied, raising his eyebrows. "I'm not sure if I should say zero percent or one hundred percent."

Before Adisa could rephrase the question, the judge spoke.

"Do you believe the hair samples come from the same person?" the judge asked the witness.

"No. And I'm one hundred percent sure of my answer. In addition, I placed the samples under a microscope. Magnified, it was clear that the hair came from different people. One person had curly brown hair; the other person's hair was straight and black."

Adisa saw the judge glance at her client and then turn to her.

"Where and how was the GBI sample obtained?" the judge asked Adisa.

"As I mentioned in my brief, the State stipulates the hair sample was removed from beneath the fingernails of Mr. Chesney, the victim. He testified at trial that he briefly fought with the assailant."

"That's correct," Kildare replied, half rising from his chair. "And identified the defendant from a lineup as the perpetrator of the crime."

"A lineup that did not meet the requirements of *Kirby v. Illinois,*" Adisa quickly responded. "At that point Mr. Larimore had already been charged with the crime and had the right for a lawyer to be present."

"The lineup issue was extensively litigated in the defendant's prior appeals," Kildare responded with more vigor. "If Ms. Johnson believes this is relevant to the current motion, she is going to have to —"

"It's not relevant, Your Honor," Adisa interjected. "The extraordinary motion for new trial is based on the DNA evidence."

"Then stick to it," the judge said.

Adisa kicked herself for chasing an evidentiary rabbit that had long ago escaped into the woods. She rested her hands on a lectern while Dr. McHenry provided the necessary details about the DNA testing of the hair samples.

"Once you isolated the DNA profile from the hair samples delivered by the GBI lab and determined that the hair did not come from Mr. Larimore, what did you do?" she asked.

"I entered the data into CODIS and discovered —"

"The judge is familiar with CODIS," Adisa interrupted, "but please explain for the record."

"CODIS is the Combined DNA Index System maintained by federal, state, and local law enforcement systems. It allows comparison of DNA samples with the profiles on record from convicted offenders and is extremely valuable, especially in serial crimes."

"Were there any matches on CODIS?"

"Yes, for an individual named Vester Plunkett within a degree of accuracy of 99.58 percent. In my opinion, the hair supplied to me from the GBI lab came from this individual."

"Mr. Plunkett is currently incarcerated

and serving a forty-year sentence at the Big Sandy federal penitentiary in Kentucky," Adisa said to the judge. "He was convicted five years after the Chesney robbery of three felony theft offenses, including one in which a bank guard was shot and severely wounded."

"Is that correct, Mr. Kildare?" the judge asked.

"Yes, sir," Kildare replied.

"Anything else, Ms. Johnson?" the judge asked.

Adisa had several more follow-up questions on her laptop, but the way the judge spoke indicated he'd heard what he wanted, or needed, to hear.

"No, sir, subject to any redirect."

"Mr. Kildare, you may proceed."

Kildare stood and looked over at Adisa's client for a moment. "No questions for Dr. McHenry, Your Honor," he replied.

"The witness is excused," the judge said.

The forensic pathologist left the witness stand. Adisa let out a deep breath. She knew the DNA evidence was strong, but postconviction relief in a criminal case was always a long shot. Courts were notoriously reluctant to disturb what a jury had decided. As she watched Dr. McHenry move past, she knew the pathologist was disappointed that Kil-

41

dare wasn't going to attempt to challenge his findings or conclusions. The pathologist had told her he loved to spar with lawyers who cross-examined him.

"At this time I'd like to call Mr. Larimore," Adisa said.

"What's he going to say?" the judge asked.

"That he bought Mr. Chesney's car from Vester Plunkett for six hundred and fifty dollars without any knowledge that the vehicle was stolen. At the time the crime occurred, Mr. Larimore was fishing alone at a pond about five miles away."

"What's the State's position?" the judge asked Kildare.

"Judge, Ms. Springer in our office instructed me not to oppose the motion if Your Honor deems the DNA evidence sufficient to grant a new trial."

"I so find," Judge Boswell replied quickly, catching Adisa off guard.

Adisa was stunned. The judge turned to Kildare. "Is the State going to retry the defendant?"

"No, sir. As you know from Ms. Johnson's brief, Mr. Chesney passed away three years ago. I'll contact his family and tell them what happened today. We do not oppose the defendant's immediate release from custody without the necessity of a bond. I anticipate an indictment will be issued shortly charging Mr. Plunkett with the crime."

Adisa felt an extreme sense of satisfaction. Six months of work vindicated in less than an hour. She turned to her client, who was in shock.

"You're going to be free," she said, smiling.

"It will take forty-eight hours to process the paperwork," Kildare replied. "In the interim, Mr. Larimore will be kept at the Fulton County Jail."

"Ms. Johnson," the judge said. "Please prepare a proposed order for Mr. Kildare's review, then submit it to me by five o'clock tomorrow afternoon."

"Yes, sir."

"The Court will be in recess for fifteen minutes," the judge said before leaving the bench.

Adisa stepped over to Kildare. "Thank you," she said. "I wasn't sure how you viewed the case."

Kildare watched the judge exit the courtroom. He then faced Adisa. "John Adams once said, 'Facts are stubborn things; and whatever may be our wishes, our inclinations, or the dictates of our passions, they cannot alter the state of facts and evidence.' My job is to convict the guilty, not the innocent. Once I received Dr. McHenry's report, the merit of the motion was decided in my mind. I wish every issue I faced was so clear."

Adisa had considered Kildare smart but perhaps a bit lazy. Now she realized he might simply be efficient.

"I guess you want to take a minute or two to celebrate with your client," Kildare said. The prosecutor turned and spoke to the officer who'd escorted Larimore into the courtroom. "You can take off his shackles."

Larimore wiped tears from his eyes with the backs of his still-bound hands and held them out as the deputy removed the cuffs from his wrists. The deputy knelt down to free the inmate's feet. Adisa watched, wanting to imprint the moment as a lasting memory.

"Is your firm going to represent Mr. Larimore in his claim for reimbursement from the State for wrongful imprisonment?" Kildare asked.

"I doubt it, but that will be up to my bosses. All my time has been pro bono."

"The government's response to any damage claim will be handled by the attorney general's office," Kildare continued. "I'll let you know the name of the person to notify."

"Okay, thanks."

Kildare left, leaving Adisa alone in the courtroom with her client and the deputy, who stepped away to give them privacy.

"Thank you, ma'am," Larimore said in the gravelly voice that had bristled with anger and animosity the first time Adisa met him face-to-face without a wall of glass between them. Now the voice cracked with emotion, and Adisa saw more tears in the corners of her client's eyes.

"You're welcome," she replied.

"No, I mean it with all my heart," Larimore persisted, roughly swatting away the moisture in his eyes. "You believed me even when no one else did."

Adisa wasn't sure how to respond. Saying something about the importance of the Constitution for every American didn't seem to fit. She settled on a brief explanation of the judge's decision to make sure Larimore understood exactly what had happened.

"I got it," he said, nodding as she finished. "And I know that you were the one God picked out for me. I know it sounds crazy, but if I can ever do anything to help you, I'll be there as quick as I can."

"You're right to be thankful," she said. "I prayed a lot about your case myself."

"Come on," the deputy said to Larimore.

"We'll put you up for the night in the special suite we have for big-shot prisoners. It has a whirlpool tub, sauna, and your choice of snacks."

Larimore managed a grin that revealed several missing teeth. "Just don't throw me in the hole with anyone who's crazy enough to stick me with a shiv out of spite to make a name for hisself."

"Yes," Adisa quickly added. "Is there a safe place for Mr. Larimore to stay while he's processed for release?"

"Yeah," the deputy replied. "We'll keep him in a cozy spot with a camera stuck up in the corner of the cell so we can watch him twenty-four/seven."

THREE

The middle-aged woman with shockingly blond hair who served as Police Chief Ben Lockhart's assistant returned the phone receiver to its cradle. Luke scooted closer to the edge of his chair.

"Officer Nelson, he'll see you now," the woman said.

Luke licked his lips. Rapid heartbeat, dry mouth, nightmares, sudden sweating, and waves of anxiety had been intrusive companions during the ten days since he shot Deshaun Hamlin. Immediately placed on administrative leave with pay as required by police department regulations, Luke had spent most of his time at home. Jane's support had proved as unwavering as her faith that he would be vindicated when all the facts came out. But it was hard for even her to be cheerful. The sunshine and joy in their lives came from Ashley, who at fourteen months was oblivious to everything except hunger, a dirty diaper, discovering the world at her fingertips, and the love in her parents' faces.

Luke opened the door to the office. Chief Lockhart was leaning back in his chair. A big man with a thick neck and an ample stomach, he immediately returned the seat to an upright position.

"Make yourself comfortable, Luke," Lockhart said in his slow southern drawl. "And let me get one thing out of the way. I didn't ask you to come see me because I'm going to fire you."

"Thank you, sir," Luke said with a sigh of relief.

Lockhart scratched the top of his large head that was covered with closely cut black hair. "And I guess you heard the two bullets that missed the suspect didn't put anyone else at risk."

"Yes, sir. Bruce Alverez sent me a text message letting me know. That's a relief."

"It's also a relief that half the shots you fired missed the Hamlin boy. From the scores you racked up on the range in April, I found that surprising. But things are different when it's for real."

"Yes, they are."

Lockhart ran his thick index finger around the inside edge of his shirt collar. "Nelson, we're going to have an off-the-record conversation. If you bring it up, I'll deny it happened. I don't want you to mention what I'm about to say to anyone, not even your wife. Understood?"

"Yes, sir."

Lockhart shifted in his chair. "From your first day on the job, you've been one of the most loyal, conscientious officers on the force. You remind me of myself when I first got into law enforcement."

"I appreciate that."

"And I believe what you wrote in your report reflects your state of mind at the time you pulled your weapon and shot the Hamlin boy. Ordinary citizens don't realize the pressure a police officer faces when making split-second decisions. Do I wish this hadn't happened? Of course, but nobody I've talked to has heard you make a racist comment or treat anyone differently because of the color of their skin. That's the only way to be in this day and age."

The chief paused. Luke wasn't exactly sure where his boss was going with the conversation, but every police officer, even in a town like Campbellton, knew that both the perception and the reality of police interaction with the black community were a big deal, with strong opinions on both sides. There were two black officers on the force. Luke had enjoyed working with both of them.

"It was tough fighting prejudice when I worked in Atlanta," Luke offered, "but since coming here I've tried not to let anything influence me except what I'm supposed to do as an officer. My old unit commander in Atlanta was always reminding us that when it comes to color, justice is blind."

"But we should always keep our eyes open."

"Yes," Luke replied, still uncertain as to the purpose of their conversation.

Lockhart turned in his chair and picked up a photo from his credenza. It was a picture of a younger, much slimmer version of the police chief in an Army uniform with a desert setting in the background. He placed the photo so Luke could see it.

"Did you know that I served a tour of duty in Iraq when I was in the Army?" Lockhart asked.

"No, sir."

"Most of the time I was holed up on a base where the worst things we fought were boredom and body odor. But for six weeks I was in a unit assigned to clear out pockets of opposition fighters in Mosul. We ended up in several firefights. Five of the men in our company didn't make it. Others came back with scars inside and out."

As the police chief talked, Luke felt a touch of anxiety rising in his chest. He tried to control his breathing. Lockhart didn't seem to notice.

"During that time I killed at least four, maybe five men," the police chief said. "We were fighting a war and people die in battle, but it's not something that's easy to forget. One night we were on patrol, and I shot an Iraqi who startled me when I came around the corner of a narrow street. When we checked his body we couldn't find a weapon other than a nasty-looking knife strapped in a sheath under his clothes. He never pulled it out."

"Did you get into trouble?"

"There was an investigation that involved talking to the other soldiers in my platoon, and after a couple of months a JAG officer issued a report exonerating me. The wait was brutal. Later, I found out that the colonel who commanded our unit went to bat for me in a big way. It was a war zone, and everyone was on high alert. When that happens it's easy for our senses to be so amped up that everything is magnified." Lockhart paused. "Kind of like lightning on a stormy night."

"I heard a gunshot," Luke immediately replied. "I'm positive. It was stormy, but —"

"Okay." Lockhart held up his hand. "Put that aside for now. Here's what's more important. In your situation, District Attorney Baldwin is the JAG officer, and I'm your colonel. We're working closely together on the police department's internal investigation. Do you catch my drift?"

Luke now knew the purpose for the meeting but couldn't believe what he was hearing. Chief Lockhart was going to huddle up with the DA and make sure no criminal charges would be filed.

"I think so."

"I only wish civilian life was as simple as things in the military," Lockhart continued. "But we're not in a war zone here in Campbellton, and it's a lot more complicated than Mosul, Iraq. No matter what you hear or read in the media, remember the story I just told you."

Luke was encouraged and confused at the same time. "I'll try," he managed. "Are you going to talk to the DA and help me out?"

"Like I said, he knows my thoughts on the situation, and we're in close communication," Lockhart replied cryptically. "No one wants a bunch of negative publicity and a huge lawsuit against the city."

"Who's handling the internal investigation?"

"Detective Maxwell. He's the obvious choice."

Luke swallowed. To him, Mitch Maxwell was the worst choice if the goal was to prevent charges from being filed against him. The longtime detective seemed impervious to the opinions of others.

"Mitch is the best and that's what you deserve," the chief continued. "And on the publicity front, remember what I told you the night it happened. Don't talk to any reporters. It's not good for you, and it's not good for the department. The press doesn't care about you, only about selling papers."

"I haven't and won't."

"Have you met with Dr. Flanagan?"

"Yes, sir. He gave me some pills that are supposed to help me sleep. I'm not sure —"

"Don't tell me anything else," Lockhart said abruptly. "What you and the psychiatrist talk about is between the two of you. But keep going to see him if you want to. There's no deductible for the visits. The department covers all the costs."

"I appreciate that."

"Good. And don't stay cooped up all the time. You and Jane need to sneak out for dinner in Gainesville where you won't be recognized."

"There's a chance my mother-in-law will come up from Florida for a few weeks and help out. If she does, we could do that, although being with Jane and Ashley together has been the best therapy I've had."

Luke stopped. He sounded like someone dealing with situational depression caused by poor self-esteem.

"Are you sure it's a good idea for your mother-in-law to camp out at your place?" Lockhart asked with a smile. "If she's anything like mine, she doesn't come to help; she comes to take over."

"Jane's mom is great," Luke replied, avoiding a fake macho response.

"Good. And we'll schedule a patrol car on each shift to check your street and make sure everything is quiet. If you see anything suspicious, let us know ASAP." The chief tapped his fingers on the desk for a moment. "Have you been able to keep up with the condition of the Hamlin boy at the hospital?"

"Not really. All I know is that he's still in a coma. I was hoping you could give me an update."

"That's the gist of it. The wound to his upper chest was on the right side and will

54

heal over time. It's a good thing you didn't pop him on the left side. It would have killed him instantly."

Luke licked his lips.

"But the bullet to the head has him on the fence," Lockhart continued. "He has a lot of swelling in the brain, and they can't risk trying to remove the bullet until that goes down. For all our sakes, let's hope he pulls through. An aggravated assault charge is a lot easier to deal with than an indictment for murder."

The tightness in Luke's chest returned, only worse. The police chief stood to signal an end to the meeting.

"And remember, we're here for you, son."

On his way out of the station, Luke passed Detective Maxwell in the hallway. The blond-haired detective didn't look at him.

It was six blocks from the courthouse to the thirty-seven-story building where Dixon and White maintained its Atlanta office. The firm occupied floors thirty-five to thirty-eight. The corporation division where Adisa worked filled the entire thirty-sixth floor. Her primary job, and that of the six other lawyers in her subgroup, was to uncover traps and pitfalls of multimillion-dollar business mergers and acquisitions. Few people outside the legal community realized the enormous stress that came with putting together major corporate deals, a pressure that often exceeded the tension experienced by seasoned trial lawyers.

Catherine Summey, the senior partner in the group, had instilled the perspective in her team that it was better to kill a shaky deal than keep it alive. One of her favorite analogies was "Even a tiny bacterium can turn deadly if allowed to enter the body."

While she waited at the curb for a taxi, Adisa offered up a quick prayer of thanks for her courtroom success. One of her favorite verses was Proverbs 21:1: "In the LORD's hand the king's heart is a stream of water that he channels toward all who please him." Time after time in her six-year career she'd seen evidence of the Lord's intervention on her behalf with people in positions of power — including judges, corporate CEOs, and senior partners in law firms. Others might view the instances as co-incidence. Adisa knew better. She'd worked hard to prove that Leroy Larimore was one of the tiny percentage of inmates who were in fact innocent of the crime for which they were convicted, but she gave the Lord significant credit for Judge Boswell's ruling. And if Larimore's interaction with her helped wash away a few stains of his long-held bigotry, that was an added bonus.

Adisa slipped into the rear seat of the cab. Her cell phone vibrated, and an unknown number popped up.

"Hello," she said.

"This is Sharon Rogers, a reporter with the *AJC*. Are you the lawyer representing Leroy Larimore?"

Adisa sat up straighter. Any reversal of a conviction based on newly analyzed DNA evidence would justify at least a brief mention in the *Atlanta Journal-Constitution* and serve the interests of the law firm.

"Yes, I'm an associate with Dixon and White. Our firm agreed to represent Mr. Larimore pro bono."

"Is it true the DNA evidence proved another man already in prison committed the crime?"

The reporter's summary was accurate but skipped a lot of information.

"Yes."

"So your client is going to be released?"

"It's my hope that Mr. Larimore will be released within the next forty-eight hours and begin the challenging task of rebuilding his life after spending fourteen years in prison for a crime he didn't commit."

Proud of the spontaneous news bite she'd

delivered, Adisa prepared to get out of the cab as it stopped in front of her building. She handed the driver a twenty-dollar bill, motioning for him to keep the change.

"Are they going to prosecute the man who actually committed the crime?"

"You should ask Mark Kildare with the Fulton County DA's office that question."

"He never returns my calls."

Adisa wondered what the reporter had done to irritate the sanguine prosecutor.

"What about the pending burglary charges against your client in South Carolina?" the reporter continued. "I understand there's no statute of limitations on criminal charges there."

Adisa stepped away from the flow of pedestrian traffic on the sidewalk and stood to the side of the front doors of her office tower. She quickly gathered her thoughts.

"Mr. Larimore was a juvenile when that incident took place, and the case wasn't transferred to general sessions court, which handles felony criminal matters. That means he wasn't charged as an adult. I'm not licensed to practice in South Carolina, but I investigated that issue as part of my work on his behalf in this case."

"But he's not a truly innocent man, is he?"

Adisa was beginning to understand why

58

Mark Kildare didn't talk to the reporter. It was easy to imagine the sensational slant the article might take.

"In the eyes of the law, he's innocent," Adisa replied. "The juvenile case was dismissed for want of prosecution."

"By his grandmother, correct?"

"That's true. But regardless of what happened when Mr. Larimore was fifteen years old, he spent fourteen years wrongly incarcerated in the state of Georgia. Today, the system corrected that wrong."

"Got it."

"Are you recording this conversation?" Adisa asked, raising her eyebrows.

"Of course. I don't want to misquote you. Are you going to represent Larimore in his claim for damages from the State for locking him up for all those years?"

"That will be up to my bosses at the law firm, but there's no doubt he should be compensated for a decade and a half spent behind bars. He was as much a victim as Mr. Chesney."

Adisa didn't like the sound of her last statement but couldn't think of a quick fix.

"Who's your boss?" Rogers asked.

"Catherine Summey is the supervising attorney in this case. She's a partner at Dixon and White in the Atlanta office."

59

"How many of these cases have you handled?"

"This is the first, but I worked for a couple of years as a prosecutor in Cobb County. It's not unfamiliar territory for me."

"What kind of work do you do at Dixon and White?"

"Forensic accounting for corporate mergers. I spend a lot of time piecing together financial puzzles so our corporate clients can see what they're getting into. Working to unravel the evidence that exonerated Mr. Larimore was a similar process."

"Interesting. What is your hourly rate at Dixon and White?"

"I'm not going to answer that question because it's not pertinent to my representation of Mr. Larimore."

"What's next for you?" the reporter asked, unfazed. "Would you be willing to take on another criminal case?"

"No, but I'm glad for the opportunity to represent Mr. Larimore. I need to go now."

"Sure. Will you be available if I circle back with you before I run the article?"

"I'll try."

The call ended. Pulling the catalog case containing the file and her laptop behind her, Adisa stepped into the marble-floored entrance of the office tower. A security checkpoint blocked the bank of elevators that served floors twenty through thirty-eight. Adisa swiped an access card that triggered an electric lock on a glass door. She recognized the security guard on duty, who greeted her by name.

Waiting for an elevator door to open, Adisa suffered a second moment of anxiety about what Sharon Rogers might include in the newspaper article. If the story took a negative slant, it would send the wrong kind of waves rippling up to the large offices on the thirty-eighth floor. Adisa offered a quick prayer for the Lord to direct the reporter's heart as skillfully as he had Judge Boswell's.

Adisa's first stop was to see Catherine Summey. The managing partner of the subgroup was staring at the screen of her computer. Fifty years old, Catherine had been a free spirit in her younger days and still let her blond hair flow down her back. Over her boss's shoulder, Adisa could see the Atlanta skyline to the southeast of Peachtree Street. Catherine looked up and smiled.

"I already know," she said, her green eyes sparkling. "It came across as a local news item five minutes ago. Congratulations."

"Thanks."

"Come in and tell me about it."

61

One of Catherine's strengths was the ability to listen. The competing demands on her boss's time were as tough to balance as a juggler trying to keep multiple plates spinning at the tops of long poles, but the Princeton Law School graduate always made Adisa feel like she had her undivided attention when they talked. Catherine didn't interrupt Adisa until the phone on the partner's desk buzzed. One of her two assistants spoke.

"Mr. Katner wants to move up his appointment with you by ten minutes," the young man said.

"I'll be there," Catherine replied promptly.

Adisa hadn't yet told her boss about the conversation with the newspaper reporter; Catherine, however, pointed to the ceiling. Linwood Katner, the managing attorney in the Atlanta office, had a massive office that occupied an entire corner of the thirty-eighth floor. Katner made Adisa uneasy. The first year she worked for the firm, he had either ignored her or confused her with one of the two black female paralegals who worked in the corporations department. He'd never solicited Adisa's input in a meeting, which left Adisa no option but to let Catherine do the talking for her.

"Rumor has it a huge deal is coming our

way," Catherine said, putting her index finger to her lips. "Big enough that it's going to be a two-thousand-hour project. I need you to finish up your work on the Sipco matter as soon as possible so you're available when it hits."

Adisa wasn't even halfway through her review of the proposed merger but had already identified a couple of red flags in the financial data.

"How quick?"

"Prepare a memo by tomorrow morning. We'll discuss it first thing."

"Okay," Adisa replied, knowing she would be working into the night.

Adisa walked quickly to her office, a small space barely big enough for a desk, a chair, a stand for her laptop, and a juvenile schefflera plant that extended its leaves hopefully toward a window that let in a narrow sliver of light. But Adisa would have been grateful for a closet. Beside the window was a framed poster of a waterfall with the caption "My Cup Runneth Over" beneath it. Few of Adisa's coworkers suspected that the words were part of a Bible verse.

As a third-year associate, Adisa had received a decent bonus in December that enabled her to buy new clothes and make headway on a six-figure student loan debt, which hung over her head like a sword on a silken thread. Someday she hoped to buy a townhome in the midtown area near the office, but that would have to wait at least another couple of years.

On the corner of Adisa's desk was a picture of her older sister, Shanika, holding twin daughters who would turn four years old in a few weeks. Standing behind Shanika with his right hand on his mother's shoulder was her six-year-old son. Shanika had worked as a bank teller for several years, but after the twins were born she became a stay-at-home mom. Her husband, Ronnie, was a traveling salesman for an industrial equipment manufacturing company.

Next to Shanika's photograph was a picture of their great-aunt Josie. Josephine Adams had raised the two girls after their parents' marriage blew up and no one else wanted them. In the photo, a much younger Aunt Josie was hanging white sheets on a clothesline to dry. In the black-and-white picture the sheets were flapping in the wind, and the rangy woman had a contented smile on her face. Aunt Josie had worn many hats in her long life: a spinster who raised two girls, a retired business owner, and an intercessor who for decades had prayed as she walked the streets of her hometown. She carried a crude walking stick during her spiritual outings, earning her the nickname of "Walker Woman."

While her computer was booting up, Adisa went to the break room for a fresh cup of coffee. On the way she passed several coworkers, but no one stopped to chat. Idle conversation in the middle of the workday wasn't part of the firm culture. Returning to her office, she opened the electronic folder for the Sipco matter. The phone on her desk buzzed.

"Your sister, Shanika, is on the phone," the receptionist said. "She says it's an emergency."

FOUR

"What's happened?" Adisa asked rapidly. "Is it about Mom?"

Their mother had struggled with addiction issues for over twenty-five years. The last they'd heard she was unemployed and living somewhere in New Jersey. The sisters weren't sure where and didn't know how to contact her.

"No, it's Aunt Josie. She's had a stroke. They admitted her to the hospital in Campbellton about an hour ago."

"How serious is it?" Adisa asked as a wave of anxiety rolled through her.

"They put her in a regular room, not ICU. I haven't talked to her, but she was lucid enough to give the EMTs a slip of paper with my name and number on it when they picked her up in the ambulance."

Adisa relaxed slightly at the news that her aunt wasn't in a life-and-death crisis. A skinny woman with more nervous energy than a ten-year-old, Aunt Josie spent time not only prayer walking but also growing a vegetable garden. She still could hoe an entire row of green beans without taking a break. And the only medicines she took on a daily basis were a pill to treat hypertension and a baby aspirin.

"Even though she's not in critical condition, should they transfer her to a hospital here in Atlanta?" Adisa asked. "They don't have tons of resources in Nash County."

"I agree. Ronnie is out of town overnight in Macon, so there's no way I can get up there to check on her and make sure she's getting the attention she deserves."

Shanika lived in a rural area that was a two-hour drive from Campbellton.

"What about Ronnie's mother?" Adisa asked. "Can't she watch the kids for you?"

"She has a nasty upper respiratory infection, and I don't want it to infect everyone at our house. I just finished a round of amoxicillin with the twins, and if they pick up a new bug, I'll need to go to the hospital myself."

Adisa glanced at the clock on her computer taskbar. It was 2:47 p.m. If she left immediately, she could beat the worst of rush-hour traffic and be in Campbellton within ninety minutes.

"I'll talk to Catherine and see what she says about leaving early," Adisa replied.

"This is our aunt Josie," Shanika responded. "She's more important than the legal problems of a billion-dollar company that already has hundreds of lawyers available to do their bidding."

"I know, I know. Don't try to put a guilt trip on me. But I can't bolt out the door without making arrangements for a project that's time sensitive. It shouldn't be a problem if I can be back by early in the morning."

Shanika didn't respond.

"Did you hear me?" Adisa asked.

"Yes, but did you hear yourself? I hope you put checking on Aunt Josie in the hospital at the top of your to-do list. I've already told Ronnie he has to be home before noon tomorrow so I can get up to Campbellton myself."

Adisa heard a high-pitched scream in the background.

"Keisha! Stop!" Shanika yelled, and the phone went dead.

Keisha was the older of the twins and dominated Kendal, her younger sister. Keisha even tried to boss Ronnie Jr., her big brother. Adisa lowered the receiver. She knew better than to call back. Settling intrafamily disputes involving Keisha could take as much time as mediation in a lawsuit.

The relationship between Keisha and Kendal reminded her of Shanika and herself when they were little. So far, Adisa had resisted the urge to point out the obvious similarity in the relationships and tie it to the biblical principle of reaping what you sow. But that didn't keep her from thinking about it.

Adisa and Shanika were six and eight when they first arrived at Aunt Josie's house. Before that, the girls had been like feral animals, often left alone for hours at a time while their father was at a tavern after his shift at a lumberyard and their mother was in her bedroom in a drug-induced stupor. It was amazing that the girls hadn't been seriously injured or burned down the ratty apartment building where they lived on the outskirts of Savannah.

Removed from their parents' custody by the Chatham County Department of Family and Children Services, the sisters were placed with their great-aunt Josie, the only close relative willing to claim them. From that point it had taken Josephine Adams several years of consistent discipline and countless hugs to bring order to the girls' lives.

Shanika was a two-sport athlete in high school with a type A personality. Adisa was more shy and bookish. Only in college did Adisa begin to flourish in an environment where she was surrounded by other smart, academically minded people. Law school was an even richer petri dish, and Adisa's analytical skills came to life at a high level. She'd graduated in the top twenty-five percent of her class.

Slipping her cell phone into the pocket of her suit jacket, Adisa went to Catherine Summey's office, but she was still upstairs in the meeting with Mr. Katner. Next in the chain of command was Lorenzo "Nick" Balsamo, a junior partner with dark hair and thick black-framed glasses. Nick could sit in front of a computer and work nonstop for hours at a stretch but had zero interest in the management aspects of law practice. Adisa found him parked in his usual spot staring at his laptop. He glanced up as she tapped lightly on the doorframe.

"What is it?" he asked, squinting his eyes slightly.

Adisa summarized the situation as quickly as possible. "I'd like to take the rest of the afternoon off so I can drive to Campbellton and check on her," she said as she finished.

"Go," Nick replied with a dismissive wave

of his hand. "But if Catherine gets upset, don't drag me into it."

"Then what does 'go' mean?"

Nick had already refocused on the computer screen. Adisa returned to her office and sent Catherine an e-mail. She was confident enough in the relationship with her boss that leaving work early to tend to a family emergency wouldn't be a serious problem.

Adisa parked her small imported car in a numbered spot on the sixth floor of a deck adjacent to the office. If she tried to leave between 5:00 p.m. and 6:00 p.m., it could take ten minutes to reach street level. At this midafternoon time, though, she was quickly on the streets of Atlanta, and four blocks later, she turned onto a ramp for the interstate highway that would take her away from the city. Her cell phone vibrated. It was Shanika.

"The receptionist told me you left," her sister said. "Are you on your way to Campbellton?"

"Yes," Adisa replied.

"Thank God you'll be there to find out what's really going on," Shanika responded.

"What do you mean?"

"I'm getting mixed signals from the doctor who first called me and the nurse on duty. The doctor said he thought Aunt Josie probably had a TIA. I looked it up and that's a —"

"Transient ischemic attack or ministroke," Adisa finished.

"Yeah, but the nurse on the floor told me Aunt Josie is slurring her words and complaining about not being able to see clearly. She uses reading glasses, but otherwise her vision is okay."

"I should be there in time for late-afternoon rounds by the physician. Hopefully, they've called in a neurologist by now. What's the name of the doctor you talked to?"

"Dr. Smith or Sanders or Stephens; I'm not sure. He was in the ER."

"As soon as I know anything specific, I'll call you back," Adisa said. "How are the kids? Did Keisha start a fire or hit Ronnie Jr. in the head with a block?"

"No, but she had a death grip on Kendal's hair and wasn't going to let go. Like mother, like daughter. Did I ever apologize to you for doing that? It was a dirty way to fight."

Adisa smiled. "I'm not permanently scarred. And my retaliation was often worse than what you did. If you promise not to bring up my biting, I won't bring up your hair grabbing."

"Deal. Drive safely, and call as soon as you know something."

An hour later, Adisa turned off the radio tuned to a classical station and exited the interstate. It was another forty-three miles on two-lane roads to Campbellton. The grass in the pastures was May green from the spring rains, and she passed many small farms with twenty or thirty cattle, a large garden spot, and an occasional chicken house. By midsummer, the humid Georgia heat would descend with such oppressive force that only biting flies stirred from noon till six.

Aunt Josie's house didn't have air-conditioning when Adisa and Shanika were little, and they spent many summer nights in their bedroom with a window fan vainly trying to suck out the sticky, hot air that built up in the house during the heat of the day.

Normally, Adisa enjoyed the drive to see Aunt Josie and loved crossing into Nash County. The rolling hills felt comfortable, and the branches of the trees held out their arms in welcome. Campbellton was not only Adisa's childhood home; it was home to the first happy memories of her life. It had been over four months since she'd made the trip.

Aunt Josie seemed satisfied with a Sunday-afternoon phone call every week, but Adisa felt guilty, knowing there was no substitute for a hug and a kiss.

The hospital was on the east side of town. It was a little past five o'clock when Adisa pulled into the parking lot. On her way to the main entrance, she passed the parking spaces reserved for doctors. Campbellton Memorial Hospital drew patients from three surrounding counties, and it was possible for a physician to make a decent living in the area. The expensive cars in the physician lot reflected prosperity. Opposite the doctor spaces were five clergy spots. There wasn't a BMW or late-model Lexus among them.

Next to the sliding glass doors for the entrance was a green box containing the *Campbellton News*. The daily afternoon newspaper was a stubborn, ten-page dinosaur sustained by a local population that still liked a paper in the driveway at the end of the workday. Adisa read a bold headline that proclaimed "Local Police Officer Under Investigation for Shooting Black Teenager." Adisa slowed and read the portion of the article that was visible before continuing inside to the information desk.

"Room number for Josephine Adams,

please," she asked a white-haired volunteer on duty.

The woman typed the name into her computer. "Second floor, room 2265," she replied.

Adisa made her way to the elevators behind the information desk. As the doors were about to close, a man's hand appeared in the narrow opening. In his grasp was a black Bible. The doors pressed against the Bible and jerked back open. A stocky young black man who looked to be about thirty years old and was wearing a dark suit, a white shirt, and a tie with a gray design joined her.

"Sorry," he said.

"That was a different use of the Scriptures," Adisa said.

The man patted the Bible. "This book is good for a lot more than people give it credit for," he said in a pleasant baritone voice. "I'm Reggie Reynolds, pastor of Zion Hills Baptist Church."

The minister's hair was clipped short, and he sported a thin, well-groomed mustache. The fingers of his left hand that gripped the Bible looked strong. Adisa extended her right hand and he shook it.

"Adisa Johnson," she said.

"What brings you to the hospital?" the

minister asked.

The elevator doors opened, and they both got out.

"My great-aunt, Josephine Adams," Adisa replied. "She had a stroke this morning."

"I'm sorry to hear that," the minister said and then paused. "It seems like I've heard that name somewhere, but I can't place it."

"She's a longtime member of Woodside Gospel Tabernacle, but you may have seen her around town. She likes to go for long walks and carries a big stick with her."

"Yes," the minister said and nodded. "I've seen her but never met her. A woman in my congregation told me your aunt prays for the city."

"And the county. That's Aunt Josie."

"Would it be okay if I came by to visit while she's here? I'd like to meet her. I know her home church is between pastors."

"I'd better check with her first," Adisa replied. "She may not be able to have visitors."

"Of course," the minister replied as he reached into his pocket and took out a card.

The ivory-colored card listed "Rev. Reginald Reynolds" as "Senior Pastor and Overseer."

"Thanks, Reverend Reynolds," she said.

"Call me Reggie. And don't hesitate to

call if I can help you or your family."

The minister pressed the up button for the elevator.

"You're not visiting someone on this floor?" Adisa asked.

"No, I'm going to the third floor."

As she walked down the hallway, Adisa remembered Zion Hills Baptist as one of the larger churches in the area. Reggie seemed young to be a senior pastor.

She came face-to-face with a set of double doors that were closed. A sign beside the doors read "Ring for Assistance." Adisa pressed a red button and waited.

"May I help you?" a female voice asked.

"I'm here to see Josephine Adams."

"Come to the nurses' station."

A buzzer sounded, and the doors slowly swung outward so Adisa could pass through. The nursing area was directly in front of her. A middle-aged woman with brown hair looked up as Adisa approached. Two health-care workers wearing white masks passed by on their way down the hall.

"Why the extra precautions?" Adisa asked. "I thought my aunt had a mild stroke."

"It's not her. There are several patients who have to be in sterile environments. Your aunt is here until a regular room becomes available."

"Okay," Adisa said with relief. "Am I in time to speak with one of her doctors? My sister and I are the closest family she has."

The nurse pulled out a folder and flipped it open. "Dr. Dewberry, the neurologist, should be here within the next hour or so."

"I'll wait in my aunt's room."

"She's at the end of the hall on the right."

Adisa made her way past the rooms marked with signs warning about avoiding the risk of infection. She reached 2265 and knocked lightly on the door. No one answered, and she slowly pushed it open.

Jane Nelson was introducing finger foods to Ashley's diet, and the little girl was pushing pieces of slippery banana across the tray of her high chair. The couple's first child had her mother's blond hair and blue eyes and a dimple in the exact same spot as her father. Ashley giggled when a piece of banana became stuck on her finger. Carefully lifting the finger in the air, she admired it for a moment and then guided it into her mouth where she clamped down with her two lower teeth. Letting out a startled cry, she jerked the banana out of her mouth and flung it across the room where it remained on the white front of the refrigerator.

At that moment Luke came inside after

working out in a home gym he'd set up in the garage. He wiped his face with a towel and threw the afternoon newspaper on the kitchen table.

"Take a look at this," he said.

Jane scraped the banana from the refrigerator and picked up the paper.

"I think you should throw it away," she said after she read the lead story about Luke and the shooting. "Just because they print something doesn't make it true."

"Yes, but Chief Lockhart told me he was going to work with the DA. Now all this talk about the grand jury makes me nervous. Lockhart practically guaranteed me I was going to be cleared after an internal investigation by the police department."

"You told the truth. You believed your life was in danger and had to act quickly. What if that boy had pulled out a gun and shot you? Where would that leave Ashley and me?"

"I know, I know."

Ashley successfully maneuvered two squishy pieces of banana into her mouth and swallowed them.

"I was reading my Bible this afternoon during Ashley's nap, and a verse really jumped out at me," Jane said. "Do you want to hear it?"

"Sure."

When he was a teenager, Luke was active in the youth group at his local church. Since then, his religious commitment had lessened as work duties increased. As a police officer in Atlanta and now in Campbellton, he often volunteered to work on Sundays as a way to increase his income. He didn't do anything to quash Jane's interest in God, but he attended church with her only about once a month.

"Here it is," Jane said as she returned to the kitchen with an open Bible in her hands. "It's Matthew 10:26: 'Do not be afraid of them, for there is nothing concealed that will not be disclosed, or hidden that will not be made known.' That's what I'm going to pray."

Luke was puzzled. He didn't want to disagree with Jane. She knew much more about the Bible than he did. But he wasn't sure why she found the words helpful.

"I'm more worried than afraid," he replied slowly. "Partly for myself, but mostly for you and Ashley. And I know what happened the night of the shooting. The problem is convincing the people in charge that I'm right about it."

"The verse really spoke to my heart."

"And I want you to pray what you think

you should," Luke quickly added. "For me, I feel a little hypocritical praying now that I'm in trouble."

"You shouldn't."

Luke pointed at the newspaper. "Did you read about the big rally they held at that black church on the west side of town?"

"They're fighting a battle based on what's happened in other parts of the country, not here," Jane said, shaking her head. "You and Rob Atwood have been close as brothers since you worked together as security guards at the mall. He was one of the groomsmen at our wedding, and you've always gotten along fine with the black men on the police force."

"Rob is in California and can't vouch for me, and I don't know the guys here well enough for them to go to bat for me in the face of what people are saying about me."

Jane cut off more pieces of banana and placed them on Ashley's tray.

"When you first joined the police department in Atlanta, I remember Rob saying that a lot of blacks are suspicious of police officers because of the way they, or members of their families, have been treated over the years."

"I faced that night after night in the city, but it hasn't been a big issue here in Campbellton."

Jane pointed to the newspaper article. "It is now."

"And we don't need the newspaper to rub our noses in it," Luke said.

He picked up the newspaper and dropped it into the recycling bin on the pantry floor. Ashley reached for her sippy cup, which was perched precariously on the edge of the tray, and knocked it onto the floor. Luke retrieved it and handed it to her. The little girl raised it high and began to drink like a lumberjack chugging a beer at a bar. Luke smiled.

"I like that look," Jane said as she reached over and touched Luke on the hand. "I'm trying to be strong and full of faith, but in a couple of hours you may have to drag me out of the ditch of depression."

Luke wrapped his hand around hers and gently squeezed it. "I'll be here for you."

FIVE

Her eyes closed, Aunt Josie was lying with the head of the bed slightly elevated. Adisa quietly stepped closer. The faint rattle in her aunt's throat let her know the elderly woman was asleep. She was wearing a pale-blue hospital gown with the sheet pulled up just beneath her bony shoulders. There was an IV in her left arm. Adisa glanced at the label on the bag. It was glucose. Adisa eased over to a chair at the foot of the bed and sat down. Although raspy, the sound of Aunt Josie's steady breathing was better music to Adisa's ears than the intricate notes of the Mozart concerto she'd listened to during the drive from Atlanta.

Watching her aunt sleep, Adisa remembered a time when she was a teenager and came down with the worst case of flu in her life. For three nights Aunt Josie let Adisa sleep propped up in the older woman's bed, so as not to disturb Shanika, while Aunt

Josie dozed in a worn-out recliner. Many times, Adisa awoke to the soothing touch of a cool rag on her burning forehead.

Aunt Josie moved her head slightly and groaned. Adisa jumped up from the chair and came closer. Her aunt's hair seemed grayer than the last time she'd seen her.

"Aunt Josie," she said softly. "It's Adisa."

The older woman's eyes fluttered and then opened. Adisa waited for her to say her name. Aunt Josie's lips moved, but the only sound that escaped her lips was something that came out like "baba sole lit to."

"What?" Adisa asked.

Aunt Josie continued with words that sounded equally incomprehensible. Adisa glanced at the door and wondered if she should get a nurse. Instead, she touched the hand that didn't have the IV and squeezed it gently.

"I've come to see you," she said. "Is there anything I can get you?"

Aunt Josie closed her eyes for a moment. When she opened them more gibberish came out of her mouth. Her aunt had always been a woman of precise speech with no wasted words. The effects of the stroke were worse than Adisa had suspected. Panic began to rise up in her chest. The door to the room opened. A young male doctor with thick, reddish-brown hair briskly entered the room.

"I'm Dr. Dewberry, the neurologist taking care of Ms. Adams," he said.

Adisa introduced herself.

"I'm glad you're here," the doctor continued. "Your aunt had an MRI of her brain shortly after admission. I just reviewed the results with the radiologist."

"What's wrong? She's talking nonsense."

"She's had a brain hemorrhage," the doctor replied. "And she probably doesn't recognize you or realize that her speech is impaired. My hope is that she's going to stabilize without the need for surgery. Dr. Steiner, a neurosurgeon, is going to review the MRI this evening."

Adisa looked at Aunt Josie, who mumbled a few sounds and licked her lips.

"How bad do you think it is?" she asked.

"Bad enough that it's a good thing the next-door neighbor who found her immediately called 911." The doctor patted Aunt Josie on the arm. "As you know, she's mildly hypertensive, but there was no way to predict that she had a blood vessel in her brain that was weak and about to rupture. From the scan it appears the bleeding is confined to the intracranial areas that control movement on the right side of her body."

"I live in Atlanta. If she needs brain surgery, I'd prefer to move her to Emory or Piedmont."

"Certainly," Dr. Dewberry replied easily. "But I suggest you delay that decision until we hear from Dr. Steiner."

"And when do you expect that to happen?"

"Anytime from six to midnight," the doctor said, glancing at his watch. "As soon as I know anything, I'll notify you."

"I need to get back to Atlanta by morning."

"Does your aunt have a health-care power of attorney?"

"Yes. I'm a lawyer and prepared it a few years ago. The POA designates me as the primary decision maker and my sister as secondary."

"Then I hope one of you will be available to give us direction about surgery and anything else that comes up."

"My sister is driving up from Augusta tomorrow afternoon."

"Good. Does the hospital know how to get in touch with you? The next day or so will be critical."

"No, but I can leave my cell phone number at the nurses' station."

"And it'll be necessary to have a copy of the health-care power of attorney on file to make sure we comply with HIPAA."

"Sure, I know where she keeps it in her house."

"Okay," the doctor responded and turned to leave.

"Thanks for taking care of her," Adisa said, not wanting to come across as ungrateful.

"You're welcome," Dr. Dewberry replied. "She's in good physical condition for an eighty-year-old woman. Hopefully, she'll bounce back strong."

After the doctor left, Adisa leaned over and gave Aunt Josie a quick kiss on her wrinkled cheek. Her aunt's eyes remained closed.

"I'm going to your house to pick up the health-care power of attorney," Adisa said. "The hospital needs to have it on file. I won't be gone for long."

Hoping for a response, Adisa stared intently at Aunt Josie's face. Her aunt twitched her nose but gave no indication she understood. With a heavy heart, Adisa left the hospital room. She stopped at the nurses' station and asked where she needed to drop off the legal papers.

"After five o'clock everything can be handled here," the nurse replied, writing down Adisa's name. "I'll record your contact information in the file and put you on the list for twenty-four-hour access."

"Thanks."

It was less than a ten-minute drive from the hospital to Aunt Josie's house. Adisa needed gas for her car and stopped at the Westside Quik Mart. After paying for the gas at the pump, she went inside the store to buy a bottle of flavored vitamin water. Two workmen were installing a Plexiglas barrier in front of the cash register similar to what she'd seen at convenience stores in rougher parts of Atlanta. A bold sign on the barrier announced "Cashier Has Less Than $100 Cash and No Key to Safe." Adisa glanced up and saw two large surveillance cameras pointed directly at the spot where she was standing.

She left the store. A few blocks later she turned onto East Nixon Street, the main access point to the older neighborhood where Aunt Josie lived. Most of the modest houses had been built in the 1950s and '60s. The dwellings were small but the lots spacious. Without any neighborhood restrictions or oversight by the city, the condition of the houses varied widely. Some were neat and meticulous, with green grass, flowers, and neatly trimmed bushes. Others were surrounded by weeds, with ripped screens in the windows, peeling paint, and multicolored shingles on the roof due to irregular repairs.

Adisa saw a cluster of floral displays surrounding a picture in the grass beside the road. She slowed to a stop. In the middle of the flowers was a large photograph of a young black man. Adisa didn't recognize him, but it had been more than ten years since she'd lived in Campbellton. The young man was wearing a coat and tie. Stuck among the display was an orange basketball with signatures scribbled on it.

Her aunt's house on Baxter Street was one of the few mostly brick homes in the neighborhood. The exterior walls were redbrick up to the level of the windows on the front and entirely brick on the sides and rear. Aunt Josie used to tell the girls the wicked wolf would never blow her house down.

The businessman who sold the house to Aunt Josie really was a wolf who utilized an installment plan that bordered on usury. In spite of the oppressive terms of the contract, Aunt Josie paid off the house when Adisa was in the sixth grade and threw a big party to celebrate.

Adisa pulled into the driveway and parked behind her aunt's fifteen-year-old sedan that had less than fifty thousand miles on the odometer. The grass in the front yard of the flat lot was in good shape. Even though Adisa had offered to pay for a lawn service, Aunt Josie still insisted on cutting the grass herself. Mature bushes reached to the bottoms of the windows and lined the narrow sidewalk that connected the concrete driveway to the entrance. There wasn't a garage or carport. Taking groceries inside during a rainstorm meant getting wet. Aunt Josie didn't plant flowers in the yard, but Adisa knew the inside of the house was filled with color from flowers, ferns, and other kinds of potted plants. She got out of the car and walked around the side of the house.

The backyard was adjacent to baseball fields and basketball courts owned by the local parks and recreation department. The area reserved for Aunt Josie's garden had been tilled, but it wasn't clear what the older woman had planted except for a line of ten tomato plants. The clothesline in the photo in Adisa's office was gone, replaced many years before by an electric dryer.

A neighbor, Mr. Walter Broome, was sitting in a chair on the back stoop of his house. The gray-haired man had worked for the city as a heavy-equipment operator for over forty years before he retired.

"How's your aunt?" he called out.

Adisa walked over and gave him a quick summary.

"I was the one who called 911," Mr. Broome said. "Mary sent me over to borrow some vanilla extract for pancake batter, and when Josie didn't answer I went inside and found her lying on the floor in the living room."

"I'm glad you did."

"And I was thanking the Lord that her door was unlocked." Mr. Broome pointed up at the sky. "Her angel was working overtime."

"Yes," Adisa agreed.

"I called Brother Mack," Walter continued, referring to one of the deacons at the church Aunt Josie attended. "He's out of town with his wife but will be back Sunday morning."

"Shanika is driving up tomorrow," Adisa said, "so everyone should probably check with her to get the latest news."

"Can't Josie have visitors?" Mr. Broome asked in surprise.

"No, they've put her in a room on the quarantine floor because of a shortage of beds."

As soon as the words were out of her mouth, Adisa regretted them. Mention of the word "quarantine" was likely to spark crazy speculation. She knew it was pointless to ask Walter and his wife, Mary, to keep quiet. Fresh gossip was better than iced sweet tea with a thick slice of lemon on a hot afternoon in August. Adisa quickly changed the subject.

"What's going on with the memorial on East Nixon Street?" she asked. "I didn't know the young man in the picture. Was he hit by a car?"

"Where have you been?" Mr. Broome asked in surprise. "I was sure that story made it into the newspaper in Atlanta. Deshaun Hamlin was shot in the middle of the road by a white police officer looking for a young black man to kill. Thankfully, Deshaun didn't die, but he's hanging on to life by a thread with a bullet in his brain. It would have been on TV, the Internet, and everywhere else if it had happened in a big city. But nobody cares about a place like this. Or what happens to a fine young man like Deshaun. Thelma Armistead is his grandmother. He was living with her during his junior year in high school."

Adisa remembered Mrs. Armistead as a jolly, overweight woman known for wearing hats and baking delicious desserts. It was sad to think about her grieving the tragic shooting of a grandson.

"Now that I think about it, I did see a headline in a newspaper at the hospital about the shooting. It looks like the district attorney's office may file charges against the officer," she said.

"There's a petition with over seven hundred and fifty signatures on it asking him to do exactly that. Even a few white folks signed it. I wish you were practicing law here in Campbellton. You wouldn't be afraid to prosecute a police officer."

"That's not my area of the law now."

"But it could be," Mr. Broome insisted hopefully.

"No, I've moved on. The local DA's office will make that decision."

"But do you really think they'll do the right thing? Jasper Baldwin, the DA, only got elected because of his uncle's money."

Adisa didn't want to get dragged into a sinkhole of Nash County politics. She glanced over her shoulder at her aunt's house.

"Maybe folks should get the governor's office involved," she suggested. "He could bring in a special prosecutor if the local

DA's office doesn't want to handle the case."

"Could the governor appoint you to do it?" Mr. Broome perked up. "Everybody knows how smart you are."

Desperate to escape, Adisa began backing away. "I need to take something from the house to the hospital," she said. "Thanks for letting Brother Mack and folks at the church know about Aunt Josie."

"No problem. And let us know if we can help in any way. Mary and I think the world of Josie. After Mary had her hip surgery last summer, Josie took care of both of us." Mr. Broome patted his stomach. "I love to eat but can't cook anything except a fried egg. Josie fed me and helped Mary with her bath."

Adisa told Walter she would keep him and Mary posted on Aunt Josie's condition as she waved and turned to walk back to the house. She picked up her aunt's copy of the local newspaper and carried it inside. Aunt Josie's walking stick was in its usual place behind the door. All the bark had been stripped from the five-foot piece of wood. The spot Aunt Josie grasped as she walked was totally smooth and the wood darkened by the oils from the older woman's hand.

In the den a ball of gray yarn lay on the

floor beside her aunt's recliner, a partially finished scarf draped across the armrest. On a low table next to the chair was a half-empty cup of green tea. Adisa picked up the delicate teacup, an antique made of fragile cream-colored china, took it into the kitchen, and poured the tea down the drain. Aunt Josie hated dirty dishes piling up in the sink, so Adisa washed the cup in warm sudsy water and returned it to its assigned place in the cupboard above the toaster. When Adisa closed the cupboard she was hit by a wave of sadness that her aunt might never be able to do a simple task that had been part of a sixty-year routine for her.

"No, Lord!" Adisa said out loud. "She's going to be better soon!"

Drying her hands and pushing back gloomy thoughts, Adisa went into her aunt's bedroom. A chenille spread decorated with a large multicolored peacock in the middle covered the bed. Against the far wall was a small desk with two side-by-side drawers. The health-care power of attorney was in an envelope with "Dixon and White" printed as the return address. Adisa took out one of the two signed and notarized copies.

Returning to the kitchen, she stuck her finger into the dirt in a pot that contained an explosion of multicolored coleus. Aunt

Josie had more than forty houseplants. The hardy schefflera at Adisa's office was the only plant child in her life. The soil in the kitchen pot was moist, a sign that it had been cared for within the past twenty-four hours.

On her way out the door, Adisa grabbed the newspaper that she'd dropped on the small kitchen table. There would be plenty of time at the hospital to read every word about the local shooting along with the wedding announcements and reports about prospects for the soybean harvest.

Adisa delivered the health-care power of attorney to the woman on duty at the nurses' station. Aunt Josie was in the same position. Scooting a chair close to her aunt's side, Adisa opened the paper. Not wanting to read anything gloomy, she skipped the article about the police officer and focused on upbeat news. She read aloud, even though there was no sign Aunt Josie was listening.

"Here's one I bet you already know about," Adisa said. "Brianne Morehead took a trip to Europe in the spring and is going to talk about it Saturday morning at the library. She especially liked Venice."

"Venus?" Aunt Josie croaked.

With a start, Adisa stopped reading and stared at her aunt; Josie's eyes remained closed.

"Aunt Josie," she said, leaning closer. "It's Adisa. I'm here with you at the hospital. You've had a stroke."

Aunt Josie wrinkled her nose and sniffed. On the tray table beside the bed was a cup of water and a wooden stick with a small yellow sponge on the end. Adisa dipped the sponge into the water and ran it along her aunt's lips. Aunt Josie weakly tried to close her mouth on the sponge. The IV dripping from the bag wouldn't do anything about a parched tongue. Adisa moistened the sponge again and held it so her aunt could press her lips against it. She repeated the motion seven or eight times before Aunt Josie relaxed, and Adisa was satisfied the older woman's thirst was at least partially quenched. A male nurse about Adisa's age entered the room and saw Adisa with the sponge stick in her hand.

"Did she show any interest in the water?" the nurse asked.

"Yes."

"That's good. I couldn't get her to take any a few hours ago."

Adisa watched as the young man checked

her aunt's vital signs and repositioned her pillow.

"Dr. Dewberry said we're waiting on an opinion from Dr. Steiner, the neurosurgeon."

"I saw the referral in the chart," the RN replied. "We'll make sure you get a chance to talk to her."

"Dr. Steiner is a woman?"

"Who graduated from medical school at Johns Hopkins," the young man replied with a smile. "She treated my mother last summer. She's an excellent surgeon. My shift doesn't end until 11:00 p.m., so I'll be sure to facilitate the call with Dr. Steiner if she tries to contact you."

"Thanks."

The nurse left, and Adisa resumed her seat by her aunt. "Your neurosurgeon is a female," she said to the sleeping woman. "You taught me there's no ceiling to the sky. I need to remember that."

Six

Adisa waited to call Shanika until she was reasonably sure her sister's kids would be finished with their showers and tucked into bed. Aunt Josie was still asleep, so Adisa picked up the newspaper and read the front-page article about the police officer who shot the young black man. At the top of the article was the same picture of Deshaun Hamlin that Adisa had seen on East Nixon Street. Beside the black teenager's picture was a photo of a young white police officer with "Officer Nelson" beneath it.

District Attorney Jasper Baldwin will likely seek an indictment against Campbellton police officer Luke Nelson in the shooting of sixteen-year-old Deshaun Hamlin. Per police department policy, Nelson is currently on administrative leave. Hamlin remains in a coma at Campbellton Memorial Hospital. Police Chief Ben Lockhart stated that his office is fully cooperating with the district attorney. There are no known witnesses, but several residents reported hearing multiple gunshots.

Confidential sources confirm that Officer Nelson contends Hamlin threatened him with a gun and fired first. Members of Hamlin's family deny that the youth was armed or dangerous. Nelson has refused to respond to repeated requests for comment. One of the newer members of the Campbellton Police Department, Nelson previously served as an officer with the Atlanta Police Department. There is no record of any disciplinary action against him.

Last night a meeting of concerned citizens took place at Zion Hills Baptist Church. Hamlin and several members of his family are members of the church. A number of pastors and community leaders spoke to a crowd of 350 people. Several held up signs demanding "Justice for Deshaun." Reverend Reggie Reynolds, pastor of the church and spokesman for the group, pledged to maintain public pressure until legal action was taken against Officer Nelson. When informed this morning about the DA's current refusal to present the case to the grand jury, Reynolds expressed doubt that local authorities would indict a police officer without pressure from the governor's office. Reynolds stated, "Deshaun was unarmed at the time of the shooting and didn't threaten the officer in any way. An unarmed black teenager was gunned down in the middle of the street in our town, and the man responsible for shooting him must answer for it."

Adisa understood why Reverend Reynolds would rally public sentiment and demand a full investigation into the shooting of the young member of his congregation. In a town like Campbellton, the community power brokers were adept at brushing matters under the rug. The newspaper could play a big role in trying to prevent that from happening. She checked the byline for the author of the article. It was written by reporter Jamie Standard. Adisa didn't know if Standard was black or white, male or female. But it was easy to understand why folks were upset. Adisa could sympathize with Mr. Broome's frustration, but there wasn't anything she could do about it.

Even if the DA presented the case to the grand jury, there was no guarantee an indictment would be issued. The grand jury was supposed to be representative of the racial profile of the overall population. Within the city limits of Campbellton, slightly more than thirty percent of the residents were black. That percentage fell to twenty percent when including everyone who lived in Nash County. And for the past 150 years, the twenty to thirty percent of the population classified as African American had never effectively flexed its political muscle beyond the election of an occasional city council member. Adisa couldn't remember a black sheriff or district attorney and didn't know if any black officers served on the police force.

She turned to the crossword puzzle and began filling it in. At an early age she'd shown a knack for identifying the right words, and Aunt Josie saved the puzzles for her. Adisa found the puzzles relaxing. Thirty minutes later, she wrote in the last word and glanced up at her aunt.

"Done," she said. "It's a lot easier than the one in the *New York Times*."

Aunt Josie remained in a deep sleep. There was a knock on the door, and Adisa turned sideways in her chair as someone entered. It was Dr. Dewberry.

"Glad you're here," the neurologist said. "I spoke with Dr. Steiner. She doesn't think your aunt is going to need surgery."

"Great," Adisa said with relief, reaching over to pat Aunt Josie on the hand.

"Not necessarily," Dr. Dewberry replied. "It's more a case of the hemorrhage being in a place we can't get to without running the risk of making Ms. Adams worse, not better."

"Oh," Adisa replied, her relief evaporating. "What does that mean as to her recovery?"

"A longer recuperation period before we know what she'll regain and what she's lost."

"How long?"

"I can't say. All I can give now are possible scenarios."

"Please, give me your honest opinion."

Dr. Dewberry pulled up a chair and sat beside the bed. "We'll keep your aunt here in the hospital for a few more days, and if she improves, transition her to a skilled nursing facility. Medicare will authorize up to ninety days of care that will include physical and occupational therapy. If she doesn't progress, you and your sister will need to find a bed for her in a long-term-care nursing home."

Adisa glanced sadly at Aunt Josie. The thought that the formerly vibrant woman might spend her last days strapped into a wheelchair or lying inert in a bed was too painful to consider.

"We just don't know right now how she'll recover," Dr. Dewberry continued. "If she does well, she may not need an entire ninety days of skilled care and could go home. Who lives with her now?"

"No one. She's lived alone for over ten years."

"It's likely she'll need home health assistance. A social worker here at the hospital or the one who works at the skilled nursing facility can let you know the options. For now, we're going to monitor her here. As she regains cognitive function, she'll probably benefit from visitors. I wrote the order for her to be moved from the quarantine area by tomorrow morning, which will make access to her easier for friends and other family members."

"Okay," Adisa said and nodded. "I know tons of people from her church will want to come by, but I don't want that to happen until she can enjoy them."

"Yes, it will be a good idea to limit visitors at first." The doctor paused for a moment. "Caring for a loved one who's had this type of brain hemorrhage is an unknown journey. There will be twists and turns you can't plan for."

After the doctor left, Adisa looked at Aunt

Josie, leaned over, and gently kissed her aunt's wrinkled hand.

"We're in this together," she whispered.

Adisa stepped out of the room and walked down the hallway to call Shanika. She gave her sister an update.

"Or they don't want to operate because of her age," Shanika interjected when Adisa mentioned Dr. Steiner's recommendation against surgery. "This is worse than I thought. I've been imagining all afternoon that by the time you arrived she'd have been making sure every corner of her hospital room was scrubbed clean and the toilet bowl was as sanitary as a baby's bottle."

"No, I'm afraid it's going to be a while before she's going to notice details like that." Adisa paused. "Maybe never."

"The thought of her lying there alone and confused makes me want to cry. At least you'll be with her in case she has a lucid moment. We'll talk more when I get there tomorrow. Can you try to set up a meeting with the neurologist? I think it would be good if we talked with him together."

"I'm going back to Atlanta in the morning," Adisa said. "It was tough enough to sneak away for the afternoon. Failing to show up tomorrow would be an unexcused absence."

"This isn't like skipping a day of school," Shanika replied with an edge to her voice. "If I'd known you were going to bail on her, I'd have already started making arrangements to hire a private sitter."

Adisa felt her face flush with anger. She'd already sacrificed more than Shanika.

"I'll be here when I need to, but you'll see for yourself that there won't be any major decisions made tomorrow, the next day, or the day after that. Both of us are going to put some miles on our cars over the next weeks and months as we figure out what to do for her. We'll talk after you have a chance to check out the situation tomorrow."

"I know you want to cut this call short, but we're not going to give Aunt Josie the leftovers of our lives."

"Bye, Shanika," Adisa said.

Steaming, Adisa slipped her phone into her purse. Her sister was a master at laying on a guilt trip. Ronnie probably never won an argument in their household. Adisa returned to Aunt Josie's room and prepared to settle in for a long, sleep-deprived night.

"Are you sure you should go?" Jane asked Luke.

"I'm the reason for the meeting," he answered. "People need to see that I'm not some trigger-happy monster. If I don't show up at a rally supporting me, what message will that send?"

"Just remember, anything you say will be twisted and taken out of context."

"How many speeches have you heard me give in the years we've known each other?" Luke asked, trying to manage a smile. "Look, public opinion is a big deal. The DA has to run for election next year. The other side is bashing me and spreading all sorts of lies. I'm not going to hide out in the house. It makes me look like I'm guilty of doing something wrong."

"It's just —" Luke stopped his wife with a gentle touch of his index finger to her lips.

"I'll be home before Ashley finishes her bath," he said.

"Be careful."

"I will. I promise."

Luke owned an older-model pickup truck that he'd bought from one of his uncles. He'd then carefully restored it. Before Ashley was born, Luke referred to the red truck as "his baby." Now it had second billing.

It was a five-minute drive to the rally, which was being held at a high school gym. As he passed familiar houses on streets he'd come to know by heart, Luke thought about how different the world looked to him. He'd enjoyed the lower stress of the job in Campbellton and welcomed the new family responsibility that fell on his shoulders with the arrival of Ashley. But now he was struggling more and more under the crushing mental weight of the shooting. He'd hoped the passage of a few weeks would make the burden easier. It hadn't. Luke tried to keep a positive attitude in front of Jane, who remained a rock of stability, but inside he felt himself beginning to crumble.

Luke parked his truck beside the space reserved for Dr. Letha Cartwright, the high school principal. Dr. Cartwright was a well-respected black woman with a reputation for strict, impartial fairness that helped tamp down racial tensions at the high school. Several men joined Luke on the sidewalk.

"Are you Officer Nelson?" a middle-aged dark-haired man asked him.

"Yes," Luke replied.

"It was a good thing you did," the man said. "It sent a message that needed to be heard loud and clear — law enforcement in this town isn't going to back down from anyone."

"Yeah, and white folks need to stand up for you when the blacks are trying to take you down," said another one of the men.

Luke didn't respond. He didn't want the responsibility of representing the entire police department. He especially didn't want to be categorized as a white supremacist. They reached the gym entrance, and Luke held the door open for the others. He wasn't being polite. He didn't want to be seen in close proximity to the men and somehow be linked to their views. Inside the cavernous gym was a cluster of eighty or ninety people sitting on the bleachers. Luke saw several homemade signs: "Support Your Local Police," "We Believe Officer Nelson," "Protect Police Rights," and "Police Lives Matter." Luke recognized several faces, but most of those present were strangers. The crowd clapped when he appeared, and he awkwardly acknowledged their support. Dr. Cartwright was standing to the side but didn't clap her hands.

"We believe in you, Luke!" shouted a woman sitting halfway up the bleacher seats.

"Don't listen to the lies!" yelled a man Luke didn't recognize.

"We'll speak up for you!" another man called out. "Just tell us what to say!"

A middle-aged man Luke didn't know came to the front. "I'm Bob Jenkins, a local business owner. I want to thank each of you for coming out this evening. My family and

I are praying for Officer Nelson and his family. It's important that every citizen of Nash County demonstrate support for our local police who work tirelessly to protect our community. Your presence here is a practical way to show that."

The businessman stepped back and motioned for Luke to come forward. He nervously cleared his throat. The room became extra quiet.

"Thank you," he said. "Because there's an ongoing investigation, I can't make any public statements about what happened, but my family and I really appreciate the support."

"What about Deshaun Hamlin?" a woman's voice interrupted. "He's lying in the hospital on life support. And you put him there!"

Instantly, several people sitting around the woman began confronting her in loud voices. Luke glanced up and watched as one of the men who had walked into the gym with him swore at her.

"She has a right to ask her questions!" a man sitting ten feet from the woman said, rising to his feet and pointing his finger at Luke. "And Officer Nelson is a coward if he won't answer her!"

"Get out of here!" responded a man Luke

didn't recognize. "We're here to support the police, not accuse them!"

Luke raised his hands in an effort to bring quiet, but the restless crowd refused to calm down. He turned to Mr. Jenkins, who had retreated to a seat on the bleachers. Arguments were breaking out everywhere. A photographer Luke hadn't noticed began taking pictures. Dr. Cartwright rose to her feet. She was a large woman with eyeglasses hanging from a chain around her neck. She stood beside Luke.

"Quiet!" she roared in a voice loud enough for crowd control of an auditorium full of rowdy teenagers.

Either the volume of Dr. Cartwright's command or her innate authority caused the group to settle down.

"The school board gave you permission to have this public meeting," Dr. Cartwright said, her voice projecting to the four corners of the room. "But I'm going to put a stop to it if you can't at least act like ninth graders."

The room became more still.

"How many of you have children who attend this school? I know there are some of you because I recognize your faces."

About thirty hands went up.

"Keep your hands up. And how many of

you have children or grandchildren who attend a school somewhere else in Nash County?"

Most of the people in the bleachers raised their hands. Dr. Cartwright slowly let her eyes go back and forth as if taking names for detention.

"Those children are watching and listening to see how you respond to this situation. And what you do and say is going to teach them a lesson they'll carry with them for the rest of their lives. It's your choice whether that lesson is good or bad."

"You're saying that because we're white!" a male voice called out.

Luke braced himself for the explosion he knew was coming from the principal, who stared in the direction of the man who spoke.

"All of you may be white," the educator responded calmly. "But I said the same thing in a Sunday-night meeting at my church, which is all black. And this past Wednesday morning I had a meeting with the faculty of the school and told them we're going to use this as an opportunity to model the kind of society we want our students to live in. If change is going to come, it'll start with people who have a firm foundation to stand on. It's time this community took the next step — from integration to reconciliation. If you want to know the details of our plan, I'm available to talk with you one-on-one."

For Luke, the shooting wasn't an opportunity to learn; it was an ordeal to survive. The next fifteen minutes were a blur filled with the shaking of hands and mumbled thanks. The people in the room expressed many sentiments, all supportive. He particularly thanked Mr. Jenkins for his comments.

"I couldn't keep quiet," the businessman replied. "My younger brother works in law enforcement, and I know what you guys go through every day."

When the man approached who'd called Luke a coward, Dr. Cartwright stepped in between them, and the man didn't try to push past her. Luke accepted a quick hug from a woman who worked at a local insurance agency. He'd helped her one day when her car was broken down on the side of the road.

"We're praying for you," the woman said. "And your family."

"That means a lot. I'll tell my wife."

As soon as he could, Luke began looking for a graceful way to exit. He decided talking to Dr. Cartwright would be the best way to signal that he was finished interacting with the crowd.

"Thanks for what you said," he said to the educator. "I'd like to hear more, and maybe be a part of the process you described. Of course, that can't happen until I'm officially cleared."

The principal eyed him for a moment. "Do you believe justice should be done even if you don't like the result?" she asked.

"Certainly, but I didn't do —"

"I'm not asking you to say something about what took place the night of the shooting," Dr. Cartwright said, interrupting him. "But you have to be at the right place in your own heart and mind before you can have the moral authority to speak to this type of societal problem."

Luke opened his mouth but closed it without speaking. He suddenly felt like a student called on in class who hadn't read the assignment. He knew the educator was right about one thing — his offer of help was hollow. He'd not really thought much about the bigger picture, the broader implications of the shooting beyond the threat to himself and his family.

"Uh, I'm not sure I understand what you mean," he replied.

"Someday I hope you will," Dr. Cartwright replied. "I really do. Maybe then you can speak, and it will have an impact."

When Luke arrived home, Jane jumped up from the couch in the den where she was reading her Bible and hugged him tightly.

"It wasn't that bad," Luke said, stroking her hair. "There were a few hecklers."

"It's not that," Jane managed before she pulled away. "Check the living room."

Luke stepped across the foyer into the small formal space. Normally, Jane kept an arrangement of fresh flowers in the middle of the low coffee table. Tonight, the flowers were gone. In their place was a large brownish-colored brick with bits of mortar stuck to it.

"Someone threw that through the window while I was giving Ashley her bath."

"Did you see anything?" Luke asked sharply.

"No." Jane shook her head. "I guess whoever did it knew you wouldn't be here."

"How long ago?"

"About fifteen minutes."

"Did you call the police?"

"I thought about it but wasn't sure that's what you would want me to do." Jane sniffled. "I just wanted you to come home."

Luke pulled back the curtains. Two panes

in one of the windows were shattered. Jane had already covered the holes with pieces of cardboard taped to the frame.

"Where's the glass?" he asked.

"I cleaned it up. Should I have left it on the carpet?"

"No, no," Luke replied as he rubbed his temples with his fingers. "I was just thinking that this is a crime scene."

"It is," Jane answered slowly. "And I'm scared what may happen next."

Between the uncomfortable chair and interruptions by the nurses checking on Aunt Josie, Adisa was glad when 5:30 a.m. arrived. Swishing water around in her mouth, she looked at her reflection in the mirror. Stopping by her apartment for a quick shower, a change of clothes, and fresh makeup would be mandatory before she ventured into the office.

"Shanika is going to visit later today," Adisa said to her aunt. "Let me know if she tries to boss you around, and I'll straighten her out. She doesn't scare me like she used to."

Aunt Josie didn't respond. After a final glance, Adisa quietly left the hospital. Getting in her car, she tuned the radio to the AM station that broadcast local news. The announcer led off the morning news with the latest updates about Officer Luke Nelson and the shooting of Deshaun Hamlin. The radio report added one piece of information, not included in the newspaper article, about a rally that had been held to show support for the police officer the previous evening. Adisa said a quick prayer that the problems surrounding the shooting wouldn't spill over into violent confrontations in the streets.

Seven

"Good morning," Catherine said when she saw Adisa in the hallway. "How's your aunt?"

"Serious but stable. My sister is driving up to check on her later today. I came back to complete the memo in the Sipco matter. I should have it to you by noon if that's okay."

"Good, and I had a message on my voice mail from a reporter at the *AJC* about the Larimore case. Were you interviewed?"

"On the way back from the courthouse. I couldn't believe how fast the news leaked out."

"What did she ask you?"

Adisa attempted to reconstruct the conversation, but Aunt Josie's health crisis had pushed the details from the edge of her memory.

"It sounds like Ms. Rogers has a liberal bent," Catherine said.

"Maybe," Adisa answered. "She bounced all over the place with questions that didn't seem to have a sequential structure."

"Everybody's thoughts aren't as organized as yours," Catherine said with a smile. "I won't have time to call her back until later today or tomorrow."

Adisa went into her office. Before diving into work, she checked her computer. No e-mail from Sharon Rogers was in her queue. Ten minutes later, Adisa's phone buzzed.

"You're needed in conference room G for a meeting with Mr. Katner," said one of the administrative assistants who worked in their section.

"Now?"

"Yes, all the lawyers and staff on Catherine's team are required to be there."

Holding a gathering of every lawyer in the subgroup wasn't unusual, but doing so without circulating an agenda in advance was odd, especially if Linwood Katner called the meeting. Other colleagues were making their way to the largest conference room on the floor. Katner was sitting at the head of the table with Catherine to his right. Adisa immediately suspected the meeting had to do with breaking the news about the massive new merger Catherine had mentioned the previous day.

There was a minimal amount of small talk as everyone took their seats around the table. The managing partner's salt-and-pepper hair was carefully combed to the side. Dark eyes that never missed a detail peered out from beneath bushy eyebrows. Adisa glanced at Catherine, who looked puzzled.

"I have news," Katner began without any preamble. "The firm has decided to shut down the Atlanta merger and acquisition group and transfer all its responsibilities to the Boston office. Some of you will be offered positions in Boston. The rest will receive a severance package."

Several people involuntarily gasped. Adisa glanced at Catherine, who was clearly as shocked as anyone else in the room. Katner slid a thick envelope across the table to Catherine.

"Ms. Summey will inform you about your status by the end of the day. I've set the schedule for your individual meetings, which will begin in this room at ten thirty. Until then, please return to work. That's all."

Katner left the room. With apprehensive glances at their coworkers, the men and women around the table slowly pushed back their chairs to stand and began to file out.

"Adisa," Catherine said. "You're at the top of the list. I'll see you at ten thirty."

"Yes, ma'am," Adisa replied as the people who remained in the room stared at her.

She knew what they were thinking: Was it a good thing or a bad thing to be up first? Adisa numbly made her way back to her office, not sure if she should, or could, work on the memo in the Sipco case during the hour and a half until her time to return to the conference room. Knowing the professional thing to do was to finish well regardless of her fate, she turned on her computer and pulled up the documents she needed to analyze. Over the next ninety minutes, she didn't do the best work of her career, but she did the best she could. Then, after a quick trip to the restroom to check her appearance, Adisa sent up a simple prayer entrusting her future into God's hands and returned to the conference room. Catherine now sat at the head of the table with the director of human resources on her left. Grim-faced, Catherine motioned for Adisa to sit down.

"This has been a rough hour and a half that's about to get worse," Catherine said. "What have you been doing?"

"I finished the Sipco memo and sent it to

you a couple of minutes ago," Adisa said. "It's bare-bones because I didn't have time to flesh it out, but I believe you'll have the gist of what we need to request so that —"

"You'll be able to prepare a more detailed memo if I need it," Catherine said. "You're on the list for the move."

"I am?" Adisa asked, suddenly realizing that based on her history with Mr. Katner, she had assumed she'd be fired.

"Yes. The firm will buy out the lease on your apartment in Atlanta, and a relocation service will assist you in finding a place in Boston. It's more expensive to live there, so there will be an increase in your salary to avoid a de facto pay cut. All your moving expenses will be paid as well. You'll remain a part of my team, but how we'll interface with lawyers higher up the ladder than I am will be worked out later. I believe this will ultimately be good for you. You're a rising star, and the heads of the firm will have a better chance to see what you bring to the table. Any questions?"

"Will Mr. Katner be making the move to Boston?"

"No," Catherine replied in a way that let Adisa know not to ask a follow-up question.

"How soon will this happen?"

"I should have told you that up front."

Catherine paused and rubbed her temples with her fingers. "I'm still trying to get my head around this decision myself. We want you up and running within sixty days. Our first project will be the merger I mentioned yesterday. I thought it was going to be a boon for us here, but it turns out —" Catherine stopped and turned to the HR director. "Tom, anything else I should add?"

Tom Mann was a prematurely balding man in his midthirties. He'd hired and fired so many people during his tenure at the law firm that Adisa suspected he'd grown numb to the emotions of the process.

"You'll receive a packet of paperwork within a few days," he said. "Read and sign. There isn't any flexibility in the terms."

"Okay."

"Congratulations," Catherine said with a weak smile.

Leaving the conference room, Adisa felt the eyes of everyone she passed seeking clues to her fate. Over the next couple of hours the other employees and attorneys on the list made their way to the conference room. News trickled out. A clerical assistant who frequently worked with Adisa was going to stay in Atlanta and move to the thirty-seventh floor. She came into Adisa's office to tell her the news. Lucy was a couple of years younger than Adisa.

"I hope I don't have to work for Mr. Katner," Lucy said in a whisper. "I've heard he's a bear in the morning and a tiger in the afternoon."

"I doubt they'll assign anyone to him with less than ten years' experience," Adisa replied reassuringly.

"I hope you're right. I knew they wouldn't let you go. Everyone knows you're Catherine's favorite."

"She's been great to me," Adisa admitted. "But I'm not sure how much influence she had in the process. Though she met with Mr. Katner yesterday afternoon, he apparently didn't give her any idea what was coming."

"Wow!" Lucy's eyes widened. "Even the people who look like big shots to me don't always know what's going on."

"But don't repeat that to anyone," Adisa responded, alarmed that she'd let down her guard for a moment and revealed a speculative opinion about upper-level management. "Just keep working the way you have for the past eighteen months, and you'll be fine."

"It's been easy because you're so sweet," Lucy replied. "I won't be able to handle someone who yells and screams. It will make me think about my stepfather and what he put me through when I was a teenager."

The phone on Adisa's desk buzzed, which ended the conversation before any more unpleasant details about the assistant's upbringing came out. Lucy left and Adisa picked up the phone.

"Sharon Rogers from the *AJC* is calling. Do you want to talk to her?"

Adisa hesitated. She had nothing to add to the previous interview and didn't want to give Ms. Rogers another chance to try to twist her words. Besides, she needed to get to work.

"Connect her to my voice mail," she said. "And hold my calls, please."

For the next three hours, Adisa revised her memo in the Sipco matter. She found several additional troubling issues, which made her glad for a chance to update what Catherine would rely on. She didn't stop for lunch but took a quick break to eat an apple at her desk. Her phone buzzed.

"Your sister is calling," the receptionist continued. "Do you want to send her to voice mail, too?"

"I'll talk to her."

Adisa closed the door of her office before returning to her chair. "Are you on your way to Campbellton?" Adisa asked.

"No, I've been here for over an hour. I've talked to Dr. Dewberry and Aunt Josie."

"You've talked with Aunt Josie?"

"Not a lot, but she recognized me when I came into the room. The first words out of her mouth were that she wanted to go home."

Adisa had trouble connecting her last image of her aunt with the picture painted by her sister. "Sounds like she's had a miraculous recovery."

"Not really. Dr. Dewberry said it's hard to predict how quickly and to what extent someone will recover from this type of stroke. He's very pleased with her progress but cautioned that she could easily relapse."

"Is she still in the quarantine area?"

"No, they moved her shortly after I arrived. I think that may have helped wake her up. She's still having trouble swallowing, so she's on a liquid diet and someone has to assist her with eating."

Adisa listened as Shanika described feeding their aunt applesauce and broth for breakfast.

"The social worker came by a few minutes ago and talked about placement for Aunt Josie in a skilled nursing facility," Shanika continued.

"I knew that was in the works, just not

this soon."

"It won't happen for several days. Only one facility in Campbellton offers that type of care, and there's a waiting list to get in."

Adisa had assumed there would be a seamless transition to a skilled nursing facility.

"How long is the waiting list?"

"I'm not sure." Shanika paused. "But we may have to look for a place in Atlanta. The social worker said there are always beds in the metro area. I know we'd want to find one as close to you as possible —"

"That's not an option. What about a place near you and Ronnie?"

"The choices are worse than in Campbellton. Don't you remember how much trouble we had finding a place for Ronnie's grandfather? It makes much more sense for her to be close to you, even if you only drop by to see her on your way home from work."

Adisa pressed her lips together tightly for a moment before answering. "I'm being transferred to the law firm's headquarters in Boston," she replied. "They're shutting down our group in Atlanta, and over half the staff and several attorneys are losing their jobs. I was one of the lucky ones who made the cut. I just found out this morning. Everyone is still in shock, including me."

"You're moving to Boston?"

"Yes, and I'm just beginning to wrap my head around it. I've never lived someplace cold or that far from family."

"Which is what you should think about." Shanika began to speak rapidly. "This is a terrible time for you to abandon us. Can't they find another position for you in Atlanta? Your bosses obviously like you or they wouldn't have offered you the job in Boston. Once you explain your personal situation, I'm sure they'll work with you. Don't law firms have to offer you something under the family leave act?"

Adisa felt like she was being sprayed with a fire hose from five feet away. Her sister's response triggered several thoughts. Most of Adisa's energy over the past ten years had been focused on having the chance to practice her legal craft at the highest level. The move to Boston was a huge rung up on the ladder she wanted to climb. However, she didn't want to make a selfish decision.

"We don't have to decide anything about Aunt Josie today," Adisa replied. "But I can't drop everything and move to Campbellton."

"I know that," Shanika answered. "I'm

just stressed out over what's going to happen and what we should do. We're both listed on the health-care power of attorney you wrote up for her last year, right?"

"I'm first, with you as the alternate if I can't serve."

"Well, if you bail on the situation, you'll have to turn all decision making over to me."

Shanika's voice cracked, and she sounded like she was on the verge of tears. Adisa's stomach felt as queasy as it had when she was waiting her turn to go into conference room G.

"Let me see how things sort out here," she said, trying to regain her composure. "How long are you going to stay in Campbellton?"

"At least a couple of days. Ronnie took vacation time to take care of the kids."

"I'll come up Saturday morning, and we'll assess the situation then. Okay?"

"Assess the situation? You make it sound like we're talking about a leaky roof."

"You know what I mean. We'll talk. I'll be there early, no later than nine thirty," Adisa said.

"Whatever. I can't make you do anything."

The call ended. Adisa stared past the schefflera plant and out the narrow window.

The future was much less clear than the view. As frustrating as Shanika could be, she'd raised questions Adisa knew she had to answer.

EIGHT

Luke and Jane silently watched Ashley sleep in her crib. The tiny bedroom had cream-colored walls that featured hand-painted multicolored balloons. Located at the rear corner of the house, the room had a single window. Luke and Jane's bedroom was across the hall and had French doors that opened onto a small wooden deck.

Ashley had the sniffles, and she wrinkled her nose as she breathed. Jane positioned the baby's thin blanket for the third time so that it was perfectly tucked underneath Ashley's chin.

"It won't stay there," Luke whispered. "In five minutes she'll flip to her other side."

"And I'll come back in to check on her and fix it."

"She's going to kick her husband in bed more than you kick me," Luke replied.

"Do you want me to bring up your snoring?"

Ashley began breathing through her mouth with an accompanying raspy sound.

"It's cute when she snores," Luke said.

"And you like it when she kicks your stomach when you're playing with her."

They left the bedroom and went into the den. Without saying anything to each other, they'd avoided the living room.

"When will we know if they found any fingerprints on the brick?" Jane asked.

"Not long, but I'm not expecting anything to show up. Whoever threw it was probably wearing gloves."

Jane shook her head. "Do you think we should stay with my mother in Florida for a while?"

It wasn't the first time the subject of leaving Campbellton had come up. Luke had previously insisted they shouldn't move away because it would look like he was admitting guilt. The attack on his family was causing him to reconsider.

"Maybe," he replied slowly. "But I'll still have to come back and face any criminal charges filed against me."

"Don't talk like that, please. I'm praying it won't happen."

Jane's faith was personal and natural. Luke had attended church every Sunday since the shooting, but he didn't share

Jane's optimistic perspective that God might keep him from being indicted. That power rested with the DA and the grand jury.

There was a knock on the front door. Both Luke and Jane jumped. Luke went to the door and peered out the peephole. It was Bruce Alverez.

"Hey," Luke said when he opened the door. "I saw your car in the street earlier in the evening. I appreciate you keeping an eye out for me and my family."

"Sure," Bruce replied, glancing beyond Luke to the inside of the house. "Is Jane home?"

"Yes."

"The garage door is closed, so I wasn't sure both of your vehicles were there."

"Is there a problem?"

"Maybe. When I turned onto your street there was an older-model maroon car with heavily tinted windows cruising by. The driver saw me and took off."

"Why didn't you stop them?"

"I wanted to make sure you were safe first."

"Right." Luke relaxed.

"There's another thing," Bruce continued.

The officer reached into his back pocket, pulled out a folded piece of paper, and handed it to Luke.

"This isn't an arrest warrant, is it?" Luke asked in alarm.

"No, no. It's a subpoena for me to appear before the grand jury next week."

"To testify about the shooting?"

"No, a burglary, but I heard a rumor at the station that the DA might bring up your case on the same day. I have to be at Jasper Baldwin's office on Monday morning for a second interview about the shooting. There's speculation that the DA may bring in a special prosecutor. That way it would be tougher to claim you received preferential treatment, and it would get the local officials off the hook."

Luke still hoped for preferential treatment, but he also knew there were political forces in play. Chief Lockhart had shown him Bruce's report from the night of the shooting. It was so bare-bones that it didn't make half a skeleton. Luke knew his fellow officer had provided as little information as possible.

"I guess it's time for me to meet with an attorney myself," Luke said with a sigh. "But it's tough paying our monthly bills since Jane quit teaching and decided to stay home and take care of the baby."

Bruce leaned closer and spoke in a softer voice. "That's the other reason I stopped by. A meeting has been arranged for you on Saturday morning with Theodore Grayson. The chief set it up for you, but he didn't want to tell you personally in case he's asked about it later."

"Grayson? He's the top lawyer in town and probably the most expensive. Is the police department going to pay him?"

"No." Bruce shook his head. "Grayson is doing it as a favor. That's what the men who run this town do for one another. There's a lot more back-scratching going on than most people realize."

"But if I really need a lawyer, shouldn't I get one who's only looking out for me?" Luke asked.

Bruce shrugged. "I know you may not believe it, but the chief likes you and wants to help, even though at some point you may be on your own. Nobody who's in power wants to risk their position unless there's something in it for them."

"What's the status of the investigation?"

"Detective Maxwell isn't talking to anyone except the chief and the DA. The investigative file is kept under lock and key in his office."

"Are there any rumors about what he's found?" Luke asked.

"Nothing that I would believe. Do you

want to hear them anyway?"

Luke glanced over his shoulder at the den where Jane was waiting to cross-examine him about the conversation with Bruce. His imagination didn't need fresh fuel.

"No, I guess not," Luke said with a shake of his head. "Thanks for coming by."

Luke shook Bruce's hand and the officer left. Luke returned to the den.

"What did Bruce tell you?" she asked.

Jane's eyes widened when Luke broke the news that the case might be presented to the grand jury as soon as the following week.

"Will Bruce back you up when the DA calls him to testify?"

"I don't think he'll throw me under the bus."

"I hope you're right," Jane said. "Bruce and the DA are going to the top of my prayer list."

Saturday morning Adisa drove to Campbellton. It was a bright morning, and the uncertainties of life didn't seem as daunting in the light of a new day. Adisa shared the elevator with a male nurse caring for a very elderly man who appeared barely conscious as he slumped over in his wheelchair. Getting old was depressing. Adisa gently knocked on the door of her aunt's room.

"Come in," a female voice responded.

Shanika was sitting beside Aunt Josie's bed with a spoon in her hand and a container of red gelatin in front of her. Shanika was dressed casually in blue jeans and a green top. Her hair was cut even shorter than Adisa's, a practical response to managing a household with three small children. Aunt Josie was sitting up in bed with her eyes open.

"Look who's here," Shanika said as Adisa approached the end of the bed.

Aunt Josie squinted her eyes, and for a moment Adisa thought she didn't recognize her.

"Child, is that you?" she asked in a creaky voice.

"Yes, ma'am," Adisa replied, stepping to the opposite side of the bed from Shanika.

Aunt Josie's eyes followed her movements. Seeing her aunt even a tiny bit like herself made Adisa's emotions rush to the surface. She grabbed her aunt's hand and gently squeezed it. Shanika reached up and carefully repositioned Aunt Josie's head so she faced Adisa.

"I was here the evening you came into the hospital," Adisa said. "You're doing great now."

"Great?" Her aunt frowned and then

licked her lips before smacking them. "It doesn't feel great to me."

Aunt Josie glanced toward Shanika.

"Are you still hungry?" Shanika asked.

"For real food." Aunt Josie sniffed.

"Not until you can chew and swallow without choking," Shanika responded. "The occupational therapist is coming back this afternoon to work with you."

"All I need is a piece of bacon," Aunt Josie said. "That will get my strength back."

Aunt Josie considered bacon the prince of meats. A bacon, lettuce, and tomato sandwich featuring a vine-ripened tomato from her garden was a gourmet meal.

"I know she's feeling better if she's asking for bacon," Adisa said to Shanika.

"Don't talk about me like I'm not here," Aunt Josie cut in.

"Sorry," Adisa replied, looking directly into her aunt's eyes. "Now, tell me how you feel. Are you in pain?"

"I have a headache that's different from any I've had in the past. It's more toward the front than the ones that start at the top of my neck." Aunt Josie tried to raise her right hand, but it fell back to the sheet. She slowly lifted her left hand and touched her forehead directly above her eyes. "And my right arm and hand aren't working like they should. My right leg feels numb and tingly."

"Is the left side okay?" Adisa asked.

"Weak and shaky," Aunt Josie responded. "I think I could do more if it wasn't for that needle stuck in it."

Aunt Josie closed her eyes. Adisa waited for her to open them and continue. In a few moments it was clear that the older woman was sound asleep.

"That's how it goes," Shanika said. "She's talking away and passes out. She could be like this for fifteen minutes or an hour. Dr. Dewberry is very pleased with how fast she's bouncing back. He verified what you said about her condition when they brought her to the hospital."

"I wasn't lying about it."

"I know. Don't get defensive."

Adisa bit her lower lip. "You should have gone to law school instead of me," Adisa said. "I can see you baiting a hostile witness into blurting out something that destroys their case."

"You're my sister," Shanika responded calmly. "And I'm sorry for the way I've talked to you on the phone. I was worried and upset and frustrated because I couldn't be here myself and took it out on you."

The unexpected admission of fault caught Adisa off guard. "Okay," she said slowly.

"Does that mean you're fine with me moving to Boston if that's what I believe I should do, even though it would leave you primarily responsible for Aunt Josie?"

"What?" Aunt Josie asked in a creaky voice.

"Wait," Shanika said, putting her finger to her lips. "She may go back to sleep."

They sat in silence for a moment. Aunt Josie's steady breathing confirmed she wasn't finished with her nap.

"You have to decide what you think is right," Shanika replied. "It's not like when we were kids and I could force you to do what I wanted. Both of us have lives apart from Campbellton. We'll figure something out."

"Thanks," Adisa replied. "That helps."

They sat together for over an hour while Aunt Josie snoozed. Adisa asked Shanika about her kids, which was an easy conversation starter. An aide brought in a tray with Aunt Josie's lunch. As she listened to Shanika, Adisa realized it had been Christmas when she'd last visited her sister's family.

"I need to come see you," Adisa said. "It's been too long since I got a hug from Kendal and Keisha and Ronnie Jr."

Adisa's stomach growled, and she checked

the time. It was almost 1:00 p.m.

"What about our lunch?" she asked her sister.

"I'm dieting," Shanika replied. "I picked up an extra ten pounds over the past three months, so I'm drinking one of those protein shakes every day for lunch."

"I'm hungry," Aunt Josie said, opening her eyes. "How long have I been sleeping?"

"Over an hour," Shanika answered. "Your lunch is here."

Aunt Josie glanced skeptically toward the tray. "What is it?"

Shanika lifted the lid. "Broth and other assorted liquids."

Aunt Josie wrinkled her nose. "Adisa, go to the Jackson House Restaurant and get me a vegetable plate with sweet potatoes, creamed corn, and collard greens."

"That sounds good to me," Adisa replied with a smile. "I ate Chinese food last night, and you know how that doesn't stay with you."

"What day is it?" Aunt Josie asked suddenly.

"Saturday," Shanika answered.

"No, the date."

"May 18."

"One of you needs to go to the cemetery," Aunt Josie said, trying to push herself up in the bed. "Tomorrow is decoration Sunday, and there aren't any flowers on the graves."

"Isn't it usually closer to Memorial Day?" Adisa asked.

"Not this year," Aunt Josie replied.

Adisa glanced at Shanika, who shrugged. They both knew placing flowers on the family plots was a huge deal to their aunt. She'd dragged them to the ancient cemetery every spring for the ritual.

"I'll take care of it," Adisa said. "But it won't be as nice as when you do it."

"No yellows," Aunt Josie admonished. "My mama didn't like yellow."

"I know."

"Go to Bohannan's," Aunt Josie replied, relaxing in the bed. "Now, I'll try to get down some of that brown water they call soup."

Adisa left as Shanika pulled the rolling cart closer to the bed.

NINE

Luke parked behind the brick building where Grayson, Baxter, and Williams had their offices. Next to his truck was a new silver Mercedes. Even though he wasn't paying for the initial consultation, seeing the expensive car made Luke's heart sink. The monthly payment on the lawyer's vehicle was probably more than Luke and Jane's house payment, assuming that Theodore Grayson even had a car payment.

Luke went to the rear door of the office and pushed a black button. A few moments later the door opened, and he was greeted by a white-haired attorney in his early sixties. Theo Grayson was wearing a starched white shirt and gray pants. Gold-rimmed glasses sat on his nose.

"Officer Nelson," he said, extending his hand. "I'm Theo Grayson. Nice to meet you."

Grayson spoke with an Old South accent

that dripped with antebellum aristocracy.

"Thanks for seeing me."

Luke followed the lawyer a short distance down a hallway and into a spacious office with walnut paneling and original artwork. The hardwood flooring was accented by a large Oriental carpet. The lawyer's desk was the size of a small aircraft carrier and featured a leather inlay. Grayson didn't sit behind his desk. Instead, he directed Luke to a leather side chair. The lawyer sat across from him with a small coffee table between them. Everything about the room communicated prosperity.

"Would you like a cup of coffee?" Grayson asked. "I brewed a fresh pot a few minutes ago."

"No, sir," Luke replied, glancing down to make sure his shoes hadn't tracked any dirt onto the fancy carpet.

"I'm going to have a cup," Grayson replied. "Are you sure you won't join me?"

Luke hesitated. He didn't want to seem ungrateful for the opportunity to meet with the attorney.

"Okay."

"How do you take it?"

"Black."

Grayson left. Luke shifted in his chair. It felt awkward giving a drink order to the lawyer as if he were the waiter at the all-night diner the men on the police force dropped into at 2:00 a.m. for a caffeine jolt. In the midst of the sumptuous surroundings and old books, Luke also saw a sleek computer beside the lawyer's desk chair. Most of the artwork on the walls featured familiar scenes from Nash County. Luke recognized the last remaining covered bridge in the area and a large white farmhouse he suspected once belonged to the Grayson family. He knew the lawyer, a widower, lived in a Victorian house in town. Jane would love spending an hour snooping around the lawyer's office just for the history it held.

"Here you go," Grayson said, handing Luke a mug with the law firm name embossed on it in gold letters.

"Thanks."

Luke took a sip of the rich, flavorful brew. "Chief Lockhart serves us well here in Campbellton," Grayson began, "and I didn't hesitate when he asked if I'd be willing to meet with you. But let me make one thing clear at the outset. What we discuss within these four walls is between the two of us and no one else. It's confidential."

"Even though you're not my lawyer?"

"Yes, because there is a possibility I could

become your lawyer."

"There's no way I could afford to hire you —"

"That doesn't change the rules."

Grayson took a sip of coffee. Luke did, too.

"This coffee is great," Luke said.

"I'm glad you appreciate it," Grayson replied with a smile. "You can't buy it at the grocery store. It comes from a farm in Costa Rica where they pick the coffee beans by hand at the peak moment of ripeness. Do you know what they call the pod that contains the seeds?"

"No, sir."

"The cherry," Grayson replied, taking another long sip himself before setting his mug on the table. "Often, people don't know the whole story about things that are common in life. It's the same with events in the news. I've read the newspaper accounts of what supposedly happened the night of the shooting, but I don't believe everything I read in the paper, even though I own a small part of it. Tell me how you felt when Deshaun Hamlin approached you on East Nixon Street."

Luke had expected the lawyer to start with the beginning of his shift or when he received the call from the dispatcher about the robbery at the Westside Quik Mart.

"Excuse me?" he said. "Why is that important?"

"That may not be the perfect place to begin," Grayson replied. "But I want to start by identifying what you felt that night. If we can do that, it will take you back in your mind to those crucial minutes and provide the kinds of details that can be critical to a legal investigation. It's known as forensic experiential questioning; I simply call it helping people remember."

"Okay," Luke said and then paused for a moment. "When I saw Hamlin for the first time in the light of the streetlamp, I suddenly had a bitter taste in my mouth."

"Tell me about that moment."

Beginning with the bitter taste, Luke relived the encounter at a depth that exceeded the who, what, when, and where scenario he'd given when he calmed down enough to prepare a statement at the police department. While Luke talked, Grayson did nothing except drink coffee and ask questions. Theo Grayson was blowing up Luke's stereotype of a lawyer. It was the first time Luke had been able to talk in detail about the shooting without experiencing a mild panic attack or getting defensive.

"Aren't you going to take any notes?" he

asked the lawyer at one point. "Or do you have a photographic memory?"

"I don't have total recall," the lawyer said. "But if I took notes, I couldn't properly listen to you. You were telling me about hearing the sound of your heart beating."

"That happened when I thought Hamlin tried to shoot me. But as you know, he was unarmed."

"Are you sure he didn't have a gun?"

"What do you mean?" Luke sat up straighter in his chair. "Bruce Alverez checked the suspect and the area around him. He didn't find anything that could be considered a weapon except a pocketknife."

"Did you pat down Hamlin yourself?"

"No. I was pretty shook up, and we were waiting for the medics to arrive."

Grayson nodded. "Do you know who inventoried what Officer Alverez found at the scene?"

"Detective Maxwell. By that time it had started raining pretty hard, and I was sitting in my car waiting for instructions on what to do next. I don't know everything Maxwell stored in the evidence locker. He took my gun, of course."

Grayson nodded but still didn't take any notes. "Why did the dispatcher identify De-shaun Hamlin and Greg Ott as suspects in the robbery when it was an unknown assailant who stole the money and cut up the clerk?"

"Those were the names the store clerk gave when he came to for a few moments in the ambulance on the way to the hospital. The EMTs asked who did this to him. He mumbled something about Hamlin and Ott without realizing what they were asking him. The wrong information was reported to the police department and then to me."

"So the fact that you shot Deshaun Hamlin was based on incorrect information given to you by the dispatcher, correct?"

"Yeah, when information comes in to a patrol officer, it's not unusual for there to be a mistake, just not this big."

"Did you think it was wrong information at the time?"

"No."

"And you acted on it because you trusted what you'd been told about who was responsible for a serious robbery."

"Yes, I did."

Grayson sat back in his chair. "Do you know what this case is about?"

Luke didn't hesitate before answering. It was something he'd lain awake at night analyzing. "What was going on in my head that night and whether it made sense to me at the time," he said.

"Exactly," Grayson said.

Luke didn't take any satisfaction in giving the answer the lawyer wanted. The possibility that his future, and possibly his life, depended on what other people believed about him was scary. He glanced at his cup of coffee that was now cool.

"Well?" Luke asked.

"Is it okay with you that I recorded our interview so I can listen to it later?" Grayson replied.

Luke bristled. "You recorded it?"

"And didn't tell you because I knew it would stifle the flow of information. If you ask me to delete it from my system, I'll do so immediately."

"Where are the microphones?" Luke asked, glancing around the office.

"There are several," Grayson replied. "All very sensitive. The erase feature is on my computer."

"What I told you is confidential, correct? You can't tell anyone else."

"Correct," Grayson replied.

"Okay." Luke took a deep breath. "But I still want to know what you think. Give it to me straight. Do you believe the grand jury will indict me?"

"Before I answer, let me mention something else that's going to affect your case. For many years Georgia had a unique statute designed to help law enforcement officers in situations like yours. A police officer under investigation for a shooting that occurred while he or she was in the line of duty had the right to hear all the testimony presented by the grand jury and make a statement before them without being subject to cross-examination. The law changed in 2016. Now, you can still appear and testify if you want to; however, you can be questioned under oath by both the district attorney and individual members of the grand jury without the ability to have an attorney present. That's a huge change and makes it much riskier for a law enforcement officer to enter the grand jury room."

"Should I take that chance?" Luke asked. "I don't want to make things worse."

"Basic human psychology tells us it's harder to think badly of someone we know than of a total stranger. If you testify, it will be a chance for the members of the grand jury to meet you before deciding what to do about the charges. It would be better for the lawyer who ends up representing you to advise you on those issues."

"Would you consider taking the case?" Luke asked hopefully. "I don't have a lot of money, but to have someone with your experience —"

"I agreed to meet with you as a courtesy," Grayson replied with a slight smile. "I've handled my fair share of felony criminal cases, but it would take a lot to convince me to hop on that saddle at this point in my career."

Grayson was calm yet confident. Luke could easily imagine the older lawyer speaking to a jury in a grandfatherly tone that pulled the barbs from a criminal charge. His refusal to consider taking the case was deflating.

"Do I have your permission to share the information in the recorded interview with other lawyers who might be willing to help?" Grayson continued.

"Sure." Luke shrugged. "But also tell them this: I want someone who is going to fight for me. I don't want a lawyer who takes my money and then tries to bull-rush me into a plea bargain."

"Understood. And we also need to make sure any lawyer brought on board won't abandon you if Deshaun Hamlin dies and you end up being charged with murder."

After listening to Aunt Josie talk about the Jackson House, Adisa decided to go there.

Located at the west end of the main street through the center of town, the restaurant had been offering southern cuisine since the 1940s.

Saturday lunch was a slow time for the local restaurant. The busiest day of the week was Sunday dinner, and the busiest day of the year was Mother's Day, when the owners rolled out a special buffet and placed fresh flowers in the middle of each table. Seating was first come, first served, and Adisa slipped into a booth with yellow plastic seats. A teenage girl with dingy blond hair caught up in a haphazard ponytail came over with a glass of water in her hand.

"Do you want to hear the specials?" the girl asked in a lazy tone of voice and continued before Adisa answered. "We have fried pork chops and stewed okra and cauliflower casserole as the extra vegetable."

"Cauliflower casserole?" Adisa asked.

"It's the same as the broccoli and squash casseroles except they put cauliflower in it."

Adisa decided to stick to the dishes Aunt Josie had mentioned at the hospital and ordered a three-veggie plate of sweet potatoes, creamed corn, and collard greens.

"Corn bread or roll?" the girl asked.

"Corn bread. Isn't that the only kind of bread to eat with collard greens?"

"I guess," the girl replied. "Nothing but water to drink?"

"Water is fine."

The waitress left. The other customers in the restaurant included a group of four construction workers — one white, two Latino, and one black — sitting together at a table with their hard hats on the floor; several couples; and an extended family of twelve who had pushed three tables together. The large family had already received their food. There were two babies learning to eat, and small piles of discarded food were accumulating beneath their high chairs. Adisa took out her phone and began checking her office e-mails.

"Adisa Johnson?" a female voice asked, causing Adisa to look up.

Standing beside the table was a slightly overweight woman in her late forties with curly brown hair that dipped down her forehead. She was wearing black designer glasses that barely held on to her pixie nose.

"Ms. Galloway?" Adisa asked.

"Maybe I haven't changed as much as I'd feared," the civics teacher replied with a laugh. "It's been a long time since you were a junior in high school, but I recognized you as soon as I walked into the restaurant."

"Would you like to join me?" Adisa asked,

peering around the teacher.

"No, I'm meeting Lydia Fletchall in a few minutes, but I'll sit down until she gets here." The teacher slid into the seat opposite Adisa. "Lydia and I were roped into working on the graduation ceremony in a few weeks. You'd think it would run itself. I mean, how many ways can a student walk across the stage, grab a diploma, and shake Dr. Cartwright's hand before heading down to Daytona for a week? But we have to buy the decorations for the podium and make sure each student's name is correctly spelled on the program given to the parents."

Adisa remembered her own graduation and how she couldn't wait to move on to the next chapter of her life in college.

"Where's your high school diploma?" Ms. Galloway continued.

"I think it's in a drawer at my aunt Josie's house."

"I'd understand if it's disappeared. You've gotten fancier sheepskins since then. But you were always a star. How is your aunt doing?"

"She's in the hospital."

Adisa summarized Aunt Josie's status.

"I'm sorry to hear that," Ms. Galloway said. "I hope she gets better soon. She was great to you and your sister. I keep up with

Shanika on social media. Her twins are as cute as two kids can be."

Ms. Galloway had a genuine interest in her students' lives that was natural.

"And I know you've been busy with your law career," Ms. Galloway continued. "It's such a coincidence that I run into you today after reading the article this morning in the Atlanta paper about the criminal case you handled. I've watched TV shows about newly discovered DNA evidence, and it was exciting thinking about you being in the center of such an interesting case. You've come a long way since we took a field trip to Grayson, Baxter, and Williams. Didn't you end up working there during the summer?"

"Yes, and it was a great experience." Adisa took a sip of water. "I haven't seen the newspaper article."

"Oh, let me buy you a copy." Ms. Galloway immediately slid out of the booth. "There's a box for the *AJC* on the sidewalk in front of the restaurant."

"I can do it," Adisa protested. "Or check the article online."

"No, you need to hold it in your hands."

The waitress arrived with Adisa's meal.

"Enjoy your food while it's hot," the teacher said. "Cold collards are hard for even a die-hard southerner to eat."

Ms. Galloway scurried out the door. Adisa sampled the collards, which had been cooked with ham hocks, not bacon. She sprinkled a few drops of pepper vinegar on the green mixture to add spicy heat. It was easy to understand why they were one of Aunt Josie's favorites. The teacher returned.

"This is the last copy," she said, triumphantly holding up the newspaper.

"Thanks," Adisa replied.

The front door of the restaurant opened and Lydia Fletchall, an English teacher who had bled red ink on Adisa's compositions, entered.

"Gotta go," Ms. Galloway said to Adisa. "Great seeing you. The article is on A2."

The teacher left. Opening the first section to page 2, Adisa immediately saw her photograph, which must have been lifted from the law firm website. Directly beside her was the mug-shot photo of Leroy Larimore. The title of the article was "The Two-Edged Sword of DNA Evidence." Sharon Rogers's byline appeared beneath the heading.

The first two paragraphs of the article accurately described Adisa's involvement in the case and what had happened in Judge Boswell's courtroom when she presented the exonerating DNA evidence. The reporter identified Adisa as "an associate with the prestigious national law firm of Dixon and White." In the transition to the third paragraph, the reporter dropped a bomb — "DNA evidence is a double helix that can both give and take away." She then claimed that Leroy Larimore's DNA sample linked him to at least four sexual assaults on women occurring over an eighteen-month period two decades earlier in Louisiana. It took a column and a half for the reporter to lay out how the DNA sample submitted months earlier to CODIS and used to connect Vester Plunkett to the assault on Mr. Chesney had in turn implicated Larimore in cold case investigations of the sexual assaults in Louisiana. The article concluded:

Ms. Johnson asserted that other criminal acts by her client in South Carolina were no longer relevant and emphasized Larimore's right to compensation from the State of Georgia for his wrongful incarceration. It's unclear if Johnson knew about the pending charges against her client in Louisiana at the time she argued for his immediate release from custody. Neither Johnson nor anyone else at Dixon and White returned repeated calls for comment. Fulton County assistant district at-

torney Mark Kildare confirmed that Larimore is being held without bond at the
Fulton County Jail pending an extradition
request from the Louisiana attorney general's office.

Adisa read the story again, more slowly
this time. Apart from the allegations about
crimes committed by Larimore in Louisiana, which were as much news to her as to
any reader of the paper, it was factually accurate. Disturbingly, the reporter clearly
insinuated that Adisa's sole goal was to win
her case and hinted at her agenda to bury
Larimore's past. Failure to contact Rogers
and specifically deny knowledge of any
sexual assaults made her look uncoopera-
tive at best and deceptive at worst. What
made it worse was the implication that the
law firm didn't deny involvement in a cover-
up. Adisa's unselfish pro bono activity was
swallowed whole by her client's other
crimes.

Adisa refolded the paper and laid it beside
her food. She ate a bite of lukewarm
creamed corn that was a bit too peppery.
Across the room, Ms. Galloway was chatting away with her colleague. As she ate,
Adisa tried to digest how the law firm would
respond to the newspaper exposé. It ap-

peared likely that Catherine had never returned the reporter's phone call, either.

Her appetite dulled by the article, Adisa managed to eat most of the food on her plate. As she carried her bill up to the cash register, she waved at Ms. Galloway, who sent her on her way with a bright smile.

Getting into her car, Adisa wondered if she should call Catherine Summey immediately. Catherine used Saturday afternoons to organize the activities of her team for the following week. With the upcoming turnover in personnel, her boss's task would be more complicated than usual, and Adisa decided it would be best not to pile something else on her plate. If Catherine had read the article and was concerned about it, she would contact Adisa.

There were several florists in Campbellton. Bohannan Flowers was owned by a member of her aunt's church, and Mr. and Mrs. Bohannan provided the majority of wreaths and sprays for weddings and funerals at Woodside Gospel Tabernacle. Adisa parked in front of the simple building. A bell connected to the door dinged when Adisa entered. A few moments later, Mrs. Bohannan appeared from the back of the store.

"Look who's here!" the friendly black

woman in her fifties exclaimed.

"Hey, Mrs. Bohannan," Adisa replied.

Mrs. Bohannan's face suddenly fell. "Is Josie okay?"

Adisa quickly filled her in.

"Joe and I have been out of town and just got back last night," Mrs. Bohannan said with a concerned look on her face. "Let me put something together for you to take to her hospital room. I know exactly what she'll like, and there won't be a charge."

"That's nice of you," Adisa replied. "But I need some flowers to take to the cemetery. Aunt Josie hasn't missed a decoration Sunday for as long as I can remember."

"Of course — what do you want?"

Adisa glanced around at the overwhelming options in vases and two large refrigerated display cases.

"Do you have an idea what she bought last year?" Adisa asked.

"Just a minute."

Mrs. Bohannan disappeared into the rear of the shop. Adisa sniffed and inhaled the competing aromas of a large selection of flowers crammed into a small space. In organizing her plants, Aunt Josie paid attention not just to color and type, but also to scent, separating them by enough space that each fragrance had an olfactory opportunity.

Mrs. Bohannan returned with a slip of paper in her hand.

"She doesn't like the peony sprays but always orders a dahlia mix for spring decoration. I have some very nice reds, blues, and yellows."

"I'm sure that will be fine," Adisa said absentmindedly when Mrs. Bohannan finished. "I'll take a picture on my phone and show it to Aunt Josie when she's alert."

"Last year she ordered six sprays for the gravestones." Mrs. Bohannan paused and lowered her voice. "Of course, some of the old graves in that cemetery never got a proper marker and it's a guess where folks are really buried. Josie will drop a flower here and there and hope she hits the right spot."

Adisa had witnessed this activity in the past. The oldest part of the cemetery had a slave section, and Aunt Josie could trace her roots to the days when involuntary servitude of black people was the normal way of life in Nash County.

"When should I pick up the flowers?" Adisa asked.

Mrs. Bohannan glanced at a large clock with a cracked plastic cover hanging on the wall beside one of the refrigerated cases.

"Are you going to go to the cemetery after

church tomorrow? If so, I can bring them with me so they'll be as fresh as possible. That's what several customers like to do."

Adisa hadn't considered the possibility of attending the local church as part of her weekend.

"Would it be too much trouble if I picked them up today?" she asked. "I'm going to be spending my time at the hospital until I go back to Atlanta."

"Sure. Give me a couple of hours. We don't close on Saturday until six o'clock."

Adisa left the shop and headed toward the hospital. As she was pulling into the parking lot, her cell phone vibrated. It was Catherine Summey.

TEN

"Where are you?" Catherine asked as soon as Adisa answered the call.

"In Campbellton visiting my aunt," Adisa answered. "She's still in the hospital."

The phone was silent for a moment.

"Catherine?" Adisa asked.

"Yes, I'm here. I just came out of a partners' meeting. Toward the end, Linwood brought up the article about you in the *AJC*."

Adisa's heart sank. "I had no idea Larimore's DNA would be linked with any sexual assault cases in Louisiana," she said. "He told me about the juvenile court charges in South Carolina, and I ran a detailed background check on our database that came up empty except for a few traffic tickets."

"I'm sure that's true. But the firm doesn't care about the facts as much as it does perception. Linwood was playing golf this morning with some of his buddies at the Piedmont Driving Club. They grilled him about the law firm getting tangled up in liberal causes and trying to get sex offenders off the hook. One even pulled up the firm mission statement on his phone and asked Linwood if we truly believed it."

Adisa couldn't remember the specific language on the website banner, but she knew it had something to do with "serving the needs of corporate America in an ever-changing global business environment."

"Linwood didn't want to approve the pro bono work in the first place and reluctantly caved in when I pushed for it," Catherine continued.

"You pushed me, too," Adisa responded, then immediately regretted her words.

"Linwood pointed out the same thing to me, which gave me a chance to deflect blame from you."

"Thanks," Adisa said quickly.

"I also pointed out that it would have been impossible for you to uncover the connection between our client and the crimes in Louisiana. That seemed to calm Linwood down a little bit. When will you be back in Atlanta?"

"Monday morning, unless you think I should return sooner."

"No, that's fine. I think everything was okay by the end of the meeting. Linwood isn't the only vote in the room. Anyone who's worked with you appreciates your abilities."

The compliment and reassuring words didn't release the tension caused by a huge knot in Adisa's stomach. She regretted even the light lunch she'd eaten.

"Thanks for standing up for me," she said. "I should have called the reporter."

"Yes. Even a brief response denying any knowledge of the mess in Louisiana would have helped. But let's hope it blows over. The firm has much more important matters that deserve our attention."

Adisa trudged from her car to the hospital. Entering her aunt's room, she stepped into the middle of an occupational therapy session. Shanika was standing at the foot of the bed as a young man with a shaved head worked with Aunt Josie.

"Ms. Adams, try once more to bring the spoon from the plate to your mouth with your right hand."

Aunt Josie managed to raise her right hand halfway to her mouth before it flopped back onto the bed.

"This is aggravation," she muttered.

"Aggravating," Shanika corrected her.

"That, too," Aunt Josie replied. "My tongue is twisted up something fierce."

"You're doing great," the therapist said. "Don't be discouraged. Practice what we've gone over, but don't wear yourself out. I'll be back in the morning."

Aunt Josie barely acknowledged Adisa's presence before closing her eyes. Adisa gave Shanika a questioning look, and the girls stood in silence for several moments.

"Is she asleep?" Adisa asked.

"No," Aunt Josie said as her eyes fluttered open. "Where have you been?"

"I went to the Jackson House for lunch and then stopped by to order the flowers for the cemetery from Mrs. Bohannan. She'll have them ready late this afternoon."

"Oh, yes," Aunt Josie said with a slow nod. "You're sweet to do that for me. My short-term memory is awful. Tell me about the flowers."

As soon as her aunt asked the question, Adisa realized her short-term memory was flawed as well.

"I need to call Mrs. Bohannan right now!"

"Why?" Shanika asked.

"To tell her not to include any yellow flowers in the dahlia mix for the cemetery."

Without waiting for a response, Adisa

stepped into the hallway. Mrs. Bohannan answered on the third ring.

"You know, I remembered that after you left the shop," the florist said. "Josie never orders yellow flowers. I'm substituting purples. She'll love it."

Relieved, Adisa returned to the hospital room and delivered the news.

"That's okay," Aunt Josie said. "You've had a lot on your mind recently. Shanika was telling me you got a big promotion at work and will be moving all the way up to Boston. I'm proud of you but sad, too."

Adisa looked at Shanika in shock. "Uh, I didn't know she was going to do that," Adisa said.

"It was going to come out eventually," Shanika replied.

"And she knew you'd be worried that it might upset me," Aunt Josie said. "But all I've ever wanted for you girls is to love the Lord and walk in his favor for your lives. Knowing this makes me feel better than any medicine they could pump into my body through that tube in my arm."

Adisa managed a smile. There was no use mentioning to Aunt Josie and Shanika the news about the recent threat to her job. Pulling herself together, she patted Aunt Josie on the arm.

"Seeing you improve is the most important thing in the world for me," she said.

They divided the rest of the afternoon between chatting and Aunt Josie napping. Adisa let her aunt direct the conversation and gladly followed any trail the older woman wanted to explore.

Adisa left the hospital and arrived at the flower shop at 5:55 p.m. Mrs. Bohannan was standing behind the cash register. The dahlia sprays were on a table beside the doorway that led to the rear of the shop.

"I wasn't going to close until you got here," the florist said. "How's Josie feeling?"

"She's been asleep for a couple of hours, but before that she was talking and taking in liquids. The big problem is the partial paralysis on her right side. She's weak but okay on the left. It looks like she's going to have to change her dominant hand for a while."

"Can she feed herself? That's always a big deal."

"Only with the left hand. The therapist is working with the right side."

"How about walking? I can't imagine not seeing her going down the sidewalk with that stick in her hand. Something about it always makes me feel hopeful. If Josie is praying, then God is listening."

"She was able to make it to the bathroom and back using a walker. We've got high hopes for her continued progress."

"Time doesn't wait for anyone," Mrs. Bohannan replied, shaking her head. "And in our business we see it from the beginning to the end."

Adisa could see flower arrangements for newborn babies and the sprays going to the cemetery. She took out her debit card and paid for the flowers.

"Thanks so much," Adisa said. "This will mean a lot to Aunt Josie."

It was a short drive to the cemetery where a large but unknown number of ancestors on her mother's side of the family lay buried beneath the red clay. Most graves from the past one hundred years were marked. Aunt Josie owned a plot directly beside her sister with a tombstone in place. The marble marker listed her name, "Josephine Marigold Adams," along with her date of birth. The only thing to be added would be the date of death.

Years earlier there had been a church beside the graveyard, but it burned down in the 1920s, and instead of rebuilding, the congregation merged with another fellowship in town. Thus the cemetery lay in perpetual solitude. An ancient iron sign identified it as "Western Cemetery." Adisa didn't know the specific origin of the name, but the most likely explanation was that the two acres of land lay west of the center of Campbellton. Adisa parked near an ancient sycamore tree with a thick, gnarly trunk. In front of the tree was an old marble bench with the words "They rested from their labors and received their reward" inscribed on the front.

Adisa was alone, but other people had recently been there. Arrangements of fresh flowers lay in front of several tombstones. By Sunday evening the graveyard would be filled with color. Adisa took out the bundles of flowers. Her shoes barely made any indentation in the coarse grass that was dense, not soft. Going to the newer section, she carefully walked between the graves to the place where Aunt Josie's paternal grandfather, Alonzo Adams, was buried. Like Aunt Josie, he'd walked the roads of Nash County praying and quoting Scripture. Aunt Josie often joked that Alonzo walked everywhere because he didn't own a horse, but in more serious moments, she made it clear to Adisa and Shanika that Alonzo was a godly man who loved the Lord and other people, thus fulfilling the two greatest commandments. Adisa placed the flowers on the headstone and stepped back for a moment of silence. She divided four other sprays among the graves of other relatives, many of whom had lived their entire lives within ten miles of where they now rested.

With one group of flowers still in her arms, Adisa stepped into a section that looked unoccupied but was probably the most crowded piece of ground — the resting place for the bones of an unknown number of black residents of Nash County who died in the years 1820 through 1865. Many of the bodies beneath the soil were of those who had been snatched from their home villages in west Africa, sold by their black captors to English or American ship captains, and brought to slave markets in Savannah or Charleston for eventual sale to labor-starved landowners. Others were the descendants of the first generation in captivity, men and women born in a new world who died before the end of the Civil War and the great Emancipation Proclamation. Sadly, many of those freed by Abraham Lincoln's edict soon fell back into a form of serfdom caused by the oppressive sharecropper system.

Adisa's ancestors belonged to every group. She didn't know the real names of her earliest relatives, but they'd been assigned surnames such as Adams, Johnson, and Stanley by those who owned them, and first names such as Peter, Tom, Sally, and Bessy. Adisa's name had African roots. Her parents failed to research it closely and didn't know it was more commonly given to boys than girls. Adisa didn't care. It was her name, and she owned it proudly.

No gravestones marked any of her antebellum ancestors. Granite and marble tombstones cost money. The simple wooden crosses planted in the ground at the time of a slave's death had long ago returned to the soil. Only a few simple unadorned rocks that peeked up from the soil at random spots confirmed the presence of the remains of a person who'd lived and died toiling under the Georgia sun.

Aunt Josie and one of her brothers had dipped their toes into some genealogical research of the family, but the information uncovered was sparse, and Adisa didn't know many details. The first members of their clan were scattered across Nash County on different farms. There weren't any massive plantations like those in Mississippi or Texas. Few records existed, and those that did contained haphazard references to birth, death, marriage, and that tragic word, "sale."

Because no one now knew where their earliest relatives were buried, people had adopted the ritual of strewing flowers randomly in hope that a petal or blossom might fall on the place where a loved one lay. Adisa walked with measured steps across the grass while dropping single stalks. The air was still and the birds were more interested in capturing dinner than singing. Adisa reached the edge of the cemetery. With only a few flowers left in her hand, she turned and crossed the oldest section of all.

Adisa dropped her last strand of flowers. When she did, the tiny hairs on the back of her neck suddenly rose up, and she shuddered. It wasn't a creepy feeling, just a sensation that arrested her attention. Stooping, she stared at the ground. A heavy stalk laden with many blossoms had landed on top of a partially exposed rock, a smooth gray stone about six inches long and four inches across. Adisa bent over and touched the stone that was buried so deep in the ground it wasn't a threat to stub a bare toe. The unadorned rock was surprisingly cool to the touch after the warm afternoon. Close connection to the earth kept its temperature more constant than the air above.

"I wonder who's buried here?" Adisa asked softly under her breath.

She stood up but stayed in the same spot. Glancing to her left, she could see the flowers she'd dropped to the ground. Adisa inspected the entire graveyard in a way she'd never done before. She was connected to this place and those buried here. Maybe that's what Aunt Josie and others felt when they came here. If so, it was easier to understand why it might be important to them. As she stood in solitary silence, Adisa felt a strength and confidence. It was an unexpected moment of encouragement she needed after the phone call with Catherine Summey and the worry connected to Aunt Josie's illness.

Returning to her car, Adisa lowered the window and sat quietly. She didn't want to leave. Her life was so frantically busy that any quiet time she experienced was usually the result of mental and physical exhaustion. This was different. She was at rest, yet fully alive.

Adisa's thoughts then strayed to the young black man gunned down less than ten minutes from the cemetery. Racism in Adisa's lifetime was less than the hatred and cruelty of the past, but that didn't mean the slate was clean. Surrounded by departed generations who knew brutal oppression, she offered up a silent petition that things would be better before her time came to rest beneath the soil. It felt especially right that she, an Adams, should pray.

Eleven

Luke was cooking hamburgers and hot dogs on the grill in the backyard. Their property backed up against an undeveloped wooded area. Luke knew at some point it would likely sprout homes instead of pines and hardwoods.

He was using lump charcoal without any of the additives found in standard charcoal. Luke disliked the artificial flavor imparted by a propane gas grill, and when natural charcoal first appeared on the market he immediately bought it. He ground his own hamburger meat, buying boneless beef ribs that he mixed in the grinder with uncooked bacon. The fat in the bacon held the meat together so it didn't fall apart on the grill and added the unique richness only bacon can offer.

This evening Luke was focusing on cooking as a diversion from revisiting his earlier meeting with Theo Grayson.

"I think the odds are greater than fifty percent that the grand jury will indict you," the lawyer had told him.

"How is that possible?"

"Here's what the law says."

Grayson had then pulled a black statute book with gold-embossed binding from a bookcase and began to read:

A person commits the offense of aggravated assault when he or she assaults:

1. With intent to murder, to rape, or to rob;
2. With a deadly weapon or with any object, device, or instrument which, when used offensively against a person, is likely to or actually does result in serious bodily injury.

"I don't see how I could be guilty of that," Luke said. "I didn't intend to murder Hamlin."

"I can see why you'd look at it that way. But this law has been on the books a long time, and the courts allow intent to be *inferred* by action. If someone shoots another person without justification, then the necessary intent can exist. It's up to the jury to decide if that's the case."

Luke was unconvinced. "What if Hamlin dies? Do you think I'll be charged with murder?"

"Are you sure you want to talk about that?"

"Yes. Otherwise I'll be asking myself questions I can't answer."

Grayson reopened the black volume to a place he'd tabbed with a tiny yellow marker. "Either murder or manslaughter," the lawyer replied.

Luke had learned about the legal distinction between the two charges in one of his criminal justice classes, but that had been theoretical. Grayson began reading again:

A person commits the offense of murder when he unlawfully and with malice aforethought, either express or implied, causes the death of another human being. Express malice is that deliberate intention unlawfully to take the life of another human being which is manifested by external circumstances capable of proof. Malice shall be implied where no considerable provocation appears and where all the circumstances of the killing show an abandoned and malignant heart.

Luke remembered being confused about

the ancient English term "malice afore-thought," words his professor discussed with way too much enthusiasm.

"I didn't drive down the street, get out of the car, and pull out my gun intending to kill anyone."

"Which is the express malice provision in the law. You're clear there. It's the second part that presents the problem. If a jury doesn't find enough provocation for you to shoot to kill, it can conclude that you had an 'abandoned and malignant heart.' "

"That's crazy. When Hamlin started running toward me, I was scared. And then I heard a gunshot."

"Which brings in the possibility of a voluntary manslaughter charge." Grayson turned several pages and adjusted his glasses before continuing:

A person commits the offense of voluntary manslaughter when he causes the death of another human being under circumstances which would otherwise be murder and if he acts solely as the result of a sudden, violent, and irresistible passion resulting from serious provocation sufficient to excite such passion in a reasonable person; however, if there should have been an interval between the provocation and the killing sufficient for the voice of reason and humanity to be heard, of which the jury in all cases shall be the judge, the killing shall be attributed to deliberate revenge and be punished as murder.

The convoluted verbiage of the statute lost Luke, but his palms felt sweaty and it suddenly became uncomfortably hot in the office. Grayson looked up and spoke. "If you had a reason to be upset, it would be considered manslaughter, not murder. It's common in murder cases to charge a defendant with either murder or manslaughter. That way, the prosecutor has a better chance of getting at least some kind of conviction."

Anger against Deshaun Hamlin rose up in Luke. If the teenager had simply obeyed orders, stopped in the middle of the street, and put his hands over his head, he would be going to basketball practice, and Luke would be enjoying his job as a police officer.

"I believed Hamlin was going to shoot me and fired my gun in self-defense."

Grayson closed the statute book and held it up. "In that case, you're not guilty of aggravated assault, manslaughter, murder, or any other crime in the state of Georgia."

■ ■ ■ ■

The sun slipped below the horizon and shadows covered the graveyard. Adisa's thoughts lingered upon the hardships faced by those buried in the cemetery. Catastrophic upheaval could appear like a tornado and tear families apart and scar people physically and emotionally. How her ancestors faced extreme adversity was a mystery to Adisa, but she suspected that for many, faith played a major role. In a profound irony, the "peculiar institution" that enslaved them brought them to a new world where they heard the gospel and experienced spiritual freedom. Salvation of souls in the slave quarters didn't excuse bondage, but it explained why the music the slaves produced often contained an overcoming message of hope.

Adisa returned to the hospital where she found a note from Shanika on the bedside tray. Her sister had gone to Aunt Josie's house for a few hours' rest. Aunt Josie's eyes were closed and her breathing regular. There was a knock on the door. Dr. Dewberry entered.

"I'm glad you're here," the neurologist said. "I just finished reviewing your aunt's chart, including the assessments from the therapists who've been working with her for the past few days. Do you want to talk here or in a conference room down the hall?"

The way the doctor asked the question made Adisa think it would be better to meet privately. She glanced at Aunt Josie, who hadn't stirred at the sound of the conversation.

"Privately," she said.

Adisa followed the doctor into a windowless space barely big enough for four chairs and a small table.

"Based on the MRI scan and the location and scope of the hemorrhage, your aunt is doing remarkably well," the doctor said. "Other than a few problems with her short-term memory and getting tired easily, she seems close to normal from a mental standpoint."

"That sounds great."

"True, but you'll notice swings in cognition for quite some time before she settles into a baseline of functioning. At that point, the hope is that she can avoid another episode. The more challenging issues relate to her physical capabilities. She has limited use of her right arm; however, she has sufficient mobility in her left arm to feed herself and perform basic activities of daily living. Her left leg is in good shape, so we want to keep it active in therapy while we work with her right leg. I can justify keeping her in the hospital for at least a few more days. After that, she will need placement in a skilled nursing facility or with comprehensive care in her home environment."

"My sister and I are already talking about the options. Aunt Josie has lived in Campbellton her whole life. All her friends live here, and she has a lot of connections through her church. Tons of folks will visit and help out if she's at home."

"Informal arrangements are fine for a few days, but I think it's likely she will need regular assistance for weeks or months. Does your aunt have the resources to hire a home health-care worker?"

Adisa knew Aunt Josie's financial status to the penny.

"For a while."

"You don't have to decide tonight, but you and your sister will need to have a plan in place by the middle of the week."

Adisa nodded. "That gives us time to discuss it."

Dr. Dewberry left. It was after 11:00 p.m. when Shanika returned. She'd changed clothes and was wearing light-gray workout pants and a red top. Adisa told her about the conversation with the neurologist.

"Aunt Josie can afford a private sitter at home for months," Adisa said. "I know she'd prefer that, even if Medicare would pay for a skilled nursing center."

"Yes, but we should ask her," Shanika replied.

Aunt Josie stirred in bed but didn't awaken.

"Did you go by the cemetery?" Shanika asked.

"Yes," Adisa replied, taking out her phone to show her the pictures she'd taken of the flowers and graves.

"That should satisfy her," Shanika said. "Send those to me. You can take off now. I'll spend the night with her."

"She's resting well, and the nurses check on her regularly. Are you sure you need to stay?"

"Probably not," Shanika replied, looking down at Aunt Josie. "But it makes me feel better to be close by."

"Okay, but I'll be here early in the morning."

"See you then. Love you."

Adisa slept in the bedroom she'd shared with Shanika. The twin beds the girls used as teenagers were still there. A five-drawer chest rested between the beds. Once a battlefield of underwear, socks, shirts, and pants, the chest was now empty. After changing into pajamas and brushing her teeth, Adisa crawled into bed. The room had a familiar, pleasant smell, a mixture of fragrances released by the plants in the house and Aunt Josie's favorite air freshener. Before she had time to think about anything else, Adisa drifted off to sleep.

When she awoke in the morning, it took her a split second to realize where she was. She glanced at the twenty-year-old digital clock, whose raucous buzz could force the most reluctant teenager out of bed, and realized she'd overslept. Hurriedly taking a shower and getting dressed, she left for the hospital, only stopping long enough at the Westside Quik Mart to pour a cup of black coffee from the coffee service beside the cash register. A large black man with a bandage on the right side of his neck swiped her debit card with a hand wrapped in gauze. His name tag read "Stan."

Adisa remembered the connection between the robbery of the convenience store and the shooting of Deshaun Hamlin on nearby East Nixon Street.

"How are you feeling?" she asked. "I live in Atlanta, but I read about what happened in the newspaper. I'm sorry."

"It was in the Atlanta paper, too?" the young man asked with a surprised expression on his face. "Nobody told me that."

"No, I saw it in the local paper when I was visiting my aunt at the hospital. You may know her, Josephine Adams; she lives on Baxter Street."

"Older lady who goes around town carrying a big walking stick?"

"That's her." Adisa smiled.

"She's in the hospital?" Stan asked. "What's wrong with her?"

"Stroke, but we're praying she'll be able to go home soon."

"I spent the night in the hospital after they stitched me up," the clerk replied, touching his bandage. "I'm going to have a bad scar, but it could have been a lot worse."

Adisa turned to leave.

"Hey, while you're praying, would you please pray for me?" Stan asked.

Adisa faced the young man and saw the sadness in his big brown eyes. "I will," she said.

Stan hesitated and then spoke again. "And pray for Deshaun Hamlin. He's the boy who got shot. It was partly my fault."

"I thought a police officer shot him."

"Only because the cops believed I told

them Deshaun was one of the people who robbed the store. I don't remember what I said. I'd passed out, and when I came to, I must have mumbled Deshaun's name because I know him so well. Anyway, Deshaun didn't have anything to do with the robbery, and a crazy white cop shot him in the middle of the street."

"I'll pray for you and for Deshaun," Adisa said and then paused. "And one of the things I'm going to pray is that you can forgive yourself."

Aunt Josie was sitting up in bed when Adisa entered her room.

"Good morning," Adisa said. "Where's Shanika?"

"She went to the hospital cafeteria for a proper meal," Aunt Josie replied. "I offered her five dollars to bring me a sausage patty and a biscuit, but she turned me down."

"How are you?" Adisa asked.

"Fine, if I could go back to sleep and continue dreaming," Aunt Josie said with a faraway look in her eyes. "I was walking down Morgan Street where it crosses Poplar Avenue near the fire station. I had my stick in my hand, and I was shouting to the Lord at the top of my lungs, but nobody seemed to be paying attention. The people kept passing by as if I were invisible. In the dream it didn't bother me. I just kept yelling. What do you think that means?"

"You were talking to God, not to the people," Adisa answered.

"Yes and amen!" Aunt Josie replied with a slightly crooked smile. "Why didn't I think of that?"

"You would have figured it out," Adisa replied. "Even when you're praying under your breath the sound echoes when it gets to heaven."

Aunt Josie reached out with her left hand. Adisa took it in hers.

"Child, you can preach to me anytime you want. Tell me what you've been up to."

Adisa sat at the end of the bed. "I took the flowers to the cemetery late yesterday afternoon," she said.

"Oh, good," Aunt Josie said as she relaxed her head against the pillow. "Tell me all about it."

Adisa took out her phone and scrolled through the photos. As she did, Aunt Josie engaged in a monologue.

"That's Uncle Joe's grave," she said. "I'm named after him because Daddy wanted me to be a boy."

Adisa had heard all this many times before but didn't mind the repetition because it revealed a high level of mental health. She pointed to a photo of the area of unmarked graves.

"Do you have any idea how many of our relatives are buried in the slave section?"

"That's one of those questions we'll never be able to answer until we get to heaven," Aunt Josie replied, shaking her head. "But there has to be at least twenty or thirty. The church that used to be by the graveyard was founded by a former slave named Adams who started preaching at brush arbor meetings after the war. I've got notes about all that written by my grandmother. They're someplace at the house."

A reference by members of Aunt Josie's generation to "the war" had only one meaning — the Civil War.

"What was your grandmother's name?"

"Adelaide Adams. Isn't that pretty?"

"It's kind of old-fashioned."

"Well, it wasn't old-fashioned in the 1870s when she was born. Her mother and father were born in slavery. They lived on a farm in the east part of the county."

"And it was Adelaide's father who founded the church?"

"Or her grandfather; I'm not sure about all that. In slave times our people couldn't have their own gatherings and had to go to the white churches where they sat in the back of the sanctuary or in a balcony." Aunt Josie paused and looked directly at Adisa. "What time is it? It's Sunday. Aren't you and Shanika going to church?"

Before Adisa could answer, the door opened and Shanika returned. Shanika's hair was disheveled, and her eyes betrayed lack of sleep.

"Where's my sausage biscuit?" Aunt Josie demanded.

"In my stomach where it belongs," Shanika replied.

"If you're not going to get me a sausage biscuit, you and Adisa need to leave and get ready for church."

Shanika glanced at Adisa. "I didn't bring any church clothes," Shanika replied.

"Me, either," Adisa added.

Wearing a nice dress on Sunday morning wasn't optional at Woodside Gospel Tabernacle. God deserved the best, which included the clothes worn by the members of the congregation.

"There's no use arguing with you girls," Aunt Josie said with a yawn. "I haven't been able to make you do anything for years. When did I brush my teeth? My mouth feels bad."

"I brushed them right after you ate breakfast," Shanika replied. "Do you want to brush them again?"

"Yes, please."

As soon as Shanika finished, Aunt Josie closed her eyes and within seconds was fast asleep.

"It's almost like she passes out," Shanika said to Adisa.

"Yes," Adisa replied. "Let me tell you about her dream."

After Adisa finished, the sisters settled into chairs on opposite sides of the bed. Aunt Josie snored softly and then let out a series of louder snorts.

"Remember the night you put a hand towel over her face to muffle the sound?" Adisa asked.

"That didn't work," Shanika replied. "And the next morning she wouldn't let us leave our room until one of us confessed to the crime of trying to smother her."

Shanika yawned.

"Why don't you go to her house and take a nap?" Adisa suggested. "I'd like a little alone time with her, and you get grumpy when you're tired."

"Okay," Shanika said, yawning again. "But let me know if anything changes."

TWELVE

Luke hung up the phone and sat down next to Ashley's high chair. Jane was putting the little girl to bed for her afternoon nap. Ashley's food tray hadn't been cleaned following supper the previous evening. Bits of macaroni and cheese were already beginning to turn dark orange and congeal on the white plastic surface.

Luke took off the tie he'd worn to church. He and Jane had sat at the back of the sanctuary and left immediately at the end of the service so he wouldn't have to answer questions from well-meaning people. Luke was finding it harder and harder to be in public settings. Even though he hadn't done anything wrong, the urge to isolate himself was gaining the upper hand.

Turning on the kitchen sink faucet, he dampened a dishrag and started scrubbing the dried food from the tray. Once it was clean, he got down on his knees and attacked bits of chicken, pieces of macaroni, and tiny globs of applesauce on the floor. Some of the applesauce was at least two days old.

"I meant to mop the kitchen floor before we went to bed last night," Jane said, entering the room.

"I don't mind," Luke said. "But I didn't know applesauce had glue in it. This stuff has become a part of the tile."

"Let me help." Jane grabbed another rag and wet it. "You should have changed out of your church clothes before doing this."

"I took off my tie."

Jane, who was wearing an exercise outfit, crawled under the table and began cleaning the floor in a circular motion.

"I don't know how that child can toss food this far under the table," she said. "It's like she drops it on her foot and kicks it."

Luke moistened his rag again and moved toward the refrigerator. Jane turned her head and saw him.

"We don't have to do this by hand," she said. "We own a sponge mop and a bucket. And soap is an amazing substance."

"I need to do something I can control," Luke answered. "Chief Lockhart left a voice mail on my phone saying the DA has completely taken over the investigation. It's out of the chief's hands."

Jane came out from beneath the table and sat up. Luke dislodged a stubborn piece of a gray substance from the refrigerator door and leaned against it. Jane pointed up at the ceiling.

"Then we know whose hands it's in."

"But there are people at other churches in town praying that I'll be indicted. What if God listens to their prayers instead of ours?"

As soon as he spoke, Luke regretted his words. Jane's reliance on divine intervention on his behalf had been unwavering.

"Sorry," he added quickly. "It's just that I'm disappointed."

"The Lord has to sort that out," Jane answered. "I'm praying that every person on the grand jury will hear the evidence and realize you didn't do anything except your duty to the best of your ability. Being on our knees doing more than cleaning the floor is where we need to be."

Jane closed her eyes and began to pray. Luke watched her for a few moments. Two thoughts hit him. He didn't deserve such a godly wife. And he was thankful he had one. He bowed his head, too.

By the middle of the afternoon, Adisa was getting restless and decided to take a walk around the hospital grounds. When she stepped outside, the grass was wet from a rain shower. She hoped the rain hadn't interrupted the dedication service at the cemetery. Reentering the hospital, Adisa saw a group of people wearing their Sunday-best clothes. In the center was Reverend Reynolds. Adisa started to slip around to the right on her way to the elevator, but the minister saw her and called out.

"Adisa Johnson!"

Adisa stopped. There were six people standing with the minister. Even though it had been several years since their paths had crossed, Adisa immediately recognized Thelma Armistead. Deshaun Hamlin's grandmother was wearing a large white hat with a green feather stuck in the side band. She gave Adisa a tight hug.

"How's Josie doing?" Sister Armistead asked when she released her.

"We're optimistic," Adisa replied. "She may be able to go home without spending time in a nursing home. And I've been praying for your grandson."

"That boy needs a miracle," Mrs. Armistead said, sadly shaking her head. "We just left his room where we talked to the specialist. They're waiting for the swelling of his brain to go down so they can take out the bullet that's inside his head."

"Is he in a coma?" Adisa asked.

"Yes, which the doctors say is a good thing. But it's awful seeing my grandbaby lying there with a big bandage on his head."

Sister Armistead touched her right eye with a tissue she was clutching in her hands. "I don't want to burden Josie, but does she know about Deshaun? She's such a mighty prayer warrior."

"No, ma'am, but I'll tell her. She's just now coming around so she can handle news like that."

One of the men in the group touched Sister Armistead on the arm. "We need to get on home," he said.

They moved away, but Reggie lingered.

"That's a tragic situation," Adisa said when they were alone. "This morning I stopped off at the Westside Quik Mart for a cup of coffee and met the young man who mistakenly told the police Deshaun was involved in the robbery. He's blaming himself for what happened."

"He didn't pull the trigger," Reggie replied. "The white officer did."

"I told him that. Would you consider going by the store to talk to him? His name is Stan. I told him I'd be praying for him."

"Sure," Reggie said and paused for a

second. "You're a lawyer; what do you think will happen to the officer?"

"It's hard to predict. As a general rule, it's tough to get an indictment against a police officer and even harder to obtain a conviction. Most people are willing to give the police the benefit of the doubt because of the difficulty of the job."

Reggie shook his head. "I think they should be held to a stricter standard. A group of us are trying to rally community pressure to make sure Nelson has to answer for what he did in a court of law. And if Deshaun dies —" The minister stopped.

"The officer could be charged with murder."

"You worked as a prosecutor, didn't you?"

"How did you find that out?" Adisa asked in surprise.

"A man in our church mentioned it to me when I told him I'd met you." Reggie was quiet for a moment. "Would you consider serving as a special prosecutor to make sure justice is done for Deshaun?"

"Have you been talking to Walter Broome?"

"I don't know Walter, but a lawyer friend in Birmingham brought it up when I told him about the shooting."

"My experience as a prosecutor is limited

to a couple of years right after I graduated from law school. Recently, I've been working for a big law firm in the corporate merger area. They're not going to give me time off to work on a criminal case here in Campbellton. And I'm about to move to Boston. I'll be leaving the state within a couple of months."

"Oh," Reggie replied, deflated. "That changes everything. I guess I'll have to forget it."

"I'm not the only lawyer who could step in," Adisa said. "And thanks for standing up for justice. It would have been easy to use your ministry as an excuse not to get involved."

"Standing up for justice is part of my ministry."

Adisa's respect for Reggie increased. "I'm sure Aunt Josie would love to meet you," she said.

"I would like that. I'm here almost every day."

Adisa left at 4:30 a.m. the following morning to return to Atlanta. Departing any later would have pushed her into the vortex of Monday-morning rush-hour traffic. She arrived at the office after a quick detour to her apartment for a shower and a fresh change of clothes.

Before turning on her computer, Adisa checked the status of her schefflera. The dirt was dangerously dry, and Adisa went to the break room for a pitcher of water. As she waited for the water to reach the top of the container, one of the women who worked as a transcriptionist on the third shift came in for a cup of coffee. The young woman often handled Adisa's dictation.

"I hope you weren't bored last night," Adisa said. "I was out of town and didn't send you anything."

"No," the woman replied and gave Adisa a puzzled look. "I wasn't expecting anything from you."

Adisa returned to her office and carefully poured the water into the pot so that it didn't splash onto the carpet. The plant was thirsty. Adisa then turned on her computer and entered her password. An error message appeared. Typing more slowly, Adisa received the same error message. No one from the IT department would arrive at the office for another forty-five minutes. She went to the kitchen for a second pitcher of water. This time when she returned to her office, Catherine Summey was waiting for her.

"Good morning," Adisa said. "I came in

early but couldn't get started because of a computer problem."

"There's no computer problem," Catherine said with a somber look on her face. "I didn't call you Saturday evening because I knew you were with your aunt at the hospital. I fought as hard as I could, but I wasn't able to save you. You've been terminated effective immediately. Linwood went behind my back and had the votes he needed before sending out an e-mail requesting input from the equity partners. The article in the newspaper couldn't have come at a worse time with the firm looking for any and every reason to cut staff and avoid the costs of relocating attorneys to Boston. I was able to get you a severance package in line with the one offered to the people let go last week, and you can use me as a reference on your résumé. I'll do anything I can to help you land on your feet. You know what I think about you as an attorney and as a person." Catherine stopped talking.

Stunned by the devastating news, Adisa froze in place. She realized the pitcher of water was still in her hand and placed it on the front corner of her desk.

"I'm not sure what to say," Adisa managed. "I have a few personal files that I need to transfer to a flash drive or my cloud account. Nothing business-related."

"That won't be a problem. And I'll send a copy of your severance agreement to your personal e-mail account by noon today. It's the first item on my task list for this morning."

The mention of a mundane thing like a task list made Adisa's emotions rush to the surface. There would be no task list for her today or ever again at Dixon and White.

"And all this is because of a stupid newspaper article?" she asked as a tear threatened to escape her right eye and stream down her cheek.

Catherine hesitated, which caused Adisa's jaw to tighten and a touch of anger to rise up inside her.

"What else is there? My performance reviews have always been great."

Catherine looked directly at Adisa. "I can't, and won't, tell you specifics. You know personnel discussions are confidential. I didn't agree with the decision, but I only have one vote."

"Is it that I wasn't considered partner-worthy down the road?"

"Sorry; you'll have to draw your own conclusions."

Adisa's thoughts suddenly returned to the graveyard that was the final resting place of many of her ancestors. Prejudice and racism didn't die when her relatives were laid to rest or end after black people left the farms and moved into corporate America. There was still life in what should be, after hundreds of years, an inert corpse.

"I have nothing but respect for you," Adisa said in a steely tone of voice. "And I believe you went to bat for me. But I know when there's an undercurrent of prejudice. And it's not because I'm trapped in racial paranoia."

"Adisa —"

"Mr. Katner probably didn't want me included in the move to Boston, and this hiccup with the newspaper gave him an excuse to do what he wanted to do all along."

Catherine didn't respond. The look on her face told Adisa what she needed to know.

"Don't worry," Adisa continued with a sigh. "I don't want to cause another problem that would blow up in your face. You've been an awesome mentor. Assuming everything is straightforward, I'll sign the severance agreement."

"This makes me so mad!" Catherine burst out.

"Hearing you say that means a lot."

"I'll write a letter of recommendation

extolling your virtues and describing your duties," Catherine continued. "Lawyers like you with two to four years' experience at a firm like this one are a hot commodity. When I'm finished, you'll have a decent shot at any job opening in the corporate section of any quality law firm. If a hiring partner wants to contact me directly, I'll take the call."

"Thanks."

Catherine left, and after staring out the window for a few moments, Adisa began to pack up her personal belongings. The biggest problem was the schefflera plant. To avoid damaging it, she gently laid it across the backseat of her car with a large plastic bag wrapped around the pot.

With the loss of her job, Adisa became invisible to her fellow workers. Except for the man from IT who retrieved her personal files from her computer, no one spoke to her on her way out of the office. Then, as she was doing a final inspection of her office to make sure she hadn't forgotten anything, Lucy, the assistant who'd worked for her, came down from the thirty-seventh floor. Sneaking into Adisa's office, the young woman closed the door.

"I probably shouldn't be talking to you," she said in a whisper, "but it would be awful if I didn't tell you how sorry I am that you're leaving. First thing this morning I typed a memo to your personnel file dictated by Mr. Katner. It made me so mad I wanted to walk out the door myself. I mean, the way he described you —"

"Stop." Adisa held up her hand and then pointed to her head. "I don't want to carry that in here when I leave."

"Sorry," Lucy said. "I'm just upset and wanted to let you know. What are you going to do?"

"Go to my apartment and take a bubble bath. And I'm not getting out until I'm good and ready."

After her bubble bath, Adisa brewed a cup of flavored coffee and took it to the living room. Sitting on the sofa with her feet curled up beneath her, she read her Bible. She followed a daily plan that included verses from both the Old and the New Testaments along with a selection from Psalms. The words from Psalm 34 particularly spoke to her about God's care and provision for those who trusted in him.

After finishing her coffee and Bible study, Adisa put on her exercise clothes and watched an exercise DVD that combined Zumba and kickboxing. The recording was over ten years old, but Adisa still liked it. Needing to burn off energy, she kicked higher and her dance moves were crisper than normal. As she was finishing, her phone vibrated and an unfamiliar number appeared. Rather than letting it go to voice mail, Adisa picked it up and answered.

"Adisa Johnson?" asked a man with a rich southern drawl.

"Yes, who's calling?" she asked, slightly out of breath.

"Theo Grayson from Campbellton. You worked at my office one summer when you were in high school."

"Sure," Adisa replied as she plopped down on the sofa. "I ran into Peggy Galloway this past weekend at the Jackson House, and your name came up. You inspired me to become an attorney."

"That's what she mentioned after church yesterday," the lawyer continued. "She also told me about your involvement in a case that overturned an old criminal conviction based on DNA evidence."

"It was a pro bono matter I handled for the Georgia Innocence Project. There was an article about it in the *AJC*."

"I read it. What an ironic twist of events that your client's DNA sample linked him to the cold cases in Louisiana."

206

"That's one way to put it," Adisa replied ruefully.

"I don't want to take up too much of your time. Here's the reason for my call. Could you connect me with someone at the Georgia Innocence Project? I know they specialize in postconviction relief, but there's a situation involving a nice young man here in Campbellton that may require a lawyer who doesn't care about anything except the Constitution. Their network would give me a place to start."

"Sure."

Adisa gave him the names of the lawyer who referred the Larimore case and the paralegal who worked for him.

"Thanks," Grayson replied. "Next time you're in town seeing Ms. Adams, I'd love to take you to lunch and learn more about your career. Peggy told me about your aunt's stroke. I hope she gets better soon."

"And I hope you can find competent representation for the man who needs a lawyer," she said. "What's the charge?"

"Most likely aggravated assault, but it could turn into murder if the victim dies."

Adisa felt her face suddenly get hot. "Is this the police officer who shot the unarmed black teenager?" she asked.

"Yes."

"There's been way too much of that happening all over the country," Adisa said.

"I agree," Grayson responded. "And it was going on before the media started paying attention. However, each situation has to be evaluated on its own facts."

Adisa knew she couldn't ask for more details. If Grayson had talked to the officer, the conversation would be subject to the attorney-client privilege.

"Well, everyone is entitled to representation," she said, trying to sound more broad-minded than she felt. "I just hope this is a circumstance where the system works."

"Me, too. Thanks again for the info, and don't forget to call if you have time for lunch during a visit with your aunt."

The call ended. Theo Grayson had always seemed like a nice gentleman, but Adisa knew it was impossible for even an enlightened white lawyer to know how a black person felt when hearing about the shooting of a young man like Deshaun Hamlin by a police officer. Hundreds of years of overt and subtle prejudice by those in authority didn't evaporate easily, especially when current events reinforced long-held stereotypes.

THIRTEEN

Luke paced back and forth inside the house.

"Either find something to do or take that energy outside, please," Jane said from the spot in the den where she was folding clothes.

Luke stopped and stared at the mountain of laundry that covered the imitation leather couch.

"I could help you fold clothes."

Jane looked up at him. "I like to fold towels the way my mother taught me, not the way your mother taught you. Why don't you see if there's a project you can tackle in the backyard?"

Luke had already considered that option and come up empty. No dandelions dared to peek up from the soil since he last went on a weed hunt, and Jane's bushes and flowers were fertilized and watered so thoroughly they were rain-forest healthy. He'd put together a playset that Ashley wouldn't be old enough to enjoy for at least another couple of years.

The playset assembly had been a bittersweet endeavor because Luke couldn't shake the thought that he might not be around to see his daughter go down the slide. Thoughts of prison were becoming more and more frequent and intrusive.

"I'm going over to the range," he said.

"Good idea. You should have it to yourself this time of day."

Luke grabbed his personal Glock 17 from the top of the refrigerator and retrieved a Sig Sauer P226 from the gun safe in the corner of the garage. He threw the leather satchel he used to transport ammunition onto the passenger seat of his truck.

Charlie Sellers, the owner of the gun range, was sitting in a ratty brown recliner and reading a trade magazine with pictures of the latest semiautomatic rifles displayed on the cover. He quickly closed the magazine.

"Luke," he said. "What brings you down here this time of day?"

Luke shrugged. "There's no job for me to go to, and I needed to shoot a few rounds to drive away the boredom."

"Are you by yourself?" Charlie asked, peering past him.

"Yeah, why?"

"Uh, no reason. Inside or out?"

"Outside. I don't want to be confined."

As soon as Luke spoke, he inwardly kicked himself for his choice of words. Charlie didn't seem to notice.

"I'll join you," the owner said. "What are you going to shoot first?"

"The Glock."

They went to the large field at the rear of the building. Charlie sat in a folding chair beneath an open wooden covering and leaned back against the building. Luke stood at a table and loaded bullets into the pistols: seventeen for the Glock and fifteen for the Sig Sauer. He nodded at Charlie when he finished.

"Hot!" Charlie called out, even though no one else was present. "Range is hot!"

Luke found the regimented routine at the range comforting. He slipped on a set of ear protectors. Carrying the pistol with the barrel pointed at the ground, Luke moved into position about twenty yards from a row of five chest-size metal targets. He glanced back at Charlie, who raised and lowered his hand. Luke brought the gun to eye level. He took a couple of deep breaths and in rapid succession fired one shot at the first target, two at the second, three at the third, four at the fourth, and five at the fifth. The goal was to move seamlessly from target to target.

Even wearing the ear protectors, Luke could hear the dull metallic *ping* as the bullets hit the targets. It was a perfect run. He had two rounds left but reloaded with bullets from his pocket and shot another perfect round. He lowered the gun. Although he wouldn't voice his thoughts to anyone, Luke was mystified by how he could be so accurate on the range and yet half his shots missed Deshaun Hamlin. He'd been troubled by the idea that he sent two 9 mm bullets flying down East Nixon Street with deadly potential. It was a big relief when he learned they hadn't come close to injuring anyone. On the other hand, if the two bullets had struck their intended target, Luke knew his conversation with Theo Grayson would have been about a murder charge.

Laying down the Glock, he made several passes with the Sig Sauer, the pistol preferred by Navy SEALs. Luke loved the solid feel of the weapon and the locked breech, short recoil design. He always practiced more with the Glock than the Sig Sauer because he used a Glock at work. Today he split time equally between the two weapons.

When he finished he returned to the table near Charlie.

"You really should consider competitive shooting," the range owner said. "And I'm not saying that as a way to get you to burn up more ammo. You've got the gift."

"I'd feel like I was trying to show off when all I want to do is be better at my job."

"Understood." Charlie paused. "How many rounds did you squeeze off when you shot the armed robber?"

Luke, who was cleaning the Sig Sauer, looked up.

"That was stupid of me," the owner quickly added. "I know you can't answer. That young man should consider himself lucky."

When he left the range, Luke wasn't ready to return home. Instead, he turned in the direction of the Westside Quik Mart.

After a light lunch, Adisa cleaned her apartment. Her phone vibrated, and the number for Dr. Dewberry's office popped into view as she was scrubbing the kitchen sink. She quickly rinsed and dried her hands. It was the doctor himself.

"How's my aunt?" she asked.

"She's had a setback. It may be necessary to perform a follow-up MRI to see if she's suffered another stroke or hemorrhage in a different part of the brain."

Adisa was disappointed. In her mind she'd reached the place of believing Aunt Josie was going to steadily improve.

"What kind of setback?"

"The occupational therapist noticed more delay in your aunt's speech patterns and limitations in the use of her left arm, not just the right."

"When will you decide if the MRI is necessary?"

"Tomorrow. I reviewed the records from her primary care provider, and it appears that until this happened, Ms. Adams was in great shape. I want to see her regain as much mobility and function as possible. Hopefully, this is a temporary situation we can address by adjusting her medication, but I wanted to keep you informed."

"Okay, thanks," Adisa replied. "I have a lot of free time this week, so I may come to Campbellton sooner than I'd planned."

As the afternoon dragged on, Adisa felt more and more anxious. She couldn't push the thought from her mind that Aunt Josie might suddenly die before she could see her again. Adisa started watching a movie that had been in her Netflix queue for almost a month, but it didn't hold her interest.

Finally, she gave up. After throwing a variety of clothes into a suitcase and a hanging bag, she loaded them into the trunk of her car and left. She'd be stuck in the beginning stages of rush-hour traffic, but she had to see Aunt Josie.

While creeping along in traffic, Adisa decided to call a few of the law firms that might be interested in hiring her. At the top of her list was a firm that had been on the other side of a Dixon and White deal. The managing partner conducted himself in a competent, professional manner. If nothing else, he might know about job openings for lawyers with Adisa's skill set. To her surprise, she didn't have to leave a voice mail.

"Paul Austin," the lawyer said as soon as the receptionist transferred the call.

The car in front of Adisa lurched forward, and she stepped on the gas.

"This is Adisa Johnson."

"Right," the lawyer said. "I remember you at Dixon and White. You took part in the negotiations on the National Carrier deal."

Adisa swerved slightly as a car drifted over into her lane. "Yes," she replied. "But I'm no longer at the firm."

For the next fifteen minutes, Adisa repeated the presentation she'd mentally prepared while cleaning her apartment. Austin didn't cut her off by saying they weren't hiring, which gave her confidence a boost.

"What's the likelihood that you can bring a book of business with you?" the managing partner asked when she finished.

Adisa doubted any of Dixon and White's clients would follow her. Their loyalties lay with the large firm and the men and women who ran it.

"Not very good," she admitted. "All of my work was a part of Catherine Summey's group."

"That wouldn't stop you from sending out notices that you've taken a new position. My client and I were impressed with your contributions to the deal we worked on together."

Adisa remembered the woman CEO as an aggressive, no-nonsense negotiator.

"Wow," she said before catching herself. "But I wouldn't want to step on Catherine's toes."

"Steel-toed boots are a prerequisite in this business. We have a partners' breakfast on Friday, and I'll put your availability on the agenda. If something opens up before then, let me know. I want us to be in the mix."

The call ended, and Adisa's spirits soared. She made two other calls, left voice messages for managing partners, and spent the rest of the drive in a pleasant fantasy about what life might be like in a smaller, boutique firm.

The Westside Quik Mart was in a part of town Luke rarely visited except on patrol. He parked his truck at the pump closest to the exit. A middle-aged black man was filling up his car. As he swiped his credit card, Luke glanced toward the building but couldn't see inside the store. There weren't any cars parked out front. An older-model sedan sat alongside the building.

The man finished pumping gas and placed the nozzle in its slot. As he walked around his car toward the driver's side of the vehicle, the man glanced over at Luke, who quickly lowered his eyes.

Luke carefully filled his tank without allowing any of the gas to splash out on the paint. Locking the driver's-side door of the truck, he walked across the narrow lot to the convenience store. A bell chimed when he opened the door. A black man was at the back of the store bending over in front of the beer cooler. Luke couldn't see his face.

"I'll be with you in a second!" the man called out.

"Take your time," Luke replied.

He quickly surveyed the store. He wasn't

sure what he was looking for. He just wanted to check out the place where the events occurred that led to his current troubles. He noted the placement of the surveillance cameras and the obviously new Plexiglas shield in front of the cash register. The store clerk moved in his direction, and Luke hurriedly grabbed a bag of cashews from a nearby rack. As the clerk came closer, Luke saw bandages on the man's neck and hand. It was Stanley Jackson.

Luke's mouth suddenly went dry, and he turned away from the cash register and stepped over to the drink coolers. He stared unseeing at the rows of fruit and sports drinks before making a selection. He took the drink and the cashews up to the cash register. The young man didn't pay any attention to Luke as he scanned the items.

"That will be $5.59," Stan said.

Luke suddenly realized he didn't have any cash in his wallet and would have to give the clerk his credit or debit card. He slid his credit card across the counter.

"Ran out of the house without any cash," he said with a nervous laugh.

Stan took the card. "Even though it's not much, I need to see your ID before I run the card," the clerk said.

For a split second, Luke considered grabbing the credit card and bolting out the door. Instead, he flipped open his wallet so his driver's license was visible. The clerk stared at it for a second and then jerked his head up, his eyes wide.

"What are you doing here?" he asked, glancing around.

Luke licked his lips and tried to swallow. "I bought some gas and wanted a drink and a snack," he managed.

The store clerk gave him a skeptical look.

"And I wanted to see where all this mess started," Luke continued, relieved to say something that was completely true. "I'm sorry you were cut up during the robbery."

Stan didn't respond but swiped the credit card without looking Luke in the eye.

"Do you want your receipt?" the clerk asked, still averting his gaze.

"Uh, yes."

Stan looked up and fixed his eyes on Luke as he handed him the receipt. "I didn't say Deshaun robbed the store," Stan said.

"I know," Luke quickly replied. "But that's the word that went out from the dispatcher."

"And there wasn't any mention of a gun."

Luke nodded but didn't say anything. Stan looked down at his injured hand.

"I wish you hadn't shot him," Stan said. "He's a good kid."

Luke knew he couldn't speak even if he wanted to. Anything he said might be replayed in the future before a jury.

"If you'd given him a chance to explain why he was walking down the street, I would have been the only one hurt," Stan continued.

"I wanted to see where it started," Luke said, repeating himself.

"This is it," Stan answered with a sweeping motion of his non-injured hand. "They've added a couple of cameras and this plastic that I doubt could stop a pellet gun. But I wasn't going to hide out in fear. That's not who I am."

"I can see that."

"I just hope Deshaun makes it."

"Me, too," Luke replied. "I really do."

"I'm sure about that," Stan said in a sarcastic tone of voice.

Luke shifted on his feet and didn't reply.

"Well, unless you want to buy something else, I'd appreciate you moving on," Stan said after a few awkward moments of silence passed.

"I understand."

"No." Stan shook his head. "I don't think you do."

Arriving in Campbellton, Adisa pulled into

the hospital parking lot. As she entered the main doors, she glanced at the newspaper box. The headline grabbed her attention: "Grand Jury to Consider Charges Against Officer." Adisa found enough loose change in her purse to buy a copy. The local paper didn't publish articles online until the day following their appearance in the print version.

Aunt Josie was sleeping with her mouth partly open and an untouched supper tray on her bedside table. Adisa frowned. Going to the nurses' station, she introduced herself to the woman on duty.

"What has my aunt eaten today?" she asked.

The phone rang, and the nurse picked it up. Adisa stood in front of the counter and waited several minutes until the call ended.

"I'm sorry," the woman said. "How may I help you?"

"Josephine Adams in 2568. She didn't eat any supper, and I'm wondering what she's had today."

The phone rang again. The nurse answered it and raised her index finger. After another minute passed, Adisa gave up and left. It didn't look like Aunt Josie had moved a millimeter. Pulling a chair close to the bed, Adisa lightly touched her aunt's right arm. The once-sinewy muscles were already beginning to feel softer and weaker. Adisa lowered her head and sighed. There was a knock on the door, and a nurse's aide entered.

"Sorry," the young black woman said. "The call nurse asked me to come in and feed the patient."

Adisa moved to the side.

"Would you like something to eat, sweetie?" the aide asked.

Aunt Josie opened her eyes and managed a weak nod. The aide brought the tray closer and began to carefully spoon the liquid into Aunt Josie's mouth. It was a tedious process, but it was clear that she wanted nourishment. Adisa was relieved. Some appetite was better than none. She sat in a chair at the foot of the bed and picked up the newspaper. The aide glanced over her shoulder.

"Isn't that terrible about the young man who was shot by the police?"

"At least the grand jury will have a chance to hear the evidence," Adisa replied. "Lots of times that wouldn't have happened in the past."

"Yeah, but my daddy says in a few months they'll come up with an excuse to drop the charges."

Aunt Josie opened her mouth to receive

another bite.

"I've been taking care of Ms. Adams ever since she came to the hospital," the woman continued. "She's a fighter. Maybe this broth will help her regain her strength. She told me about you and your sister. Are you the one who's a lawyer?"

"Yes."

"I thought so. What do you think will happen to the man who shot the teenager?"

"I'm not sure," Adisa said. "But everybody I talk to in Campbellton wants to see justice done."

"Does that include white folks?" the aide responded.

Theo Grayson had come across more as an advocate for the officer than a champion of justice.

"I hope so."

The aide patiently worked with Aunt Josie until all the food was gone. During the meal, the older woman mostly kept her eyes closed.

"There you go," the young woman said to Aunt Josie. "Maybe those calories will give you the energy to talk to your niece."

Aunt Josie's eyes blinked open. Adisa, who was still sitting in a chair at the foot of the bed, stood up.

"Adisa?" the older woman croaked.

"Yes, ma'am." Adisa came around to her aunt's side.

"You're not leaving me, are you?"

"No, I'm here."

Aunt Josie nodded slowly and closed her eyes. The nurse's aide gently cleaned the older woman's mouth with a sterile wipe.

"Do you want me to brush her teeth?"

"No, I'll do it," Adisa replied.

"You'll be getting plenty of practice," the aide said sadly as she patted Aunt Josie on the left arm. "Now she's having trouble with the left side, too."

The young woman left. Adisa put a tiny amount of toothpaste on a moistened brush and gently worked it around the inside of her aunt's mouth. When she finished, she held a plastic cup with water up to the older woman's mouth so she could swish and spit. Adisa was relieved when her aunt realized what to do.

"Great," Adisa said, wiping Aunt Josie's mouth with a tissue. "Are you ready for another nap?"

"No," Aunt Josie said with surprising strength and then turned her head toward Adisa. "Tell me what's wrong with me. My body isn't working, and I'm confused."

Adisa scooted a chair close to the bed and told her what had happened.

"Am I dying?" Aunt Josie asked when Adisa finished.

"Not yet," Adisa replied. "You've perked up since eating supper."

"I'm ready to go," Aunt Josie said, closing her eyes. "The plans for my funeral are in the desk drawer at the house where I keep all my business papers."

Adisa had seen the envelope marked "Funeral" when she retrieved the power of attorney.

"Please, no," Adisa said. "Let's not —"

"How long are they going to keep me here?" Aunt Josie said. "Whether I live or die, I want to go home. You can hire Mary Broome to take care of me. If she could handle Walter when he was sick, she can help me. And they need the money. I've got money in —" Aunt Josie stopped and looked at Adisa in alarm. "I can't remember where I put my money!"

"I know about your money," Adisa said soothingly. "And I check the bank statements every month to make sure everything is okay."

Aunt Josie sighed again. "Thank the Lord for you, Adisa. You're better than any daughter could be to me."

And with that the older woman fell asleep, leaving Adisa wondering how she could, in fact, be better than a daughter.

Jane had fixed spaghetti for supper. Normally, it was one of Luke's favorite meals. His wife's spaghetti didn't have the runny, tepid sauce Luke grew up eating as a child. Her version of the classic Italian dish featured noodles covered in a thick, meaty sauce with plenty of onions and loads of fresh tomatoes that were cooked until they released all their slightly acidic goodness into the deep red broth. A moderate dash of garlic and a liberal covering of freshly grated Parmesan cheese made the meal complete. Luke usually ate two large servings. Tonight he barely finished his first plateful and turned down a second.

"I wish you hadn't done that," Jane said as she took away his plate and placed it in the sink. "Especially driving over to East Nixon Street where the shooting happened. Are you sure no one saw you snooping around?"

"I wasn't snooping around. I had to look at everything again in the light of day so I could try to figure some things out for myself."

"What do you mean?"

Luke stared straight ahead, unaware that Ashley was carefully laying a messy piece of

226

spaghetti across her arms.

"I keep replaying the tapes in my head of what happened, but I'm not sure they're accurate. I thought the distance from the streetlight to my patrol car was greater. That night it seemed like it took Hamlin a long time to run down the road toward me. But it couldn't have been more than a few seconds between when I first saw him and" — Luke paused and took a breath — "I shot him. I guess I was so pumped full of adrenaline that it made everything slow down. Chief Lockhart told me adrenaline will mess with our senses and perception."

"People should realize how fast you had to act."

"Yeah," Luke said as he looked over at Ashley, removed a piece of spaghetti she'd deposited on top of her head, and placed it on the high-chair tray. "I just wish there were eyewitnesses who would back me up. Of course, folks might be afraid to come forward because of the backlash they'd face in the black community."

"I want to believe the people in this town would tell the truth under oath," Jane said resolutely. "And I can't stand the thought of a bunch of lies being told about you just because you're white and Deshaun Hamlin is black."

Luke didn't respond. Ashley had managed to wrap part of a noodle around one of her stubby fingers like a ring. She held it up and admired it in amazement. The phone rang, and Jane answered it. She listened for several moments.

"Okay, thanks for calling to let us know," she said, replacing the receiver in its cradle. "That was Betsy. She says we need to see the newspaper. There's a front-page article that claims the DA is going to submit the case to the grand jury."

"I'll go out and buy one," Luke said, scooting back his chair.

"No, you clean Ashley. She's going straight to the tub. I'll run over to the dry cleaners. There's a paper box out front. I don't want you driving to the Westside Quik Mart to buy a newspaper."

FOURTEEN

It was 7:30 p.m. when Adisa pulled into the driveway of Aunt Josie's home. Walter and Mary Broome were locking the front door of their house. Seeing Mary Broome up close, Adisa couldn't imagine the seventy-year-old woman caring for Aunt Josie. It would be like trying to fit a size 6 shoe on a size 8 foot.

"How's Josephine?" Mrs. Broome asked in the high-pitched voice that had enabled her to sing soprano in the church choir for the past fifty years. "We went down to see her this morning, but she was sleeping the whole time."

"I saw the note you left on the nightstand beside her bed," Adisa replied.

"We'll get down there again soon," Mr. Broome said. "But we don't have time to talk now. There's a big meeting tonight at the rec center for the Hamlin boy who was shot."

Adisa glanced across the athletic fields to the redbrick building that served as a multipurpose community center.

"It was moved from one of the churches so everyone can feel comfortable about coming," Mr. Broome continued.

"I disagreed with that decision," Mary Broome added. "But nobody is going to listen to me. I just hope someone makes sure they start and end the meeting with prayer. Do you want to come with us?"

"I'm exhausted and ready to collapse," Adisa replied.

"I want to grab a seat down front," Mr. Broome said, looking at his watch.

"And as soon as Josephine gets home from the hospital, I'll coordinate the meals folks from the church will want to bring," Mrs. Broome said. "I know it's aggravating for her to be on a liquid diet, but I have several soup recipes that are savory enough to scratch the itch for something flavorful to put in her mouth."

"That sounds wonderful."

Mrs. Broome reached out and patted Adisa on the arm. "Seeing you is the best medicine in the world."

Adisa went inside the house. From the window over the kitchen sink, she could see the rec center. She'd praised Reggie Reynolds for getting involved in the local justice effort. Now she wasn't willing to walk 150 yards to attend a meeting. She felt like a hypocrite. Going into the bathroom, she washed her face and reapplied her makeup.

The sun had dipped below the horizon by the time Adisa left the house. Leaving her car in the driveway, she walked across the backyard. There was a small gate in the fence that served as the boundary for one of the baseball fields. The sound of chirping crickets accompanied her across the outfield toward home plate. The parking lot was as full as on a July evening when the baseball or softball play-offs were in full swing. Vans from several area churches were parked in front of the building.

Adisa slipped inside and leaned against the rear wall. Most of the people were already sitting on folding chairs set up on the floor of the low-ceilinged gym. Even though it wasn't a particularly warm evening, the mass of bodies in the room was causing the temperature to rise. She estimated that at least seven hundred people, including families with small children, were present. For a town the size of Campbellton, this was a major event. The sound of that many people greeting one another and talking in an enclosed space reached a dull roar. Reggie Reynolds, wearing a dark suit, stood up with a microphone in his hand and tapped it with his finger. There was no podium or pulpit in front of him.

"Testing, one, two, three," he said.

The crowd began to settle down.

"I'm Reverend Reginald Reynolds, pastor of the Zion Hills Baptist Church, and I want to greet each and every one of you in the name of the Lord. This meeting is open to every citizen of Campbellton and Nash County who wants to see justice for Deshaun Hamlin. We welcome all races and particularly thank our white and Latino friends who have joined us. If that's you, please stand."

About forty people stood up. Reggie clapped his hands while still holding the mic.

"We also want to recognize the members of Deshaun's family who are with us and offer our prayers and support to them during this trying time," Reggie said. "That includes Mrs. Thelma Armistead, his grandmother; Mr. Cecil Hamlin, his uncle . . ."

Ten or twelve of Deshaun's relatives were sitting on the front row. Mrs. Armistead was wearing a black hat and a white dress.

"We also want to thank Chief Ben Lockhart with the Campbellton Police Department for joining us. We met with Chief Lockhart before the meeting, and he assured us that Deshaun's shooting is being thoroughly investigated and appropriate action will be taken in cooperation with the district attorney's office."

A large, middle-aged white police officer in uniform stood and waved. The response of the crowd to the police chief was limited to scattered applause. Adisa heard a few boos. Reggie then laid out the circumstances of the shooting. Listening to him, Adisa didn't doubt the young preacher's sincerity, but as a lawyer she couldn't help wondering which parts of his narrative were true and which were false. Determining the truth, the whole truth, and nothing but the truth was an inexact science. Reggie paused for a moment to make sure everyone in the room was paying attention.

"It's time we brought our community into the twenty-first century and shattered the racism and oppression that for generations have stained the ground with innocent blood!"

Applause and a few shouts greeted his words. Reggie warmed to his task. Adisa could understand why the young minister's church was growing. He was a dynamic speaker with oratorical skills that could have easily transferred to a courtroom if he'd chosen to become a lawyer. Even though he was speaking without notes, he'd obviously given thought to what he wanted to say.

"But we're not going to meet violence with violence, are we?" he called out. "No! We're going to let the righteous authority of our cause lead us to victory!"

Several loud "Amens" greeted the minister's words. Adisa said the same word, only under her breath. While the influence of black ministers had waned in cities like Atlanta, pastors still swayed public opinion in a town like Campbellton.

"We appreciate the efforts of men like Chief Lockhart," Reggie said, "but it's our responsibility to police our own people. If you catch wind of plans for violence or see someone acting inconsistently with what we stand for, inform someone in authority immediately. There have been threats communicated to Officer Nelson and acts of vandalism at his home. This is not who we are! And it must stop!"

There were several loud "Amens" again, but the response wasn't universal. Clearly, Reggie was trying to pattern his message after the words of the young Martin Luther King Jr.

The minister finished, and another man

Adisa didn't know talked about organizational efforts. People were directed toward tables in different corners of the room. Some of the opportunities included those willing to be present in the courtroom for every appearance by Officer Nelson, volunteers to call and visit elected officials, and a group to hand out information door-to-door. As people began making their way to different parts of the room, Adisa turned and slipped out the doorway.

"Adisa!" a voice called out to her, and she turned around.

It was a former high school classmate named Darlene Singletary. "What are you doing in town?" Darlene asked.

Adisa quickly told her about Aunt Josie's condition.

"I hadn't heard anything about it," Darlene replied. She motioned toward the rec center building. "Isn't Pastor Reynolds amazing? My husband and I have been going to his church for over two years. We met there the first Sunday he preached, and he married us six months later."

"He's a good speaker," Adisa replied, glancing down at the ring on Darlene's left hand.

Darlene wasn't a churchgoer when they were in high school. Back then, the tall and slender girl with an abundance of hair had been more interested in locating the hottest party than in seeking out a prayer meeting.

"And I think he's taking the right approach to the shooting," Adisa added.

"You should visit Zion Hills if you're here on a Sunday morning. You'll be blessed."

"Maybe I will," Adisa replied noncommittally.

Stepping away, Adisa headed toward the baseball fields. In a dimly lit section of the parking lot farthest from the rec center, a group of twelve to fifteen young men were gathered around two cars and a pickup truck.

"This has gotta stop," Adisa heard one of the men say. "And I'm not going to count on a preacher who only cares about what's dropped into the offering plate to do it for me."

As Adisa came closer she saw the glint of something metal in the hand of one of the men. She quickly changed direction to move away from the group.

"Tell us when and where, and we'll be there," she heard another voice say.

Adisa reached the infield grass and glanced over her shoulder. The men remained clustered together; however, two broke away and headed in her direction. The lights of the pickup truck came on and pointed across the ball field. Adisa knew she was caught in the beams of light and nervously began walking faster across the soft dirt between the second and third bases. Her shoes wouldn't allow her to run. Kicking them off, she grabbed them up in her right hand and sprinted across the outfield to the fence. She was breathing heavily when she reached the gate and turned around. The lights of the truck still shone on the field, but she didn't see anyone. Putting on her shoes, she made her way to Aunt Josie's house, where she entered and quickly locked the door behind her.

Adisa debated whether to call the police and report what she'd heard, but she was short on details. She didn't know the names of the men gathered at the back corner of the parking lot, and all she could recall was that the pickup was blue and one of the other cars near them was a reddish or maroon color. Before going to bed, she turned out the lights and peeked out one of the windows at the front of the house. The street was empty, the houses dark.

The following morning Adisa woke up early and brewed a pot of coffee in Aunt Josie's ancient percolator. The freshly brewed coffee hit a bull's-eye on every taste-bud receptor. While she sipped it, she called Shanika.

"You're back in Campbellton?" her sister asked in surprise.

"Yeah, I'm trying to keep her plants alive," Adisa told her sister as a diversion to keep from revealing that she'd lost her job. "And there's unrest in Campbellton about an unarmed young black man who was shot by a white police officer."

"Did the young man die?"

"No, he's in a coma at the hospital."

"I haven't heard anything about it. It won't show up on the news around here unless protesters set a car or two on fire."

Adisa told her about the meeting at the rec center and her encounter with Darlene Singletary. "Darlene was wild as a bobcat in high school," Adisa said. "Do you know who she married?"

"No, I haven't followed her on social media."

"She and her husband go to the church where the leader of the rally serves as pastor. Darlene invited me to visit."

"Maybe you should go," Shanika replied. "You might meet a guy, and the preacher can marry the two of you in six months."

"I'll make sure to wear a name tag announcing my availability," Adisa joked.

Adisa hadn't been in a serious romantic relationship since her senior year in college. Nothing since then had progressed beyond the friendship level.

"You didn't meet Ronnie in church," she continued. "It was a blind date."

"Yeah, but the girl who set it up knew someone who went to church with him. That way I knew he wasn't a jerk trolling for a victim."

Adisa checked the time on the kitchen clock. "I need to head over to the hospital. I'll call later this morning and let you know how Aunt Josie is doing."

"Okay. Ronnie is in Savannah playing golf with the big bosses at his company. I know it's a business trip and he didn't have a choice about going, but it's still hard to swallow."

"What are the kids doing?"

"I let them stay up too late last night and they're sleeping in. They'll be crawling out of bed and demanding breakfast soon."

Adisa was silent for a second. It would have been easy to hang up, but she didn't.

"I have some news about the law firm," she said hesitantly.

"What? Are you moving to Boston sooner than you thought?"

"No, I'm not going at all."

Adisa told Shanika about losing her job. Even though Adisa knew her termination was unjustified, she was still embarrassed.

"I can't tell you much more because Catherine Summey finagled a generous severance package if I promise to keep my mouth shut about the details."

"It makes me sad and furious," Shanika replied with an edge to her voice. "I'm sad for you and furious that a stupid article in the newspaper about something you had no way of knowing could get you fired. There's got to be a way you could sue for wrongful termination or something. It doesn't seem right."

"I've already started looking for another job, but I'm going to focus on firms in the Atlanta area. That way I can help keep an eye on Aunt Josie so all the burden doesn't fall on you."

"What about Campbellton? If you worked there, even on a temporary basis, it would be much easier to help until she's back on her feet."

"Uh, I doubt there are any firms looking for lawyers. The total membership of the bar can't be more than thirty or forty attorneys."

"But I bet at least one of them would jump at the chance to get someone as smart as you are."

"That's not practical," Adisa answered. "Law firms don't operate like temp agencies —"

Shanika interrupted her. "How do you know without asking around? That was your problem finding your first job."

Adisa bristled. Shanika's comment was a throwback to Adisa's shy reluctance as a tenth grader to look for a part-time job. Shanika had picked up an application for a cashier position at a local drugstore and made Adisa fill it out. Shanika then took the application back to the manager and convinced him to hire her little sister. The job lasted over two years.

"This isn't the same as Shoemaker's Drug Store," Adisa said.

"Which went out of business when all the big drugstore chains came to town, but there will always be lawyers camped around the courthouse. It wouldn't hurt to ask."

"I already have a solid lead for a job with a smaller firm in Atlanta. I think the managing partner wants to hire me, and it would be a great opportunity. I could still drive up to Campbellton and check on Aunt Josie. Last night she mentioned hiring Mary Broome to care for her when she's dismissed from the hospital."

241

"Mary Broome!" Shanika exploded. "We'd have to lock up everything in the house! Not that Mary would steal, or at least I hope not. But she's so nosy she'd rifle through every drawer and closet in the house and then tell her cronies what she found."

It was a true statement and further evidence of Aunt Josie's diminished mental capacity.

"You're right," Adisa admitted.

A child's voice cried out, "Mama! Ronnie hit me!"

"Gotta go," Shanika said hurriedly.

Adisa went into the kitchen and poured another cup of coffee into a travel mug. Conversations with Shanika could still turn into black holes that sucked her in.

Luke and Jane sat close to each other in the reception area of Theo Grayson's office and listened to the receptionist answer the phone.

"Good morning, Grayson, Baxter, and Williams. How may I direct your call?"

"They're busy," Jane whispered to Luke, who was staring at a sports magazine without reading the words or absorbing the pictures. "Is that good or bad?"

"I don't know," Luke replied, returning

the magazine to a wooden rack near his chair. "But everybody knows Mr. Grayson is the lawyer to hire if you can afford to pay him."

"Why didn't he say anything about his fee when he called this morning and asked you to come see him?"

"They don't do that over the phone. But he asked me a bunch of questions about our finances, including if we had an equity line of credit on the house. I guess he's figuring out the maximum amount we can come up with."

"Don't forget about the money my mom inherited after my grandpa died and they sold the orange grove. I'm sure she'd help."

"It wouldn't be right to take your mother's inheritance."

Before Jane responded, the receptionist spoke. "Mr. Grayson will see you now. He'll meet with you in the main conference room. It's the second door on the left."

Jane grabbed Luke's hand as they walked down a carpeted hallway to a set of double doors. They intertwined their fingers, which was their way of communicating unity. Luke gave her hand a quick squeeze and pushed open the doors. Inside was a shiny wooden table with curved legs surrounded by eight leather chairs. The walls were a creamy yellow with a chair railing and multitiered crown molding around the ceiling. Portraits of men who Luke assumed were, or had been, partners in the firm lined one wall. Included were Theo Grayson and a bald man with glasses whom Luke recognized as Harold Baxter, a real-estate lawyer who served on the board of directors at a local bank. From the changes in the style of clothes in the portraits, it was clear the firm had been around a long, long time. In the earliest painting, the lawyer had thick white sideburns and piercing dark eyes, and he wore a skinny black tie. A brass plate on the frame read "Augustus Frampton, Superior Court Judge, 1925–1932."

"From what I've been told, Gus Frampton wasn't the kind of judge who would have been electable in the twenty-first century," Theodore Grayson said. "But he was a legal genius."

Luke turned around as Grayson extended his hand to Jane. "Theo Grayson, Ms. Nelson. Please have a seat."

The lawyer pulled back a chair for Jane. Luke sat beside her. Jane twisted a tissue in her lap. Grayson, a computer tablet in his hand, walked around to the other side of the table.

"Thanks for seeing us," Luke began. "We

244

know your time is valuable."

Grayson cleared his throat. "I'll get right to it," the lawyer began. "As you know, the DA is going to present your case to the grand jury, probably by the end of the week. The political pressure is simply too great to treat this as an internal police matter. There was a rally last night at the rec center not far from the shooting. Over eight hundred people were there."

"Eight hundred?" Luke asked in shock, remembering the modest gathering at the high school gym.

"The DA doesn't want to run the risk of public unrest breaking out, which would make it look like he was bowing to violence," Grayson continued. "So he's decided to let the grand jury determine the next step. If the grand jury refuses to indict, then he's off the hook."

"What do you think the grand jury will do?" Jane asked anxiously.

"It depends on how vigorously Baldwin presents the evidence. Grand jury deliberations are secret, of course, but it's easy for the DA to telegraph what he wants."

"Can someone talk to him in advance and find out?" Luke asked.

"Oh, yes, there can be a lobbying effort. That's already going on by the people who want to see you charged."

"Could you do that for us?" Jane asked. "Everybody in town respects you. I know it's a lot to ask, and we don't have much money."

"Not everyone has as high an opinion of me as you do," Grayson replied gently. "But I'm going to make a phone call to the DA on Luke's behalf as a concerned citizen. More importantly, I've been working on finding someone who can step in and help as his lawyer."

Grayson referred again to his tablet. "Based on what you told me earlier about your financial situation, you're not going to qualify for a public defender, and you don't have the kind of resources to pay what most experienced criminal defense lawyers would charge. Right now I'm focusing on organizations dedicated to representing police officers charged with crimes. I have a few leads but nothing definite to tell you."

"Is bringing someone in from the outside a good idea?" Luke asked. "They won't know the judges or the jurors."

"That's where I can assist. My value, to you and to the attorney who ultimately represents you if you're charged, will be behind the scenes. I can help investigate the case and sit at the counsel table when it's time to pick a jury. I know the jury pool in Nash County as well as anyone and can tell an out-of-town lawyer who to strike and who to keep. As for the judges, I'm up-to-date with their quirks and preferences and can pass that information along, too."

Luke shook his head before saying, "It will be impossible for us to pay you and another lawyer."

"I wouldn't charge a fee to do what I just described," Grayson replied.

Luke's mouth dropped open. Jane gasped.

"Why would you do that?" Luke asked.

"Because at this point in my career I can do whatever I want to," Grayson replied with a slight smile. "Lawyers are always reminded about their civic duty when they go to meetings of the bar association. This will give me a chance to prove I believe that's true and help a police officer who risked his life every day to protect me and every other citizen of the community I love."

FIFTEEN

Adisa spent a quiet morning with Aunt Josie. The older woman was drowsy, and when her eyes first opened, she smiled and then went right back to sleep. While Aunt Josie slept, Adisa completed two complicated crossword puzzles. She was itching to exercise, but that would have to wait until she returned to Aunt Josie's house later in the day. Around noon, the older woman came fully awake. Adisa gave her a few sips of water.

"I'm hungry," Aunt Josie said. "Where's my food?"

"It should be here in a few minutes," Adisa replied. "Your room is at the end of the hall, so you're served last."

"Where's the doctor? I want to talk to him about going home."

"If Dr. Dewberry came in this morning, it was before I arrived. I checked with the lead nurse assigned to your room, and she told me there was no change in your status or the doctor's orders."

"Then what am I doing here?" Aunt Josie asked irritably. "If I'm not getting better, I'd rather be sick at home in my own bed than stuck in here."

"Move your right arm," Adisa said softly.

The older woman shifted in her bed and then stared at her arm as if shocked that it didn't do more than move a few inches across the sheet.

"Now move the left one," Adisa continued.

Aunt Josie was able to lift her left hand to her face and touch her nose.

"That's great!" Adisa exclaimed. "Your left arm is back to where it was a couple of days ago."

"Great? It's practically useless."

"No. The second stroke, or whatever it was, could have been a bigger setback. We'll see what your therapist says when she comes in later to work with you."

"Child, I wasn't cut out to be bedfast," Aunt Josie said and sighed. "If this is what my life is going to be, I'd rather Jesus would take me home as soon as possible."

"That's up to him, isn't it?"

Aunt Josie managed a slightly crooked smile that revealed the impact of the stroke on her facial movements. "What day is it?" the older woman asked.

"Tuesday."

There was a knock on the door. Adisa opened it, and Reggie Reynolds, dressed in casual clothes and running shoes, greeted her.

"Come in," Adisa said.

Reggie entered the room. Adisa prepared to introduce him to Aunt Josie.

"Glory to God!" the older woman exclaimed.

"Aunt Josie?" Adisa said hesitantly. "This is Reggie Reynolds, pastor at the Zion Hills Baptist Church."

Aunt Josie raised her trembling left hand, pointed it at the ceiling, and then let it drop back to her side.

"What is it, Sister Adams?" Reggie asked, a respectful expression on his face.

"Pastor, the presence of the Lord came into the room with you!" Aunt Josie said in the strongest voice Adisa had heard since the older woman's stroke. "Can't you feel it?"

Reggie glanced over at Adisa, who shook her head.

"No, ma'am," he answered. "It must have been for your benefit."

"Well, I'll take it," Aunt Josie answered. "I

haven't felt a jolt like that since the move of God at Woodside Tabernacle thirty years ago."

"I'd like to know more about that," Reggie said.

"Sit here, and I'll tell you," Aunt Josie replied, patting the bed with her left hand.

Reggie and Adisa spent the next forty-five minutes listening to stories about what happened at the local church long before Adisa and Shanika arrived on the scene. It had been a watershed event in the lives of many of the people who were now the older members of the congregation.

"I've never heard most of this," Adisa said when Aunt Josie paused and asked for a drink of sweet tea.

The older woman took a long sip through the straw. "Just talking about it makes me feel better," she said. "In the presence of the Lord there is great strength."

"That's true," Reggie said.

Aunt Josie reached out with her left hand, and he took it in his right hand.

"God is going to let you see mighty things if you stay true to him and his Word," she said. "And stay humble. He opposes the proud but gives grace to the humble."

"Yes, ma'am."

Aunt Josie yawned. The older woman's

face seemed more symmetrical and less twisted.

"I need to rest," she said. "Will you pray with me before you go?"

"Certainly. That's why I came," Reggie replied and bowed his head.

Reggie prayed a shorter prayer than Adisa expected, but it included a heartfelt request that God would touch and heal Aunt Josie.

"Amen," he said.

"Come again," Aunt Josie said, yawning once more. "Even if Adisa isn't here."

Within seconds, the older woman's breathing was slow and steady.

"She can go to sleep in a nanosecond," Adisa said.

Reggie shook his head. "Your aunt is an amazing woman. When I first saw her walking around town with that big stick, I thought she had a mental problem. But when I heard what she was doing, I came to respect her faith and perseverance. I've seen her bundled up in a big coat and going down Main Street on the coldest day of the year."

"You're not telling me anything I don't know," Adisa said with a smile. "It embarrassed me when I was in high school, but heaven alone knows the good she's done."

"How did you end up living with her?"

Reggie asked, then quickly added, "I'm not trying to pry if that's a bad question."

"It's okay. Aunt Josie rescued my sister and me. We weren't orphans when she took us in, but we might as well have been."

Adisa gave Reggie a brief account of how she and Shanika had come to live with their great-aunt in Campbellton.

"She did a great job," Reggie said. "I mean, look how you turned out."

Adisa laughed. "Don't jump too quickly to a conclusion," she said. "You barely know me."

"And I hope that changes," Reggie said, standing up.

Adisa paused for a moment. The young minister possessed a nice mix of kindness and confidence.

"I'd like that," she said.

"Great."

Reggie stepped over to the door. Stopping, he turned and faced Adisa. "I have a question for you," he said.

Adisa realized the minister was going to ask her out to dinner. At this point in her life she hadn't considered the possibility of meeting someone to date in Campbellton. Before he said the words, she decided she would say yes.

"Would you like to visit Deshaun Hamlin

with me?" he asked.

Luke's mind was in a fog when they left Theo Grayson's office. He hadn't mentioned it to Jane, but at times since the shooting he'd felt like an observer watching life unfold around him. It made him wonder if he was either going crazy or having a nervous breakdown. He'd had the weird out-of-body sensation partway through the meeting with the lawyer and had difficulty shaking it.

"Do you really think Mr. Grayson is going to help me?" Luke asked as they pulled into the driveway of their house.

"Unless he was lying," Jane said and gave him a puzzled look. "But I'm still praying that the truth will come out and you won't be indicted, which will make all this unnecessary."

As soon as the car rolled to a stop in the garage, Jane opened the passenger door.

"I'd better relieve Jessica," she said. "Her mother said she's on a tight schedule."

Luke didn't follow. If he went inside, there would be nothing for him to do except watch Jane take care of Ashley. The complete disruption of his daily work routine and forced inactivity didn't help his mental status. And while Jane was praying for the truth to come out, Luke could try to find out for himself. He restarted the car's engine and backed out of the driveway. When he reached the stop sign at the end of their street, he stopped to send Jane a text message:

Going to the station for a minute. Back soon.

Eight minutes later he pulled into the police department parking lot. It was several hours until the end of the first shift, and all the vehicles except one were on patrol. He parked in the visitor area and walked into the station, a modest, single-story gray brick building. There wasn't a city jail. Prisoners were held in the county correctional center a couple of blocks to the west. The receptionist, a young woman in her twenties, looked up in surprise when he entered.

"Hey, Luke," she blurted out. "What's going on? Oh, sorry. I mean, I know what's going on. That just came out before I had a chance —"

"It's okay, Becky. Is the chief available?"

"Let me check."

Luke stepped back to avoid overhearing Becky's conversation with Chief Lockhart's assistant. She lowered the receiver and motioned for him to pass.

"He's in his office."

"Thanks."

Luke made his way down a hallway to the largest office in the building. Chief Lockhart was sitting behind his desk. He didn't get up when Luke knocked lightly on the doorframe.

"Come in," the chief said brusquely. "But next time call and make an appointment."

"Yes, sir. Sorry to barge in."

"Make it quick."

The chief motioned to the two chairs on the other side of his desk. When he was seated, Luke could see the photo of Chief Lockhart with his military unit in Iraq. He wanted to remind the chief about their last conversation but couldn't come up with anything on the spur of the moment.

"I've met twice with Mr. Grayson," Luke began. "Thanks for setting that up for me."

"Which is something you're not to repeat to anyone. No exceptions."

"I understand. Anyway, this morning he told me it looks like the DA is going to present the case to the grand jury."

Chief Lockhart nodded but didn't speak. Luke cleared his throat.

"Before that happens, would you be willing to fill me in on the details of Detective

Maxwell's investigation? Off the record, of course."

"No," the police chief replied, leaning forward. "But I can tell you that the only officer testifying before the grand jury will be Bruce Alverez."

"That's good," Luke replied as he tried to process the significance of the chief's revelation. "Bruce was the first person on the scene."

"Yes," Lockhart replied. "He was."

Adisa and Reggie walked to the elevator together. Reggie pushed the up button.

"Deshaun is on the third floor," he said.

"Why do you want me to see him?" Adisa asked.

"I think you'll understand when we get there."

"Are you still lobbying for me to get involved in the case against the police officer?"

"You shut that door when you told me you were moving to Boston."

The elevator arrived. Adisa didn't correct the minister's mistaken assumption about her future.

They reached the ICU waiting area, a small room with six plastic chairs and a vinyl sofa against one wall. Reggie approached the middle-aged white man on duty beside the door to the ICU area.

"Good afternoon, Preacher," the man said.

Reggie introduced Adisa, who wrote her name on a sheet of paper for visitors to the ICU.

"How is he doing?" Reggie asked the attendant as he added his name beneath Adisa's.

"Haven't heard about any major changes. His brother was here for a couple of hours."

Reggie turned to Adisa. "Deshaun and his older brother have been on the outs for a couple of years. It was a breakthrough that K.C. came to the rally at the rec center. I encouraged him to visit Deshaun."

"I was at the rally, too."

"I saw you."

The attendant pressed a button that released the lock on the entrance to the ICU area. Reggie held the door open for Adisa. She glanced into the rooms they passed. One was occupied by a very old man with multiple tubes connected to his body. Beside his room, she saw a young woman who, except for a single IV in her arm, looked like she was simply taking a nap.

"What's wrong with her?" Adisa whispered, touching Reggie on the arm.

"Drug overdose. There's an increasing problem in Campbellton with black tar heroin."

Adisa wasn't naive, but hearing Campbellton linked with such a powerful and dangerous street drug sounded strange. They reached Deshaun's room.

"Hello, Deshaun," the preacher said, walking directly up to the bed. He leaned over and spoke into Deshaun's left ear. "It's Reggie Reynolds from the church. I'm glad to see you today."

Adisa held back and watched. Deshaun was breathing via a ventilator. There was a large bandage on the right side of his skull. His arms were lying on top of the sheet. Adisa noticed that his hands seemed extra large.

"And I've brought someone with me," Reggie continued, introducing Adisa.

"Hey, Deshaun," Adisa said, stepping closer and trying to act as if speaking to a man who couldn't hear her were a natural thing to do.

"Tell him that you've been spending a lot of time at the hospital with your aunt," Reggie said.

"Why?" Adisa asked in a soft voice.

"Because it stimulates him. And one of these days I'm praying someone will say

259

something to him and he'll answer."

Knowing she'd jump out of her skin if Deshaun opened his eyes and spoke to her, Adisa awkwardly told him about Aunt Josie. She then talked about the neighborhood where they'd both lived and explained where Aunt Josie's house was located.

"It's not far from your grandmother's house," Adisa said. "She's a sweet lady. How many hats does she have? I bet she has as many hats as Steph Curry or LeBron James has basketball shoes. She loves you and is praying for you all the time."

The more Adisa talked, the more natural it felt. She reached out and gently touched one of Deshaun's hands that lay inert on the sheet.

"And I can see that you have big hands that are great for playing basketball. I believe you're going to get better and do exactly that."

It was the kind of statement she could make to an unconscious boy without creating false hope. She had no idea what part of the brain had been damaged by the police officer's bullet. Reggie pulled back the sheet and pointed to a place on Deshaun's chest. Adisa could see the outline of a bandage beneath his hospital gown.

"Here's where he was shot in the chest.

Thankfully, the bullet exited without hitting his spine and paralyzing him."

"What about the bullet in his brain? Are they going to try to remove it?"

"They can't attempt surgery until the swelling goes down. Dr. Steiner, the neurosurgeon, performed a craniotomy to help relieve the pressure. They'll do another MRI and decide afterward whether to risk surgery," Reggie said.

Adisa looked more closely at the bandage on the right side of Deshaun's head. Reggie pointed to a spot covered by a bandage.

"There's no question he's lost the hearing in that ear. But the bullet didn't break into fragments upon impact. If that had happened, he wouldn't have survived."

Adisa thought about the destructive path of the metal projectile and shuddered.

"It's also confined to one quadrant, which increases the chance that other parts of the brain can pick up the slack," Reggie continued.

"How do you know all this?"

"Sister Armistead asked me to be here when the family talked to Dr. Steiner."

Adisa shook her head sadly. "When I worked as a prosecutor, most of the shootings were black on black or white on white. In two years, I never worked on a homicide case that was white on black or black on white. Most of the cases were drug- or gang-related, with a few domestic disputes."

"My father was shot and killed in a drive-by shooting in Birmingham when I was five years old," Reggie said. "He was an innocent bystander walking out of a barber-shop in the middle of the day. The boy who shot him was younger than Deshaun. It was part of a gang initiation."

Adisa caught her breath. "I'm sorry. I had no idea."

"It's not a secret," Reggie replied, staring down at Deshaun. "My mother had two children younger than me, and my uncle and aunt stepped in to help out for a few months, which ended up being permanent. Like you with your aunt, I'm thankful for them. Without my uncle's influence, I doubt I'd be doing what I am today. He's a strong Christian."

"Does what happened to your father affect how you feel about Deshaun?"

"Maybe a little bit, although it's a totally different situation. A police officer is sworn to protect life, not recklessly threaten it. My job is to speak up for Deshaun because he can't speak for himself."

"Yes," Adisa said, also looking down at the unconscious teenager. "A lot of voices need to speak up for him."

When Adisa returned to Aunt Josie's room, the older woman was awake and alert.

"What have you been up to?" Aunt Josie asked as soon as Adisa entered. "And where is Pastor Reynolds?"

"He's gone, but he'll be back."

Adisa decided it was time to tell Aunt Josie about Deshaun Hamlin.

"Thelma Armistead is real proud of that boy," Aunt Josie said. "That's real sad about him getting shot by mistake."

"It was more than a mistake," Adisa responded. "I mean, a police officer has to have a very good reason to use deadly force. From what I've read, that wasn't the case."

They spent most of the rest of the afternoon chatting. Aunt Josie seemed much improved, and Adisa was able to direct the conversation onto several topics she knew the older woman liked to discuss.

"Have you had any more dreams about praying as you walk around town?" Adisa asked.

"No," Aunt Josie said and shook her head. "But I'd like to. You don't have to be somewhere to go there."

Adisa paused to digest her aunt's words.

"Jesus would speak a word and someone would be healed across town," Aunt Josie continued. "When a person prays, it goes where the Lord sends it."

"Yes, ma'am."

Aunt Josie looked at the door of the room. "The next time Dr. Dewberry comes to see me, I'm going to talk to him about going home," she said. "He sneaks in and out of here without me knowing it."

"He doesn't sneak in and out. There have been times when you've been so out of it due to the stroke or the medication, you couldn't have talked to him about anything."

"That won't be the case tomorrow," Aunt Josie said resolutely. "I'm going to be alert and pounce on him."

"Maybe I should tell the nurses to warn him," Adisa replied with a smile.

SIXTEEN

Aunt Josie drifted off for a midafternoon nap, and Adisa slipped out to grab a bite to eat. She drove to the center of town and parallel parked across from the courthouse, a cube-shaped building in the stark modern style of the 1960s. The courthouse had replaced a beautiful classic Greek Revival structure built in the 1870s that burned to the ground due to faulty electrical wiring.

Three cafés were clustered around the courthouse square. Adisa opted for a new restaurant that specialized in soups, salads, gourmet sandwiches, and pastries. The café was empty, so Adisa sat at a table that looked out on the courthouse square and ate a muffuletta sandwich.

Toward the end of the quick meal, she glanced across the street and saw Theodore Grayson walk into the courthouse. The only errand Adisa had to run before returning to the hospital was a short trip to the grocery store. Putting that off, she crossed the street and entered the courthouse.

Theo Grayson was standing at the foot of a broad staircase talking to a short, dark-haired man Adisa didn't recognize. Mr. Grayson turned around, looked at her for a second, and then smiled.

"Adisa Johnson?" he asked, extending his hand. "I don't have any contact with you since your junior year in high school, and now I talk to you on the phone and see you in person in less than a week. Are you visiting your aunt?"

"Yes, sir."

"Oh," Grayson said. "Excuse me. This is Jasper Baldwin, our district attorney."

Baldwin was meticulously dressed in a blue suit with a crisp white shirt and carefully knotted yellow tie. The DA shook her hand as Grayson explained who she was and where he thought she worked. It would have been awkward for Adisa to interrupt and inform him that she'd been fired.

"She's made it to the big time in Atlanta," Grayson finished.

"You worked in Atlanta, didn't you?" Baldwin asked Grayson.

"Yeah, I spent a year or so slaving for a big firm when I graduated from law school, but I wasn't cut out for it. They had me

266

tangled up in Section 5 securities work. It drove me crazy, so I ran back home to be closer to my grandmother's cooking."

The DA checked his wristwatch.

"I know you're in a hurry," Grayson said to the DA. "But I want a chance to bend your ear for a few minutes before you make a final decision on moving forward with Officer Nelson's case."

"You and a hundred other people on both sides of the issue," the DA replied with a harried look.

"Have you considered hiring a special prosecutor?" Adisa interjected.

"What?" Baldwin turned and looked at Adisa as if seeing her for the first time.

"It might be a good idea in a politically charged case like this to bring in someone from the outside," she said.

"That thought crossed my mind," Baldwin said slowly. "But I'm not sure where the money would come from. My budget is razor thin."

"There are creative ways to fund special projects if the county commissioners see the benefit of going in that direction," Adisa responded.

Baldwin glanced at his watch again.

"Speaking of special treatment, I'm going to get the kind of treatment I don't want if

I don't head upstairs. I'm supposed to be in front of Judge Morris right now. Nice to meet you," he said to Adisa.

The DA took the stairs two at a time. Grayson remained behind with Adisa.

"It sounded like you were lobbying for a job," the older lawyer said. "How would serving as a special prosecutor fit in with your required billable hours at Dixon and White?"

"I'm no longer working at Dixon and White."

Grayson raised one of his white eyebrows. "I'm sorry to hear that," he said.

"And I'd like some advice if you have a few minutes to spare."

Grayson glanced over his shoulder. "There's a small conference room in the corner where lawyers meet with clients before going upstairs to the courtroom. Let's see if it's empty."

Adisa followed Grayson, who tapped lightly on the door, and when no one answered he pushed it open. Inside was a tiny room containing a small square table surrounded by four plastic chairs.

"What was this?" Adisa asked. "A broom closet?"

"Close," Grayson replied. "This was where they kept janitorial supplies when the city government used prisoners from the jail to clean the building. Now that's handled by an outside service with employees who pose less of a security risk."

Adisa could imagine a posse of black men mopping the floors and cleaning the tall, narrow windows. She and Grayson sat down at the table.

"How can I help you?" the older lawyer asked, adjusting his glasses.

Adisa briefly told him about the impact of the *AJC* article.

"I thought I was going to Boston and getting a big promotion," she said. "Now I'm not sure what to do. I have a solid job lead with a boutique firm in Atlanta that works in the merger and acquisition field, but I'm concerned about Aunt Josephine and who's going to make sure she gets the care she needs. My sister and I are the only real family she has."

"And you're thinking about moving back to Campbellton?" Grayson asked.

"I don't want to, but my sister put the bug in my ear about it, and I have to at least consider the possibility on a temporary basis."

"The roots of home are harder to cut than most people realize," Grayson replied. "Especially for families like ours that have

269

been here for many, many generations."

If she hadn't been to the cemetery so recently, Adisa wouldn't have identified with the older lawyer's words. Now she did.

"I've felt that connection even though I wasn't born here," she admitted. "It's strange."

"But not surprising, and I respect you for not pushing those thoughts away."

"That's not an option when I look at my aunt lying in a hospital bed. Who knows what would have happened to my sister and me if she hadn't taken us in."

Grayson was silent for a moment. "If you came back to Campbellton, what type of law would you like to practice?"

"I couldn't be a general practitioner. I'd be a malpractice claim waiting to happen."

"No one does general practice anymore, at least not well," Grayson replied. "All of us find a niche or two and try to develop our skills to a high level. It makes the practice of law more enjoyable and profitable. Litigation has been my wheelhouse for years with occasional forays into government law."

Adisa remembered Grayson handling criminal cases when she interned at the firm.

"Do you still take criminal cases?"

"Less and less," Grayson answered. "It takes a lot of fire in your belly to tackle a big-time criminal case. But there are still a few bundles of dry wood left in my gut if the right situation comes along."

Adisa gave him a puzzled look at the odd description. "Would that include the white police officer's case?" she asked.

"Like I mentioned in my call, I'm trying to find a lawyer for him. What kind of practice would you enjoy?"

"I enjoy any form of corporate work, especially if it involves numbers. I love unraveling financial statements and working with forensic accountants."

"Businesses are bought and sold in Nash County, and a lawyer who isn't intimidated by accounting concepts would have a real edge."

"Does your firm handle that type of work?" Adisa asked.

"Yes." Grayson paused. "Michael Williams handles most of our business clients, and he's planning a once-in-a-lifetime vacation to France with his wife this summer that's going to take him out of the office for over two months. There might be a way to cobble together enough work to keep you busy and help us out if you believe you should be in town to look after your aunt."

Adisa barely hid her shock. "That's very kind of you —" she began and then stopped.

"It's not an offer, but if you'd like, I can bring it up with my law partners," Grayson said.

Adisa felt herself being pulled in different directions. She sensed she was on the verge of an offer from Paul Austin's firm in Atlanta and had just planted a seed in Jasper Baldwin's mind about being hired as a special prosecutor. But working for Theo Grayson in a low-stress environment as a fill-in lawyer would be a perfect position to hold while Adisa helped Aunt Josie recuperate.

"Could you let me think about it first?" she responded. "I know that sounds arrogant to ask you to wait, but small choices can have big consequences."

"Wise answer," Grayson replied. "Especially for someone your age."

"Some of my friends in law school called me an 'old soul,' " Adisa replied with a smile. "I don't think they meant it as a compliment."

"Send over a résumé if you want me to talk to Baxter and Williams. They both remember your time with us as an intern."

The older lawyer handed Adisa a business card and stood up.

"Thanks so much for talking to me," Adisa said.

"Sure, and I appreciate the contact at the Georgia Innocence Project. I spoke with the paralegal, and she gave me the names of a couple of lawyers who might be interested in representing Officer Nelson. The most promising lead is with an organization whose sole purpose is to help police officers charged with murder in the line of duty. Deshaun Hamlin is alive, but this group may jump in even if Luke is charged with aggravated assault."

"Do they only represent white officers?" Adisa asked.

"I don't know," Grayson replied, raising his right eyebrow. "But that would smack of a kind of racism I wouldn't want to introduce into what's already a tense situation."

After a high-energy Zumba/kickboxing workout in the den at Aunt Josie's house, Adisa showered and selected one of Aunt Josie's potted plants to take to the hospital for a visit. She knew her aunt would prefer one of her own green friends to a strange plant bought at the store. Sitting in her car at a stoplight, Adisa felt a headache coming on and pulled into a drugstore. Walking down the aisle, she encountered a young couple with a toddler girl in the husband's arms.

"I think she'll be fine with a generic pain medicine," the woman said. "She cares more about the flavor than whether it's a brand name."

"But I want it to work," the man replied, glancing up at Adisa as she approached.

"Luke, it will do the job so long as it's pink," the woman said.

Adisa, who was standing in front of the adult pain relievers trying to decide whether to go generic or name brand for herself, froze for a second and then cut her eyes toward the couple. The little girl was pulling on her father's right ear.

"Here," the mother said, handing the package to her husband. "And grab a syringe to shoot it into her mouth. My old one must have fallen out of the diaper bag when we were at the church nursery on Sunday."

Everything about the man spoke of law enforcement. Although not very tall, he was muscular and wore his brown hair clipped short in a military style. Adisa glanced down at his brightly shined black shoes. The wife caught Adisa staring at them and quickly reached out for her husband.

"Come on," the wife said. "Let's go."

"But what about the syringe, honey?" the man protested. "Ashley isn't going to take medicine from a spoon."

The woman was already walking up the aisle toward the cashier. Adisa saw the type of syringe used to administer liquid medicine to babies and small children. It was hanging on a metal hook beneath the blue bulbs used to clean out children's noses. She quickly grabbed the syringe and handed it to the man.

"Here," she said. "This is the kind my sister uses with her kids."

"Thanks," the man said appreciatively. "I'm new to the father thing."

He got up from a crouch. Adisa didn't move. She watched as he joined his wife. The baby girl in his arms continued to play with the man's ear. Adisa knew she'd just met Officer Luke Nelson.

Seventeen

Adisa thought about her encounter with the white policeman as she adjusted the plant on the windowsill in the hospital room. Nelson might be a family man with a cute little girl, but that shouldn't influence the justice system. Bad choices hurt good people. The young man lying in a coma on the third floor of the hospital was proof of that.

"Can you see the plant if I put it here?" she asked Aunt Josie.

Her aunt moved her right hand enough to reach the control for the bed and elevated her body.

"That's great!" Adisa exclaimed as the head of the bed moved closer to vertical. "When did you start doing that?"

"During therapy today," Aunt Josie replied, her jaw slightly clenched. "The controls have to be really close to my hand."

Adisa turned the plant so the thicker

foliage faced her aunt.

"That's fine," Aunt Josie replied. "It's one of my favorite coleus and will need to be re-potted in a couple of months before it gets root-bound."

Adisa resumed her place in a chair beside the bed. "Show me again how you operate the controls," she said.

She watched as the older woman slid her right hand to the side, raised her index finger, and placed it on the button that controlled the bed. She lowered it and then raised it. Adisa leaned over and kissed her aunt's fingers.

"Don't get carried away," Aunt Josie said. "It's not that big a deal."

"It is to me," Adisa replied.

They spent the next half hour doing therapy. Adisa was thrilled with the older woman's progress.

"Mercy," Aunt Josie finally said. "That's enough."

Adisa's phone vibrated and she glanced at the caller ID. It was Paul Austin from Atlanta.

"Let me run out into the hall and take this," she said.

Holding the phone to her ear, Adisa walked rapidly from the room.

"Ms. Johnson. I wanted to touch base with

you. I discussed your availability with my partners during a firm meeting late this afternoon. Everyone is impressed with your experience at Dixon and White, but we're not going to make a new hire at this time. The situation may change in six months or so, but it wouldn't be fair to ask you to wait under such uncertain circumstances."

Adisa swallowed her disappointment. "Was the negative publicity in the *AJC* about the pro bono work I did in the criminal case a problem?"

"No. That passed out of the public eye by the time the paper landed in the recycle bin the following morning."

Adisa wasn't sure if Austin's opinion made her feel better or worse about her termination at Dixon and White, but it made her like him more. She wasn't ready to give up on the job quite yet.

"After our conversation the other day, I thought about a company I might be able to cultivate as a client. It's not a company represented by Dixon and White. They work in the financial management area and broker deals worldwide."

"How solid is your relationship with this company?"

"At the beginning stages, but the possibility was raised by the company CFO."

"That could change the situation. Our primary concern is plugging you in at maximum efficiency."

"Okay. Thanks again for considering me."

"And I look forward to hearing from you."

The call ended. Adisa quietly peeked into Aunt Josie's room. Worn out from therapy, the older woman was asleep. Returning to the conference room where she'd talked with Dr. Dewberry, Adisa said a quick prayer and placed a call to the woman CFO who'd expressed interest in hiring her as their attorney.

Luke held Ashley in his arms while Jane gently inserted the plastic syringe filled with pain reliever into the baby's mouth.

"You love pink medicine," Jane said soothingly.

Ashley frowned and turned her head to the side, but Jane kept the syringe in place so that a tiny bit of medicine entered the little girl's mouth. Ashley's resistance evaporated. Within five seconds all the pink medicine had made its way from the syringe into Ashley's mouth. Jane kept the syringe in place so Ashley could lick the tip.

"You weren't kidding," Luke said. "She loves that stuff."

"Better than the name brand. I'd better

give her a bath now. She'll be sleepy as soon as this hits her system."

Luke gave Ashley a quick kiss on the top of her blond curls and handed her to Jane. The house phone beside the refrigerator rang and he answered it.

"Luke, this is Theo Grayson."

Luke stood up slightly straighter. "Yes, sir."

"I'd like to meet with you again. When can you come to the office?"

"Uh, this afternoon about four o'clock?"

"Perfect. I've decided to be with you at the courthouse when the grand jury meets tomorrow."

Adisa fixed breakfast at Aunt Josie's house before leaving for the hospital. The previous night she'd combined praying and worrying about her future employment. She tossed and turned until 2:00 a.m. She hadn't heard back from the woman CFO and wondered if she'd imagined the level of interest the woman had in working with her. Finally, deciding there was no harm in sending a résumé to Theo Grayson, Adisa got out of bed, sent her résumé, and fell asleep.

She was driving to the hospital when her phone vibrated. It was an unknown number.

"Adisa, this is Theo Grayson. I hope I

didn't catch you at an inconvenient time."

"I'm on my way to the hospital."

"Thanks for sending your résumé. You were up late last night."

"Yes."

Adisa hadn't considered Grayson's reaction to an e-mail sent after midnight.

"But I'd guess that happened a lot at Dixon and White," the older lawyer continued.

"More than I wanted it to."

"Listen, I don't want to disrupt your time with your aunt, but do you think you could slip away today for lunch with me?"

Adisa felt her heart jump into her throat. "You've discussed my résumé with Mr. Baxter and Mr. Williams?" she asked.

"Yes, and I'm ready to talk and ask you a few questions in person."

"Will the other partners be joining us?"

"No."

Adisa waited, but the lawyer didn't volunteer any additional information.

"Okay," she replied slowly.

"Would you prefer the country club or the Jackson House?"

Adisa had never eaten a meal at the Campbellton Country Club. Going there as the guest of Mr. Grayson, who was probably a charter member, might be an interesting experience.

"Which has the better food?" she asked.

"It depends on what you're in the mood for. Chicken salad or fried chicken."

"Chicken salad."

"Then I'll meet you in the atrium of the country club at noon."

After a full morning at the hospital that included helping Aunt Josie with a shower, Adisa went to her aunt's house to change clothes before driving to the country club. As she was applying the finishing touches of her makeup, Shanika called.

"Let me talk to Aunt Josie," Shanika said.

"I'm not at the hospital. I'm about to leave for lunch with Theo Grayson at the country club."

"The lawyer? What does he want to talk to you about?"

Adisa quickly filled her sister in on the possibility of working at Grayson, Baxter, and Williams. She didn't mention the call to the woman CFO.

"That sounds great," Shanika said.

"There's no offer on the table. Not yet."

"But if he wasn't interested, why would he get back to you so quickly and invite you to lunch at the country club?"

"You're right," Adisa admitted. "But I'd

hate to make a mistake by accepting a temporary job and losing out on something more permanent."

"You thought the job in Atlanta was long-term."

"True," Adisa admitted.

"One thing I've learned being a mother is that life changes fast. I'll be praying for you. Let me know how it goes."

Adisa turned onto a tree-lined boulevard that snaked its way from the highway to the clubhouse. To her right was the golf course, which was a lush green from the spring rainfall. By August, only frequent nighttime watering would keep the fairways and greens alive beneath the baking Georgia sun. The clubhouse featured a white-columned entrance and a covered portico. She pulled to a stop for valet parking, and a lanky teenager took her car keys and handed her a claim check. Adisa checked her appearance in a full-length mirror in the lobby.

"Ms. Johnson?" asked the maître' d, a middle-aged man in a blue suit and crimson necktie.

"Yes."

"Mr. Grayson is waiting for you."

Adisa's phone vibrated, and she took it from her purse. The caller ID was for the company she'd contacted after talking with Paul Austin.

"Just a minute," she said, holding up her index finger. "I need to take this call."

"Certainly. The lounge is to your left."

Adisa rapidly walked into a wood-paneled room with green leather chairs.

"Ms. Adisa Johnson?" a woman asked.

"Yes."

"Hold for Ms. Trentham, please."

"It's nice hearing from you," the CFO said when she came on the line. "It's such a co-incidence that you called. I was thinking about you earlier this week."

"You were?"

"Yes, we've decided to hire your firm to represent us in a transaction that's becoming tougher with an arbitrage house in Singapore, and I was going to request that you be part of the legal team."

Adisa swallowed. "I'm no longer at Dixon and White," she said. "But I'm talking to another law firm that might be able to provide the type of services you need."

"Do they work in Asia?"

"I'm not sure, but I could find out."

"Are you an associate there?"

"Not yet," Adisa admitted. "I'm talking to them about a position."

"If you had something in place, I'd be glad

to discuss it with you, but we need to move quickly. Is Catherine Summey still at Dixon and White?"

"Yes."

"I'd better give her a call. I know they have experience in foreign mergers and acquisitions."

"A lot of experience," Adisa said resignedly. "It's an area I'd like to develop in the future."

"I'm sure you will. Nice talking to you and good luck."

The call ended. And Adisa realized she was not yet a big enough fish to swim in the legal ocean that reached across the Pacific.

The maître' d led Adisa into a spacious dining room with a large chandelier in the center. The tables were covered with white cloths and napkins embossed with the country-club crest. Not only was Adisa the only black person in the room; she was the only female. Grayson was sitting at a table near the bar area. He saw her and stood as she approached. The maître' d pulled back the chair for Adisa.

"There's a first time for everything," Adisa said to Grayson when they were alone. "Where are the women?"

"Women?" Grayson raised his eyebrows.

"What makes you think women are allowed?"

Adisa's jaw dropped. Grayson smiled.

"Wait!" he said, pointing past her shoulder. "Here they come."

Adisa turned around as a group of ladies wearing golf attire entered the room.

"You just happened to arrive before the morning groups finished eighteen holes. In a few minutes there will be as many women here as men. And there are all races on the membership roll. The only thing that matters is an applicant's ability to pay the membership fee and yearly dues."

"Okay," Adisa replied. "I guess I was a little on edge about coming here."

A waitress arrived and took their orders for the walnut chicken salad.

"The chicken salad is the best," Grayson said when the waitress left. "It has grapes, a few cranberries, crisp celery, and premium chicken. If you don't like it, I'll order you something else."

"I'm sure it will be delicious," Adisa responded with a smile.

Grayson raised his hand in greeting to someone across the room. Adisa took a sip of water. Her heart was beating faster than normal, and she hoped Grayson couldn't pick up on any nervousness in her voice.

"I know you probably haven't heard anything yet from the firm in Atlanta that's interested in you —" he began.

"Actually, I have," Adisa said and then told him about her phone call with Paul Austin. She left out the bad news she'd received just minutes earlier.

"I'm sorry that door is temporarily closed, but it sounds like a great opportunity. I hope it works out eventually," Grayson replied.

"You do?" Adisa asked in surprise.

"Of course. Why wouldn't I want you to practice the type of law you're interested in with a firm that has a high level of expertise?"

A second wave of disappointment washed over Adisa as she realized Grayson had scheduled the lunch as a nice way of breaking the news that he didn't have a job for her, either. She'd prepared herself to critically evaluate an offer. Now she felt foolish for presuming Grayson, Baxter, and Williams would want her.

The waitress arrived with their food. The chicken salad was nestled on a large, perfectly formed piece of iceberg lettuce. In a small side cup was a medley of fresh fruit that included strawberries, blueberries, and kiwi. Grayson took a bite of chicken salad and nodded his head.

"It's a great batch. Try it."

Adisa scooped up a small portion of chicken salad with her fork. The crunchy walnuts, sweet grapes, and juicy, tender chicken weren't overpowered by the mayonnaise. The salad had the perfect balance of sweet, tangy, and meaty.

"It's good," she agreed.

Grayson ate contentedly. Although the chicken salad was delicious, Adisa found herself staring at her plate.

"I'm glad the firm in Atlanta doesn't have a position for you now," Grayson said, stopping to take a sip of water. "Because I do. The partners met first thing this morning and agreed that we'd like you to take care of Mike Williams's clients while he's out of the country. He liked the idea that you weren't going to stay in Campbellton long-term or have any interest in stealing his business."

"Of course not," Adisa replied quickly. "That didn't enter my mind."

"Which doesn't surprise me at all. Your moral compass is fixed on truth as firmly as that of anyone I've known in a long time. That was clear when you were a teenager, and I don't believe that's changed."

"Thank you," Adisa replied, a bit overwhelmed by the compliment.

"Because you'll need to spend extra time away from the office taking care of your aunt, we'd like to pay you a percentage of the hours you bill. What were you making at Dixon and White?"

Adisa told him. Grayson's eyes widened.

"That's impressive. I estimate you'll make about twenty-five percent of your previous salary and work twenty-five to thirty percent less. Health benefits included."

By living at Aunt Josie's house, Adisa quickly calculated that the proposal would allow her to stay current on her student loans, car payment, and other bills. She might even be able to save some money because she wouldn't be maintaining a big-city lifestyle. She felt comfortable with Theo Grayson. He was different from Catherine Summey but would offer another type of beneficial mentoring. Above all, Adisa felt an inner peace linked to the ability to keep an eye on Aunt Josie.

"Think about the offer while we eat," Grayson said. "There's one string attached, but I think you're up to it."

The older lawyer dug his fork into the chicken salad, put it in his mouth, and continued to chew with satisfaction.

"I love this stuff," he said.

Adisa laughed. "Mr. Grayson, how can you turn a scoop of chicken salad into the epitome of dining excellence?"

Grayson pointed his fork at her. "Chicken salad like this proves that something ordinary can go to extraordinary heights if combined with the right ingredients. I've tried to be like that myself, and I believe that's true about you."

Adisa's emotions suddenly rushed to the surface. Grayson lowered his fork to the table and eyed her closely.

"What's wrong?" he asked.

Adisa shook her head. "Nothing. That was very kind of you to compare me to yourself."

The older lawyer raised the cloth napkin to his lips. "That's the role of my generation. My father didn't or couldn't encourage me, but I'm thankful someone else came along and did."

Adisa placed her fork beside her plate. "I don't need to think about the offer. I'm going to accept the job."

Grayson held up his hand to stop her. "I haven't gotten to the string. You need to hear that first."

"What is it?"

Grayson stared at her for a few seconds before he spoke. "I want you to help me represent Officer Luke Nelson."

EIGHTEEN

For the second time during the short meal, Adisa lost her appetite.

"Please, hear me out," Grayson continued, responding to the reaction showing on her face. "After I reviewed your résumé, I spoke with your former boss at the DA's office in Cobb County. He told me you were a quick learner and almost ready to sit first chair in a murder case. He believed an aggravated assault case, even one with a high profile, was well within your capabilities."

Adisa's head was spinning as her mind flashed back to courtrooms during criminal trials and scenes she'd tried to systematically purge from her memory: victims' families sitting stoically during jury selection, weeping when photos of their loved ones were introduced into evidence; the pathos of the defendants' relatives plunged into a swamp of vicarious guilt and shame; the pressure on the prosecutors not to mess up the case on an erroneous interpretation of the law or failure to gain admissibility of a crucial piece of evidence; and the slipperiness of some defense lawyers who seemed willing to blur the lines of ethical conduct to win at any cost.

"I was glad to land the assistant DA job out of law school," Adisa replied. "But that wasn't the career I wanted."

"But you were good at it."

"And miserable most of the time. When the opportunity came to become an associate at Dixon and White, I didn't hesitate a second. Once I settled in there, the practice of law became something I looked forward to when I got out of bed in the morning. And I was a prosecutor, not a defense lawyer. It's a very different mind-set. I handled most of the research but didn't question a ton of witnesses and only gave a few closing arguments to the jury."

Grayson ignored his chicken salad and leaned forward. "I'm not asking you to do this on your own. Ensuring Officer Nelson's right to good representation has challenged me, too. If you agree to help, it'll be with my assistance. We'll share the load, which makes the burden much easier."

Adisa shifted in her chair. "That's not possible."

"Oh, it's like riding a bicycle. You'll be surprised how quickly you regain your confidence."

"That's not what I mean," Adisa replied. "It's not possible for me to represent an officer who shot an unarmed black teenager. I'd rather be appointed special prosecutor. That's a role I could put my heart and soul into."

"Prosecution, defense." Grayson held his hands out in front of him and alternately raised them up and down. "Both are necessary parts of the process."

"No." Adisa shook her head. "It's not that simple."

Grayson ate a final bite of chicken salad. "And I'm not going to pretend that it is," the older lawyer said. "Also, I won't insult you by asking if you could defend a black teenager who mistakenly shot a white officer who'd left his gun in his patrol car. Jasper Baldwin is going to present the case to the grand jury this afternoon. Until then, we won't know for sure that Luke is going to be charged."

"But you and I both know he will be."

"Yes," Grayson said with a nod of his head. "The facts of the shooting and the political realities are going to dictate a result. Beyond that, the system needs to work as it should. We agree on that, don't we?"

"Are you cross-examining me?"

"Only until I uncover the truth."

Adisa bristled. "Bringing up my moral compass was a setup."

"No, I meant it."

Adisa was silent for a few moments. "Yes," she finally sighed. "Officer Nelson is entitled to competent representation if he's charged with a crime. But I'm not the person to do it."

"Here's what I'd like you to do," Grayson said, leaning back in his chair. "Talk to Jasper Baldwin and see what he has to say. Then let me know your decision."

"Why do you want me to talk to the DA?"

Grayson patted his slightly pudgy midsection. "My gut has more than chicken salad in it. And it tells me you'll only consider my offer after you explore all your options."

While he waited for Jane, Luke paced back and forth throughout the house.

Each time he checked his watch, he tried to imagine what would happen at the courthouse.

"Jessica!" Jane called out to the babysitter from the master bedroom. "Don't forget to give Ashley her pink medicine. It's in the refrigerator, and the syringe is in the top left drawer of the chest beside her crib."

"I see the syringe," Jessica replied from the baby's room. "Should I let her play with it?"

"No, it's not a toy."

Although grateful that Mr. Grayson was going to be with him at the courthouse, Luke was still frustrated about the decision not to testify. After all, he was the only person on earth who knew the truth. It would be impossible for the grand jury to decide what to do without the testimony he alone could provide. And doing nothing seemed like surrender, which was contrary to his nature.

"I'm ready," Jane said as she appeared with a grim look on her face.

She was wearing the same gray dress she'd worn to the funeral for Luke's grandmother. Luke started to question her wardrobe selection, but he realized that was as pointless as debating whether the medicine syringe could do double duty as a toy. He was wearing a blue sport coat, khaki pants, and red tie. His shirt was too small at the neck, forcing him to unbutton the top button.

They rode to the courthouse in silence. Jane stared out the window. Reflexively,

Luke almost parked in one of the spots at the courthouse reserved for law enforcement officers but swerved to the right and found an open place nearby.

"By habit," he muttered.

They reached for the other's hand and joined their fingers together as they walked up the sidewalk to the main entrance.

"There he is!" a male voice called out.

Luke turned and saw a middle-aged man holding up a sign that read "No Charges Against Officer Nelson." The man was surrounded by a group of ten or twelve people. The group quickly made their way toward Luke, who wanted to continue into the courthouse but knew he had to acknowledge their presence.

"We're here to let the DA and grand jury know there are people in Nash County who believe in law and order!" called out the man holding the sign.

"Thanks for your support," Luke replied.

"Are you his wife?" a woman in the group asked Jane.

Jane nodded.

"I think it's horrible what they're saying about your husband and want you to know that I don't believe a word of it. My little boy and I are praying for you and your family every night."

"Thank you," Jane answered gratefully.

"And we're working on our own petition," another man in the group added. "The other side got the jump on us, but we've already got three hundred registered voters demanding that the DA nolle pros your case."

Luke eyed the speaker more closely at his use of the legal term for a DA's prosecutorial discretion not to file charges against someone. Over the months Luke had been on the force, several of his arrests had been dismissed via nolle pros.

"We're going for a thousand signatures," the man continued.

"And then we'll go for another thousand," the woman who'd spoken to Jane added.

"My family and I appreciate all you're doing," Luke replied.

They continued toward the courthouse. Before they entered, a deputy with the sheriff's department came out and stopped them.

"This way," he said.

Adisa and Reggie left Deshaun Hamlin's hospital room.

"It doesn't get any easier," Adisa said after visiting the comatose young man for the third time. "Initially, I was glad to see him alive. Now it's depressing to think this might be the only existence he ever has."

"That's one reason I talk normally to him. It's a way to build my faith that someday he'll respond. And Dr. Steiner told the family yesterday that surgery is looming on the horizon."

Adisa's stomach turned over at the stress related to Deshaun's condition.

"When can I see you again?" Reggie asked when they reached the hospital elevator.

"I'm here every day," Adisa replied, sounding more casual about seeing the minister than she felt. She'd found herself thinking a lot about Reggie while she sat in Aunt Josie's hospital room.

"I'm leading the worship service at the church tonight," he said. "Would you like to come? I won't make you sit on the front row or call on you to pray in front of everyone."

"I'd like that," Adisa replied with a smile. "And praying in public isn't a problem for me. As a lawyer, I've had to open my mouth in environments a lot more hostile than a church service."

"Great. We begin at 7:00 p.m."

After Reggie left, Adisa peeked into Aunt Josie's room. The older woman's power nap was over, and she was sitting up straighter in her bed than Adisa had seen before.

"Did someone help you sit up?" Adisa asked.

"No, I did it myself," Aunt Josie answered. "Where's Pastor Reggie?"

"He left after we prayed with Deshaun."

"Any change?"

"Dr. Steiner, the neurosurgeon, says the swelling in Deshaun's brain is slowly going down, which means the possibility for surgery to remove the bullet is increasing. If he survives the surgery, the future is completely unknown."

Aunt Josie pointed up with her increasingly strong right hand. "And we know who holds the future," the older woman said.

Adisa left the hospital for the courthouse. She'd called Jasper Baldwin's office and told him she wanted to talk to him about the case against Officer Nelson. To her surprise, the DA agreed to meet with her.

"I mentioned your name to our receptionist and found out how extensive your family's contacts are in Nash County," Baldwin said.

That comment made Adisa realize that the DA viewed her as a person with political influence. She didn't try to convince him otherwise.

"You'll be glad to know that I'm presenting the case against Officer Nelson to the grand jury this afternoon," the DA continued. "Why don't you swing by at one thirty so we can chat for a few minutes?"

"That would be great."

On the way, she made up her mind what she wanted to do. If Jasper Baldwin was open to the possibility of her serving as special prosecutor, Adisa would turn down the job offer from Theo Grayson. However, even if the DA told her he wasn't going to bring in a special prosecutor, Adisa would still turn down Grayson's offer and pray for something else to open up. Putting herself in the position of trying to exonerate the man who had wrongfully sent Deshaun Hamlin into the dark abyss of a gunshot-induced coma wasn't something she could do under any circumstances.

There weren't any parking spaces near the courthouse, and Adisa had to walk three blocks. She encountered a group of about twenty people, all white, gathered in support of the police officer. Several held signs. Adisa didn't make eye contact as she passed by and climbed the broad steps leading to the main courthouse entrance.

Inside, she came face-to-face with a large group of at least 150 people, mostly blacks with a smattering of whites. They were milling around the hallway in front of the clerk's office. The size of the second group explained the parking problem she'd encountered. A middle-aged black man Adisa didn't recognize seemed to be leading the group. He was confronting a pair of white deputies who were blocking the stairwell to the second floor. The black man was yelling and pointing his finger at one of the deputies.

"Are you going to use that gun to shoot me like Nelson did Deshaun? These people have a right to be heard!"

Adisa edged closer.

"I don't have a gun!" the man continued, holding up his hands. "But I have a voice! We all have a voice!"

Several others in the group shouted out in agreement. The deputy didn't respond, but stayed in place with his arms folded across his chest.

"Adisa!" she heard someone call out.

Theo Grayson had entered through a side door of the courthouse and was motioning to her from a spot near the small conference room.

"That's the cop's lawyer!" a female voice in the crowd called out when Grayson appeared.

Most of the group turned toward Grayson

as Adisa quickly made her way forward. By the time she reached him, two men were haranguing the older lawyer in profanity-laced language.

"Excuse me," Grayson said as he attempted to move toward the staircase.

Someone pushed him and he lost his balance, crashing into Adisa, who was barely able to keep him from falling down.

"Get out of the way!" she said when she regained her footing. "He has a right to be here!"

A woman standing near Adisa faced her with a hate-filled glare. "What are you doing here?"

A deputy appeared and quickly opened a way for them by holding his nightstick in front of the group. Foul language pelted them like golf ball–size hail as they made their way to the stairs. Once they were on the steps, Adisa glanced back and saw a group of six law enforcement officers, some from the city and others from the sheriff's department, begin to herd the crowd toward the front door of the courthouse. One of the deputies who'd been stationed at the bottom of the stairs accompanied Adisa and Grayson.

As Adisa climbed the stairs, words from the crowd followed her to the top of the landing. Hearing her name, she jerked her head around but couldn't identify anyone she knew. She and Grayson walked a short distance down a hallway. It grew quieter. Grayson was wearing a blue suit and yellow bow tie that seemed comically out of place in the chaos they'd just escaped. The older lawyer's hair was mussed, and he looked disheveled. Adisa felt embarrassed by what they'd experienced.

"Sorry I got you in the middle of that," he said to Adisa.

"I'm the one who feels like I should apologize."

"We took Officer Nelson up the same elevator we use to transport prisoners to the courtroom," the deputy said. "That way, we avoided the mob."

"What are you doing here?" Grayson asked Adisa.

"I have an appointment with Jasper Baldwin."

"Me, too," Grayson replied. "At one o'clock, and I'm running late."

Grayson ran his fingers through his hair, which only made it worse. Adisa resisted the urge to help the older lawyer with his grooming needs. They continued down the hallway to a door with opaque white window glass and the words "Nash County District

Attorney" stenciled on it in black letters. Grayson opened the door for Adisa.

Luke and Jane sat close to each other in the waiting area of the district attorney's office. The receptionist studiously avoided looking at them. Luke wasn't sure what Jane was thinking. He was trying not to think. The door to his right opened, and Theo Grayson entered, accompanied by the sheriff's deputy who'd brought them up in the secure elevator and a young black woman who looked vaguely familiar. Grayson saw them and extended his hand.

"Luke, Jane," Grayson said. "This is Adisa Johnson, a lawyer who grew up in Campbellton but now lives in Atlanta."

Luke nodded without saying anything. It felt like the walls of the DA's office had giant ears, and anything he said would be public record. The black attorney sat as far away from Luke and Jane as the small reception area would allow. She crossed her legs and began to look at her cell phone. Luke ignored her.

"What are you going to say to the DA?" Jane asked Grayson in a whisper.

"I'm going to strongly suggest that he delay any action until the police department has time to complete a thorough investigation of the incident. It's the fairest course of action consistent with due process of law for everyone involved."

"Do you think he'll listen to you?" Luke asked. "Chief Lockhart couldn't make any headway with him."

"This will be lawyer to lawyer," Grayson replied. "And at least he's giving me a chance to present an argument. He didn't have to agree to that. My hope is that he'll be willing to talk to you off the record with me in the room."

"Me?" Luke's face paled. "You didn't tell me that."

"Would it have done any good if I had?" Grayson responded. "You would have just worried and driven yourself crazy. If Baldwin agrees, I want you to tell him what happened just like you did at my office. I'll make sure you stay on track."

Luke glanced at Jane, whose eyes were big as saucers.

"Before I meet with him, you need to sign an agreement authorizing me to act as your attorney," Grayson said, taking a single sheet of paper from his briefcase and handing it to Luke, who quickly read it.

"You're going to represent me for one dollar?" Luke asked in shock.

"That's temporary," Grayson replied.

"After we get through today, we'll see where we are and what it's going to cost to move forward. I didn't want you unrepresented and at risk."

"Thank you," Jane said, surprised and pleased at Theo Grayson's generous offer.

Luke scribbled his signature on the line above his name.

"Mr. Baldwin will see you now," the receptionist said to Grayson.

Grayson left. Luke glanced at Jane, who'd closed her eyes and bowed her head. He knew she was praying. Luke offered up a silent petition for help but wasn't sure his words made it past his skull. When he glanced again at the black woman lawyer, he caught her staring at Jane. The lawyer quickly looked away and began talking to the receptionist.

"Your turn," Grayson said to Adisa when he returned to the reception area after fifteen minutes in Jasper Baldwin's office. "His office is the first door to the right."

Adisa's posture was excellent, but she tried to stand even straighter. She knocked on the doorframe of the DA's office, which also had a door with the opaque white glass in the top half and "Jasper Baldwin, District Attorney" stenciled on it in black letters.

"Come in," the DA said, motioning for her to have a seat. "Did you get re-acquainted with Sofia?"

"Yes, her older sister and I graduated from high school the same year."

"And you're related to Malcomb Adams, Val Adams, Larry Graham, and Roberta Kendrick?"

"And all their uncles, aunts, children, cousins, and grandchildren. I don't know how many relatives I have in Nash County, but it's a lot."

Baldwin nodded. "What can I do for you?"

"I'd like to follow up on my suggestion to you the other day about bringing a special prosecutor into the case against Officer Nelson."

"We don't know yet what the grand jury is going to do."

Adisa gave the DA a wry smile. "I worked on the major felony team in Cobb County for over two years. Is there any real doubt in your mind?"

"Okay," Baldwin replied. "Make your pitch."

Adisa handed the DA a copy of her résumé and quickly outlined her experience as a prosecutor and as a defense lawyer for Leroy Larimore in the recent pro bono case.

Baldwin's face remained inscrutable as she talked.

"If you call the attorneys I worked with at the DA's office in Cobb County, I believe they'll give me a good reference," Adisa said. "The partner who supervised my work at Dixon and White will do the same. But the most important fact is that I was raised in Campbellton and care about what happens here."

"And who's going to pay you to serve as a special prosecutor?" Baldwin asked. "I have no money budgeted for this type of position."

Adisa was ready for the question. "I'd do it pro bono."

Baldwin let out a loud guffaw.

"I'm totally serious," Adisa said. "I'd consider it more of a public service than the case I recently handled in Atlanta."

Baldwin put his fingers together in front of his chest. "That's putting your money, or the lack thereof, behind your convictions," he said thoughtfully. "Tell me what you know about the facts of the shooting."

"Nothing except what I read in the newspaper and heard from people in the black community."

"The evidence is strong," Baldwin said. "The proof is coming together nicely, and I intend to show the citizens of Nash County that justice will be color-blind as long as I'm their district attorney."

"That's commendable," Adisa said.

The DA eyed Adisa for several seconds with a look she couldn't interpret. She prayed. Baldwin cleared his throat.

"Your offer is intriguing, but the people elected me district attorney, and they expect me to at least supervise a case of this magnitude."

"I'd be acting on your behalf and under your supervision."

Baldwin paused again.

"Would you at least consider it?" Adisa pressed harder.

"You've really caught me off guard," Baldwin replied. "But I'll check out your references and get back to you."

"That's all I ask."

NINETEEN

"Let's go down the hallway to a place where we can talk in private," Grayson said to Luke and Jane.

They followed the lawyer to a room beside an old-fashioned ceramic water fountain.

"I didn't get anywhere with Baldwin," Grayson said after he closed the door. "He's going to present the case to the grand jury later this afternoon."

"I feel betrayed," Luke said, shaking his head. "One day I'm working as hard as I can to bring good cases to the DA so he can put criminals behind bars. A few weeks later, he's coming after me for doing my job."

Jane grabbed Luke's hand and squeezed it.

"Your world has turned upside down," the lawyer agreed. "I want to see it put right, but that's going to take time and effort."

"I've been thinking again about the grand

jury," Luke replied slowly. "It made a huge difference when Kip Abernathy spoke up for himself ten years ago. That was way before I came to town, but Kip called me the other day and told me how it turned out. He ran over a kid on a bicycle and killed him. They were going to charge him with negligent homicide until Kip explained what happened. He walked out of the grand jury room and went straight back to work for the sheriff's department."

"I know," Grayson replied. "But that was under the old law when a law enforcement officer could testify before a grand jury without having to answer any questions."

"You keep bringing that up, but I'm not convinced it makes that much difference."

"It does because now the DA will have a chance to cross-examine you under oath."

"I don't have anything to hide!" Luke burst out. "I'll tell what happened. There's nothing fancy to it."

"Do you know all the questions the DA might ask you?" Jane asked anxiously. "What if he gets you upset or confused?"

Luke shot a scowl in the direction of his wife. "Whose side are you on?" he asked.

"We're both on your side," Grayson replied before Jane could say anything. "And I can't make you do or keep you from doing anything. My job is to give you the best advice I can. Let me put it to you straight. I don't think whether or not you testify today is going to change the outcome."

"What do you mean?"

Grayson gave both of them a somber look. "Your account of what happened that night on East Nixon Street might win at trial, but it won't keep you from being indicted. When presenting a case to a grand jury, the DA doesn't have to prove you're guilty beyond a reasonable doubt, only that there's probable cause a crime occurred. Even if most of the grand jurors have questions or qualms, they can indict and let a regular jury hear all the evidence and decide whether you're guilty or not guilty."

Luke knew this in his head, but it was maddening to be caught in the web of legal technicalities. He felt his face redden.

"Honey," Jane said, "I believe we should listen to Mr. Grayson and follow his advice."

"All right," Luke said, biting off his words. "Then what are we doing here? We could be at home waiting for a phone call. I feel like I put Jane in danger bringing her to the courthouse."

"As I said, I wanted you here in case Baldwin was willing to meet with us. It was a long shot, but a good defense isn't limited to one cannon blast. It's a lot of little skirmishes."

"What's next?" Luke asked.

"Stay here. If the grand jury indicts you, I don't want you to have to spend a night or two in jail."

Luke heard Jane gasp. They'd carefully avoided using the word "jail" in their conversations.

"I'll let the bailiff on duty know you're in here so no one will disturb you," Grayson continued.

"I feel like I'm already locked up," Luke muttered.

As she left the DA's office, Adisa saw Theo Grayson exit a conference room.

"Are we enemies or friends?" the older lawyer asked her.

"Friends," Adisa replied.

It was impossible not to like Mr. Grayson.

"Can you tell me what happened with Baldwin?" Grayson asked.

"I asked him to bring me in as a special prosecutor. He's considering it."

"And you're also considering my offer?"

"Not really," Adisa said bluntly. "As much as I'd like to work with your firm, I can't go down that road if it involves representing Officer Nelson."

"I understand," Grayson said, patting his chest over his heart. "I respect your decision even if I don't agree."

They walked side by side in silence to the top of the staircase. The older lawyer's hair was still in disarray.

"Thanks again for wanting to help me," Adisa said.

"You're welcome," Grayson replied. "And please keep me in the loop about your aunt's condition."

Three hours later, Theo Grayson returned to the room where he'd left Luke and Jane.

"Sorry for the delay," he said. "The grand jury has retired to deliberate. The DA called more witnesses than I'd anticipated."

"You weren't in there, were you?" Jane asked.

"No, no. But there's not a law against sitting near the entrance to the room where they meet and seeing who goes in and out."

"Who testified?" Luke asked.

"Stan Jackson, the convenience store clerk. Deshaun Hamlin's grandmother; one of his uncles; Gregory Ott; Dr. Steiner, the neurosurgeon who's treating Deshaun; and, of course, Bruce Alverez. Officer Alverez was in there the longest."

Luke was silent for a moment. "Do you

think Bruce threw me under the bus?" he asked.

"He talked with me briefly when he finished," Grayson answered. "He said he told what he saw and heard, but wouldn't give me any clues about the DA's questions."

"Bruce is a good man."

"I'll try to talk to him again in a few days and find out where his testimony is going to fall," Grayson said. "Even though he was the first person on the scene, he can't speculate about what happened before he arrived."

"Yeah," Luke replied with a shrug. "Chief Lockhart didn't testify?"

"No. And neither did Detective Maxwell, which reinforces the notion that the investigation is ongoing. Baldwin didn't want the grand jury to know the police department hasn't decided exactly what took place. If he had, the jurors might have told him to come back when the case is ready to present."

"I'm getting railroaded," Luke said with a sigh.

There was a knock on the door. Jane jumped.

"Come in!" Grayson called out.

One of the bailiffs opened the door. "Mr. Grayson, you asked me to let you know what the grand jury returned," the deputy said without making eye contact with Luke. "One count of aggravated assault with a deadly weapon."

"Thanks, Mickey," Grayson replied.

After the door closed, Jane took a tissue from her purse and pressed it against her eyes.

"I'm deeply sorry," Grayson said. "I've already made arrangements for you to voluntarily go to the jail to be booked, and a magistrate is standing by to set bail. I don't know how much that will be, but I know someone who's willing to post bond for you."

Luke's head was spinning at the thought of going to jail to be photographed and fingerprinted.

"Wait — who's going to put up bond?" he asked.

"Clayton Jones."

"We bought a used minivan from his dealership last year," Jane said.

"When he found out I was representing you, he called to see how he could help," Grayson said. "My firm has represented Clayton for years. He knows there are people in the community who won't like it if he vouches for you, but that didn't stop him from offering."

"I'm not sure how to thank him," Luke said.

"The crowd downstairs is one group," Grayson replied. "But not everyone in Campbellton feels the same way. I'll give you a ride to the jail in my car so Jane can go home."

They stepped into the hallway. The photographer Luke recognized from the rally at the high school was waiting for them, along with a woman Luke didn't know. The photographer began taking pictures. Luke stepped in front of Jane.

"Leave her out of this!" he demanded.

The photographer ignored him. The woman spoke to Grayson.

"Any comment about Officer Nelson being indicted by the Nash County grand jury?" she asked.

"The wheels of justice are turning, Ms. Standard," Grayson replied. "We believe that when all the evidence is presented, Officer Nelson will be exonerated."

"What sort of evidence?" the reporter asked.

Grayson began moving down the hall with Luke and Jane trailing behind him.

"Convincing evidence. The grand jury didn't hear from multiple persons who have knowledge about this case or those involved in the ongoing investigation into what took place."

The reporter spoke to Luke. "Officer Nelson, now that you know Deshaun Hamlin was unarmed, are you sorry you shot him?"

"Because this is now a legal case, Officer Nelson cannot comment," Grayson cut in.

"He doesn't regret shooting an unarmed teenager in the head and chest?" the reporter continued and then refocused on Grayson. "Are you going to argue that the shooting was justified?"

"Our arguments will be made at the proper time in the proper place," Grayson replied.

They reached the elevator that had brought Luke and Jane to the second floor. The bailiff who'd delivered the news of the grand jury's actions pressed the call button.

"Is Ms. Adisa Johnson also going to represent Officer Nelson?" the reporter asked. "Was she meeting with DA Baldwin as part of the defense team? And is that part of your strategy for negating the racial implications of this case? To bring in a black attorney who grew up here to represent a white officer?"

Luke's face registered his shock, and the photographer took his picture.

"Ms. Johnson has no current involvement in this matter," Grayson said.

"But you're not ruling her out for the future?"

Grayson didn't reply. The elevator arrived. Grayson, Luke, and Jane got in, and the door closed to a final flurry of photos.

"Why was she asking about the black lawyer?" Luke asked sharply. "Does the reporter know something we don't?"

"It's complicated," Grayson replied with a sigh. "Which is one of several reasons why I didn't answer the question."

Adisa arrived at the hospital in time for Aunt Josie's dinner, which included mashed potatoes and stewed squash cooked so long that it had turned into yellow mush. But to Aunt Josie, the introduction of anything other than liquids was ecstasy. The older woman was able to maneuver small forkfuls of food into her mouth with her left hand. As she chewed, she closed her eyes in contentment.

"Child, this is like manna in the wilderness. And don't tell me how bland it is. Let me believe this is fresh from my garden."

"Yes, ma'am," Adisa said with a smile. "I'm not going to tell you what you already know — the potatoes came from a box instead of the ground."

Aunt Josie's hand shook slightly as she raised a fluffy white bite to her mouth. "It's hard to fake real mashed potatoes," the older woman said. "Do you remember how you used to pick out the bits of skin when I'd make them with red potatoes?"

"It was a texture thing."

"And part of growing up. Life has a lot of skin in it. You can't pick it out like you did when you were little. That's where most of the vitamins and minerals are hiding."

"Why are you saying that?" Adisa asked.

" 'Cause it's true," Aunt Josie said, licking her lips. "But you already know that."

After dinner, Adisa brushed her aunt's teeth.

"If it's okay, I'm going to Reggie's church this evening," Adisa said as her aunt swished water around in her mouth.

"I think that's a great idea," Aunt Josie replied after spitting the water into a plastic bowl. "I don't want you wasting your life hanging around me just to brush my teeth."

"Aunt Josie!"

"Go to church," Aunt Josie said with a smile. "If my sense of humor is coming back, it's time for them to let me out of this hospital."

Adisa leaned over and kissed her aunt on

the forehead.

"Have a good time," the older woman said. "I bet Reggie is a great preacher."

Adisa stopped off at Aunt Josie's house to change clothes. She wasn't sure if people dressed up every time they walked through the doors at Zion Hills Baptist, but it was always better to be overdressed than under-dressed. She found a green dress of Shanika's that her sister hadn't been able to wear since giving birth to Ronnie Jr. It fit Adisa perfectly.

The church parking lot was half full when she arrived. Attendance was healthy for a midweek service. Adisa parked in an area of newly paved asphalt divided by freshly painted lines. Bible in hand, she walked to the front entrance and climbed three broad steps. She could already hear singing from inside the brightly lit sanctuary.

A twenty-person choir was praising so loudly they sounded like a group two or three times larger. The director was a young woman about Adisa's age who played an electric keyboard with one hand and directed the choir with the other. The director ran her fingers down the keyboard, pounded out a few new chords, and the choir took off on a new song. The words to the song were displayed on two screens to the right and left of the pulpit platform. The sanctuary was traditional in design, but there had obviously been technical upgrades to the sound and media systems. Adisa sat near the front.

Reggie strode out onto the platform. He was wearing a coat and a tie, but most of those in attendance were dressed more casually. The preacher made eye contact with Adisa and pointed upward. Adisa wasn't sure what that was supposed to mean but smiled and nodded. Several more songs followed. Adisa found herself swaying in rhythm. Several people nearby lifted their hands, and a few shouted. When the last song died down, Reggie turned around and offered up an opening prayer.

"Welcome to you all, especially our first-time visitors," he said.

Adisa assumed he would ask the visitors to identify themselves, but Reggie didn't go in that direction. Instead, he announced the theme for the meeting.

"This evening is for testimonies," he said. "Usually you hear me preach, but tonight you're going to speak the truth of God's grace, goodness, and power to one another. I've talked to a few of you in advance. You will get things started, but after that, the pulpit is open to anyone who wants to give

God praise and glory. First up is Gloria Nichols."

A woman in her midthirties walked onto the platform.

"Please keep it to five minutes," Reggie said to the woman with a twinkle in his eyes.

"Five minutes!" the woman exclaimed. "You told me I could talk for ten minutes!"

Reggie turned to the congregation. "Five minutes or ten minutes?" he asked.

"Ten!" a chorus of voices replied.

"Time starts now," Reggie said and then stepped from the platform to the front pew.

Gloria told how the Lord had been working in her relationship with her troubled twelve-year-old daughter. She was followed by a man named Kenneth, who was celebrating a year of sobriety and the restoration of his marriage. Adisa knew Kenneth's sister-in-law and saw her sitting in the congregation.

"Who else wants to share?" Reggie said after he led the congregation in prayer for a man named Roger.

"I do!" a strong female voice called out.

Adisa and those around her strained to see who'd spoken.

"Of course, Sister Armistead," Reggie said. "Someone please help her to the platform."

TWENTY

Luke felt numb when the detention officer at the jail took his photo and rolled his fingerprints. He wondered if the mug-shot picture would be published in the newspaper the following day. Afterward, he sat alone for half an hour on a chair in the hallway near the booking station. There was nothing to do except stare at the concrete floor painted a glossy gray and marred by scuff marks left by the black-soled shoes of detention officers. No one was in the nearby drunk tank, and the jail was quiet as a tomb. The door near the booking area clanged open, and Theo Grayson appeared.

"Let's go," the lawyer said. "Magistrate Caldwell set your bail at $100,000, and Clayton Jones posted a property bond. He's aware that one of the superior court judges could increase bail on his own accord or upon request of the DA's office. Just make sure you don't say or do anything that will give the judge assigned to the case an excuse to revoke bond or increase it to a level that Clayton won't touch."

"What would make the judge do that?"

"Harassing a witness or making statements that you might leave town."

"I wouldn't do either one of those things."

"Then I suggest you stay away from Stan Jackson and don't investigate the case on your own," Grayson said.

"I didn't hassle him."

"That's not what the DA claims."

"What?!"

"Hold on," Grayson said in a calm voice. "This happens. People are already saying crazy things about you."

"Yeah," Luke admitted. "But it's tougher coming from someone like the DA, who's in law enforcement."

They left the booking area and went through another secure door. Outside, Luke took a deep breath. Even his limited time in the confined area had felt like a crushing weight. He couldn't imagine what it would be like as his day-to-day existence. They got in Grayson's fancy car.

"I'm still working on finding a lawyer who can take on primary responsibility for your case," Grayson said as he pulled out of the parking lot. "Judge Andrews knows my role is limited. If I were thirty years younger, he could force me to represent you, but that's not going to happen now."

"I wish it would," Luke replied.

"One step at a time. Let's get you home to Jane and your little girl. If the reporter from the newspaper tries to ask any more questions, refer her to me."

"I've always refused to talk to them, which hasn't done me any good."

"But it hasn't made things worse."

Luke wasn't sure how things could get worse. Grayson turned onto the main road away from the center of town.

"How is Hamlin doing?" Luke asked. "Has there been any improvement in his condition?"

"As far as I know, he's still in a coma, which disqualifies him from having surgery to remove the bullet," Grayson replied.

"I sure hope he makes it."

"Yes," Grayson said, glancing to the side at Luke. "We all know his death would make things a lot worse."

On the arm of one of the younger parishioners, Thelma Armistead made her way slowly to the front of the sanctuary. Reggie took the older woman's hand and assisted her up the steps and onto the platform.

Sister Armistead was wearing a turquoise dress. Reggie spoke into the microphone.

"Sister Armistead, we're all continuing to pray for Deshaun's recovery and that justice will be done to the white officer who shot him. Thankfully, the Nash County grand jury met earlier today and issued an indictment charging Officer Nelson with aggravated assault."

Several "Amens!" and claps greeted Reggie's words. Sister Armistead put her hands on the edges of the pulpit and leaned forward so that her mouth was close to the microphone.

"It's because of Officer Nelson that I'm here," she said in a voice that carried across the sanctuary.

Reggie reached over and pulled the microphone an inch or two away from the older woman's lips.

"The Lord has dealt with me over the past few days," Sister Armistead continued. "And he's convicted me to say something that some of you may not understand or agree with."

Not wanting to miss anything, Adisa leaned forward. Sister Armistead closed her eyes and put her hand on her heart. Adisa suddenly wondered if the older woman was about to collapse on the platform. But she opened her eyes, looked toward the ceiling, and lifted her right hand high in the air.

"Lord, I forgive Officer Luke Nelson for shooting my Deshaun!" she cried out. "Lay not this sin at his door! I forgive him! I forgive him! I forgive him!"

Adisa stared, transfixed by the passion and anguish on the grandmother's face.

"And I ask you to forgive him!" Sister Armistead continued. "I want no part of judgment! Only mercy! Mercy! Mercy! For him, for Deshaun, for me!"

Reggie seemed as stunned by the moment as Adisa. Sister Armistead turned toward the preacher.

"That's all, Pastor," she said in a soft voice.

Sister Armistead slowly made her way to the top of the steps. A man on the front row jumped to his feet and helped her to one of the front pews. Reggie returned to the microphone.

"Does anyone else, uh, have a testimony they'd like to share?" he asked.

Two more people came forward, but Adisa's mind and heart couldn't move from the place Sister Armistead had taken her. When the meeting ended, Adisa positioned herself so she could watch the way people interacted with the older woman. She wondered if anyone would aggressively confront an elderly, well-respected woman whose grandson was lying in a coma at the local hospital. The looks on several faces made it clear they disagreed with what Sister Armistead said. Leaning on the arm of one of the men Adisa had seen at the hospital, Sister Armistead made her way slowly down the aisle. After she left, Reggie came over to Adisa.

"That was powerful," Adisa said. "But I'm guessing Sister Armistead didn't let you know in advance what she was going to say."

"No, she didn't," Reggie said and then lowered the volume of his voice. "But I wish she had. People want justice, not judgment, and she's muddied the waters. I know Thelma is trying to work through things the best she can, but it sounded like she's struck a bargain with the Lord that if she forgives Officer Nelson, God will raise up Deshaun."

"I'm not so sure about that," Adisa replied. "It seemed like pure passion to me."

"But dubious theology, which puts me in damage control mode."

"What do you mean?"

"On the issue of whether it's necessary for someone to ask forgiveness in order to be forgiven. Does Jesus forgive our sins if we don't ask him to? I don't think so. If that's the standard he laid down, how can anyone, even Thelma Armistead, forgive someone who hasn't admitted to doing something wrong and asked for forgiveness? Several of the deacons were telling me I have to publicly rebuke her."

Adisa jerked her head backward.

"Yeah, that's how I reacted," Reggie said. "I'd rather Thelma believe something wrong about forgiveness than wound a woman who's already hurting at such a deep level. But the head deacon claims I have to bring correction when necessary. Otherwise people will assume I agree with her and quit responding to the call for justice."

"I don't know," Adisa said slowly. "What Sister Armistead said challenged me in a good way."

"How?"

Adisa hesitated. Reggie spoke first.

"When I invited you to come tonight, I was going to ask you to grab a bite to eat with me after the meeting so we could relax and talk. Now I'd like to decompress with someone who isn't a member of the congregation."

"Let's do it," Adisa replied immediately.

While Adisa waited for everyone to clear the sanctuary, several people she knew came over and asked about Aunt Josie. When the last person left, Reggie joined her.

"Where do you want to go?" he asked, loosening his tie.

Adisa thought for a moment. There weren't a lot of options for dining out in Campbellton at 8:30 p.m. on a Wednesday.

"You pick," she said.

"What about the Lincoln Drive-In?" Reggie suggested. "It's open, but we'd have to eat in the car."

"I haven't eaten there in years. They used to have great milk shakes."

"And still do."

The Lincoln Drive-In had changed little since the days when Adisa was a high school student. The teenage boys and girls who worked as carhops wore Rollerblades to move around. Adisa drove and followed Reggie. They parked and she got into his car, which was spotlessly clean.

"It doesn't look like you've been squirting ketchup around in here," Adisa said when she slipped into the passenger seat.

"The night is still young."

A four-foot-square sign listed the items on the menu. Most of the pictures of the food didn't look like they'd been updated in years.

"I'm hungry," she said.

"I know you want a milk shake."

"For dessert."

"I usually get the same thing when I bring kids from the youth group here," Reggie said.

Adisa read the sign. "Okay," she said. "Press the green button with the clown face on it."

Reggie reached out the window and pressed the enormous button.

"What's the story behind the clown button?" he asked.

"I don't know," Adisa replied. "It's been on there for as long as I can remember. I should ask Aunt Josie. She might know."

A chubby teenage boy with red hair rolled up to their window. Adisa leaned over and made sure she spoke loud enough for the boy to hear her.

"I'll have a cheeseburger with the works, add slaw, an order of chili cheese fries, a large limeade, and a small peanut butter chocolate shake."

Reggie, a surprised expression on his face, glanced sideways at Adisa.

"I said I was hungry," Adisa said.

Reggie ordered a double cheeseburger with bacon, onion rings, and a drink.

"I'm glad you ordered onion rings," Adisa said when the carhop skated away. "That's always been a dilemma for me. Chili cheese fries or onion rings."

"I'll share," Reggie replied. "I've never tried the chili cheese fries."

"You'd think it would be a soggy mess, but they use little string potatoes that stay crispy. You'll love them."

Reggie took off his tie and laid it across the backseat.

"I thought some more about Thelma Armistead," he said. "I really don't have the heart to say anything that would hurt her, especially during such a tough time for her family, so I'm going to talk about the issue of our forgiveness of others in a sermon without specifically mentioning what she said. The deacons will have to be satisfied with that approach."

"When she was speaking, I felt the Lord convicting me about my attitude toward the police officer."

"It can be a challenge to love a wrongdoer without usurping the Lord's role as the only one who can forgive him," Reggie quickly responded.

"I wasn't finished," Adisa replied. "I was just taking a breath."

"Sorry." Reggie turned slightly in his seat so he faced her. "Go ahead."

"I realized that I jumped to judgment without knowing much more than I read in the newspaper or heard from a neighbor.

And when I made up my mind prematurely, it led to an attitude against Nelson that isn't consistent with Jesus' command to love my neighbor as myself." Adisa paused. "Or with the presence of the fruit of the Holy Spirit in my life."

"You certainly need to make sure your conscience is clear, but I don't think there's much disagreement about the facts of the shooting."

"Maybe not, but neither of us knows exactly what happened, and until the full story is told, it's not right to automatically reach the conclusion that the officer's actions were racially motivated."

"Except for two hundred years of history," Reggie replied flatly. "Look, you and I both know that the likelihood a young black man will be shot is much greater than for a young white man. That's the sad reality of the world we live in."

"I'm not denying that. But Sister Armistead's words made me consider the possibility that the shooting wasn't about race at all."

"The officer will never admit that it was, maybe even to himself," Reggie said. "But those attitudes run deep, and lots of white folks are unwilling to face the impact racism has on them in subtle ways. And against

Deshaun the racism wasn't subtle; it was brutal. You have to look to the past to understand the present."

"You're probably right," Adisa sighed. "And I hate that you are."

The carhop skated up with their order and balanced the tray on Reggie's open window. Reggie distributed the food. They ended up with cups and bags all over the front area of the car.

"I'll pray a blessing," Reggie said when they were situated.

"Looking at all the calories in this food, it had better be a good one."

While they ate Adisa dropped the topic of the shooting. She was still trying to process the impact of the evening on herself and didn't want to argue with the minister. However, as she munched on a chili cheese fry, she pondered his comment about the influence of the past on the present. And she sensed there was something the Lord wanted to say to her about that, too.

Unable to sleep, Luke tossed and turned. He glanced at the clock on the nightstand. They'd been in bed for over two hours. Not wanting to disturb Jane, he slipped out of bed and headed toward the couch in the den.

"I'm awake," Jane said before he reached the bedroom door. "I think I woke you up."

"No."

"You're wrong," Jane replied. "You fell asleep for at least a few minutes. Believe me, I can tell."

Luke didn't argue. He knew he was guilty of what he called aggressive breathing, otherwise known as snoring. He sat on the side of the bed. Jane propped her pillow up against the headboard. A full moon cast light through the cracks in the blinds of their bedroom windows.

"Do you want to talk?" she asked.

Luke's mouth was dry. "I need a drink of water," he said and left the bedroom.

When he returned, Jane had turned on a lamp. Luke sat on her side of the bed near her feet. He looked down at the carpeted floor.

"I haven't been able to stop thinking about the questions the reporter from the newspaper kept firing at me at the court-house," he said.

Luke glanced up at Jane, who was looking at him and clearly not going to speak.

"Do you remember what she asked?" he said.

"Not really. I just wanted to get out of there and was glad Mr. Grayson did all the talking."

"She asked if I was sorry."

Luke's chest felt tight. He pressed his lips tightly together. After a few moments passed, he felt Jane wrapping her arms around his shoulders.

"I wish with all my heart this hadn't happened. And I try not to think about Hamlin lying in a coma at the hospital with a bullet in his brain. If he wakes up, who knows how he'll have to spend the rest of his life. I believed I was doing the right thing, but now it's impossible not to second-guess myself."

Jane didn't say anything. Instead, she pulled him closer. Luke knew there was nothing she could say. Her touch in his moment of weakness told him all she could. Whether his actions on East Nixon Street were right or wrong wouldn't change the fact that she loved him. He felt himself begin to relax. Jane released him. Luke hugged her and kissed the top of her hand.

"Thanks, I needed that," he said.

"Good."

"And are you sure it's okay for me to tell you how I'm struggling without making you feel insecure and unprotected? I don't want to burden you any more than you already are, and —"

Jane reached out and touched his lips with her index finger to stop him from continuing. Luke returned to his side of the bed. Knowing he could go to sleep, he laid his head on the pillow. Jane turned out the light.

It was almost 1:00 a.m. when Adisa reached the bottom drawer of the oldest chest in Aunt Josie's guest bedroom. Over the past three hours, she'd waded through faded photographs of people she didn't know and read letters written by people long dead. It was obvious that the family archives had ended up in her aunt's house. She went down several rabbit trails of information that piqued her interest, but she didn't find what she was looking for. She wasn't sure it existed.

Taking out a manila folder that was so old the yellow tint from the thick paper stock was almost gone, Adisa opened it. The last remaining fibers holding the folder together gave up, and she lifted off the detached top. Beneath it were several sheets of unlined paper covered with cursive writing in dark black ink. The title of the top sheet caught her eye — "Westside Free Church." It was the church that had once stood beside the cemetery. In spidery black ink, a long-ago scribe wrote that the cemetery preceded the church by at least fifty years. The existence of a burial place for slaves before the church was built made sense in light of the legal prohibition against the public assembly of blacks in the antebellum era.

Turning over the sheet of paper, Adisa found a list of over thirty names, some first names only, without any explanation of their significance. Her best guess was that the people recorded on the sheet were either early members of the congregation or deceased residents of the cemetery. Several had the last name Adams. Seeing the names of long-departed relatives made Adisa's heart beat a little faster. These were her people, her heritage. Likely uneducated and illiterate, they were nevertheless the people whose blood ran in her veins. She ran her finger down the list, and the same tingly feeling that had swept over her at the cemetery returned.

The next two sheets of paper included the names of early pastors and deacons at the church. There were dates by some names, but most were undated. Several men named Adams served as deacons but none as pastor. Several other sheets listed information about marriages and deaths. Toward the bottom of the stack she found a paper that should have been on top: "Compiled by Adelaide Adams — 1921." From the spindly handwriting, it was clear that Adelaide had prepared the other sheets as well. The very last sheet in the folder contained six sentences:

The property for the church was deeded to the Trustees by Harold Grayson III around 1868 or 1870. I heard this from my mother but don't know if it's true. At one time the Grayson family owned a large farm in the area. Raphael Adams, my great-uncle, worked as a sharecropper for the Grayson family. I remember hearing Uncle Rafe preach at the church when I was a child. He never mentioned anything about this to me.

Apparently, the connection between Adisa and the Grayson family went back much further than her summer job at Grayson, Baxter, and Williams. The entry raised the real possibility that some of her ancestors were slaves owned by Harold Grayson until they were forcibly freed at the end of the Civil War. Adisa sat on the floor, leaned her back against the wall, and tried to process how that made her feel toward the modern-day Grayson who'd offered her a job. Would that provide another rationale for refusing to work at his law firm? How did the challenge that came from Thelma Armistead's lips about forgiving Officer Nelson factor into the situation?

Half an hour later, Adisa fell asleep with Sister Armistead's words ringing in her ears and images of long-dead ancestors toiling under the hot sun for the Grayson family swirling in her mind.

TWENTY-ONE

Adisa was up before dawn. She threw on workout clothes and, with a fresh cup of coffee in her hand, left the house and returned to the Westside Cemetery. The sky was turning from gray to blue as the sun sent a few scout rays over the horizon. Adisa took a long sip of coffee before getting out of the car. The air was fresh, the temperature cool. She took a deep breath void of any tinge of pollution. Campbellton had its advantages over Atlanta.

The remnants of the vibrant floral bouquets that had covered the cemetery in color were now wilted and dying. Adisa saw some of the dahlias she'd brought. What had been beautiful was now faded. The blossoms were turning brown, the stalks brittle. She began to pick them up. What was true for flowers was true for people. Adisa thought about the verse from 1 Peter chapter 1: "All people are like grass, and all their glory is like the flowers of the field; the grass withers and the flowers fall, but the word of the Lord endures forever." The words of Scripture rang true in her heart. But what was the word of the Lord for her? What did he have to say to her that transcended every competing voice? What did he think about the path before her? Only his will could withstand the relentless onslaught of time.

Adisa reached the spot where she'd found the simple stone marker. She knelt in the damp grass and touched the cool surface of the rock. There was no way to know for sure, but she hoped she was near the grave of Raphael Adams. She bowed her head and offered up a prayer for guidance to the Lord whom her ancestor and others like him served in the midst of unfathomably difficult times. If they found a way to live in the enduring reality of the word of the Lord, there had to be a way for her to do so, too.

And in that moment, Adisa felt a presence that flooded her heart with peace, confidence, hope, freedom, faith, and courage. It happened so fast that it took a few moments to identify what she'd received. Tears welled up in her eyes at the goodness of God.

Adisa had been a Christian since childhood, but in that moment, on her knees in the cemetery, she entered a new realm of her faith. She realized in a deep way that like the children of Israel, she was the descendant of slaves, but now she was the daughter of a King, called to live in the land of his promises. Tears flowed from her eyes and onto the grass. After several minutes passed, she took a deep breath, wiped away her tears, and rose to her feet. Straightening her shoulders, she looked to the east where the sun peeked above the rim of the earth. A small smile crossed her lips. For a reason not rooted in analytical thinking or ethnic identity, she knew what she should do. Sometimes an inner witness speaks without need for a logical explanation.

When Luke awoke, he enjoyed a split second of forgetful peace before the crushing weight of his circumstances returned. He lay on his back, staring at the ceiling, and tried to figure out how to manage the next sixteen hours before returning to bed. The sound of Ashley whimpering in her bedroom was a welcome distraction.

"I'll check on her," he said to Jane, who had begun to stir beside him.

"She's wet for sure," Jane said. "I'll get up in a second and fix her breakfast."

"No, let me do it," Luke answered.

Jane rolled over in bed and looked at him

with her eyes fully open. "Are you sure?"

"Yes, I've fixed her food before."

"I know, but . . . ," Jane began and then paused. "No, that would be great. I'm going to try to sleep a few more minutes."

Luke went into Ashley's room. The little girl was lying on her side facing away from him and whimpering into the back of her right hand.

"Good morning, angel," Luke said.

Ashley immediately flipped over and faced him with a smile as brilliant as a sunrise on a clear day.

"Thank you," Luke said as he approached the crib.

He changed the little girl's diaper and took her into the kitchen. From her vantage point in her high chair, Ashley carefully watched him prepare breakfast. Noticing her attentiveness, Luke decided to entertain her.

"Do you want rice or oatmeal cereal?" he asked, holding up both boxes and selecting one based on a vague wave of her hand that had nothing to do with an act of her will.

He did the same with the other breakfast choices, including peaches and bananas, two different kinds of yogurt, and alternate brands of vitamins. When everything was mixed together, he sat down beside her high chair and began to carefully spoon the mixture into her mouth.

"We'll show Mommy what a neat baby looks like," he said to the little girl as he scraped away stray cereal that had escaped the corner of her mouth.

Ashley was as hungry as a lumberjack, and in only a few minutes reached the bottom of the bowl.

"If you're interested in working as a nanny, you're hired," Jane's voice said from behind him.

He turned and saw his wife standing with her arms crossed in the kitchen doorway.

"But I'm not sure saying that you can do a better job than Mommy is the right message to send to a child," she said.

"You heard that?" Luke asked. "How long have you been standing there?"

"Long enough to enjoy the sight of a father loving his daughter."

Instead of joy, pain filled Luke's heart. "She won't remember this if I'm sent off —" He stopped.

"Please don't talk that way," Jane said. "It ruins the moment for me."

Theo Grayson stared at the account of the transfer of land from his family to the West-

346

side Free Church more than 150 years earlier.

"I didn't know anything about this," he said to Adisa. "The earliest documents for land transfers in Nash County are on microfilm, and you have to use one of those OCR machines that are almost as old as I am to read them."

"I'd like to see the records," Adisa replied. "They might tell a little bit more about the original trustees. What can you tell me about Harold Grayson III?"

"He was the third of four," Grayson replied. "They stopped with Harold Grayson IV, who was my great-grandfather. The first Harold came to this area with a horse, an ax, and a plow. I don't know a lot of details. My spinster aunt was into genealogy. Her records probably went to one of my cousins in Savannah. I'm sure I could uncover a bunch of information about my family if I went onto one of those ancestry sites."

Adisa paused for a moment. "Do the old microfilm records document the sale of slaves?"

Grayson put down the sheet of paper. "Occasionally, slaves were transferred with the land. Are you wondering about the connection between our ancestors?"

"I know there was a sharecropper relation-ship, but we don't have to go there," Adisa said. "At least not now."

Grayson locked eyes with Adisa. "I ac-knowledged to myself a long time ago that what my family did was wrong and the excuses they used were false. But I've never had a chance to say that to someone whose forebears suffered at their hands. That likely happened in our family lines, and I'd wel-come the opportunity to make things right —"

"You can start by letting me rescind my rejection of the job offer you gave me," Adisa said.

"What?" Grayson asked in surprise. "I don't understand."

"And I'm not sure I do, either, except that I know in my heart I'm supposed to work for you, even if it means helping defend Officer Nelson."

Grayson couldn't hide his shock. "Why?" he managed.

"Two things," Adisa answered. "One that's easy to understand; another that's as ob-scure as my family history."

Adisa told Grayson about Sister Armi-stead's testimony at the church followed by the trip to the cemetery. It seemed odd opening up on such a deeply personal level to the older lawyer, but it simply felt both right and necessary. Grayson listened without interruption.

"Does this sound crazy to you?" Adisa asked at one point.

"Not the way you describe it," Grayson answered thoughtfully. "What Deshaun Hamlin's grandmother said at the church is amazing, and I'm impressed that you followed her lead. I mean, if everyone who's been deeply hurt by another person forgave —" Grayson stopped.

"The world would change," Adisa said.

Grayson nodded. "And you're obviously a much more spiritual person than I am. You're like Raphael, and I'm like Harold III."

"You don't know what Harold III believed. He obviously wanted to support God's work. Otherwise he wouldn't have donated land for a church."

"That's true, but if Raphael Adams were here, I think he'd see himself in you."

A shiver ran down Adisa's spine. It was the second time a comment by Grayson had touched her in a place much deeper than her mind.

"It may not make logical sense," Adisa said, "but if after hearing all this you still want to hire me, the answer is yes."

As soon as the words were out of her mouth, Adisa quickly checked to see if her heart agreed. Nothing rose up to protest. She was at peace but sensed war was about to break out. Grayson pointed up with his right index finger.

"I'd be afraid not to. However, our trip to the deed room will need to wait. It's time for you and Luke to get together. You and I may have an agreement, but he's obviously going to have to sign off on it, too."

"Okay," Adisa said. "And I need to call Jasper Baldwin and tell him I'm not interested in serving as a special prosecutor."

The phone in the kitchen rang and Jane answered it. Luke watched her eyes widen as she listened.

"This morning?" she asked and then nodded. "Okay, I'll have to scramble to get a babysitter."

She listened another moment before hanging up the phone. "That was Mr. Grayson's paralegal. They want both of us to come to his office."

"Why?"

"She said he will explain when we get there."

Luke backed the car out of the driveway.

Jane was in the passenger seat sending a last-minute text message to the babysitter who'd picked up Ashley.

"I wonder why Mr. Grayson's assistant wouldn't tell you the name of the lawyer he wants us to meet," Luke said.

"She just said it was someone to interview," Jane said as she sent the text. "What will you ask him?"

"How many cases have you won? Will you believe me when I tell you the truth? Are you a fighter or will you try to talk me into a plea bargain?"

They walked together through the front door of the law firm. The reception area was already beginning to feel familiar.

"We're here to see Mr. Grayson," Luke told a receptionist he didn't recognize. "I'm Luke —"

"Yes, Officer Nelson. Please have a seat. I'll let him know that you and your wife are here."

A couple of minutes later, Mr. Grayson opened the door that led to the interior area of the office. Inside the conference room was the female attorney they'd briefly met at the courthouse.

"Luke and Jane," Grayson said, motioning toward the woman, "I'm sure you remember Ms. Adisa Johnson. I've asked her to meet with us and discuss the possibility of representing you. I'd still be in charge, but she would play a big role."

Luke and Jane simultaneously turned to each other, their mouths dropping open. Grayson sat at the end of the table with the black lawyer to his right. Luke and Jane sat across from her. Luke quickly studied the woman's face. It was hard to tell what she was thinking.

"Do you know Deshaun Hamlin?" he asked.

"No," the young woman responded evenly. "Did you?"

Luke shook his head. "But since this happened I found out he played on the high school basketball team."

"And I've been to his hospital room several times with his pastor to pray for his recovery," the woman continued. "Would you have a problem with that?"

Luke heard Jane gasp.

"No," Luke replied. "I want him to recover. For several reasons, not just because it would be good for me."

"And I'm going to continue to pray for him," Adisa responded. "Most likely from a distance since I'm not sure how his family will view any involvement I have in your case."

Jane spoke. "It's a shock for us to meet you."

"Yeah," Luke added. "We don't know anything about you except what Mr. Grayson mentioned in the DA's office and what he just said."

The woman looked at Grayson, who nodded his head. For the next few minutes, Adisa told them about her educational and professional background and experience. Luke liked the confident way she spoke. He knew that a lot of former prosecutors ended up working as defense lawyers because they already knew the ins and outs of criminal law.

"Because I need to be in Campbellton to help take care of my aunt, I've accepted a job offer with Mr. Grayson's firm. He's asked me to help with your case."

"And you want to do that?" Jane asked.

"I didn't at first," Adisa replied. "But a couple of things have happened that changed my mind."

She told them about Thelma Armistead's testimony the previous night at the Zion Hills Baptist Church. When she got to the point where Deshaun's grandmother forgave Luke and cried out for mercy, Jane's eyes filled with tears. Adisa stopped.

"That's unbelievable," Jane said, sniffling.

Luke, too, was stunned. He tried to imagine the scene in his mind as he stared at the top of the shiny table.

"It challenged my attitude," Adisa continued. "As a lawyer, I believe the Constitution and the Bill of Rights guarantee everyone a fair trial, but as a black woman it's hard to put aside years of hearing how African Americans have been singled out for differential treatment by white police officers."

"I've never done that," Luke replied.

"From your point of view," Grayson interjected. "But that's going to be a factor we have to deal with in the case, especially with black jurors."

Luke didn't like being accused of racism by anyone, but before he responded, Jane spoke.

"He's right, Luke," she said.

Luke grunted and kept his mouth shut.

"And I'm not going to take this case just so you can have a black lawyer sitting beside you in the courtroom," Adisa said. "People will accuse us of that, but it's not true. This isn't for show. After hearing Ms. Armistead and praying about it myself, I'm willing to help if that's what you want."

Hearing all this talk about praying and forgiving and asking God for mercy was so foreign to Luke he wasn't sure how to respond. He felt Jane tap his leg beneath the table. He looked at her as she firmly nodded her head.

"Mr. Grayson," Luke said, "what do you think?"

"I wouldn't recommend bringing in Adisa if I didn't think it was a good idea."

"Okay," Luke said and shrugged. "I guess so."

Grayson slid a sheet of paper and a pen across the table toward him. "This modifies our agreement and adds Adisa as one of your attorneys. As you know, the previous agreement set the fee at one dollar subject to modification. That won't change."

"Wait — you're still not going to charge me?" Luke asked in surprise. "I thought that was just to get us through the day with the grand jury."

Grayson looked at Adisa. "I had another figure in mind," the older lawyer said. "But after listening to Adisa's story this morning, I decided I need to do something bold, too. I hope my law partners don't have heart attacks when they find out."

Luke quickly signed the agreement before the lawyers changed their minds.

"Good," Grayson said. "Now I'd like Adisa to listen to the recording of our first interview."

Grayson hit several keys on his tablet, and in a few seconds Luke had the weird experience of listening to his own voice. A couple of times, he raised his eyes enough to try to gauge Adisa's reaction to his story. The black lawyer's face betrayed nothing.

Adisa tried to control her breathing as the recording began. She didn't want to react in an unprofessional way. As Nelson methodically described what had unfolded on East Nixon Street, Adisa gripped the arms of the chair tightly and desperately wished she could change what she knew was about to happen. If only someone else had been on the scene to disrupt the chain of events.

When the police officer described Deshaun running toward him, she barely kept herself from crying out, "Stop! Stop!"

She clenched her teeth behind her tightly closed mouth as Nelson described firing the shots that cut down Deshaun in the middle of the street. The policeman's voice betrayed no emotion until the second officer arrived on the scene and told him the black teenager was unarmed and possibly bleeding to death. At that point, Nelson was silent for a few seconds before he continued. After the officer finished describing the gruesome scene, Grayson brought him back to the call he'd received from the dispatcher about the robbery at the convenience store. A few minutes later, Grayson turned off the recording.

"Any follow-up questions?" he asked Adisa.

"Not at this time," she said, hoping her voice didn't quiver.

"Then we're done for now," Grayson said. "Luke, you need to be back here this afternoon at three o'clock. The judge wants to meet with us and the district attorney to discuss the case."

"Isn't that unusual?" Luke asked.

"Yes, it is," Grayson replied. "And I'm not sure what he has in mind."

After Luke and Jane were gone, Adisa and Grayson returned to the conference room. Adisa had bottled up so much inner tension she was about to explode.

"That went well," the older lawyer said.

"How do you define 'well'?"

"Luke agreed to make you part of the defense team."

"True, but unless things change, he's going to be a very shaky witness. How many times have you listened to the interview?"

"Three."

"Once was enough for me to see huge

problems. He sounds robotic and quickly defaults to blame-shifting. Those two traits are a lethal combination for a witness. Even when he's telling the truth, which is tough for me to identify beyond his name and occupation, it sounds like he's hiding something. At best, he comes across as callous. A jury could easily conclude that he would calmly shoot an unarmed young man whether he's black, white, yellow, or brown."

"But he was upset after the shooting."

"Caused by what? I didn't hear any remorse. If the shakes he described were triggered by fear, what was he afraid of? That he was about to get in big trouble?"

"My natural optimism can be a weakness," the older lawyer replied wryly. "It didn't strike me the same way. Your perspective is going to be valuable to this case."

"Even if Nelson was scared and thought he was in danger, he was wrong. It's all going to come down to whether a jury thinks his fear was reasonable under the circumstances —"

"And justified shooting someone who wasn't in fact a lethal threat. Remember, he thought Hamlin fired at him first."

"Please, call him Deshaun," Adisa replied. "I can't dehumanize him."

"Will you call Officer Nelson Luke?"

"Yes," Adisa said after a brief pause. "But Deshaun didn't shoot, which undermines Nelson's, uh, Luke's credibility. If I were prosecuting this case, I'd ask Luke ten different questions designed to make him admit Deshaun didn't have a gun and therefore couldn't have fired at him. I'd bring the officer's gun into the courtroom and lay it on the railing in front of the jury box and make sure every juror understood that it was the only gun on East Nixon Street the night of the shooting. I'd hammer that point so hard the lid on Luke's coffin would be shut for good."

"I'm glad you called Jasper Baldwin and turned him down."

Adisa shook her head. "You can thank Thelma Armistead, Raphael Adams, and God for that," she said and then paused. "With a little help from John Adams, the second president."

Luke and Jane picked up Ashley from the babysitter on their way home.

"What do you think about Ms. Johnson?" Jane asked.

"It's going to take time and proof for me to trust her," Luke replied.

"If Mr. Grayson believes it's a smart move adding her to the case, I don't see how we can disagree." Jane's tone of voice lacked conviction.

"Come on," Luke prodded. "Tell me what you really think. I can tell when you're holding out on me."

"Okay," Jane replied. "I'm trying to keep your hopes up when it's next to impossible for me to do so for myself. I'm at my wit's end about everything that's happened. I prayed you wouldn't be indicted, but you were. I've prayed for someone to help you and thought Mr. Grayson might be the answer. He's on the case, but in the back of my mind I'm worried he's going to dump you onto Ms. Johnson, who sounds like she has a lot more experience prosecuting cases than defending them. Regardless of what they said during the meeting, it looks to me like Mr. Grayson wants to have a black lawyer sitting beside you in court. That could backfire. You're not a racist and you didn't shoot Deshaun Hamlin because of the color of his skin. You believed he was going to kill you. Setting you up with Ms. Johnson makes it look like we're trying to play the race card ourselves. I didn't say anything back there, but I've tried to be like Deshaun's grandmother and forgive the people who've said horrible things about you, because I know in my heart they aren't true."

"You said what I felt way better than I could," Luke said.

Ashley started to whimper, and Jane turned sideways in her seat to place a pacifier in the baby's mouth.

"All I want to do right now is go home, lock the door, and try to forget about everything except Ashley," she said.

On her way to the hospital, Adisa called Shanika and told her the news about the job.

"See, I was right as usual," Shanika said when Adisa finished. "I knew you were supposed to contact Mr. Grayson about a job. He's liked you ever since you worked for him when you were in high school."

"It's not that simple. He told me there was a string attached to the offer. The string ended up looking more like a rope."

"What do you mean?"

Adisa told her about the requirement that she assist in the representation of Luke Nelson. Shanika remained silent.

"Are you there?" Adisa asked.

"Yeah," Shanika replied. "But I'm not sure your brain is still attached to your body. I wanted you to work for Mr. Grayson so you could be in Campbellton to help look after Aunt Josie. I never would have expected you to sell your soul for a paycheck."

Adisa knew this was the preamble to future reactions from the black community. She couldn't tell everyone the complicated, unexplainable spiritual process that had brought her to her decision. Soon she'd have to come up with a shorthand answer. Now, she didn't have one.

"Do you want to hear the whole story?" she asked.

"It's going to take something good to convince me you're not crazy."

Adisa reached the hospital parking lot and stayed in her car for fifteen minutes talking to Shanika. When she finished, her sister was open but skeptical.

"I didn't know any of that stuff about the old cemetery and church," Shanika said. "What was it again that made you dig through all those records?"

"It's hard to explain," Adisa said, realizing herself the tenuous connection between Sister Armistead, Reggie's comment at the drive-in, and her genealogical quest. "Reggie mentioned the importance of the past, and I couldn't get the idea out of my head."

"Okay," Shanika replied. "But I hope you don't get run out of town."

"Me, too. Listen, I'm at the hospital. I need to check on Aunt Josie and then return to the law office for a meeting with a judge this afternoon."

"Not so fast," Shanika responded. "What's going on with you and Preacher Reggie? It sounds like he's doing more than proselytizing you as a potential tither to the church budget."

"I'm pretty sure he's interested in me," Adisa said. "And I like him, too. But it's not a good time to try to juggle a relationship. There's too much other stuff going on."

"And when do you believe there'll be enough time in your life to do that?"

"Hey, you convinced me to pursue a job with Theo Grayson," Adisa said, a smile on her lips. "Don't try to take over every detail of my life."

"If I did, it would be the best thing that ever happened to you."

"Be praying for me instead."

"Oh, I will. I really will."

TWENTY-TWO

Adisa found Aunt Josie awake, alert, and enjoying a lunch of "soft" foods. While her aunt ate, Adisa told her about the road that had brought her to Theo Grayson's office and the agreement to represent Luke Nelson. The only time Aunt Josie interrupted was to ask again about what happened at the cemetery.

"It's so interesting to hear you say that," the older woman said. "I've always felt close to the Lord at the graveyard but never mentioned it to anyone. I was afraid they'd jump to the conclusion that I was communicating with the dead. I mean, they're not really dead because they're with the Lord." Aunt Josie stopped. "That just shows why I never brought it up."

"I know," Adisa replied. "And I'm not trying to analyze it, even though that's the way I'm wired. But you, me, Shanika, her kids — we're all connected in some way to those who've gone before us. They didn't leave us any earthly wealth, but I believe there's a spiritual inheritance available if we'll reach out and claim it."

Aunt Josie slowly lowered her fork to her plate and raised a trembling left hand in the air above her head.

"Hallelujah!" she shouted in the loud voice she'd used when Reggie first entered her hospital room. Adisa immediately looked toward the door to see if the minister had returned. They were alone.

"Adisa, you're a never-ending source of blessing to me," Aunt Josie continued. "It's like Naomi and Ruth. You're better than the daughter I never had."

Adisa reached over and squeezed the older woman's left hand. "I love you," she said.

"And when it's my time to leave this world, I want you and Shanika to receive every blessing I can give you. Maybe one of the reasons you came back to Campbellton was to claim yours in person."

Adisa started to release Aunt Josie's hand but then continued to hold it for several moments. "Thank you," Adisa said.

"You're welcome," Aunt Josie replied. "The Lord's doing a powerful work in your heart."

"So you're not upset with me for agreeing

to represent the police officer who shot Thelma Armistead's grandson?"

"How could I be after the powerful testimony Thelma gave at Reggie's church? You're brave, and you've given me something new to be praying about while I lie here with nothing else to do."

There was a gentle knock on the door. This time it really was Reggie.

"We were just talking about you," Aunt Josie said, her face lighting up.

"Actually, it was your church," Adisa added. "I told Aunt Josie what Sister Armistead said last night."

"Which continues to stir up more controversy than I've been able to manage," Reggie said, shaking his head.

"Well, it sure touched Adisa," Aunt Josie said.

"I know," Reggie said. "But I wanted to come by and pray with you."

"I'd like that," Aunt Josie said. "I'm feeling better, and your prayers have been like daily bread."

The three of them closed their eyes. Reggie prayed. Adisa listened. The young preacher never seemed to offer up a perfunctory, one-size-fits-all prayer. She could tell he was really trying to craft petitions tailor-made for Aunt Josie's particular needs. He finished with a strong request that she be able to return home soon. Regardless of her words to Shanika about it being an inconvenient time for a romantic relationship, Adisa was attracted to the minister in a real, deep way.

"Amen," he said.

"Amen," the two women echoed.

"Today has been better than most Sundays in church," Aunt Josie said.

"Why is that?" Reggie asked.

"Adisa can tell you," Aunt Josie replied with a yawn. "You two run on. It's time for my second nap of the day."

Her heart beating a bit faster, Adisa followed Reggie out of the hospital room.

In the afternoon mail, Luke received a letter informing him that as a result of the indictment, he would no longer be on administrative leave with pay from the police department. The notice wasn't a surprise, but it was tough to realize that he wouldn't be able to provide for his family.

"I'm going out for a few minutes!" he called to Jane, who was in the laundry room at the rear of the house.

Jane stuck her head out of the doorway and brushed a stray strand of hair away from her face. "Why now?" she asked. "You have to be back downtown in a few hours."

"I need to go —" Luke started.

"Okay, okay," Jane said with a wave of her hand. "I get it."

Relieved he didn't have to give a detailed explanation, Luke bolted from the house. When he passed the Lincoln Drive-In, he saw Bruce Alverez's police cruiser and pulled in beside his former colleague. Bruce motioned him over, and Luke got in the police car. It felt like coming home.

"Are you sure it's okay for me to join you?" Luke asked.

"I need someone to help me eat these chili cheese fries," Bruce replied. "If I eat all of them, my next stop will be the ER at the hospital."

Bruce signaled for one of the carhops and ordered Luke a limeade.

"I miss this," Luke said.

"You can order this food anytime you want to."

"I mean the job."

"You don't miss the morning I had. I've already been on a domestic violence call in which the husband ended up in the ER, and then I had to break up a fight on the west side of town."

"The husband went to the ER?" Luke asked.

"Yeah, his wife broke a bottle over his head. He deserved a headache for cussing her out and threatening to take the kids to Arkansas, but she went over the top. The Department of Family and Children Services is going to step in and check on the kids." Bruce paused. "Will you take the corn dog off my hands? I know you like them."

Bruce handed the corn dog to Luke as well as a couple of packets of mustard. Luke carefully squeezed the mustard along the length of the corn dog. The corn dogs at the Lincoln Drive-In were much better than the ones at the county fair. Luke took a tangy bite.

"What kind of fight did you have to break up on the west side?"

"Actually, it wasn't far from the spot where you shot the Hamlin boy."

Luke was about to take another bite of corn dog but lowered it instead. "On East Nixon Street?"

"Yeah, one of the smaller houses for rent. It's the yellow one with the brown roof. A bunch of teenagers who should have been in school were in there. Mike Dailey and I both responded to a call that came in from a neighbor. When we showed up, most of the kids took off running. The only ones left were the Ott boy and an older kid who was in his early twenties. Both of them had blood on their faces but refused to say who started the ruckus. There wasn't anything to do except tell them to stay away from each other and go to the doctor. Mike and I checked the house for drugs and weapons but didn't find anything."

Luke ate a couple of bites of the corn dog.

"How are you doing?" Bruce asked and then quickly added, "Sorry, that's a dumb question."

"It's okay," Luke replied.

Neither of them said a word while Luke finished eating the corn dog. He thought about telling Bruce about the black lawyer agreeing to represent him but couldn't see the point in doing so.

"Thanks," he said, dropping the corn-dog stick into an empty bag. "Someday I hope I'll be back in one of these cars."

"Yeah," Bruce said. "See you around."

"I hope it's not in court," Luke blurted out.

"Things happen in life. I have to do my job."

Luke got out of the car and closed the door. He knew Bruce Alverez doing his job was going to be tough on both of them, but worse for Luke.

■ ■ ■ ■

"Have you eaten lunch?" Reggie asked
Adisa as soon as they were in the hallway
outside Aunt Josie's room.

"No, I thought I'd grab a salad in the
hospital cafeteria," she said.

"Sounds good to me, too," he replied.

They rode the elevator to the first floor.
The small cafeteria was located at the rear
of the building and wasn't much more than
a glorified snack bar. All the salads were
prepackaged and lined up in a glass-front
cooler. Adisa selected one with tomatoes
that looked fresh, although she knew the
flavor would be vastly different from the
ones grown by Aunt Josie. They sat at a
table for two. Only one other person was
eating, a doctor who paid no attention to
them as he concentrated on his phone.
Reggie checked his watch.

"I need to eat fast if I'm going to see Deshaun and get back to the church for a one
thirty appointment."

Adisa carefully poured dressing over her
salad. She had little appetite but placed a
solitary cucumber slice in her mouth. It was
a notch above a piece of thin round cardboard.

"I have some big news," she said, trying to sound chatty. "I accepted a job this morning as an associate with Theo Grayson's law firm. He's the one I worked for when I was in high school. He knows about Aunt Josie's condition and is willing to be flexible with my hours."

"What about your job in Atlanta?"

Adisa gave him a quick summary. She could see him getting upset as he listened.

"I can't believe —" he started.

"Please, I'm trying to move on," Adisa said. "But I wanted you to know."

"Okay. I'm sorry for the way you were treated, but I'm glad you're going to be in Campbellton."

Adisa chewed and swallowed a tasteless bite of salad. "And handling a very challenging case."

"Can you tell me anything about it?"

Adisa stirred her salad around in the clear plastic box for a moment with a disposable fork. When she answered, she wanted her voice to sound calm with a hint of confidence.

"Part of my responsibilities at Theo Grayson's firm will include representing Officer Nelson in his criminal case," she said more rapidly than she wanted to.

"What?!" Reggie spoke so loudly the doc-

372

tor on his phone glanced over at them.

"You heard me," Adisa said, lowering her voice. "Mr. Grayson and I are going to serve as cocounsel for Officer Nelson."

"And your job will be to try to get him off for shooting Deshaun in the chest and head?" Reggie asked. "I can't believe what I'm hearing!"

"I knew you wouldn't understand," Adisa answered in a tone she feared sounded like an accusatory teenager. "But lawyers do things like this all the time. It's not about my personal feelings but about protecting someone's constitutional rights."

She stopped. Reggie simply stared at her. She suspected he didn't know what else to say.

"It doesn't mean I believe what the officer did was right or even justified," Adisa continued.

"This is crazy," Reggie said, pushing his chair away from the table.

"And I probably shouldn't have said that," she added quickly. "Please don't quote me about the Constitution since I can't discuss any aspect of the case due to attorney-client confidentiality rules."

"Quote you?" Reggie replied, still apparently struggling for words. "Why would I want anyone to know what you're doing?"

Adisa stabbed the salad with her fork so vigorously that one of the tines broke off. "I don't want to eat that," she said, picking up the white piece of plastic.

"Does your aunt know about this?"

"Yes, I told her this morning. Thelma Armistead's testimony at the church played a big part in my decision," Adisa said, preparing to lay out the whole sequence of events that influenced her.

"That's not a reason to do anything," Reggie cut her off. "I told you she's on shaky theological ground."

"And I'm not a theologian," Adisa answered. "But her words spoke to my heart, and along with some other events, everything fell into place. I believe I'm doing the right thing."

"If you defend the white officer, you can't expect me to defend you," Reggie said. "You're going to be on your own."

It took a lot to make Adisa mad, but the young minister's response lit the fuse of her temper. She felt her face get hot.

"It's going to look like a betrayal of your family," he continued. "And the inevitable reactions you'll face all over town will be terrible."

"Starting with you?" Adisa asked, her eyes flashing.

"Hey," Reggie said, holding up his hands. "I'm just being honest with you."

Adisa picked up her salad container, walked over to the trash receptacle, and threw it in. She left the snack bar without looking back.

Twenty-Three

Cindy Berman, the law firm administrator at Grayson, Baxter, and Williams, led Adisa down the hallway to a wood-paneled office that was twice as big as her space had been at Dixon and White. Two windows provided a nice view of the flowering bushes in the side yard of the building. There was a large wooden desk and a brand-new computer setup. A vase of fresh flowers rested on a side table between two leather conference chairs that faced the desk.

"This is gorgeous," Adisa said, standing still in the doorway. "How long has it been empty?"

"Oh, four or five years," Cindy answered. "The partners don't hire people just to take up space, but Mr. Grayson didn't waste time making up his mind about you. Congratulations."

Still stinging from her encounter with Reggie, Adisa managed a smile.

"Thanks," she said. "And I appreciate you getting this set up so quickly."

"There wasn't much to do except bring in the flowers. There's a new employee packet on the desk. Did Mr. Grayson go over any of that with you?"

"Nothing much except my salary and hours."

"It's self-explanatory, but let me know if you have any questions."

"I will."

Cindy left. Adisa walked around the office, touching the furniture and trying to acclimate to her new professional surroundings. She took a few quick photos of the office on her phone so she could show Aunt Josie and Shanika. She flipped through the employee information that was much less extensive than what she'd received at Dixon and White. She heard a light tap on her doorframe and glanced up. It was Theo Grayson.

"It's very nice," Adisa said before the older lawyer could ask. "And Cindy gave me the official employment paperwork to review and sign."

"Good," Grayson said, pressing his hands together. "Luke will be here in a little while, and we'll walk over to the courthouse."

"Okay. What about the files from Mr. Williams?"

"Mike is in Atlanta this afternoon but wants to meet with you first thing in the morning. His paralegal is preparing and prioritizing a list of matters that need attention."

"I look forward to jumping in," Adisa said.

"There will be challenges, but Mike and I talked about how you may be able to bring us more fully into modern practices. We're excited and hope you are, too."

Adisa hesitated before she answered. "The negative reactions to my involvement in the Nelson case have already started," she said.

"Who?" Grayson asked, a puzzled look on his face. "I sent over a brief press release to the newspaper, but nothing will be public about your involvement until tomorrow."

"Aunt Josie was fine, but I told a new friend, and he let me have it."

"I'm sorry," Grayson replied. "I'm going to defend your decision every chance I get."

"And I appreciate it," Adisa said, recognizing the stark contrast between the positions of the white lawyer and the black preacher. "But the gaps in the bridge on this issue are so huge that I don't feel capable of bringing the two sides together."

"All you can control is your own response," Grayson said. "That's what De-shaun's grandmother did, and look at the effect it had on you."

Adisa nodded. "True. And I need to keep her words in the forefront of my mind."

Adisa, Theo Grayson, and Luke Nelson crossed the street and walked down the sidewalk toward the courthouse. Adisa knew it was the first of many times the three of them would make the short journey. Unlike the day before when the grand jury had issued its indictment, no one paid special attention to them. Adisa felt nervous but tried to relax.

The main floor of the courthouse was empty, and they walked directly upstairs to the judge's chambers. In Atlanta, they already would have passed at least two levels of security and multiple metal detectors. In Nash County, September 11 had happened far, far away.

"This courthouse is completely unprotected," she observed.

"They only operate the metal detectors on days the judges are sitting on the bench," Grayson replied.

They reached Judge Andrews's chambers and the first level of security. The door to the area where the judge worked was locked.

Grayson pressed a button for an intercom. A woman's voice answered and Grayson responded.

"Theo Grayson, Luke Nelson, and Adisa Johnson, a new lawyer with our firm, here to see the judge."

The door buzzed, and Grayson held it open for the others to enter a small waiting area with only two chairs. Sitting in one of them was Jasper Baldwin, the district attorney. He stood to shake Theo Grayson's hand and gave Adisa a puzzled look.

"Ms. Johnson," the DA said. "What brings you here?"

"She's graciously accepted a job offer with our firm," Grayson cut in. "And she will be cocounsel with me in Officer Nelson's case."

"What?!" Baldwin exploded. "So all the talk about coming to work with my office so you could prosecute Officer Nelson was a sham. I'm going to let the judge know about this conduct and request that you be held in contempt of court!"

The judge's secretary, who was watching the conversation with wide eyes, picked up the phone, which had buzzed.

"He'll see you now," she said.

Baldwin shot past them into the judge's chambers. Grayson followed. Luke touched Adisa on the arm and held her back.

"What's he talking about?"

"I'll explain it later," Adisa said in a hushed voice. "But Mr. Grayson and I haven't done anything wrong."

The judge's office was modestly furnished with a scratched-up wooden desk facing six chairs. A long wooden bookcase filled with old books covered one wall. The judge, a trim, athletic man in his fifties with sandy hair mixed with gray, was sitting behind his desk.

"Your Honor," Baldwin said, his voice still filled with emotion. "Before we go any further, I need to report to the Court a serious breach of professionalism and ethics by Mr. Grayson and Ms. Johnson."

"And who is Ms. Johnson?" the judge asked.

Grayson introduced Adisa to the judge, who shook her hand and motioned for everyone to sit down. Grayson positioned himself next to Baldwin, with Adisa to his right and Luke next to her.

"Do you need a court reporter to transcribe this?" the judge asked.

"Yes," Baldwin immediately responded.

"Fine with me," Grayson replied.

"Meet me in the main courtroom in five minutes," the judge said. "Ms. Dixon will need time to set up her machine."

The judge grabbed his robe as the lawyers and Luke left his chambers.

"I can't believe you'd pull a stunt like this," Baldwin said to Grayson as soon as they were back in the reception area.

"We'll see you in the courtroom," Grayson replied evenly.

"What's he talking about?" Luke asked again as the DA stormed off.

Grayson began to speak, but Adisa jumped in first. "When you met me the other day, I was talking to the DA about coming to work for his office. We discussed a job that would have included prosecuting you, but I decided I should work with Mr. Grayson and help you for the reasons I told you yesterday. Mr. Baldwin and I didn't discuss the facts of your case, so I don't believe I broke any ethical rules."

"How can I trust someone who wanted to prosecute me?" Luke asked. "If Jane and I had known that —"

"Adisa made her choice, and I'm satisfied with how she went about it," Grayson said. "It will be up to us to prove that to you and your wife."

Luke didn't respond.

"We can't talk about this right now," Grayson said. "We need to get to the court-room."

The main courtroom in the Nash County Courthouse had a 1950s look with high ceilings covered in soundproof tiles, plain white walls, and rows of long, utilitarian brown benches. It was a room designed not for aesthetics or to create an atmosphere of judicial solemnity but to accommodate a large crowd of people on jury selection and criminal arraignment days. When empty it seemed especially sterile.

Judge Andrews wasn't on the bench, but the court reporter was setting up. Jasper Baldwin was seated at the table used by the prosecution in criminal cases. Adisa hadn't been in the courtroom since she interned for Theo Grayson. The space that once seemed majestic and overwhelming to a high schooler now looked pedestrian and dull. The judge, wearing his black robe, took his place on the bench. Baldwin immediately rose to his feet.

"Call *State v. Nelson,*" the judge said without any preamble. "Mr. Baldwin, I understand there's a matter you want to bring up with the Court."

"Yes, sir. The day the grand jury issued its indictment charging Officer Nelson with aggravated assault in the shooting of Deshaun Hamlin, Ms. Adisa Johnson spoke privately with me and asked me to consider hiring her to serve as special prosecutor in the case. The next day, she called and left a voice message informing me that she'd decided not to pursue the job. At no time did she notify me that she was, in fact, going to join Mr. Grayson's firm and become cocounsel for the defendant. Her deceptive efforts to obtain inside information from me about this case and the charges against Officer Nelson should disqualify her from representation. I therefore move the Court to issue an order removing her from the case and imposing any additional sanctions you deem warranted. I will also be filing a formal complaint against Ms. Johnson with the state bar association."

While Baldwin spoke, Adisa shifted and fidgeted in her chair like a third grader counting down the seconds until recess. As soon as Baldwin sat down, she prepared to stand up and defend herself but felt a surprisingly strong grip on her left arm from Grayson, who kept her in her seat.

"I'll speak to this issue, Your Honor," the older lawyer said, rising to his feet.

Adisa bit her lip to keep from talking.

"Even if everything Mr. Baldwin says is true, it doesn't support removal of Ms. Johnson," Grayson said. "The DA didn't talk about the merits of the case with her.

Their conversation focused on the possibility of a job for her as special prosecutor. If Your Honor wants to receive testimony on any aspect of the discussion, Ms. Johnson is present and willing to answer any and all questions from you or Mr. Baldwin."

Adisa quickly started to mentally run through every detail she could remember from her time in Baldwin's office.

"Mr. Baldwin," the judge said, "will you state in your place that everything you've represented to the Court is true and correct to the best of your knowledge and belief?"

"Yes, Your Honor," the DA replied.

"Very well. There's no need for testimony from Ms. Johnson. I'll take the motion under advisement and notify the parties of my decision by five o'clock tomorrow afternoon. This hearing is adjourned."

The judge left the courtroom. As soon as he was gone, the DA turned to Adisa, Grayson, and Luke.

"That may be the way you've learned to practice law in Atlanta," he said to Adisa, "but that's not the way it's done in Nash County."

The DA stormed out of the courtroom. Luke looked at Grayson and Adisa and asked a question Adisa didn't anticipate.

"Why did we come here to see the judge

in the first place?" he asked.

"He wanted to discuss scheduling your arraignment, timing for discovery, whether to allow cameras in the courtroom, and how long it would be before the case might be ready for trial," Grayson answered. "But one thing about being a trial lawyer is that the unexpected always happens."

"And I didn't count on being represented by an attorney who was looking for a job to prosecute me," Luke said to Adisa.

"That's why I went into such detail about it with you and your wife the other day," Adisa replied patiently. "But if after hearing the DA's allegations you don't want me involved, I'll understand."

"Why don't we wait on discussing that until Judge Andrews rules on the DA's motion to disqualify Adisa," Grayson interjected.

"If he grants it, I won't hold you to the job offer with your firm," Adisa said to Grayson.

"Understood," the older lawyer replied.

Luke held back and let Grayson and Adisa leave the courtroom ahead of him. The behind-the-scenes chaos with the lawyers had seriously shaken his confidence. Adisa was unknown to him, but he'd not questioned Mr. Grayson's judgment. Until now.

Grayson and Adisa had their heads together as they walked down the hallway outside the courtroom. Luke stepped closer.

"Remember," Grayson was saying to Adisa, "I told you I was going to defend your involvement in the case. I just didn't think the attack would be from this angle."

"And is this going to take time away from working on my case?" Luke asked as they reached the top of the stairs.

"This is a minor hiccup," Grayson replied. "The judge will deny the motion."

They exited the courthouse with Grayson and Adisa still talking about what had just happened.

"I'll let you go ahead," Luke said to the two lawyers. "I have an errand to run downtown."

"Sure," Grayson replied, briefly turning away from Adisa. "We'll be in touch."

Luke walked directly to the law offices of Fillmore and Dudley. He entered an empty reception area. A middle-aged woman behind a desk was filing her nails but quickly sat up straighter when he approached.

"I don't have an appointment," Luke began. "But I'd like to either talk to Mr. Fillmore or leave a message for him to call me."

"Your name, please?" the woman asked.

"Luke Nelson. I'm a police officer —"

"Oh, I know who you are. Let me inform Mr. Fillmore that you're here."

Luke left an hour later. Sam Fillmore was a chubby lawyer with a baby face. Luke had seen him many times in court handling criminal cases and decided it wouldn't hurt to get a second opinion. When Luke told him what had just happened in court, Fillmore got so excited he knocked over a cup of coffee, spattering Luke's khaki pants.

"Good thing they're already brown," Fillmore quipped as he buzzed his assistant and told her to bring in a paper towel. "I hate to talk negatively about a brother at the bar, but it sounds like Theo Grayson is trying to dump your case into the lap of a rookie lawyer who barely knows her way to the courthouse."

"How many felony cases have you tried to a verdict?" Luke asked.

"Oh, I lost track of that a long time ago."

"What about since I joined the police force about a year and a half ago?"

Fillmore paused. "It's been a slow spell, except for a ton of DUIs, but that just means I can't wait to scratch the courtroom itch and sink my teeth into a case that has meat on the bone."

Luke wasn't sure he wanted Fillmore to either scratch or gnaw at his expense. "Thanks for taking the time to talk to me. I appreciate you seeing me without an appointment."

"It was perfect timing," the lawyer replied. "Make the switch soon. The longer you let Theo and his new associate mess up your case, the harder it will be to build a solid defense. And I'm not intimidated by negative public opinion. If a lawyer is a fighter, even the people he beats up respect him and hire him when they get the chance."

"How much would you charge?"

"It depends. What is Mr. Grayson charging you?"

Luke hesitated. It didn't feel right to reveal the nominal fee.

"It doesn't matter," Fillmore continued. "Representing you is better than a year's worth of Internet advertising. Theo wants to build up business for this young black lawyer and doesn't mind using you to do it."

"Let me think about it," Luke replied.

"Are you going to talk to any other lawyers?"

"I was considering Fred Bentley. I know he's at the courthouse a lot and seems to have almost as many cases on the docket as the public defender's office."

Fillmore shook his head. "Don't get sucked into the hype that Freddie will dump on you. He's made so many people mad at the DA's office they won't agree to a recess so he can go to the bathroom."

"I thought being a fighter was good."

"You have to fight smart," Fillmore said as he tapped the side of his head. "And make every blow count. I'll pile the motions up to the ceiling in the DA's office without letting them know which ones are for real."

"Doesn't that make the judges mad?"

"They get over it," Fillmore replied with a wave of his hand. "But it will make Jasper Baldwin and his lazy assistants work, which is the one thing they hate more than anything else. When they see my name on the pleadings in your case, they'll be on the phone trying to work something out."

"I'm not interested in a plea bargain," Luke replied.

"Of course. That's just an illustration."

Luke left, partly impressed but significantly unsettled.

He arrived at the house in time to watch Jane spoon the final bite of supper into Ashley's mouth.

"Well?" Jane asked hopefully. "How did it go? You were gone a long time."

"I felt like I was in a pinball machine getting knocked all over the place."

Aunt Josie finished brushing her own teeth right before Dr. Dewberry entered the room and briskly approached the bed.

"Ms. Adams, I'm putting your picture on the wall of my office," he announced.

"I know I'm good-looking," Aunt Josie said with a smile, "but I've lost some of my luster since I've been in here."

Dr. Dewberry patted the older woman on the arm and looked at Adisa. "Your aunt is exceeding every goal in therapy, and while it's great that she's improving, it forces us to discuss where she needs to go from here. I can't justify ongoing hospitalization."

Adisa told him about accepting the job with Grayson, Baxter, and Williams.

"If Adisa is going to be living in Campbellton, does that mean I can go home?" Aunt Josie asked the doctor hopefully.

"Only if you can make arrangements for someone to be with you during the day while Adisa is at work. Would you be spending the night at your aunt's house?" he asked Adisa.

"If she'll have me."

"Hush, child. That house and everything I have is yours."

"Theo Grayson understands my personal situation with Aunt Josie and is going to work with me," Adisa said. "I'm going to fill in for Mike Williams while he's out of the office for a couple of months and back up Mr. Grayson in a big criminal case he's taking on. I'm going to make arrangements in the next few days to empty my apartment in Atlanta and move everything into a storage unit in Campbellton."

The doctor's eyes went from Aunt Josie to Adisa and back to his patient. "Ms. Adams, I'd prefer sending you to a skilled nursing facility for several weeks, but we can give this a try if that's what you want to do," he said.

"Yes!" Aunt Josie said as strongly as her voice allowed. "And I'll work so hard to get better that I'll prove you made the right decision."

"Okay, I'll write orders for regular visits by skilled care providers to assess your status. It won't be safe for you to be alone in a house for more than an hour or so, at least in the beginning."

After the doctor left, Adisa took her tablet from her purse and opened it to a blank screen. "We have our own business to tend to — finding a caretaker who can stay with you during the day. Shanika already crossed

Mary Broome off the list."

"Mary is a friend, but I agree with Shanika," Aunt Josie said. "I'd like to hire someone from my church, but there aren't many young people in the congregation or folks looking for a job. Why don't we ask Reggie if he knows someone who would be interested in helping out?"

"No," Adisa said. "I'm not sure Reggie's a good referral source."

"Why not?"

Adisa didn't want to go into an explanation of why she and the young preacher had a falling-out. She scrambled to come up with an explanation that wouldn't upset Aunt Josie yet would stay within the boundaries of the truth.

"He hasn't lived here that long. Let me check with Horace Bramblett at the AME Church."

"Most of his members are older than I am!" Aunt Josie answered.

"Then I'll go to someone else."

"I still think Reggie should be at the top of the list," Aunt Josie grumbled. "And if you don't ask him, I will the next time he comes to visit."

Adisa successfully avoided the topic of Reggie Reynolds for the rest of the evening.

But she knew eventually she'd have to tell Aunt Josie what happened.

TWENTY-FOUR

When Luke woke up in the morning, Jane's spot in the bed was empty. He peeked into Ashley's room. The little girl was asleep in her crib with her favorite blanket tucked beneath her chin.

"I'm in here," Jane called out softly when he stepped back into the hallway.

Luke went into the rarely used living room. Jane, her pillow under her head, was lying on her back on a secondhand sofa given to them by her mother. A cream-colored sheet covered her legs and feet.

"How long have you been here?" Luke asked. "Did I snore?"

"Not since pollen season ended," Jane replied. "But I couldn't sleep after our talk about what happened at the courthouse and didn't want to wake you by thrashing around in bed."

Before the shooting, Luke had been a sound sleeper. Even fatherhood hadn't sensitized him to Ashley's whimpers. He sat at the end of the couch and briefly massaged Jane's right foot, waiting until she made eye contact with him.

"Our lives are totally out of our control right now," Jane continued. "And I don't know who to trust."

"Mr. Grayson assured me that he is going to be in charge —"

"Luke," Jane cut in. "Be realistic. It's great that Mr. Grayson says he wants to help, but the other lawyer you talked to about your case is right. Ms. Johnson is going to end up being the one who represents you. That's the way it works. The older lawyer passes a case down to a younger lawyer, especially for a client who isn't going to pay his way financially."

Luke shifted uneasily. "I don't think that's going to happen," he said.

"It will." Jane looked directly at him. "And God help us if Ms. Johnson doesn't do her job. I had a sense she was reluctant to get involved when we met with her, and now I know why. I bet she'll try to convince you to accept a plea bargain the first chance she gets."

Luke was usually the suspicious, guarded one in the marriage. Seeing Jane in that role was unsettling.

"Do you think I should follow up with Mr. Fillmore? He really wants to represent me."

"I don't know." Jane pulled the sheet up beneath her chin and looked at Luke with sad eyes that made his heart ache. "But I wish I could wake up and find out this has all been a horrible nightmare."

Adisa came out of her meeting with Mike Williams impressed with the corporate lawyer's clients and the breadth of legal services he provided. Even in the short time Adisa had practiced in Atlanta, she'd bought into the theory that only attorneys who worked for big firms in the city functioned at the highest levels of competency. Although Mike's clients weren't multibillion-dollar companies, they still faced serious challenges, but on a smaller scale.

"I can't wait to get started," Adisa said when he finished describing one project that required the kind of technical forensic accounting she loved.

Mike, a tall, slender man in his late forties with a head of curly brown hair and blue eyes, chuckled.

"I never thought I'd hear a lawyer speak those words," he said. "But it's music to me. The ability to keep some of that work in the firm instead of farming it out to CPAs is going to be good for revenue and help us keep closer tabs on what's going on."

"That's my passion," Adisa replied. "I love any kind of puzzle."

"I didn't see this side of you when you interned that summer in high school," Mike replied. "You were a serious, earnest young woman, but you were so quiet it was hard to tell what was going on inside your head. You spent all your time grinding away on research projects with your eyes glued to the computer."

"I still like working by myself when possible. I can be around people for a while and then I need to get away and recharge."

"That's going to be tough working with Theo. He's the ultimate people person."

"I know."

Mike closed the cover of his laptop. "My wife and I leave on our trip in two weeks. Let's do all we can to iron out the kinks before that happens."

"What about the Nelson criminal case?" Adisa began. "How should I allocate my time?"

"*State v. Nelson* gets first priority. Just try to be efficient in structuring your workload."

"Okay."

Grayson was out of the office all morning for a meeting with a client, and Adisa used the time to begin working on the files Mike had given her. The hours flew by, and it was close to noon before she took a break. Leaving the office, she grabbed a Reuben sandwich at a deli. She reached the hospital the same time as the delivery driver for the *Campbellton News,* who was restocking the container at the front door.

Tapping her foot nervously, Adisa waited for him to finish and then immediately purchased a paper. She quickly scanned the front page. There was no story about Luke's case, Mr. Grayson, or her. Apparently, news that the local chicken processing plant was going to be closed longer than usual for a USDA inspection ranked higher than information about the most high-profile criminal case on the superior court docket. She flipped through the paper. At the bottom of the next to last page was a notice without a byline that quoted verbatim the three-sentence press release prepared by Theo Grayson announcing her association with the law firm as cocounsel in the Nelson case. Until now, she'd never considered herself an advocate for press censorship, but she couldn't help wishing she could instantly become invisible at any mention of Luke's case.

Adisa folded the paper and slipped it

beneath her arm as she walked to the elevators. She arrived at the same time as a middle-aged black couple she didn't recognize. The woman glanced over at her and then leaned over to whisper to her husband.

"Excuse me," the woman said. "Aren't you Adisa Johnson?"

"Yes," Adisa answered.

"I thought I recognized you," the woman said. "Josephine Adams is your aunt, isn't she?"

"That's right. I'm on my way to visit her now."

"We're here to see Deshaun Hamlin, the boy who was shot by the white police officer," the woman continued. "He goes to my church."

The elevator opened, and the three of them entered.

"How do you know my aunt?" Adisa asked.

"From the garden club. We're in it with Thelma Armistead, Deshaun's grandmother. Anyway, when everyone brought in pictures of their grandchildren, Josie brought in photos of you and your sister. In one of them she was with you when you graduated from law school."

Adisa remembered the picture. Wearing a new dress, Aunt Josie beamed with pride as they stood together in front of a massive oak tree.

"How's she doing?" the woman continued. "I heard about her stroke, but someone said she's doing better now."

"Yes. We hope she'll be released to come home soon."

"Great. Tell her Sissy Forrest asked about her."

"I will."

The elevator opened. Adisa pushed the button to keep the door from closing.

"And keep praying for Deshaun. He's off the ventilator, which is great news. But the policeman who shot him has hired a big-shot lawyer who will pull every string to get him off the hook. God's people can't let that happen."

Pressing the newspaper more firmly beneath her arm, Adisa got off the elevator and let the door close behind her.

Aunt Josie was awake and sitting up in bed when Adisa entered the room.

"That smells yummy," Aunt Josie said, eyeing Adisa's sandwich. "Is that sauerkraut?"

"Yes, I picked up a Reuben at the deli on Market Street. But I'm sure the sauerkraut isn't as good as what you make with the cabbage from your garden."

"Let me have a little bite anyway," the older woman said.

"What about your lunch? It's past time for them to bring it to you."

"It's come and gone, leaving me half starving."

"I don't believe that," Adisa said with a smile. "But I'll be glad to share with you so long as you don't take too big a bite and choke."

Adisa took the sandwich from the bag and carefully cut off several baby-size bites. She handed one to Aunt Josie, who took it in her left hand and put it in her mouth.

"That's something that will cause my taste buds to wake up," Aunt Josie said as she slowly chewed.

Adisa took a bite and handed another tiny piece to her aunt.

"I saw a woman named Sissy Forrest in the elevator," Adisa said. "She told me to tell you hello."

"She's in the garden club. She and her husband moved to Campbellton from Villa Rica a couple of years ago."

"She goes to Reggie's church and said they've been praying for you."

"I'm not surprised," Aunt Josie replied. "I had the best visit with Reggie. He left about half an hour ago. I tried to get him to stay,

402

but with your new job I didn't know when you'd be here."

Adisa didn't say anything. She'd doubted the minister would come by after their blowup in the hospital cafeteria. She handed Aunt Josie another tiny bite of sandwich and cut off two more for later. The satisfaction the older woman was receiving from the food made Adisa want to give her all of it.

"But you can see him on Sunday," Aunt Josie continued before putting the bite in her mouth.

"What do you mean?" Adisa asked.

Aunt Josie shook her head while she chewed. Adisa waited impatiently.

"Eat," Aunt Josie said when she finally swallowed the food. "And please hand me something to drink."

"I'm not going to Reggie's church on Sunday," Adisa said.

"You have to," Aunt Josie replied. "He's getting together a list of women who might be interested in staying with me at the house while you're at work. He knows a bunch of reliable folks who need to make extra money. I knew we should have gone to him first."

"But why do I have to go to his church?" Adisa protested. "He can drop off the list, and we'll interview them here at the hospital or at home if you're released before the weekend."

"Go to church, child!" Aunt Josie retorted. "And give me another bite of sandwich. That sauerkraut is strong enough that I'd better brush my teeth again before the nurse comes in to check my vitals. Otherwise she's likely to faint when she catches a whiff of my breath."

When she returned to the office, Adisa completed her review of one of Mike Williams's cases, typed a memo, and sent it to the corporate lawyer. She was deep into her research regarding potential experts in the Nelson case when there was a knock on her door. It was Theo Grayson.

"Let's go," he said rapidly to Adisa. "Judge Andrews wanted us in his chambers with Jasper Baldwin half an hour ago."

"In chambers?" Adisa asked, getting up from her chair. "I thought he was going to call and tell us how he was going to rule."

"He hasn't and don't ask me why he wants to see our faces."

Grayson looked flustered. "This has been a tough day," the older lawyer said. "A judge in Clarke County chopped off my client's head and handed it on a platter to the other side in a motion hearing, and it's going to take a trip to the court of appeals to see if I can get it sewn back on. That's why I'm late."

As they walked across the street, Adisa considered trying to tell him about her memo on expert witnesses, but there wasn't time to explain where she was in the process, and she didn't want to leave anything out. They walked up the steps and entered the courthouse.

"Let me do the talking," Grayson said as they climbed to the second floor. "Unless, of course, the judge asks you a specific question."

"I'm counting on you to defend me," Adisa replied.

Grayson rewarded her with a wry smile. "A promise is a promise," he said.

They reached the judge's chambers and entered. As soon as the secretary saw them, she picked up the phone and notified Jasper Baldwin that they'd arrived. The DA came in a couple of minutes later. The secretary knocked on the door to the judge's office and motioned for them to enter.

Judge Andrews was sitting behind his desk with his robe on a wall hook. "Sit where you like," he said as soon as the three lawyers entered.

The DA brought up the rear and shut the door.

"I'm not happy with the way this case has started," the judge said. "We all know how volatile these situations are across the country, and now it's come to Campbell-ton. That means I don't want any extraneous activity going on that fuels the fire of public unrest."

Adisa wasn't sure where the judge was heading with his comments.

"Is that clear?" he asked.

"Yes, sir," Baldwin replied. "I'm here to do the job the citizens of Nash County elected me to do."

"Yes, Your Honor," Grayson replied. "It's our intention to limit publicity and focus on the case. I'm not seeking notoriety to build a criminal defense practice, and Ms. John-son is in Campbellton on a temporary basis to help care for a great-aunt who's suffered a stroke."

"Good," the judge replied and then glanced down at a folder open on his desk. "I've considered Mr. Baldwin's motion to disqualify Ms. Johnson, and while I find the timing of her conduct professionally ques-tionable, it does not warrant removal from the case if the defendant wants to retain her services."

"Thank you, Judge," Grayson replied.

Adisa glanced at Baldwin, whose face was impassive.

"Unless either side objects, I'm going to ban cameras from the courtroom at all stages of the proceedings against Officer Nelson," the judge continued. "Are either of you aware of any requests from the media to be present?"

"No," both Grayson and Baldwin replied.

Adisa suspected that level of statewide interest in the case wouldn't develop unless Deshaun died. She offered a quick, silent prayer for the young man's continued improvement.

"What is the condition of the young man who was shot?" the judge asked.

Baldwin spoke. "I've not had any contact with the family for over a week, but —"

"He's still in a coma," Adisa cut in. "But I understand he's been taken off the ventilator and is breathing on his own."

The judge raised his eyebrows and looked at her in surprise. "What is the basis for your information?" he asked.

Adisa now regretted speaking up. "As Mr. Grayson mentioned, my great-aunt is in the hospital, so I've been spending time there," she said, trying to sound matter-of-fact. "I saw a friend of Deshaun's family in the elevator earlier today, and she passed along the good news."

"Very well," the judge replied, turning his attention back to Grayson and Baldwin.

"I'm going to make sure the defendant's right to a speedy trial takes place," the judge continued. "If either the State or defense counsel starts dragging out this case, you'll find me strongly encouraging you to keep moving. If a nudge doesn't work, I won't hesitate to resort to other means. How soon can the State comply with the criminal discovery statute?"

"As soon as the defense files the necessary requests," Baldwin replied.

"Good. I'm going to set a morning arraignment for a week from Monday. Mr. Baldwin, are you satisfied with the current level of the defendant's bond?"

"Yes, unless there's a change in circumstances."

"Does either side anticipate use of expert witnesses? If so, I want to get that process started."

"The treating doctors who will testify about the extent of injury caused by the gunshot wounds," Baldwin replied.

"Mr. Grayson?" the judge asked.

"Not at this —"

"If Dr. Steiner removes the bullet from

Deshaun's head, we'd like to have it examined by a ballistics expert along with the bullet that passed through the young man's body," Adisa said.

"Right," Grayson said, correcting himself.

"And it will also be necessary for the defense to call an expert to testify as to proper police conduct under similar circumstances," Adisa added.

"We'll address that issue, too," Baldwin responded.

"There may be the need for a reconstruction expert to evaluate the scene and testify about setting and conditions the night of the shooting," Adisa said. "Things look different at night than they do during the day."

The judge leaned forward slightly. "Ms. Johnson, there's no need for a witness to testify that the sun sets in the west and it gets dark soon thereafter. Did you hear what I said earlier about not engaging in obstructionist behavior to delay this case moving forward?"

"Yes, Your Honor, but you asked about experts, and I thought it would be my obligation —"

"For you and Mr. Grayson to get on the same page," the judge interrupted. "I realize we're early in the proceeding, but for the reasons I stated earlier, I expect this case to receive top priority by the State and the defense. Give me a status report on experts after the arraignment on Monday."

As soon as Adisa and Grayson exited the courthouse, the older lawyer turned to her.

"It would have helped if you'd given me a heads-up about the outside witnesses you want to testify in the case," he said.

"It's in a memo I was working on while you were in Clarke County but couldn't give you because we had to rush over here."

"I'd like to read it before I leave the office today."

"Yes, sir. I'll finish it as soon as I'm at my desk."

They waited for a traffic light to change and crossed the street.

"And who's going to pay for these witnesses?" Grayson asked as soon as they were on the other side of the roadway. "Hired guns to talk in court are expensive."

"Maybe Luke can come up with the money for that part of the case since we're only charging him one dollar to represent him."

"If he's not willing to foot the bill for outside help, then we'll do without it," Grayson replied.

Adisa didn't say anything else during the rest of the short walk to the office. Grayson didn't need any more prodding or poking from her. Everyone was entitled to be grumpy from time to time.

Luke and Jane loaded Ashley and the food for their picnic into the car.

"Maybe we should drive to Mexico and continue to a Central or South American country that doesn't have an extradition treaty with the US," Luke suggested.

"I'd prefer Badin Lake," Jane replied with a weak smile.

Knowing his attempt at dark humor had fallen flat, Luke was silent during the first part of the thirty-mile trip to the state park. Because it was a weekday, the picnic area beside the small lake was deserted. Jane threw a white sheet over a concrete table, and Luke put Ashley's high chair at the end where the little girl could see the water.

"Leave everything in the cooler for a few minutes," Luke said to Jane.

"It's past time for Ashley to eat, and your stomach is like a clock that goes off at noon," Jane responded.

"I know, but let's walk around the lake first. I'll push Ashley in her stroller. She'll be distracted by the new sights, and both of us will forget about our stomachs."

Jane put a floppy hat on Ashley's head to

protect her from the sun. The path around the lake was flat and covered in tiny pea gravel.

"They designed this with strollers in mind," Luke said when they'd taken a few steps. "It's not bad at all."

Jane came alongside him and pushed a few strands of hair away from her face. She lightly placed her hand on Luke's shoulder. He glanced at her and smiled. The path wound its way through a grove of hardwood trees. Luke heard a loud *plop* at the edge of the water.

"There goes a frog," he said. "I wish I could catch one and show it to Ashley."

"She wouldn't appreciate it for another year or so," Jane replied. "I would be afraid she'd try to put it in her mouth."

Luke pushed a little harder as the stroller rolled over a root that had invaded the path.

"I wonder where I'll be in another year or so," he said.

"Please, Luke," Jane said. "That's not why I brought it up."

"I know, but it's something we should talk about. One of the mistakes we've made so far is ignoring what might happen, which makes it twice as tough to deal with when it does."

Jane didn't reply. She walked beside him

with her head down.

"If things don't go well, I want you to leave Campbellton and move in with your mother," he said. "Orlando is such a big place that no one will care who you are or ask where your husband is. And if it ever came up, you could say I'm working in Georgia, because the prison officials will have me cutting right-of-way along the highways. As a former cop, I wouldn't be safe with the general prison population. I've heard they have dorms in some facilities where they keep prisoners who would be at risk of being attacked."

"I appreciate you trying to plan ahead," Jane said. "But I'd rather make this a getaway day."

"Okay," he replied. "So long as you don't ever forget that I love you and Ashley."

Jane slipped her arm through his and gave his strong bicep a squeeze. "No matter what happens, I know that will always be true."

They made their way around the lake. Close to the picnic table, a frog hopped out of the weeds near the edge of the water. Ashley saw it and squealed with delight as it plopped into the pond.

"See, she likes frogs," Luke said. "Now I know what to buy her for Christmas. Stuffed, not live, of course."

"And we'll both watch her open the package as we sit around the tree in our house," Jane said resolutely.

TWENTY-FIVE

Adisa stopped by the Jackson House Restaurant and ordered a four-vegetable plate to go. Ten minutes later she was on her way to the hospital with the fragrance of sweet potatoes, creamed corn, collard greens, okra, tomatoes, and two fresh pieces of corn bread filling the inside of her car. She fully intended to share what she could with Aunt Josie, but the idea of letting the older woman eat most of the collard greens was difficult to accept. When she entered the elevator and turned around, she caught a glimpse of Thelma Armistead approaching. Adisa tried to push the button to reopen the doors but couldn't maneuver the heavy Styrofoam container of food in time to do so.

Aunt Josie was sitting up in bed with Dr. Dewberry standing beside her.

"You're just in time for the good news!" Aunt Josie exclaimed. "Tomorrow is freedom day! I'm going home!"

Adisa glanced at Dr. Dewberry.

"You're a lawyer, so you know about a trial," the neurologist said. "For this one you're going to have to be the jury and give me a verdict on how your aunt functions and any problems that come up. I'm arranging for an occupational therapist to make sure the house is set up to accommodate Ms. Adams's restrictions, and I'll write an order for a physical therapist to work with her on increasing her mobility, manual dexterity, and strength. It's going to take a lot of hard work."

"That's all I've ever known," Aunt Josie said exuberantly. "And you know I'm going to do my part."

"I don't doubt that for a moment," the doctor replied with a smile. "I wish all my patients had your grit and determination."

"We're in the process of finding someone to stay with her during the day," Adisa said.

"That's what she told me. It needs to be someone strong enough to help if she trips or falls. She's been ambulating better here in the hospital, but she's going to be at risk for the foreseeable future. She needs to respect what her body tells her about limitations."

Aunt Josie raised her right hand and made

an attempt at a military salute but ended up poking herself in the eye.

"That's an example of trying to do too much," the doctor said. "Your right hand is still more like a puppet on a string."

"What time will she be discharged?" Adisa asked.

"Midmorning."

"And you should call Reggie as soon as possible about someone who can come to the house and help us."

Dr. Dewberry reached over and patted Aunt Josie on the arm. "I'll stop by again early in the morning, and my office will be in touch about scheduling a follow-up appointment."

The doctor turned to leave and then stopped and faced them. "Oh, one other thing. I know you've both been interested in how Deshaun Hamlin is progressing. He's in prep for surgery. In a few hours Dr. Steiner is going to try to remove the bullet that's lodged in his brain."

After Dr. Dewberry left, Aunt Josie immediately closed her eyes and prayed for Deshaun.

"It's in God's hands," she said when she finished. "And I believe that the Lord's angels will assist with the surgery."

Adisa nodded.

"Now, let me guess what's in the box without looking," Aunt Josie said. "Put it on the hospital tray but don't raise the lid."

Adisa placed the container on the narrow rolling table. Aunt Josie inhaled several times.

"Are you planning on sharing this food with me, or are you going to torture me by making me watch you eat it?" the older woman asked.

"Torture wasn't a consideration, but I'm starving. And you've been eating and snacking all day."

"Don't insult the collard greens, sweet potatoes, stewed tomatoes, and corn bread from the Jackson House you've brought by comparing them to what they've put in front of me here at the hospital. Am I right?"

"Mostly. There's also creamed corn, and it's okra and tomatoes, not stewed tomatoes."

"Even better."

The older woman ate slowly, and Adisa did the same to make sure she didn't eat too much before Aunt Josie received all she wanted.

"Feed yourself," Aunt Josie insisted. "Don't wait on me. I'm such a slowpoke."

"No, this is fine. Let me cut some more collard greens for you."

"That sounds so strange," Aunt Josie replied. "Who in the world cuts collard greens with a knife?"

Adisa divided the stringy vegetable so that Aunt Josie could take smaller bites. The older woman chewed contentedly.

"Tell me about your job," she said when she swallowed. "How are you getting along?"

Adisa filled her in on what she could in general terms. While she talked, Aunt Josie focused on eating creamed corn.

"Has anybody been hateful to you for agreeing to help represent the officer who shot Thelma's grandson?" Aunt Josie asked.

Adisa hesitated.

"Oh, I already know about Reggie," Aunt Josie continued. "He's like most men who spout off at the mouth before their minds are in gear."

"What did he say to you?" Adisa asked in surprise.

"He told me about the two of you getting into a spat at the hospital snack bar."

"Did he seem sorry about it?"

"No." Aunt Josie shook her head. "He was trying to convince me that he was right and I should jump on his side and pressure you to quit the case."

"That's not right!" Adisa replied, her voice

rising. "He should leave you out of this."

Aunt Josie touched the side of her head. "In Reggie's mind, he believes he'll be doing you a favor. I started to tell him how stubborn you could be but decided that wouldn't do any good."

"Shanika is the stubborn one."

"Maybe," Aunt Josie slowly admitted. "But once you set your mind, you're determined to move forward. Remember, just because two of God's children disagree about one thing doesn't mean they can't talk about other things."

"That's true, but I don't want to listen to him accuse me of betraying my roots. These things are more complicated than he's willing to admit. It's not just about the color of someone's skin."

"If you want to stamp out prejudice, there has to be an admission that it exists."

Adisa thought about her preliminary effort to confront Luke. The officer wasn't willing to seriously consider that he might have erred in firing his weapon at Deshaun, much less dig out any slivers of latent racism that influenced his finger pulling the trigger. Aunt Josie pointed at her skinny, dark right forearm.

"I've taken this arm with me my whole life, and its color has made a difference in how folks look at me and treat me. I can't change that, and I hope the hardships I've faced have made me stronger. But God looks at the heart. Reggie knows that's true in his spirit; he just needs to apply it. Be patient with him. Politicians and people on TV are pretty good at talking about problems, but they're pitiful when it comes to solutions." Aunt Josie pointed to the ceiling with a slightly bent left index finger. "The kind of love that removes bricks in the wall of prejudice only comes from above. Anything else is like a Band-Aid on cancer."

"Yes," Adisa agreed. "But you don't hear many people say things like that, even folks who go to church."

"The only part of the world we can change is the part we touch. I'm glad you're working for Theo Grayson and can be here in Campbellton to help look after me, but your biggest job in life is to show God's unconditional love to a world that desperately needs to see it."

"Between you and Thelma Armistead, I can't ignore the power of love," Adisa said.

"There's value in gray hair beyond good looks," Aunt Josie replied with a smile. "Now, could I have that last crumb of corn bread, please?"

After Aunt Josie went to sleep, Adisa

stayed at the hospital to pray for Deshaun during his surgery. She walked the halls, spent time in the tiny chapel, and sat on a bench under the night sky in the garden outside. The only place she avoided was the waiting area for family members. It was after midnight when she passed through the lobby and saw a group of ten people congregating near a large potted plant. Reggie was among them. Adisa started to do a quick about-face, but the young preacher saw her and immediately started walking rapidly toward her. Adisa waited. Reggie's face was serious, and she couldn't tell anything about the success or failure of the surgery by his expression.

"How is Deshaun?" she asked anxiously. "Aunt Josie's neurologist told us about the surgery."

"He's alive," Reggie replied. "Dr. Steiner was able to remove the bullet."

Adisa burst into tears of relief as the pent-up stress of the past few hours was suddenly released in a torrent. She'd left her purse in Aunt Josie's room and didn't have any tissues. Reggie reached into his pocket and handed her a clean handkerchief so she could wipe her eyes. He then put one arm around her shoulders and gave her a quick hug. Adisa didn't pull away as she blinked back tears.

"Thanks," she said. "I'm so glad to know. Aunt Josie prayed earlier and seemed confident about the outcome."

"Pastor!" one of the members of the group called out.

"I have to go," Reggie said to Adisa. "Maybe we can talk later."

"I'd like that," Adisa replied and held out the handkerchief.

"No, you keep it. That way I know I'll see you again."

Adisa smiled through her remaining tears. She admired how Reggie naturally moved through life as a pillar of support for those around him, including her.

After a short night's sleep, Adisa was back at the hospital to assist with Aunt Josie's discharge home. Shortly after ten o'clock they turned onto Baxter Street and the house came into view. The exertion of getting ready had exhausted the older woman, who spent part of the short drive from the hospital with her eyes closed and her head resting against the back of the seat. Her breathing made Adisa wonder if she'd dozed off.

"You're home," Adisa said softly.

"I know," Aunt Josie replied, opening her

eyes. "I was making sure the first thing I did before getting out of the car was thank the Lord for bringing me here."

Adisa retrieved a walker from the trunk and placed it beside the passenger door. Aunt Josie struggled to get out. Adisa helped.

"There's so many little things I've taken for granted," Aunt Josie said. "Who would have thought the door to your little car would seem heavier than the barn door at my great-uncle's place on Cuthbertson Road? It rested on iron rollers and would squeal and complain something fierce. It took both me and your grandfather working together to push it open so we could sneak inside to play on the hay bales."

Adisa held Aunt Josie's left arm to steady her as she stood up and leaned on the walker. The older woman walked resolutely to the front stoop but stopped at the first step.

"You'd better help," Aunt Josie said. "I'll use the railing, too."

With Adisa beside her, Aunt Josie navigated up the three steps. When they made it through the front door, Aunt Josie stopped and inhaled.

"I don't smell any dead plants."

"There may be a couple on life support,

but I don't think there have been any fatalities," Adisa answered. "Where do you want to sit or lie down?"

"Not in my bedroom. I want to use that for sleeping."

Adisa followed her aunt into the living room and helped her to lie down on a cream-colored sofa.

"A pillow would be nice," Aunt Josie said. "And maybe the afghan I keep at the foot of my bed. You've got the air-conditioning turned way down. Aren't you worried about running up my power bill?"

"I'll pay it," Adisa answered as she left the room to get the pillow and multicolored throw.

No sooner was the older woman tucked in than she promptly fell asleep. She didn't stir as Adisa unloaded the car and set up her laptop on the kitchen table. One of the first things she did was prepare the standard form request for information guaranteed to a defendant under the Georgia criminal law statutes, and she added a specific request for production of the bullet taken from Deshaun's brain by Dr. Steiner. Typing the words brought back some of the emotion she'd felt the previous night at the hospital. Reggie's handkerchief was still on the nightstand beside her bed.

Adisa began researching the qualifications of expert witnesses in the areas she'd identified at the hearing in front of Judge Andrews. After collecting ten names, she checked on Aunt Josie, who remained sound asleep. Going into the guest bedroom, Adisa closed the door and started making phone calls. Now that she was in the case and not debating her role, Adisa's determination kicked in. Emerging two hours later, with several breaks to check on Aunt Josie, she felt like she'd plunged into icy water. To prepare the case properly was going to be more expensive than she'd thought. Standing in the middle of the kitchen, she called Theo Grayson.

TWENTY-SIX

Luke parked his truck in front of the shooting range. The only other vehicle in sight belonged to Charlie. Luke checked his pistol to make sure it was empty. There were two boxes of bullets in his satchel. Without the benefit of a paycheck, he knew he'd have to carefully ration his remaining supply of ammunition.

He spent the next thirty minutes efficiently pinging the targets from various distances. Toward the end of the session, Charlie came outside to watch. After hitting nine out of ten targets at 150 feet, Luke turned around with a satisfied expression on his face. Charlie was no longer alone.

Beside him was Jamie Standard, the newspaper reporter, along with the photographer who'd been with her at the courthouse. The photographer kept his camera raised for a few more moments and then lowered it. Luke ripped off the ear protectors and threw them to the ground. The photographer took more pictures.

"What are you doing here?" he demanded.

"Recording your shooting session," the reporter replied. "It sounded like you didn't miss. Am I right?"

Luke stormed back to the table. "This is private property," Luke said to the range owner. "Can't you kick them out?"

Ms. Standard turned toward Charlie. "Mr. Sellers, how often does Officer Nelson come here to practice? And is he usually as accurate as what we just saw?"

"Uh, I don't want to get involved," Charlie replied, glancing nervously at Luke.

"I'm out of here," Luke said, brushing past the reporter. He then turned around and pointed his finger at her. "And I'd better not find you snooping around my house and trespassing on my property."

"Is that a threat?" the reporter replied.

"No, but you ought to show some respect for a person's privacy."

His anger boiling, Luke stormed through the indoor range and into the parking lot. The reporter had parked her vehicle, a small import, beside his truck. Luke had to resist the urge to bang his door into the car. But that would have messed up the paint job on his truck. He spun the tires of the truck in the gravel lot as he drove away. What had been a sanctuary for him since the shooting had been violated. Several miles down the road, he called the gun range. Charlie answered.

"Did the reporter hang around after I left?" Luke asked.

"Yeah, but when I wouldn't give her anything except my name, rank, and serial number she gave up. The photographer took a few more pictures of the front of the building. I wouldn't let them take a photo of me."

"Anything else come up about me?"

"Not really. I told her I give anyone who works in law enforcement a discount because I believe it's my public duty to support the police. I'm sure she thinks I'm a gun nut, but it won't be the first time the media labeled a person who believes in the Second Amendment an extremist. I guarantee you that if she writes an article and mentions the range, there will be a big uptick in business the following week."

"That's good, but I'm sorry I lost my temper."

"I thought you made your point without totally blowing a gasket. Look, these media types forget that these situations involve real people with real feelings. She was baiting you. You rolled the hook around in your mouth for a few seconds but didn't swallow it."

"I guess I shouldn't come around for a while," Luke replied.

"No, you're welcome anytime."

The chatty occupational therapist finished taking notes after a thorough inspection of Aunt Josie's house. Adisa scribbled down notes of the therapist's suggestions. Off and on during the visit, the older woman apologized that her home wasn't sparkling clean.

"Ms. Adams, if my house looked this nice, I'd invite my mother-in-law over for coffee and pastries," the young woman said with a smile. "I know your niece was taking notes, but I'll send you a copy of my report as soon as it's finished."

"I'll get in touch with someone tomorrow to install the items she needs in the bathroom," Adisa said. "And it's good to know you don't recommend a ramp in front."

"So long as she doesn't try to climb the steps without assistance."

"She's not escaping on my watch," Adisa replied.

After the therapist left, Aunt Josie returned to her place on the sofa. "It doesn't take much to wear me out," she said with a sigh.

"I don't have the energy to fix supper."

"For now, I'm your chef," Adisa said with a smile. "Tell me what you want, and I'll whip it up."

"A nice soup would be good," she said. "And that would give me something to eat for leftovers."

"Chicken noodle?" Adisa asked. "I know there's chicken in the freezer, and I can use the pressure cooker."

"I only use thighs for soup," Aunt Josie began. "The dark meat has more flavor."

"I agree. Tell me what else you want to include, and I'll make a quick trip to the store."

Five minutes later, Adisa pulled into the parking lot at the supermarket. She was picking out a fresh bunch of celery stalks when her phone rang. It was the number at Aunt Josie's house. Adisa quickly pressed the receive button.

"Are you okay?" she asked.

"No, I don't have enough of the seasoning mix I use in my chicken soups. You know the brand I like."

"Where are you?" Adisa asked.

"In the kitchen at my spice cabinet. But I used the walker and didn't use the step stool to look at the top shelf of the cabinet. The seasoning mix was right where I could see it."

"Okay, I'll get some," Adisa replied. "And don't scare me by calling me like that."

"But we need that mix for the soup."

"Yes, ma'am."

The call ended. If Adisa was going to live in the same house with Aunt Josie, she was going to have to channel her aunt's desires and preferences and temporarily adopt them as her own. As she made her way down the spice aisle, she saw a familiar figure standing in front of the shelves. It was Reggie. He turned and saw her.

"Hey," he called out as a big smile creased his face.

Adisa pushed her cart forward. "How's Deshaun today?" she asked.

"Stable in ICU. And I saw that your aunt was discharged. How is she doing?"

"Glad to be home."

Reggie pointed to the rows of spices. "Can you give me some advice? Except for an occasional rack of ribs, I'm not much of a cook, but I was going to try to make spaghetti."

"From scratch?" Adisa asked.

"I found a five-star recipe," Reggie said as he held up his phone so she could see the screen, "but I can't figure out which type of

Italian seasoning it's talking about."

Adisa glanced at the list and then the shelf of spices. "Either one of these would work," she said, pointing to two placed side by side.

Reggie selected one and put it in a basket he was carrying with him. "What's for supper at your house?" he asked.

"Oh, I'm making chicken noodle soup to celebrate."

"Did you find someone to stay with your aunt while you're at work?"

"Not yet."

"I prepared a list of five candidates if you're interested. Three of them attend the church, and the other two are family members of people I know well."

"Thanks," Adisa said. "We need to move on that immediately. I can't leave her alone for more than an hour or two at a time. Why don't you save your spaghetti experiment for another day and join Aunt Josie and me for soup?"

"Are you sure?"

"Yes," Adisa said. "Look, I'm tired of acting like an eighth grader whose feelings were hurt on the playground. You're entitled to your opinion about my involvement in Officer Nelson's criminal case, and even if we disagree, it doesn't mean we can't be friends."

"I agree," Reggie replied with a broad smile. "Except I was the eighth grader. Should you call your aunt and make sure it's okay for me to show up unannounced?"

"She'd be mad if she found out I ran into you and didn't invite you over."

"My grandmother made the best chicken noodle soup. It's one of my favorites."

"Hold on. If you're going to measure what I fix against some ideal that's impossible to meet, I'd rather not —"

"No, no. Don't worry. I've done enough marital counseling to know a man's an idiot if he unfavorably compares his wife's banana pudding with what his mother made."

Reggie returned the Italian seasoning to its place on the shelf and walked beside Adisa through the store. All their previous interaction had focused on intense, serious situations, and Adisa enjoyed the casual stroll down the aisles. Reggie pointed out some of the things he liked to eat.

At Aunt Josie's house, Reggie parked on the street and Adisa pulled into the driveway. She got out of her car and heard someone call her name.

"Adisa!"

Walter and Mary Broome were standing on the stoop in front of their house. Mary motioned for her to come closer. Adisa glanced at Reggie.

"I'm about to fix supper!" Adisa said, holding up the plastic grocery sacks.

Mary pointed at Reggie and nodded her head approvingly.

"Aunt Josie came home from the hospital this morning!" Adisa continued.

Walter and Mary came down the steps and headed in their direction. Reggie caught up to Adisa, who whispered to him, "Do you know the Broomes? They go to Aunt Josie's church."

"No, but I think I'm about to meet them."

"Be prepared for the gossip about you being here to boomerang to your church by Sunday morning."

"Fine with me."

Adisa allowed herself a split second to enjoy the compliment. Reggie transitioned to his best ministerial persona and greeted the older couple.

"Oh, we've heard all about you and the good work you're doing," Mary said. "And we appreciate you leading the fight to make sure something is done to punish the officer who shot Deshaun."

"The district attorney will see to that," Reggie said, glancing at Adisa. "My job is to make sure the public's voice is heard."

"Come in and say hello to Aunt Josie,"

Adisa said, wanting to change the subject. "That is, if she isn't napping. The trip from the hospital wore her out."

The Broomes followed Adisa and Reggie into the house. Aunt Josie was awake. Mary gave her a hug and burst into tears. Adisa and Reggie took the groceries into the kitchen. For all her nosiness, Mary loved Aunt Josie. Walter stood back with his hands clasped in front of him.

"Cut it out," Aunt Josie said to Mary. "I'm home. That's cause for celebration."

"That's what these are for," Mary said as she grabbed a tissue from a box on the end table next to the sofa. "It's so good to see you in your house surrounded by your plants."

"And Adisa." Aunt Josie motioned to the kitchen where Reggie and Adisa were sorting out the groceries.

"I have a thousand questions to ask you," Mary said, "but I'll save those for tomorrow. When would be a good time to come over? I'd be glad to sit with you for a while so Adisa can take a break."

"That would be wonderful," Aunt Josie answered. "Adisa has taken a job with Theo Grayson's law firm and needs to go back to work on Monday."

"That settles it, then," Mary answered.

"I'll be here at eight Monday morning and stay as long as you need me. Come on, Walter."

Walter shook Reggie's hand and gave Adisa a knowing smile. The Broomes left.

"Did you see what else I picked up at the grocery store?" Adisa asked, sticking her head out of the kitchen so she had an unobstructed view of Aunt Josie.

"Yes, I did, and that's another answer to prayer. Reggie, come in here and sit with me while Adisa fixes the soup."

Reggie joined Adisa in the kitchen doorway. "If it's okay, I'll stay in here and help. We can talk while we eat."

"Suit yourself," Aunt Josie said with a wave of her hand.

"I don't mind," Adisa said. "The kitchen is small, and there's not much prep work to do."

"I'm great at cutting carrots," Reggie replied. "I can even peel them if you have one of those peeler things."

Working together, they managed to load the pressure cooker in less than ten minutes. Reggie's carrot-peeling skills were crude but adequate. He did better with the onions and didn't shed a tear.

"Those onions are making me cry over here," Adisa said as she poured in the chicken broth and measured the different spices.

"I'm immune," Reggie answered. "It was a job my grandmother always gave me when I was a kid."

Adisa sealed the lid and set the cooker on the stove. "Thirty minutes until supper," she said.

They joined Aunt Josie in the living room. She was looking at the local newspaper.

"You didn't go outside to pick up the newspaper, did you?" Adisa asked in alarm.

"No, Walter brought it in." Aunt Josie managed to turn the page with her left hand. "Here's your name."

"Don't read that now," Adisa said quickly.

"Not your name," Aunt Josie said. "It's about Reggie."

"Is that the article about the outreach our church is doing at the youth detention center?" he asked.

Aunt Josie nodded. "But I'd rather hear about it from you in person," she said.

Reggie told them how they were pairing up boys in trouble with men in his congregation for supervised activities. Soon the timer went off for the pressure cooker.

"It should cool for a few minutes," Adisa said as she got up. "You keep talking, and I'll listen."

Reggie pulled out his phone. "There's not much more to tell, but I've come up with a list of possible sitters who are either members of my congregation or recommendations through my contacts."

Adisa listened as Reggie discussed the candidates with Aunt Josie. It was obvious he'd taken her interests and personality into consideration. Several of the women were avid gardeners. When they sat down to eat, he prayed a beautiful prayer for Aunt Josie. Adisa waited and watched while he took his first spoonful of soup. He kept it in his mouth longer than necessary before swallowing. He took another bite, this time with a juicy piece of chicken surrounded by golden broth.

"Well?" Adisa asked impatiently. "How is it?"

"Whoever cut up the carrots could have made them smaller."

"That was you." Adisa smiled. "What about the flavor?"

Reggie ate another bite. "It's almost good enough to make me forget my grandmother's soup."

Aunt Josie's first bite didn't make it cleanly to her mouth and most of the soup ended up back in the bowl. When she saw what happened, Adisa immediately moved her chair closer.

"Let me help you."

After they finished supper, Aunt Josie returned to her spot on the sofa.

"I'm not long for this day," she said as she sat down. "My own bed is calling my name, and I'm looking forward to answering."

"And I'd better go," Reggie said. "Let me know when you want to interview some of the ladies who might be able to help."

"The sooner the better," Adisa responded. "Send me their contact information and I'll follow up."

"Don't send those two I marked off," Aunt Josie said.

"I made a note of that," Reggie answered. "Thanks again for supper."

"Walk him out to the car," Aunt Josie said. "But before you do, get Shanika on the phone."

Shanika knew Aunt Josie was coming home from the hospital. As soon as her sister answered, Adisa handed the phone to Aunt Josie.

"Yes, she's feeding me," Adisa heard Aunt Josie say a moment later. "We had home-made chicken noodle soup. It was scrumptious."

Adisa followed Reggie to the door. "Shanika doesn't have a lot of confidence in my cooking," she said as they stepped outside.

"From what I've heard, you've been surprising your sister for a long time."

"Who have you been talking to?"

Reggie motioned to the interior of the house. "She doesn't have the best filter," Adisa said.

"Honesty I can accept, and the truth is an ally. I wanted to know about you, and she was my best source."

Adisa was flattered. They walked down the steps to the driveway and stopped. She looked at the Broome house. Neither Walter nor Mary was in sight.

"Thanks for not outing me with the Broomes about the Nelson case," she said. "I'm still working on my stump speech to explain why I'm a traitor to my race."

Reggie shook his head. "I stepped over the line the other day at the hospital," he said. "When I have strong feelings or beliefs, I let them out. It's probably not the best trait for a minister, but it's how I'm wired. Talking to your aunt about that helped me, too."

"What did she say?"

"Nothing that convinced me I was wrong, but our conversation helped me understand you better."

"So we're stuck in the place of agreeing to disagree," she said.

"Yes," Reggie replied and then paused. "But with a twist."

"What's that?"

"I'm not going to tolerate anyone criticizing you in my presence for agreeing to represent Officer Nelson."

Adisa felt a lump rise in her throat. "That's sweet," she managed. "What are you going to say when it happens?"

"I'm not sure," he said. "But as soon as it's ready, I'd like to hear your stump speech. Maybe that will give me a few ideas."

TWENTY-SEVEN

Luke was cleaning the kitchen after supper when the phone rang. It was Theo Grayson.

"I should have called you yesterday," the lawyer said, "but it was late when Adisa and I returned to the office from the courthouse, and I've been out of town most of today. We met with Judge Andrews about the next steps in the case."

Grayson told Luke about the judge's decision and directives. Partway through the conversation Jane returned to the kitchen, and Luke put the call on speakerphone so she could listen, too.

"I think Adisa is right about hiring experts to assist in the preparation of our defense," Grayson said. "But there will be expense involved that you need to consider and discuss with Jane."

"Do it!" Jane said into the receiver. "Whatever it takes!"

"Hold on," Luke said. "He hasn't even

given us an idea of what he's talking about. And in another month we're going to have to use our home equity to pay our bills."

"I talked to my mother, Mr. Grayson," Jane cut in. "And she's going to help with any expenses. She was blown away by your generosity in taking the case without charging an attorney fee. Hire the best people you can. That's what Luke deserves."

"Adisa is researching candidates," Grayson replied. "And we'll make sure the cost is reasonable. You will be consulted before we retain anyone."

"Just fight as hard as you can," Jane responded.

The call ended. Luke looked at Jane.

"No," she said.

Luke didn't speak. Instead, he leaned over and kissed her on the lips, twice.

"The first one is for you, the second for your mother," he said. "She'll have to settle for a peck on the cheek the next time I see her."

Adisa called Aunt Josie for the third time. It was the first day that Simone, a woman from Reggie's church, was staying at the house. Aunt Josie was laughing when she answered the phone.

"What's so funny?" Adisa asked.

"Simone is telling me stories about her twins," Aunt Josie said. "Even though they're older than Keisha and Kendal, we need to get the four of them together the next time Shanika brings the family to see me."

"That may be this coming weekend," Adisa replied. "The one question she had was whether you were up to seeing the kids or not."

Aunt Josie was silent for a moment. "I'd love to say yes, but I'd better not," the older woman replied. "Keisha loves to jump on me and won't understand that I'm not ready for that kind of play."

"That's what Shanika and I thought, but we wanted to leave the decision up to you. It'll do Ronnie good to corral all three of them and appreciate what Shanika deals with twenty-four/seven."

"Yes, although Ronnie Jr. worships him. Speaking of worship, you can take Shanika with you to Reggie's church on Sunday. That will give her a chance to meet him."

"Are you sure you want to put those ideas in her head?" Adisa asked, rolling her eyes. "She'll torment me."

"Too late," Aunt Josie replied. "Shanika knows all about Reggie. That's given us something new to talk about."

"How long?"

"Since his first visit with me at the hospital."

Adisa could instantly picture the conversations. "How much does she know?"

"Everything."

"Even our disagreement about my representation of Officer Nelson?"

"Oh yes, but I couldn't tell which side of the fence Shanika came down on. You can ask her while she's here."

After the call ended, Adisa returned to working on the Nelson case. She'd made progress identifying potential experts who would help paint a picture of circumstances that justified the shooting. The deeper she went into preparation, the easier it became to divorce her feelings from what she was doing and let the analytical portion of her brain take over. The troubling part of that process was the similarity it bore to people throughout history who were cogs in oppressive regimes, performed their duties, and later claimed they were "simply obeying orders." Adisa brushed aside those thoughts and reminded herself that facts were stubborn things, and a jury charged with determining the truth would receive clear instructions from the judge as to their mission. Her job was to present as broad a palette of factual colors as she could. There was a tap on her door. It was Theo Grayson.

"You look deep in thought," the older lawyer said.

"It's going to take more than me thinking deep thoughts to assure Luke Nelson a fair trial. Here, look this over."

Adisa pushed the print button for the document she'd been working on and handed the three sheets of paper to Grayson, who sat down in a chair across from her desk. Adisa waited for him to read the memo.

"As you can see," she said, "I'm making progress on narrowing the field of experts in the Nelson case. It hasn't been as easy as finding a sitter to stay with Aunt Josie. I've talked briefly to two of them, but perhaps this is something you prefer to do yourself."

"The only expert I want to personally vet is the person who's going to testify that Luke's actions were reasonable under accepted police standards."

"Do you believe such a person exists?" Adisa asked.

"He'd better. That's fifty percent of our case."

"How about a she? Did you see the woman on the list? Dr. Briscoe has a PhD in criminal justice and thirty years' experience."

"Yes," Grayson said, shifting in his chair. "But I'm not sure a woman who retired from the city police department in Milwaukee is going to play well in front of a Nash County jury."

"That's not all," Adisa replied. "Dr. Briscoe is black, but she came across as police blue to me. I couldn't see her face, but she didn't verbally flinch when I told her our facts. And although we didn't get into a lot of details, she didn't hang up on me when she found out I was calling about a young white officer who shot an unarmed black teenager. Once she realized I was sticking my neck out to uphold the integrity of the justice system, a couple of things she mentioned clued me in that she might be willing to do so, too."

"Maybe I should withdraw my request to totally control the police standards expert," Grayson said. "You don't need me."

"No. I think it's important for her to interact with you so that the color of my skin doesn't overly influence her decision."

"If that's what you think, I'll contact her next week."

Adisa slid another sheet of paper across her desk so Grayson could see it. "Here's the subpoena for the bullet taken from Deshaun's brain," she said.

"And how will we respond if Jasper Baldwin finds out and serves us with a demand to turn it over to him?"

"Uh, we'll have to give it to him."

"And after he runs tests proving it came from Luke's gun, Baldwin will bring it into court along with the slug that went through Deshaun's body, line them up on the railing in front of the jury box, and then let each member of the jury handle them personally."

Adisa flinched. "The report is a safety precaution to make sure the bullets came from Luke's weapon. Remember, he claims he heard a gunshot before he fired."

"Or a lightning strike or a truck backfire. I agree we should run ballistics, but our better argument will be about Luke's state of mind, not whether he was actually in mortal danger."

Grayson returned the subpoena to Adisa's desk. She slid it into a thin folder marked "Discovery."

"And I haven't been able to find an expert in crime scene reconstruction," she said. "I'll keep searching, but we won't have a possible name to provide to Judge Andrews at the arraignment."

"He won't expect names, only that you and I are 'on the same page,' as he described it the other day in his chambers."

"Should we specifically mention Dr. Briscoe? That will show him we're making real progress."

Grayson paused for a moment. "I don't want to give Baldwin too much information before we've locked down an expert's opinion. He wouldn't hesitate to do an end run and poison a potential witness by feeding them information slanted in his direction."

"He'd do that?"

"There are city manners and country bare-knuckle rules," Grayson replied with a smile.

"Okay," Adisa said, checking the open screen of her computer one more time to see if she had overlooked anything. "Then I guess we're ready for arraignment on Monday."

"We'll keep it short. Someone will be at the courthouse from the newspaper, but based on what the judge told us, there won't be any cameras allowed in the courtroom. Unless you think otherwise, I recommend we enter and exit with only a brief comment to the press about looking forward to presenting a vigorous defense that will exonerate Luke."

"Exonerate? That makes it sound like we believe he's not guilty."

"What word would you use?"

Adisa thought for a moment. "I'd say that we are going to present a vigorous defense without drawing a conclusion as to where it will end up."

Grayson pressed his lips together tightly for a moment. Adisa knew he wasn't happy with her recommendation.

"I won't use the word 'exonerate,'" he said, "but I'm going to try to come up with something else and ask you to do so, too."

"And you're going to make sure Luke keeps his mouth shut?"

"Yes. All I want him to say is 'Not guilty,' when Judge Andrews asks how he wants to plea to the charges. Otherwise he should be as mute as a guard at Buckingham Palace."

Talking about the court appearance, even though it would be routine, made Adisa's heart beat a little faster.

"Any chance reporters from other papers will be there?" she asked.

"I hope not. The bigger story would be the judge banning video media from the courtroom, but that won't be publicized in advance."

"What time did you tell Luke to be here on Monday?" she asked.

"An hour early. That way we can bring him up-to-date on what you're doing and provide an estimated budget for expert witnesses."

Grayson told Adisa about his three-way phone conversation with Luke and Jane.

"If his mother-in-law is serious about helping, we need to ask for a reasonable deposit that we'll hold in trust until needed."

"Absolutely."

"Will you be in the office tomorrow?" Adisa asked. "I'm coming in for a couple of hours to work on a project Mike gave me. I'll leave when my sister arrives in town to see Aunt Josie."

Grayson smiled. "One of my granddaughters has a soccer game in the morning, and I'm going to be there to cheer her on. After that, I've promised to let her spend the afternoon with me doing anything she wants to do."

Adisa's eyes widened. "How old is she?"

"Nine."

"Do you realize what you're getting into? The wishes of a nine-year-old girl can be a bit unpredictable."

"And will get my mind off this place and the responsibilities I carry with me the rest of the week." Grayson rubbed the side of his nose. "And I'm enough of a manipulator to give guidance to her whims. Remember, I convinced you to work with me here."

"Don't give yourself too much credit. You had help from above."

"Any regrets?"

Adisa thought about how excited she'd been to land the job at Dixon and White and the incredible opportunity to be mentored by someone like Catherine Summey. Getting over that disappointment wasn't the work of a week or a month.

"It's okay. You don't have to answer," Grayson said when he saw she was hesitating.

The older lawyer turned to go and then stopped. "Oh, one other thing," he said. "If my granddaughter ever decides to become a lawyer, I want her to talk to you first. You can share things with her far beyond the scope of my experience."

The following morning Adisa fixed a light breakfast for Aunt Josie. The transition from hospital to home had gone smoothly. The addition of Simone to the mix had added zest to Aunt Josie's day, and their diet had been supplemented with delicious food brought over by Mary Broome.

"Are you and Simone doing anything

besides sitting around talking?" Adisa asked as she watched Aunt Josie carefully lift a bite of scrambled eggs with cheese from her plate to her mouth.

"We're doing my exercises three times a day."

Aunt Josie was able to push her fork into a small piece of sausage and smoothly maneuver it into her mouth.

"You're doing great with the fork," Adisa said.

"The reward is when it hits my taste buds. I was tired of hospital food and needed something savory in my diet."

"What about sweet?" Adisa asked. "I saw the cookies in the jar on the kitchen counter."

"Simone made them. I told her to take them home for her kids, but she insisted we keep a few here. It's her own chocolate chip recipe. You should try one."

"I did last night with a glass of milk after you went to sleep. They were good."

Adisa took a sip of coffee and checked the clock on the wall in the kitchen.

"I'm going to the office for a couple of hours," she said. "Shanika should be here by ten o'clock."

"I'll be fine."

"Should I stay to help you brush your

teeth and get dressed?"

"No, I can handle my teeth, and I'm going to stay in my robe until Shanika shows up. She'll enjoy bossing me around and telling me what to wear."

"True. And remember to keep your cell phone with you. It's on the table beside the sofa."

"Yes, yes. I'm going to read my Bible and pray. Did you see the map of Campbellton beside the sofa?"

"Yes."

"I've been using it to go on prayer walks. Today I'm going downtown and taking a few laps around several of the churches."

"The services will be better, and the pastors won't know why."

"Any updates about Deshaun?" Aunt Josie asked.

"No, but no news is good news. Maybe I'll find out something when Shanika and I visit Reggie's church."

The bell on the front door chimed.

"It's too early for Shanika," Adisa said, scooting back her chair. "I bet it's Mary Broome. What do you want me to tell her?"

"I was looking forward to my time with the Lord," Aunt Josie said with a sigh. "But I don't want to turn her away. She's been so good to us. Invite her in."

Adisa walked to the front door and opened it. Mary Broome wasn't standing on the front stoop.

"Are you Adisa Johnson?" asked a nicely dressed young white woman who looked a few years older than Adisa.

"Yes."

The woman confidently extended her right hand, and Adisa shook it.

"I'm Sharon Rogers with the *AJC*. We talked a few weeks ago about a case you handled involving DNA evidence —"

"And you wrote an article that cost me my job," Adisa said, her jaw tightening against the fury rising in her gut.

"Excuse me?" the reporter asked, her eyes widening.

Adisa hesitated. She wanted to confront the reporter with the devastating impact the insinuations in the Larimore article had on Adisa's career but wasn't sure how to do so without violating her own sense of morality.

"I'll leave it at that," she managed.

"You and your boss should have returned my phone calls," the reporter replied in a snippy tone of voice.

"If I'd called, would it have made a difference?"

The reporter paused, which let Adisa know discussion would have been fruitless.

Rogers had an agenda.

"That's old news," the reporter said. "I'd rather move on to the reason I'm here now. We've been keeping an eye on the case against the white police officer who shot the unarmed black teenager. When it came across my desk that you're representing the officer, I volunteered to drive up and talk to you about it."

"Why did you volunteer?"

The reporter laughed nervously. "I told my editor that I knew you from the previous piece, which would make it easier for us to ask you questions."

"No one on the defense team is talking to reporters," Adisa said in an effort to be professional. "We're going to try this case in a Nash County courtroom, not in the media."

"If you deny me access, I'll still write my story."

"And I'll deal with the consequences."

Sharon Rogers turned away and descended the steps. Adisa watched her for a few seconds.

"Who was that?" Aunt Josie asked when Adisa returned to the living room.

"Somebody from the past who still has a hook in me that needs to be removed," Adisa replied.

"What do you mean?"

"A newspaper reporter from Atlanta. I'm going to the office to get some work done before Shanika arrives."

"If the doorbell rings, I won't answer it."

"Good."

After Luke brewed the morning coffee, he glanced outside and saw something that looked like a discarded coat. He walked across the wet grass toward the street. When he got closer he recognized a Campbellton Police Department uniform. He carefully picked it up but immediately dropped it.

It was covered in blood.

Looking up and down the empty street, he knelt for a better look. The red substance smeared on the trousers and shirt bore a closer resemblance to paint than dried blood. Not wanting to touch it with his bare hands, he went inside the house and found a pair of rubber gloves beneath the sink.

"Is the coffee ready?" Jane called out from Ashley's room.

"Yes."

"Could you bring a cup in here for me?"

"Just a minute," he answered. "I'll be right back."

"Where are you going?" Jane asked, but Luke ignored her on his way out the door.

Everything about the uniform looked legitimate. He used a gloved hand to make sure there wasn't anything dangerous underneath it. The grass was dry, which meant it had been there during the night before dew formed on the ground. Stepping back, he took several pictures with the camera on his phone. Returning to the house, he poured a cup of coffee for Jane and took it to her in Ashley's room.

"What were you doing?" Jane asked as she cleaned Ashley's face with a washcloth. "I heard you opening and shutting the front door a couple of times."

Luke told Jane what he'd found. He watched as her lower lip trembled slightly before it steadied.

"There have always been hateful people in the world," she said in a voice trying to sound strong. "It's just that they've never turned their hate toward us."

"I'll call the police department and ask someone to take a look. It's not easy for an ordinary citizen to get his hands on a uniform."

The dispatcher on duty connected Luke directly with Detective Maxwell.

"Don't move anything, and I'll swing by," the detective said.

"I'll be here," Luke said. "Knock on the

door, and I'll come out and —"

"That won't be necessary. I'll be in an unmarked car."

After the call ended, Jane came into the kitchen and placed Ashley in her high chair.

"She has an awful case of the summer sniffles," Jane said.

Luke fed the little girl breakfast. Normally a voracious eater in the morning, she showed little appetite.

"Will you clean the humidifier and set it up in her room?" Jane said.

Luke and Jane had been married long enough that the way she phrased the question let him know that she didn't want the unit cleaned later; she wanted it done now. Luke finished his now-cool cup of coffee.

"It's in the top of her closet, isn't it?" he asked before leaving the kitchen.

"Yes, unless you've moved it without telling me."

Luke quickly exited the kitchen. He opened the small closet in the corner of Ashley's room and reached for the humidifier on the rear of the shelf. A cracking sound caused him to jump back. Spinning around, he saw a torn place in the wall that faced a rear corner of the house. Another cracking sound opened up a second tear about a foot beneath the other one. Luke immediately crouched and ran from the room to Jane and Ashley.

"Get down!" he yelled. "Someone is shooting at the house!"

Ashley had begun to cry. Luke grabbed Ashley and handed her to Jane, who immediately lowered herself to the floor, holding her daughter tightly, and leaned against the stove. Luke grabbed his gun from the top of the refrigerator and raced down the short hallway to the rear of the house. He peeked out the glass top of the door leading to the backyard and quickly scanned the wooded area behind the house. He saw no movement. He reached for the doorknob.

"Luke!" Jane called out. "Please, come here!"

Still crouching, Luke returned to the kitchen. "Two shots," he said. "High up in Ashley's room."

Ashley was crying so hard that she was having trouble catching her breath in between sobs. Her nose was a mess. Luke slid back down to the floor and put his arms around Jane and the baby. Jane was shaking uncontrollably.

Much like he'd reacted after he shot Deshaun Hamlin.

Still mad at Sharon Rogers and frustrated

with herself for her reaction, Adisa arrived at the office. She fixed a cup of hot tea in the break room and waited for her emotions to calm down.

Unlike the law firm in Atlanta, the offices of Grayson, Baxter, and Williams were deserted on weekends. Midmorning, the phone on the corner of her desk lit up. Since she didn't have any clients of her own, Adisa was surprised that a call came directly to her.

"Hello?" she answered.

"Ms. Johnson," a male voice responded. "This is Luke Nelson. I tried to reach Mr. Grayson, but he's not answering his phone."

"He's at a soccer match with his grand-daughter. Is everything okay?"

"No," Luke answered. "Shots were fired at my house this morning. The bullets came through the wall in my little girl's room."

"Was she hurt?" Adisa asked, sitting up straighter in her chair.

"No, she was in the kitchen eating break-fast. Detective Maxwell is coming out in a few minutes, and I wanted to let you and Mr. Grayson know what was going on."

"I'm sorry but glad you're all safe."

"That's not all."

Adisa listened as Luke told her about the bloody uniform. The whole scenario at the

Nelson residence made her slightly sick to her stomach.

"I'm coming over there," she said. "I need to see this for myself."

"Are you sure? I took pictures of the uniform and the holes in the wall."

"Did you find the bullets?"

Luke was silent for a moment. "No, and I can't believe I didn't think about that. I guess I'm still in shock."

"That's understandable. I'm on my way."

The call ended. Adisa realized she didn't know the address and had to check the file before leaving the office. It was less than ten minutes away. She pulled onto the modest suburban street. In her rearview mirror, she saw a black car with tinted windows following her. She parked in front of Luke's house and got out.

The black car entered the driveway. A white man in his forties eyed her suspiciously. The look communicated, in a miniscule way, what she knew many young black men experienced during even a casual encounter with the police.

"This is private property!" he called out, holding up his hand.

"I'm Adisa Johnson, one of the lawyers representing Officer Nelson," she replied, staying close to her car. "He called me about what happened."

"Then you know this is a crime scene. I'm instructing you to remain where you are."

Adisa leaned against her car. The front door of the house opened, and Luke came outside.

"This is Detective Maxwell," Luke called out to her.

Adisa didn't move. Luke spoke to the detective, who said something to him that Adisa couldn't hear. Luke gave a longer response. The two men talked back and forth several times before Maxwell turned to her. Adisa was on the verge of leaving when Maxwell spoke to her.

"You can join us," the detective said.

Holding her head high, Adisa walked down the driveway to the detective's car. Up close, Maxwell had striking blue eyes that were inherently intimidating. It was a physical characteristic she suspected would be a big asset when trying to pry information from criminal suspects. He turned his blue eyes on her.

"Do you realize there's a risk being here?" he asked.

"Yes, but I wanted to come anyway."

Luke gave Adisa a look between gratitude and desperation. She heard a siren as a second police car came barreling down the street.

"That's Officer Alverez," Maxwell said. "I'd like you and Ms. Johnson to stay in the house while we check the wooded area."

"I'd want to go, too," Luke said. "After all, it's my house —"

"And whoever was there might risk another shot if he sees you," Maxwell said. "We can't take that chance."

Luke wiped perspiration from his forehead and didn't argue. Adisa followed him inside, where Jane and Ashley were sitting on the floor of the den. The baby was surrounded by toys. Jane looked up when Adisa entered.

"Sorry about the mess," Jane said in an attempt at a normal voice that disappeared behind a quivering lip and a cascade of tears.

Adisa immediately sat down on the floor beside Ashley, who had her back to her mother.

"My nieces have one of these," Adisa said to the little girl and then picked up a hollow ball with different shapes cut into its surface so that plastic pieces could be placed inside. "Do you know where to put the square?"

Adisa handed Ashley a purple square and positioned the ball so it fell inside.

"Good!" Adisa exclaimed and then

465

glanced at Jane, who was leaning against a well-worn couch with her eyes closed.

"I found a shell fragment," Luke said, standing in the door to the den. "It was on the floor on the opposite side of the room. There are probably others."

"Maybe it would be better for the detective to take over," Adisa replied as she handed a yellow oval to Ashley and then rotated the ball so the little girl could find the right opening. "That's his job."

"Ashley and I are leaving Campbellton for Florida to stay with my mother," Jane said.

Adisa glanced at Luke, who had his arms crossed over his chest. He didn't respond. She didn't want to step into the middle of such a tumultuous marital discussion.

"But I'll come back for the trial," Jane continued. "I have to be here for that."

"Yes," Adisa said quickly. "Your presence in the courtroom will send a powerful message."

She picked up a green triangle that Ashley tried to squeeze through the hole designed for the circle. Adisa gently placed her hand on the little girl's fingers and guided the triangle to the right spot. She felt the softness of the baby's hand. Her heart jumped up in her throat over the scary events of the morning.

"Everything is okay now," she said soothingly to Ashley.

"No, it's not, and that's why I have to go," Jane responded.

"Sorry, I didn't mean to disagree," Adisa said. "I was just trying to say something comforting to Ashley. At least she's innocent and doesn't know."

"Which makes placing her life in danger even worse."

A shocking comparison suddenly hit Adisa. In the moment before Luke pulled the trigger, Deshaun Hamlin had been as innocent as a fifteen-month-old child.

Twenty-Eight

Adisa focused on playing with Ashley and trying to get to know Jane better.

"You're awesome with kids," Jane said after Adisa finished reading a couple of books to Ashley.

"I used to babysit when I was a teenager, and I've had a little bit of practice with my sister's children. But actually, it's been a while since I spent this kind of time one-on-one with a toddler."

"You're a natural and will be a great mom when your time comes," Jane said.

"I'm not in a rush," Adisa said with a smile.

"And you shouldn't be," Jane said, glancing over her shoulder at the entrance to the den and then lowering her voice. "Luke and I were just beginning to adjust to life as parents when the shooting happened. He loved his job, we'd been able to buy this house, and Ashley was born. It goes to show

how life can turn upside down in a hurry."

Adisa handed Ashley a magnetic toy that had proved its ability to fascinate the little girl and scooted closer to Jane.

"I'm praying about the case," Adisa said.

"Thanks," Jane replied. "We need all of that we can get. And the story you told about the young man's grandmother asking God to forgive Luke really touched me."

"I hope to see her when I go to her church."

Jane paused for a moment. "Do you think you could give her a message from me?"

"Maybe," Adisa said. "But some words need to be said in person."

Jane ran her fingers through her hair. "Just tell her I'm praying that Deshaun will get better. I haven't brought it up with Luke, but it's been on my heart since that day at the office."

"Okay," Adisa said and nodded. "I'll see if there's a good chance to pass that along."

There was a loud banging at the front door that startled both Adisa and Jane.

"I'll answer it!" Luke called out from the rear of the house.

A few seconds later, Adisa saw Luke quickly walk past.

"I'm going, too," she said to Jane.

By the time Adisa reached the front door,

it was already open and Luke was talking to Detective Maxwell and Officer Alverez.

"We covered the whole area," Maxwell said to Luke. "We found a spot where the underbrush was smashed down and the shooter would have had a good view of the house. We didn't find any spent shell casings, which isn't surprising. We interviewed the people who live on the other side of the woods and no one heard or saw anything. It's surprising someone would do something like that in the daylight."

Luke handed the detective a plastic bag containing several metal fragments. "Here's what I found in Ashley's room and dug out of the wall," he said. "It looks like hollow-point ammo."

The detective lifted the bag and held it at eye level. "Yeah, it broke up on impact. Not the best for piercing the walls of the house. It looks like there are copper components. We'll send it to the ballistics lab in Atlanta and see if they can figure out the caliber and the type of gun that fired it."

Adisa shuddered at the thought that one of the sharp fragments could have struck Ashley. Luke glanced over his shoulder toward the interior of the house.

"Jane is with the baby," he said. "And I don't want her to hear any of this. She's threatening to take Ashley to Florida to stay with her mother until this is over."

"I know you want your family with you, but it might be a good idea," Maxwell said, his voice softening.

Adisa saw the muscles in Luke's neck tighten.

"In the meantime, don't do anything else in the room," Maxwell continued. "If you happen to see other fragments, collect and save them, but don't dig into the walls or repair the damage. I want to come out on Monday and go over the room myself."

"Jane isn't going to like that," Luke said. "She'll want to remove any trace of the bullets as soon as possible."

"Blame it on me," Maxwell answered.

Watching the exchange between Maxwell and Luke, Adisa couldn't figure out if the detective was sympathetic to Luke's plight or not.

"And the uniform in the yard," Alverez said, turning to Maxwell. "I brought the kit you radioed me about."

"What kind of kit?" Luke asked.

"To test the stains on the uniform."

"Oh, I'm sure it's paint," Luke replied.

"I'd rather be sure," Maxwell answered. "We can do a field test, and if it's positive, I'll take the fabric in for further evaluation."

"May I watch?" Adisa asked.

Maxwell hesitated for a moment and then shrugged. "Okay, but don't get in the way."

Adisa stuffed the feeling that the detective was treating her like a fourth grader. She and Luke followed him across the yard to the uniform. Alverez opened the door of his cruiser and brought over a black briefcase.

The blue cloth was discolored in several places, with the biggest stain on the front of the shirt. Maxwell knelt for a few moments before opening the briefcase and putting on latex gloves. He took a bottle of liquid from the briefcase.

"What's that?" Adisa asked.

"It's similar to hydrogen peroxide," the detective replied. "It reacts with organic matter by foaming up."

The stain looked like brownish-red paint to Adisa. Maxwell unscrewed the top of the bottle and poured it on a corner of the stain near a pocket. Foamy white bubbles immediately appeared.

"Whoa," Luke said. "It is blood."

Maxwell looked up at him. "Yes, and it took a lot of it to cover this much of the uniform."

Maxwell slipped the clothing into a large, clear plastic bag.

"Where do you think the uniform came

472

from?" Luke asked. "It looks real to me."

"It is," Maxwell replied.

"What size are the pants?" Alverez asked.

"Are you missing a uniform?" the detective asked.

"Yes," Alverez replied. "The cleaners lost one."

Maxwell took the trousers from the bag and, with both Luke and Alverez peering over his shoulder, looked at the place beneath the waistband for the pant size.

"Thirty-six thirty-two," Alverez said. "That's my size."

"Which cleaners do you use?" Maxwell asked.

"New City on Sunset Avenue."

"I'll check it out," Maxwell replied. "And let the chief know you shouldn't be charged a lost uniform fee."

Maxwell returned the bloody clothing to the plastic bag. Alverez reached out and patted Luke on the arm.

"See you, buddy," Alverez said.

"Thanks for coming," Luke replied.

Luke headed toward the house. Adisa started to follow him.

"Ms. Johnson," Maxwell said. "Stay for a minute."

Luke turned around as well.

"Not you, Officer Nelson."

Adisa started to protest that Luke had a right to hear anything Maxwell wanted to say but stopped. The detective waited for Luke to reenter the house and close the front door.

"I'll let you know about the test results for the uniform," he said.

"Okay," Adisa said slowly. "I'm working at Theo Grayson's firm. You can call me there."

"I know." Maxwell checked the closure for the plastic bag and then directed his gaze toward her. "Mr. Grayson represented my father in a case a number of years ago."

"I hope that went well."

"It did." Maxwell gripped the plastic bag tightly in his right hand. "And I'm willing to speak with you about the Nelson matter so long as it's completely off the record."

"What do you mean?" Adisa asked, her eyes widening. "I can't commit to confidentiality without knowing what it's about."

"Trust me, you should agree."

Adisa hesitated. At some point she would have the opportunity to place the detective under oath and ask him anything she wanted to about *State v. Nelson.* But Mitchell Maxwell would also have the opportunity to select one of a thousand answers to give. She mentally scrambled for a way forward.

"Agreed," Adisa said before she talked herself out of making a commitment she wasn't sure she could keep.

"There's good beef jerky, and there's bad beef jerky," the detective said and stopped.

Adisa waited. Maxwell knelt and began to repack the test kit into the black briefcase.

"What does that mean?" Adisa asked.

The detective closed the top of the black briefcase and didn't respond.

"That's it?" she asked.

"Yeah," Maxwell said, standing up.

He carried the plastic bag containing the uniform and the black briefcase to his car. Adisa watched him back out of the driveway. Before she reached the front door, Jane appeared with a cell phone in her hand.

"You had a call so I grabbed your phone from your purse."

She handed the phone to Adisa, who quickly pressed the receive button.

"I've been here for almost an hour," Shanika said. "How soon can you join us? The weather is so nice that I'd like to take Aunt Josie out for a drive around town, but I don't think it's a good idea to do it by myself."

"I'll be there in a bit," Adisa replied. "I'm almost done."

Luke joined her and Jane in the doorway.

"What did Maxwell say?" he asked.

"He's an odd guy, isn't he?" she responded, stalling for time.

"Yeah, but he's the best investigator on the force," Luke replied. "Did he say anything about me and my —"

"I thought you didn't trust him," Jane cut in.

"Oh, that was about the way he handled a burglary case when I caught some kids breaking into the abandoned warehouse on Lancer Avenue. He criticized the statements I took from the suspects at the scene."

"He probably wanted to interview them himself," Adisa said, looking at her watch. "I need to go. My sister arrived in town a little while ago to spend time with my aunt. I'll let you know as soon as I hear anything from Maxwell about further tests on the uniform."

"Okay," Luke replied.

"And thanks for letting me play with Ashley," Adisa said to Jane. "I hope it helped."

"A lot," Jane said with a glance at Luke. "Oh, don't forget your purse."

Jane reentered the house. As soon as Adisa had her purse, she walked quickly to the street and drove away. She called Grayson's cell phone, but he didn't answer.

"Probably turned off his phone so he

could watch soccer," Adisa muttered.

Arriving at Aunt Josie's house, she saw Shanika's new minivan parked in the driveway.

Emotionally exhausted by the morning's trauma, Jane curled up with Ashley for a late-morning nap. Luke remained hypervigilant. He moved Ashley's crib into the guest bedroom, which was better protected from the rear of the house. In the process he found another bullet fragment beneath the crib. He didn't tell Jane, but he put the metal shard in a fresh plastic bag that he hid in the bottom of his sock drawer.

Checking on Jane and Ashley, who were still sound asleep, Luke took his gun from the top of the refrigerator, quietly left the house, and walked across the yard to the wooded area. As he approached the trees he felt the hair on the back of his neck stand up. His senses sharpened. He carefully made his way forward a couple of steps at a time, turning around to see if he'd reached a spot where the shooter could possibly have fired at the house. He was surprised by how soon the trees obscured the line of fire. Whoever took the shots was very close to the edge of the woods. Several broken twigs and areas of pressed-down underbrush revealed the recent presence of Detective Maxwell and Bruce Alverez. Luke got down on his knees in a likely area and crawled around looking for anything unnatural on the ground. He saw something under a leaf and pulled out part of a torn candy wrapper that looked like it had been there for weeks or months. He stuck it in his pocket.

"Luke! Luke!" he heard Jane yell with clear hysteria in her voice.

Luke scrambled to his feet and burst out of the woods. "Here I am!" he responded. "Everything's fine!"

He ran over to Jane, who was standing sideways in the open doorway at the rear of the house.

"What were you doing?" she demanded. "I can't believe you left Ashley and me alone in the house! You could have been killed. We could have been killed."

Luke opened his mouth to speak but knew words would be meaningless. He reached out to wrap his arms around Jane, afraid she would angrily push him away. To his surprise, she collapsed against him and buried her head in his chest. He took a deep breath and exhaled.

"I'm sorry," he said.

A way to justify his actions began to form in his mind, but instead of immediately offering an explanation, he simply continued to hold his wife. Luke was mad at himself for not considering Jane's reaction when she woke up and he wasn't in the house. And he was seething with rage at the unknown assailant who'd put his family in mortal danger. Finally, he felt Jane begin to relax.

"I'm sorry," he repeated.

Jane pulled away and placed her hands against his chest. "When I couldn't find you in the house, crazy, scary thoughts began racing through my head."

"I'm sorry," he said for the third time.

"What were you doing in the woods?"

"Checking things out, but that was a mistake," he replied. "I should have stayed here with you and Ashley."

Jane nodded. "Yes. For a while I'm going to need to know where you are every minute. It's the only way I can keep my mind from spinning out of control."

"I understand," Luke said. "And that's what I'll do."

Jane brushed a stray strand of blond hair away from her forehead. "Which means I'm not going to take Ashley and stay with my mother in Florida," she said. "I can't keep up with you and what you're doing long-distance. For that, I need to be here."

Luke hugged Jane again. This time tighter.

Adisa and Shanika helped Aunt Josie into the front seat of Adisa's car. They drove slowly down the street. Aunt Josie clearly enjoyed reconnecting with her world.

"The Clancys need to cut their grass," the older woman observed when they reached the corner. "I wonder if they're out of town visiting their granddaughter in Massachusetts. I cut their grass for them when they went to see her last year."

"That's not an option this year," Adisa said.

"Amen," Shanika echoed.

They turned onto East Nixon Street and approached the flower display in the grass beside the spot where Luke shot Deshaun.

"Those are the flowers for Thelma's grandson," Adisa said to her aunt. "Your eyes were closed when we passed on the way home from the hospital."

Adisa pulled to the curb.

"And you're in the middle of this mess," Shanika said to her sister, shaking her head.

Adisa thought about all that had happened that morning at Luke and Jane's house. "Yes," she replied. "Right in the middle."

"Roll down my window," Aunt Josie said.

"If I was walking down this street, I'd stop and pray for Deshaun."

Once the window was open, Aunt Josie slowly raised her right hand and gripped the window frame. Adisa could see the veins standing out on her aunt's hand. It was a hand that had worked for decades to provide for herself and others and taken time to do small things like braid Adisa's hair when she was a little girl.

"Lord," Aunt Josie finally said. "Don't let go of Deshaun. Keep him in your strong hand where the devil can't touch him. Amen."

Aunt Josie released her grip and slowly returned her fingers to her lap.

"That boy is fighting more than one battle," the older woman said. "And he needs reinforcements from heaven."

"The main battle is to live and recover," Adisa replied.

"I prayed what I believed I was supposed to pray," Aunt Josie answered. "God's purposes and his will are bigger than anything we can imagine. And attacks come from more than one direction."

Adisa eased the car forward. "Do you think it's God's will for me to drive us to the Jackson House for take-out banana pudding? My treat."

"That's definitely God's will," Aunt Josie said, turning her head so that Adisa could see a big smile on her face. "If it turns out there isn't any banana pudding in heaven, I want to make sure I eat my fair share on earth."

"Reggie likes banana pudding," Adisa said.

"Then maybe you'd better ask for the Jackson House recipe so you can make some for him," Shanika said.

"Oh, he likes Adisa for a lot more reasons than her cooking," Aunt Josie said.

"He liked the soup I made the evening you came home from the hospital," Adisa protested.

"Yes," Aunt Josie answered. "But I stand by my words."

TWENTY-NINE

Sunday morning appeared with dark clouds in the sky ready to drip rain. Adisa fixed coffee for Shanika and herself. Aunt Josie, still restricted from anything containing caffeine, drank herbal tea.

"Are you sure it's okay for Shanika and me to drink coffee in front of you?" Adisa asked.

"Go ahead," Aunt Josie said. "I'm just thankful to be in my own house on Sunday morning. The only thing better would be getting ready for church. But my problems shouldn't keep you girls from going."

"I'm not sure it's smart to leave you alone," Shanika began. "What if you need help?"

"Don't argue with me like you did when you were a teenager and wanted to skip church so you could meet Calvin Norris in the dugout at the ball field."

Shanika's mouth dropped open. "How did

you know about that?" she asked. "And I only did it a couple of times before his mother found out he didn't really have a stomachache and made him go to church himself."

"I didn't know about you and Calvin," Adisa said. "Aunt Josie, I'd like to hear more."

"Scoot, both of you, and get ready," Aunt Josie said. "You're wasting time."

Adisa and Shanika left the house wearing heels and nice dresses. Adisa's dress had a blue theme. Shanika's outfit was white and bronze.

"The church Ronnie and I started attending about six months ago is casual for everything except weddings and funerals," Shanika said, adjusting her top.

"It was the same with me in Atlanta."

Adisa backed her car down the driveway.

"What do you and Reggie talk about?" Shanika asked.

Adisa summarized some of her conversations with the young minister.

"Are you attracted to him?" Shanika asked while Adisa waited for a traffic light to turn green.

"When he looks at me, I feel like I'm the center of his universe in that moment."

"Wow," Shanika replied. "That's intense."

"But I'd like to see what you think about him."

"If that's what's going on with you, it doesn't matter what I think."

"Could you repeat that? It sounds wonderful hearing those words from your bossy lips."

Shanika laughed and tapped Adisa softly on the arm. They reached the church. The parking lot was almost full, and Adisa had to squeeze into a tiny spot next to a power pole. The sky thundered when they exited the car.

"I hope lightning doesn't hit that pole and cause it to fall and crush your car while we're in church," Shanika said.

"If it does, I'll take it as a sign there's no future for Reggie and me."

Several people recognized the sisters and wanted an update on Aunt Josie's condition. Thankfully, no one mentioned Luke's case.

The sanctuary was buzzing with voices. Adisa and Shanika found seats toward the front. Thelma Armistead was sitting on the other side of the sanctuary surrounded by a group of older women. The choir, wearing brilliant red-and-gold robes, entered from a side door followed by Reggie. Shouts of "Amen!" and "Hallelujah!" burst forth from the congregation.

"That's a bit much, don't you think?" Shanika whispered to Adisa.

Adisa didn't respond. The choir launched into a lively chorus. Shanika had a strong voice, and Adisa moved into her sister's vocal slipstream. An older woman standing next to them patted Shanika on the arm and pointed to the choir loft. The worship was designed to lift the members of the church from the dust of daily life and transport them into the heavenly realm. Group singing can assume a life of its own, and it didn't take long for the congregation to sway and sing as a unit, not a collection of individuals. Adisa clapped her hands in rhythm. There was a pause, and Reggie stepped to the pulpit. A tall, skinny man who was playing an electronic keyboard provided background music.

"That was good singing, church!" the preacher called out. "But I think you can do better!"

"Amen!" the congregation responded in anticipation of a rapid ramp-up in enthusiasm.

But Reggie didn't back away from the pulpit.

"And I'm going to give you a new reason to praise the Lord!" the minister continued.

"What's that, Preacher?" several voices called out.

Reggie grabbed the microphone from its holder on the front of the pulpit and waited several seconds for the anticipation to build before he spoke.

"As most of you know, a neurosurgeon successfully removed the bullet from Deshaun Hamlin's brain several days ago. And around eight o'clock this morning, Deshaun opened his eyes and drank a sip of water!"

Adisa quickly glanced over at Sister Armistead, who stood with her eyes closed and her hands raised high in the air. The choir started a new song, and the older woman left her seat and began to shuffle dance across the front. Adisa suspected none of her former colleagues at Dixon and White would have adequately appreciated the older woman's response to the wonderful news about her grandson. But like a tea bag in water, Adisa had steeped long enough in the black church culture of her hometown to appreciate Thelma Armistead's celebration. Adisa glanced at Shanika, who, like most everyone else in the sanctuary, had her eyes glued to the older woman, who swayed back and forth for a moment before taking a few steps forward. Other women joined her in a chorus line of thanksgiving that stretched across the front of the sanctuary.

"It's like King David dancing before the Lord," Adisa whispered into Shanika's ear.

Shanika nodded her head. "It is holy."

As she watched the ensuing celebration, Adisa couldn't keep from thinking about the implications of Reggie's news for Luke's case. Deshaun entering the courtroom and walking slowly to the witness stand would have a huge impact on a jury. And if the teenager was unable to walk on his own and made his appearance confined to a wheelchair, it would be even more dramatic.

Adisa tried to refocus on Sister Armistead and the group of women who'd labored alongside her in intercession for Deshaun. Adisa had prayed, too. But her prayers in the hospital room now seemed disconnected from her present reality. She remembered the intense reluctance she'd felt when first confronted with the prospect of representing the police officer. Had she made a terrible mistake?

The music slowed, and Sister Armistead and the other ladies made their way back to their seats. Sister Armistead collapsed, and several people began to fan her. The older woman lifted her hands in the air again, as if signaling that though she was tired, the fatigue she felt was the kind that comes after winning an exhausting battle. The choir transitioned to a more intimate song. Adisa closed her eyes and kept them shut until the choir sang its last note.

"What did you think of the sermon?" Shanika asked Adisa when Reggie pronounced the benediction and people began to move about the sanctuary.

"He's a good speaker, but I thought he was going to talk about forgiveness, not why God didn't allow Moses to cross over into the Promised Land."

"Forgiveness?"

"Yes," Adisa replied, glancing in the direction of Thelma Armistead. "I'll explain later. I need to talk to Deshaun's grandmother for a second."

Adisa left Shanika and made her way through the press of the crowd toward Sister Armistead. The older woman was surrounded by those intent on communicating a personal word of thanksgiving. Adisa reached the edge of the group but couldn't get closer. She felt a light tap on her shoulder and turned around. It was Reggie.

"Shouldn't you be shaking hands with people as they leave?" she asked.

"I did, but when you didn't show up I came looking for you. That had to be your sister sitting with you."

"Yes." Adisa looked again toward Thelma Armistead. "I wanted to let Sister Armistead know how thankful I am about her good news and give her a word of explanation about why I'm representing Officer Nelson."

"She already knows about it," Reggie replied.

"Oh." Adisa stopped. "You told her?"

The minister nodded. "Yes. I didn't want her to read about it in the newspaper and question your motives."

"You questioned my motives," Adisa replied. "How did you explain it to her?"

"Even though I disagreed with you, that didn't keep me from truthfully relaying what you said to me."

"How did she react?"

Reggie smiled slightly. "Like the saint she is. The words she spoke at that Wednesday-night service didn't leave her lips and fall to the ground. They took root in her heart. I don't think Thelma has a shred of animosity toward Officer Nelson. That's hard for me, even as a minister of the gospel, to believe. It has to be the result of incredible grace, the kind Jesus showed to those who nailed him to the cross."

Adisa stopped trying to move forward. She could see a woman with tears in her eyes giving Sister Armistead a big hug.

"It made me reexamine what I believe about forgiveness," Reggie continued. "Until I'm sure what to say, I need to keep my mouth shut. So I shelved the forgiveness topic and pulled out a sermon I preached several years ago at a church that was thinking about calling me as their pastor."

" 'LaGrange is to Alabama what Mount Nebo was to the land of Canaan,' " Adisa replied, quoting a line from the message.

"Yes, I added that later. Anyway, the church in LaGrange didn't identify me as their Joshua. I was disappointed then, but I'm glad that I'm here in Campbellton."

"Me, too," Adisa said. "I'd better get back to Shanika. We left Aunt Josie home alone and should check on her soon. Simone is working out beautifully. She was a great suggestion. Thanks again."

"Let me meet Shanika."

Adisa led Reggie over to her sister, who was talking to Darlene Singletary, the former high school party girl. Shanika held out her hand and spoke before Reggie introduced himself.

"Adisa has told me so much about you," Shanika gushed. "And we really appreciate you treating Aunt Josie like one of your own sheep when she was in the hospital."

491

"You're welcome," Reggie replied. "Your aunt is a great lady."

"And Adisa has all her good qualities," Shanika replied.

"I don't doubt it," Reggie said, smiling playfully at Adisa. "Plus a lot more of her own."

Adisa rolled her eyes.

"I know you're super busy," Shanika continued, ignoring Adisa. "But we'd love for you to come over for a visit while I'm here."

"How long are you staying?"

"I have to go home tomorrow to take care of my kids."

"Uh, I'm speaking at the service tonight, and I have several obligations this afternoon," Reggie said. "But the next time you're in town we'll make it happen."

Reggie nodded to Adisa and stepped away to talk to a group of men.

During the return trip to Aunt Josie's house, Adisa told Shanika about Thelma Armistead's reaction to the news that Adisa was representing Luke Nelson.

"Reggie's right about her sainthood," Shanika said.

"Yeah, but her reaction is going to be the exception rather than the rule when the word gets out."

"You're a lot tougher than you used to be," Shanika said. "That's another quality Reggie needs to know about. The last thing a man wants in a woman is for her to be a crybaby about everything. A guy needs to believe you're strong and won't call for his help unless it's the kind of situation where he wants to step in."

"I can't believe that's the way you and Ronnie treat each other!"

Shanika smiled and cut her eyes toward Adisa. "Okay, I'm kidding," she said.

Simone arrived while Adisa was getting ready for work the next day. The caretaker and Shanika hit it off immediately and began talking about twins. Adisa had just started the car to leave when the front door of the house opened and Shanika ran up to her. Adisa cut the engine and got out.

"Hey! Aren't you going to tell me good-bye?" Shanika asked. "I'll be on the road as soon as we finish eating lunch."

Adisa gave her a hug. Shanika held the embrace longer than normal before releasing her.

"That barely scratches the surface of my appreciation for how you've stepped in to help Aunt Josie," Shanika said. "It's meant the world to me that you've been here in

Campbellton. Otherwise I'd be going crazy with worry."

"It worked out," Adisa answered simply.

"I know, but that doesn't keep me from being grateful. And I also admire you taking a job with Mr. Grayson's law firm. Aunt Josie told me you took a huge pay cut. God is going to bless you for being unselfish. And the next time I visit, I promise not to act like a teenager about Reggie, although he is a gorgeous man who has totally fallen for you. Your 'hard to get' approach has worked way better than any strategy I could have cooked up."

Adisa smiled and shook her head. Her sister could effortlessly transition from the divine to the ridiculous in a matter of seconds.

"Thanks," Adisa said, giving Shanika another quick hug.

"And keep me in the loop," Shanika added. "I don't want to have to beat news out of you."

"Or pull my hair."

"Exactly."

When Adisa arrived at the law office, she saw Luke's truck parked in front of the building.

THIRTY

Unable to sleep as he thought about being in court the following morning, Luke got up at 5:00 a.m. and sat in the kitchen drinking coffee until Jane, bleary-eyed, joined him. They sat together in silence.

"Don't give up hope," Jane said after a big yawn. "The sermon yesterday about Daniel in the lions' den was exactly what I needed to hear."

The minister's message hit Luke squarely between the eyes, but he hadn't been able to absorb it as easily as Jane did. He hoped an angel would show up to rescue him, but his faith wavered.

When Luke arrived at the law office, the front door was still locked and he rang the bell. A few seconds later, a man he didn't recognize opened the door with a puzzled expression on his face.

"I'm Officer Luke Nelson," Luke began.

"Sure, come inside. I'm Mike Williams,

one of the other lawyers in the firm. You can sit in the conference room until Theo arrives. Your arraignment is this morning, isn't it?"

"Yes, sir."

Luke followed the lawyer to the room where he and Jane had met with Mr. Grayson and Ms. Johnson.

"Would you like some water?" Williams asked. "No one has brewed a pot of coffee."

"No, thanks."

"I'm glad Theo convinced Adisa to join the firm. She's a very talented young attorney."

"She seems to be."

"They'll be with you shortly."

Williams closed the door and left him alone. Luke divided his time between nervously looking at his phone, getting up to roam around the conference room, returning to his phone, and staring at the portraits of the firm patriarchs on the wall. Per instructions from Mr. Grayson, Luke was wearing a pair of gray slacks, a white shirt, and a tie with a blazer. He'd nicked himself badly in the neck while shaving, and though the blood no longer flowed, he sported an inflamed, irritated patch of skin that felt like it was the size of an interstate billboard. He stepped down the hallway to the restroom and checked himself in the mirror. As he looked into his eyes, he didn't see a man who would maliciously shoot an unarmed teenager of any color. Instead, he saw a man who'd made a reasonable, professional choice under difficult circumstances. Steeled with resolve, he returned to the conference room. Finally, there was a light tap on the door and Adisa Johnson entered.

"How long have you been here?" the female lawyer asked.

"Oh, maybe an hour," Luke replied.

"Couldn't sleep?" Adisa nodded. "I understand, but as you know, the arraignment today is going to be routine. You're not going to have to say anything except 'Not guilty.' Mr. Grayson will be here shortly, but he wanted me to outline what we've done about locating expert witnesses for the case."

Luke tried to follow Adisa's explanation. He understood the reasoning for each expert, but the multiple names she tossed into the mix became confusing.

"Dr. Briscoe is what kind of expert?" Luke asked. "Forensic evidence?"

"No, police conduct. She trains those who train officers."

"And she believes I did the right thing?"

"Don't jump ahead. She didn't render an

opinion. We'll have to pay for that, but she didn't cut me off when I mentioned the basic facts."

"How much will that cost?"

"There are stages of expense. It begins with a charge to conduct a file review, followed by consultation, preparation of a written report, and finally testimony in court. I've put together a rough estimate of what you're looking at, but remember, this could change a lot based on what the best available people cost."

Adisa slid a sheet of paper across the table to Luke, whose eyes widened when he saw the bottom-line figure. The door to the conference room opened, and Theo Grayson entered with two cups of coffee in his hands.

"Good morning," he said. "Sorry I'm a few minutes late."

Grayson placed one of the cups in front of Luke. "You prefer it black, don't you?" the lawyer asked.

"Yes, sir. Thanks."

Luke took a sip of coffee. It was the same expensive blend he'd sampled the first time he met the older lawyer.

"Adisa filled me in on what happened at your house over the weekend," Grayson said. "I'm very sorry your family was endangered and thankful they're okay."

"It's been rough," Luke replied. "But Jane has been a trouper."

"I've been going over with Luke where we are in identifying expert witnesses," Adisa said, pointing to the piece of paper she'd just given him.

"And that's enough for a down payment on a nice house," the officer said, placing the coffee on a coaster.

"Let me take a look," Grayson said as he sat down beside Adisa and read what she'd prepared.

"That's accurate," Grayson said when he finished. "Maybe even a bit on the conservative side."

"Conservative or liberal, there's no way I can ask my mother-in-law to come up with that kind of money," Luke answered. "We'll have to go with who we can find locally. One of my instructors at the community college was a retired sheriff from Banks County. I haven't called him since this happened, but I believe he'd be willing to testify for me. He taught one of my criminal justice classes."

"He might be a fine witness," Grayson said. "But Adisa and I want people who won't wilt under pressure. Please talk it over with Jane. She seemed confident that your mother-in-law would step up and help.

We're not asking that she pay us, only that she let us find the best tools out there to build a solid defense."

Luke knew that if Jane were sitting beside him, she would volunteer her mother's bank account. "I haven't discussed any specific dollar amount with her," he said slowly.

"Which is why I prepared this for you," Adisa answered. "Show it to Jane. Talk it over with your mother-in-law, and let us know what she's willing to do. We only want to spend money if we believe it's going to make a difference."

"And we're under pressure from Judge Andrews to identify who we may call as witnesses," Grayson said. "We don't have to let him know specific people this morning. That would be unreasonable, but we need to tell him we're diligently moving forward in the process."

"Okay," Luke replied with a shrug. "But if this turns out to be a huge waste of money —"

"It will be money spent by someone who cares about you," Grayson said. "But that's not the issue this morning. You've attended criminal arraignments in the past, but it's different when you're the person in the spotlight."

"There's one other thing I need to mention," Adisa added. "It has to do with Deshaun Hamlin's medical status."

"What is it?" Grayson asked quickly. "Is he worse?"

"No, better. He opened his eyes and asked for a drink of water."

Hearing the news sent a shock wave through Luke. Although he'd tried to imagine how he would feel if the black teenager either died or improved, nothing had prepared him for what he felt in that instant. Massive relief was quickly replaced by intense fear. He saw Adisa watching his face.

"What are you thinking, Luke?" she asked.

"I'm not sure," he began. "I mean, I'm glad he's coming out of the coma, but I'm worried about what he might say and how it's going to impact me."

"That's the way it hit me when I heard the news yesterday morning in church," Adisa responded. "It also means another type of expert may be necessary, someone who can run what's called neuropsychological testing on Deshaun."

"He'll have to improve for that to reveal much beyond what the treating doctors can tell us," Grayson said.

"True," Adisa said. "But it needs to be brought up with the judge."

"And you're sure this is true about his

improvement?" Grayson asked. "I'd hate to make a representation to the court that turned out to be false."

"It came from the mouth of his pastor with the grandmother sitting in the sanctuary."

"Okay," Grayson said.

"There's one other thing," Adisa said, clearing her throat.

She told them about her encounter with Sharon Rogers from the Atlanta newspaper.

"She said she was going to be at the courthouse," Adisa said. "And we all know a lot of people in Campbellton subscribe to the *AJC* or read it online."

"Point her out and leave her to me," Grayson said and then spoke to Luke. "All you need to do this morning is say, 'Not guilty.' And say it like you mean it. People will be watching and listening."

"That won't be a problem."

"Good. Adisa and I need to get a few things together before we step across the street. Would you like to wait in here?"

"Yes," Luke said. "The fewer people I see, the better."

"Are you sure we shouldn't say something to him about the beef jerky?" Grayson asked

502

as soon as he and Adisa were alone in the hallway.

"I'm not sure."

"I know it was on the list of items found in Deshaun's pockets on the night of the shooting, but I hate bringing up matters in court when I don't have a basis to do so. It smacks of bad faith."

"And Maxwell didn't tell me anything beyond it being 'bad jerky.' "

Grayson paused for a moment. "Let's throw it out there and argue that the package may contain some form of contraband," he said with a shrug. "The worst thing that can happen is getting chewed out by the judge. It won't be the first or the last time that happens. Prepare a motion for the State to produce it and a proposed order. I'll head over there with Luke."

"Yes, sir."

Adisa returned to her office and quickly typed the motion and order herself. Inside the courthouse, she stopped by the clerk's office to obtain stamped copies for delivery to Jasper Baldwin and the judge.

When she entered through the rear of the courtroom, Adisa was shocked by the number of people packed into the right-hand side of the large room. Almost all of those present were black. Then she realized what she should have anticipated. People had come out in force to observe every second of Luke's case. Standing against the wall, she tried to identify anyone she knew by studying the backs of their heads. It was tough to do, but she thought she saw Reggie seated toward the front. She was troubled that he hadn't mentioned anything after church but immediately pushed the thought to the side. He had as much right to be there as she did.

Not looking to the right, Adisa walked down the aisle. As she passed, she heard murmuring but couldn't make out what was said. Grayson and Luke were sitting on the other side of the wooden railing that separated the spectators from the lawyers and their clients. Jasper Baldwin and a young woman who Adisa assumed was a paralegal or an assistant district attorney sat at one table. Judge Andrews had not yet taken his place on the bench.

Adisa quickly spotted Jamie Standard from the local newspaper. Sitting beside her was Sharon Rogers from the *AJC*. The Atlanta reporter made brief eye contact with Adisa before looking away. Adisa inwardly steeled herself for the personal interaction she knew would take place between them at some point during the morning. This time she resolved not to lose her cool.

"All rise!" the bailiff called out.

Everyone in the courtroom stood as Judge Andrews entered from a small door to the side of the raised bench.

"The Superior Court of Nash County is now in session," the bailiff continued. "Honorable Malcomb Andrews presiding."

"Be seated," the judge said.

THIRTY-ONE

Adisa slipped through the opening in the railing and joined Grayson and Luke. From her place at the front of the courtroom, she began to identify some of the members of the black community who'd come out in such impressive numbers. Reggie was in the front row with Thelma Armistead beside him.

"Mr. Baldwin," the judge said, turning toward the DA. "Call your first case on the calendar."

Adisa leaned over to Grayson. "Where are we on the calendar?" she whispered.

"Last case."

"Last!" Adisa was so jumpy she had trouble keeping her voice low. "Why?"

"Any number of reasons," Grayson replied, keeping his eyes on Judge Andrews. "I'm guessing the judge wants to thin out the crowd, but I don't think that's going to work. Do you recognize anyone?"

"Yes. The woman in the dark-green dress is Deshaun's grandmother. The man beside her is the pastor of her church. There are others I know, but I don't want to attract attention by staring at them."

"I understand. Why don't you scoot your chair at an angle so you're facing the bench?"

Adisa did as Grayson suggested, but the move felt unnatural. She knew her every twitch was being scrutinized. She'd never felt so exposed and vulnerable. She coughed lightly into her hand. Out of the corner of her eye, she could see Luke shifting nervously in his chair. Multiple deputy sheriffs were present to provide extra law enforcement.

Judge Andrews, Jasper Baldwin, and the assistant DA moved efficiently through the calendar. The defense lawyers rose, called their clients forward, and conducted their business in the open area in front of the bench. It was a hodgepodge of arraignments, revocation of bond motions, bench warrant requests for defendants who'd failed to show up in court, and sentencing for those pleading guilty. Several people came forward and entered guilty pleas on drug-related charges. Apparently, the manufacture and sale of crystal meth was an active criminal enterprise in Nash County. The devastated appearance of the women defendants and the cruelty of their addiction made Adisa forget her own sense of vulnerability for a few moments. The women all received probated sentences that included a treatment plan except for one repeat offender/dealer who was given a five-year jail sentence.

"I busted her one time," Luke said, leaning over to Adisa. "She tried to cut one of the other officers with a kitchen knife but didn't remember it the following morning."

As the calendar progressed, the number of defense lawyers in the courtroom thinned. Adisa's anticipation increased.

"State v. Mooney," the judge announced. "Motion to suppress."

Mooney was a landlord charged with possession of stolen goods stored in an apartment he owned. His attorney contended the individual who opened the door and allowed the police to enter didn't have the right to be in the apartment and thus lacked authority to consent to a search. Five witnesses testified. As the testimony dragged on, Adisa saw both reporters leave the courtroom, and the crowd with Reggie began to thin out as people who'd taken time off from work had to leave.

When the final witness in *State v. Mooney* left the stand, the lawyers gave their brief closing arguments to the judge. Judge Andrews repositioned his glasses and stared at Jasper Baldwin for several seconds. The DA seemed nervous. Based on what she remembered about Fourth Amendment law, Adisa suspected Judge Andrews would grant the motion and exclude the evidence.

"Motion denied," the judge said. "Mr. Baldwin, prepare an order. I also strongly urge the lawyers to consult and discuss whether the defendant wants to proceed to trial or change his plea."

The defense lawyer and Baldwin quickly huddled.

"What's going on?" Adisa asked Grayson.

"The judge knows he was on shaky ground in denying the motion and now wants the DA to offer the defendant a sweet deal to plead guilty."

Adisa wasn't used to such a high level of manipulation by judges. Theo Grayson was right about differences in rural and urban justice.

The lawyers separated.

"My client wishes to change his plea to guilty," the defense lawyer said.

"And the State has a recommendation for sentence, Your Honor," Baldwin replied.

It took another five minutes to wrap up the case.

"Court will be in recess for fifteen minutes," the judge said.

"All rise!" the bailiff called out.

Everyone stood as the judge left the courtroom.

"I'm heading to the men's room," Grayson said, turning to Adisa.

Luke and Grayson left Adisa alone. She watched them walk up the aisle to the rear of the courtroom. The aggressive looks people gave them as they passed made Adisa shudder. She couldn't run that gauntlet. Reggie left the group around Sister Armistead and came over to the railing.

"Good morning," he said.

"I'm not sure about that," Adisa replied, shaking her head. "And are you sure you should be seen talking to me?"

Reggie glanced over his shoulder. Several people were watching them.

"I'll tell people I was trying to convince you to repent," Reggie replied.

"That's not funny."

"It's the best I can do. I'm resigned to the fact that we're on different sides of the case, and I'll have to accept the criticism that comes because I'm blind when it comes to you."

Adisa quickly caught her breath. Beneath his reply was the phrase "Love is blind." But now wasn't the time to allow herself to dwell on Reggie's subliminal message.

"Thanks," she whispered. "We'll talk later, but not here."

Adisa saw the two newspaper reporters returning to the front of the courtroom.

"I'll call you," Reggie replied, moving away.

Adisa approached the bailiff. "Is there a private ladies' restroom?" she asked.

"Yes, next to the jury room," the bailiff replied, pointing to a door immediately beside him.

Adisa left the courtroom. When she returned, Grayson and Luke were sitting at the table reserved for defense lawyers and their clients. Behind them, Sharon Rogers and Jamie Standard were talking to Reggie. Rogers saw her and moved a step closer to Reggie. The move made Adisa's skin crawl. She rubbed her hands down her arms and walked over to the defense table. Baldwin and his assistant resumed their places at the prosecution table.

"When should I serve DA Baldwin with a copy of the motion?" Adisa asked Grayson when she sat down and placed the folder containing the motion and proposed order in front of her.

The older lawyer checked his watch. "The judge will be back in a couple of minutes. Slip it to him then. I don't want to answer any questions about it outside the presence of the judge."

Adisa tapped the folder with her index finger. Her desire to turn around and find out if the reporters were still talking to Reggie was like a bad itch she couldn't scratch. She tried to focus on the molding that ran around the top and base of the judicial bench. The door behind the bench opened, and everyone stood. Adisa took the motion from the folder and placed it on the prosecution table in front of Jasper Baldwin. He glanced down at it without looking in her direction.

"Your Honor, *State v. Nelson* is the only case remaining on the calendar," the DA said.

Grayson, Adisa, and Luke moved to the open area in front of the bench. Baldwin stayed at his spot behind the prosecution table. The judge read the indictment into the record. The phrases "aggravated assault," "threat of serious bodily harm," and "contrary to the laws of the State of Georgia" sounded particularly ominous coming from a judge's lips.

"How does the defendant plea?" Judge Andrews asked.

"Not guilty!" Luke said in a loud, clear voice.

The judge handed the indictment to Grayson, who turned it over and wrote "Not guilty" on the back. Luke signed his name beneath the words.

"Unless there is objection by the State, defendant's bond will remain in effect," the judge said.

"No objection," Baldwin replied. "We're in the process of turning over discoverable materials to defense counsel. We've not received any information from them regarding expert witnesses."

"Ms. Johnson will speak to that, Your Honor," Grayson replied.

Adisa cleared her throat. She knew the eyes of everyone in the courtroom were fixed on her back. She quickly summarized her efforts. The judge nodded.

"Very well," he replied when she finished.

"There's one other matter," Grayson said. "We filed and served a motion this morning requesting the opportunity to examine certain items we believe were on Mr. Hamlin's person the night of the shooting."

"What sort of items?" the judge asked.

"A bag of beef jerky," Grayson replied.

"I received a copy of the motion a couple of minutes ago," Baldwin said. "Absent a showing of justifiable cause, the State opposes the motion."

The judge raised his eyebrows. "Mr. Grayson, your response?"

Grayson looked at Adisa, who knew she couldn't reveal what Detective Mitchell had said to her.

"To determine if the bag contained any illegal substances, contraband, or stolen property," she said.

There was an audible gasp from the people assembled in the courtroom. Adisa cringed.

"What is the basis for this allegation?" Baldwin shot back sharply.

Adisa licked her lips. "That will be determined by the results of what the bag contains. We recognize appropriate safeguards will need to be in place to guarantee chain of custody of the material and prevent contamination."

"Judge, this is nothing more than a fishing expedition!" Baldwin retorted. "Defense counsel have no idea what they're looking for."

Adisa started to respond, but the judge cut her off.

"The defendant faces a serious felony

charge," he said. "And the Court is inclined to allow his attorneys leeway to explore all reasonable avenues for his defense."

"The operative word is 'reasonable,' " Baldwin quickly interjected, holding up the motion. "And that's missing from this document. It contains nothing substantive."

"Your argument is noted," the judge replied. "But I'm going to grant the request. Anything else?"

"We've prepared an order for your review and signature," Adisa said, handing it up to the judge.

"Is your expert identified in the order?" Baldwin asked.

"No," Adisa replied. "That doesn't go to the legal basis for allowing —"

"But it goes to the type of order I'm willing to sign," the judge interrupted, handing the sheet of paper to her. "Come back when you can be specific."

"And may the State respond and object to the designation of the expert?" Baldwin asked.

"Yes," the judge said.

"That's all from the defense," Grayson said.

"There's one other thing," the judge said, looking past the lawyers at the crowd assembled in the courtroom. "The attorneys are aware that I'm not going to allow video cameras in the courtroom. That includes cell phone videos or still photos of the parties or any aspect of the proceeding. If you choose to attend further court sessions in this case, leave all cell phones at home or in your car. Violation of this instruction will subject the individual to contempt of court. You have a right to observe. You don't have a right to disrupt. To avoid the necessity of contacting the courthouse about further proceedings in this case, I've instructed the clerk of court to post on our website the date and time *State v. Nelson* will appear on the Court's calendar."

The judge rose and left the bench. Luke immediately turned to Grayson and Adisa.

"What's going on with the beef jerky?" he demanded.

"We'll talk about it at the office," Grayson replied, putting his finger to his lips.

"I should have been told!" Luke replied, his eyes flashing. "I have a right to know what you're doing in my case!"

Hearing the exchange, Baldwin looked at them. "I should have called your client as a witness to explain the reason for the motion," the DA said to Grayson and Adisa.

"The judge wouldn't have allowed it," Adisa replied, moving into position so that she blocked the DA's eye contact with Luke.

"Let's go," Grayson said to Adisa.

The three of them headed to the railing opening. Waiting for them on the other side were the two reporters and the people who'd come to observe the proceedings.

"How do you know there was a package of beef jerky in the victim's pocket on the night of the shooting?" Rogers asked.

Grayson didn't respond.

"Please, no questions," Adisa said to Rogers.

The reporter ignored her and pushed closer to Luke. Grayson led the way up the aisle. The reporters kept pace.

"Isn't it enough that you shot Deshaun?" a male voice called out. "Now you're trying to drag him through the mud!"

"That's crooked lawyering!" a female voice chimed in. "You'll burn for it, and Nelson is going to prison."

"Officer Nelson, what did you say to your lawyers at the end of the hearing?" Rogers asked. "Did you know in advance about the motion?"

"No," Luke replied. "I have no idea what they're doing."

Grayson stopped and spun around. "No comment. No more questions."

"It looks like your client is interested in

clearing his name even if you're not," Rogers shot back. "Why did you keep him in the dark about your trial strategy? Is that your usual practice?"

"No comment," Adisa repeated.

"Was Officer Nelson at home when the gunshots were fired at his residence on Saturday morning?" Rogers continued. "What does he know about the bloody uniform found in his front yard?"

Grayson continued walking. The two deputies at the rear of the courtroom stepped forward to escort them out. Adisa felt a hand on her left arm. She couldn't believe the reporter would try to physically stop her and jerked away. Glancing over her shoulder, she realized it wasn't Sharon Rogers who'd touched her but Thelma Armistead. Adisa stopped. Luke and Grayson continued with the deputies. Sister Armistead, her eyes moist, resumed her hold on Adisa's arm.

"Deshaun is a good boy," the older woman said, her voice intense. "He's never given me any trouble."

While Sister Armistead spoke, a crowd surrounded them. Adisa wanted to pull away, but the older woman showed no interest in voluntarily releasing her.

"I understand," Adisa said. "We don't

know anything yet."

"Your aunt raised you right," Sister Armistead continued. "If nothing else, be true to that."

"Yes, ma'am."

Sister Armistead released her grip on Adisa's arm. Reggie elbowed his way up to them.

"Hey, I have a question for her, too!" a man called out.

"Please, move out of the way," Reggie said, stepping in front of Adisa.

"She has a lot of explaining to do!" a woman added.

Reggie glanced at Adisa, who followed him through the swirl of bodies. Twenty feet farther up the aisle the crowd thinned and they made it to the courtroom door. Immediately on the other side was Sharon Rogers, who'd gone ahead of them.

"You can't suppress the truth," the reporter said to Adisa.

"And it's your job to accurately report it," Adisa replied.

Reggie stepped in between them. He took Adisa's arm and they walked down the hallway to where other people, who hadn't entered the courtroom, had gathered.

"Jail time! Jail time!" several voices chanted.

"Nelson and Mr. Grayson must be downstairs," Reggie said.

Adisa and Reggie reached the top of the stairs. A photographer on the steps snapped their picture. Adisa involuntarily raised her hand to shield her face.

"Don't do that!" Reggie said. "You're not ashamed of what you're doing."

Adisa moved closer to Reggie as they descended the stairs. Luke and Grayson had apparently left the courthouse because the crowd was beginning to disperse. Adisa and Reggie stepped outside into what remained of a sunny morning. They stayed close together until they reached the sidewalk.

"Whew," Adisa said, finally releasing her hold on Reggie's arm. "Thanks. That was scary."

"Not nearly as bad as what young black men feel when being hassled by the police," Reggie replied.

"I know," Adisa sighed. "I understand why people are furious with Luke and upset with me."

"And that talk about Deshaun and the beef jerky made it ten times worse. The judge couldn't hear the murmuring going on around me, but people were really getting upset."

"Including Thelma Armistead. I can't

blame her, either."

"Why was the reporter asking Officer Nelson about gunshots and a bloody uniform?"

"I'm sorry," Adisa replied, "but I can't discuss it. Things are bad all around. The only good news is that Deshaun is better."

"I'm heading over to the hospital to check on him as soon as I finish here."

They walked a block and stopped for a traffic light to change to green so Adisa could cross the street.

"I'm okay now," she said to Reggie. "Go to the hospital. You don't have to walk me back to the office."

"But I want to."

Adisa didn't argue. She wanted to face Reggie, look directly in his eyes, and thank him for caring about her. The light changed, and he stepped off the curb.

"When will you be able to talk about what's going on?" he asked.

"As long as the charges are unresolved, I have to be careful not to comment about information, even if it becomes public."

"Was that the reporter who wrote the article about you in the *AJC*?" Reggie asked. "I saw the press badge around her neck."

"Yes. How did I treat her?"

"Given the chaos, you did fine."

"Good. I lost my temper the other day when she came by Aunt Josie's house, and I didn't want a repeat performance."

They reached the law office and stopped in front of the building.

"Thanks again for rescuing me," Adisa said. "I'm sorry for the backlash you're going to get."

"Oh, I can spiritualize it," Reggie said with a smile. "Jesus commands us to love sinners."

"That certainly applies to me," Adisa said with a slight shake of her head.

Adisa reached out and squeezed Reggie's hand before turning toward the law office.

"Send Adisa to the conference room as soon as she returns from the courthouse," Grayson said to the receptionist when he and Luke entered.

"Why do we have to wait for her?" Luke asked the back of Grayson's head as they walked down the hallway. "What does she know that you don't?"

"In here, please," Grayson replied, holding the door for Luke.

Instead of following Luke into the room, the lawyer closed the door. Luke spun around when he realized he was alone. He was standing in the far corner of the room beneath the portrait of Augustus Frampton when Grayson returned five minutes later with Adisa behind him. The lawyers sat at one end of the table. Luke remained on his feet.

"The woman asking the questions at the courthouse was right," Luke began. "I don't like being kept in the dark."

"And you deserve to know," Adisa began. "An anonymous but reputable source suggested there was something questionable about the beef jerky in Deshaun's pocket on the night of the shooting. Mr. Grayson and I thought we should check out the tip. Since we doubted the DA would voluntarily let us run any tests, we decided at the last minute to file a motion to compel the prosecution to cooperate. We won the motion, or at least got our foot in the door, so long as our expert is accepted by the judge."

"So you really don't know anything?" Luke sat down at the opposite end of the table from the lawyers.

"No, but the law is on our side," Grayson said. "If the bag contained something stolen from the convenience store or illegal drugs or something else that incriminates Deshaun, we have a right to know about it."

"I don't remember anything odd about it," Luke said and then paused for a moment. "It was Mitch Maxwell who talked to you, wasn't it? That's why he asked you to stay behind outside my house on Saturday."

"We'd rather not confirm or deny anything, even though you're our client," Grayson answered. "We want to honor our commitment of anonymity to our source in case he or she has something valuable to pass along later."

Luke nodded. "I get it now. But when it came up in the courtroom, my mind went crazy thinking there was a bunch of stuff you weren't telling me. It didn't help having that lynch mob breathing down my neck. The judge should have stuck around after he left the bench. And who was that lady who knew what happened at my house over the weekend? I didn't mention it to anyone."

"The reporter from the *Atlanta Journal-Constitution* I mentioned earlier," Adisa answered. "She came by my aunt's house one morning and tried to interview me, but I refused to talk to her."

"Okay," Luke relented. "But promise you won't hold out on me in the future."

Adisa and Grayson glanced at each other. "Agreed," Grayson replied.

After Luke left, Adisa turned to Grayson.

"Why do you think he overreacted to the motion about the beef jerky?" she asked.

"He's grasping at every straw trying to control his future when the reality is that it's out of his hands already."

Adisa thought about her own experiences at the courthouse. "I realized this morning how little control I have, too."

"There's one thing you can control — moving forward with identification of our experts," Grayson offered.

"Don't you want to wait for Luke to talk to his mother-in-law?"

"Based on what Jane said the other day, I believe she'll help out. We're in deep, and I'm not going to do anything halfway, regardless of Luke's monetary contribution."

"Okay," Adisa replied, her eyes wide at the implication behind Grayson's words. "You're the boss."

Adisa returned to her office. Within an hour she sent an internal e-mail to Grayson letting him know she'd located a chemist from Atlanta who was willing to evaluate the beef jerky. Dr. Samuel Massey had worked for the Georgia Bureau of Investigation for eight years followed by six years in private practice. A couple of minutes after she sent the e-mail, Grayson appeared in her doorway.

"Does he know that we don't know exactly

what we're looking for?" he asked.

"Yes, and he seemed intrigued by the challenge."

"Then notify Baldwin and the judge. I'm sure there won't be a problem getting someone with Massey's qualifications approved. If what made the beef jerky 'bad' is something other than a chemical substance, I just hope it can be discovered easily."

Adisa worked through lunch. Toward the end of the day, Grayson returned to her office.

"You're a machine," the older lawyer said.

"Sometimes I'd rather work than eat," Adisa said, stretching her arms out in front of her. "I'm much closer to spending more money in Luke's case. Have you heard from him?"

"Yes, we just got off the phone. He spoke to his mother-in-law."

"And?" Adisa asked.

"She's cashing in part of her retirement to come up with the money and says she'll borrow more if needed. My guess is she's desperate to avoid her granddaughter growing up with a daddy who's in prison."

"I'm sure you're right."

"That's not all." Grayson pulled a folded-up newspaper out from behind his back. "The afternoon paper arrived a few minutes ago. We made the front page and the third page."

The older lawyer handed the paper to Adisa. There were two photos from the morning session at the courthouse. The first was of Luke and Grayson exiting the courtroom surrounded by people. The other picture captured Adisa and Reggie descending the stairs at the exact moment she tried to cover her face with her right hand.

"Oh no," she said. "That looks terrible."

"It's not half as bad as the text."

THIRTY-TWO

"Defense lawyer admits engaging in fishing mission," Adisa read as she quickly scanned the article. "That's what Baldwin said, not me!"

Adisa stopped as she remembered her words to Thelma Armistead when she tried to explain that they weren't sure what they would find when they obtained possession of the beef jerky. She looked at Grayson, who was staring at her. Adisa repeated what she'd told the older woman.

"It's not a quote," Adisa said.

"And the reporter doesn't claim it is."

Adisa kept reading. When she reached the final paragraph about her and Reggie, her eyes slowed as if caught in quicksand.

"This is terrible," she said. " 'Ms. Johnson was accompanied from the courthouse by Rev. Reginald Reynolds, pastor of Zion Hills Baptist Church, one of the most visible leaders of those calling for police accountability in the shooting of Deshaun Hamlin. Neither Johnson nor Reynolds could be reached for comment about the nature of their personal or professional relationship.' " Adisa stopped.

"Did Jamie Standard call you today?" Grayson asked her.

"Yes, but I refused to accept the call because we'd agreed on a 'No comment' policy. My history with reporters is one problem after another. But I do need to call Reggie. He's going to be in hot water with some of the members of his church over this."

"You can't let this distract you from our main goal — defending Luke," Grayson admonished. "In some ways, getting the public's attention away from him works in our favor."

"How?"

"I know it doesn't seem that way to you right now," the older lawyer continued. "Seeing yourself in a photo like a Hollywood actress leaving alcohol rehab is unsettling. But I'm looking at the big picture. The public is much more interested in gossip than truth. If people are talking about you and Reggie, then potential members of the jury pool won't be as focused on the charges against Luke."

Adisa shook her head. "Mr. Grayson, I don't see any relevance to this sort of distraction. All it will do is cause embarrassment for Reggie and me."

"In any event, I agree that you should call him. It was chivalrous of him to come to your aid."

"Chivalrous? Yes, that describes how it felt to me. I just hope Reggie doesn't suffer for a good deed."

Simone greeted Adisa curtly on her way out the door. Adisa entered the den where Aunt Josie was sitting on the sofa with the afternoon paper on the coffee table before her.

"I guess I don't need to read the news to you," Adisa said. "Simone did that already."

"Yes, and it didn't matter what I said. She blames you for getting Reggie into trouble. I could have fired her for the way she talked about you, except —" The older woman stopped.

"You agreed with her?" Adisa asked incredulously. "Nobody knows me better than you do, and you've seen the kind of man Reggie is."

"That's true, but good people can make wrong choices. I've kept my peace and supported you because I love you, but after listening to Simone and spending some time in prayer, I'm not so sure about you representing this police officer. The Bible says a good tree bears good fruit and a bad tree bears bad fruit. The fruit I see on the limbs of this criminal case looks bad to me."

Adisa didn't know what to say. "I'm sorry you feel that way," she managed after a few moments passed.

"And the remedy for any mistake is repentance, not remorse," Aunt Josie continued. "I'd rather you quit the job with Theo Grayson and let me support you while you're helping me than see you ruin your and Reggie's reputations."

Reeling at the repeated body blows that had come from the woman whose opinion she valued more than that of anyone else on earth, Adisa turned away toward the kitchen.

"I need a drink of water," she said.

"There's sweet tea in the refrigerator," Aunt Josie responded. "And fresh lemons cut up in a plastic bag. Simone brewed it for our lunch."

Adisa went to the refrigerator but avoided the tea. She leaned against the counter and sipped water from a plastic cup. The reactions from Grayson and Aunt Josie to what happened at the courthouse were totally different and completely wrong. Her phone vibrated in her purse and she took it out. It was Reggie. Adisa wanted to talk to him but wasn't sure she was prepared for the words that waited for her on the other end of the line.

Luke and Jane finished a quiet supper as both of them absorbed the events at the courthouse and the impact of the newspaper article. Luke wasn't sure what to make of the drama involving Adisa and the black preacher. Jane was deeply troubled by it.

"It's like the conversation she had with the DA about a job," she said as she wiped Ashley's high chair clean with a wet cloth. "It's crazy to think she'd openly sabotage your case. I mean, she rushed over here on Saturday and seemed so sincere in her concern for us and Ashley."

Luke walked over to the sink before facing Jane. "I think it will turn the black community against me more than it already is. Nobody, black or white, likes a shyster lawyer who manipulates the justice system."

"Maybe you should talk to Mr. Grayson about it when Adisa isn't around," Jane suggested. "Find out how much time she's been spending with the preacher. Information about your case is supposed to be confidential, but if she's dating him, I'd be afraid she's telling him stuff she shouldn't."

"And not telling me things she should," Luke replied.

"Hello," Adisa said quietly when she accepted the call.

"Where are you?" Reggie asked.

"In my aunt's kitchen."

"Can she hear you?"

Adisa glanced around the corner. Aunt Josie was lying on the couch with her eyes closed, but that wasn't a guarantee she was asleep.

"I'll go outside," Adisa said.

She sat down on the top step of the stoop. Neither Walter nor Mary Broome was in sight.

"I'm glad you called," she said. "But first I need to apologize for putting you in such a terribly awkward spot. You were being considerate of my safety, which I appreciated then and now."

"Maybe, but I pushed too hard trying to impress you," Reggie replied. "And I'm not sure what's going to come of it."

"What do you mean?"

"The saying 'A picture is worth a thousand words' should be multiplied by ten. The photo and article in the newspaper caused

533

an explosion here at the church. I'm not blaming you, but it's bad."

"Other people are," Adisa said and told him about Simone's conversation with Aunt Josie and the older woman's reaction. "If this sways Aunt Josie's opinion, I can imagine the impact on the members of your congregation."

"Four of the six deacons have already called me, and the two who didn't are the ones who like me the least. We aren't supposed to get together until the end of the month, but I'm sure there'll be a special meeting."

"They wouldn't —" Adisa started and stopped. She wished she could see Reggie's face.

"Anything can happen," he said. "I've stepped on a bunch of toes, and the reputation of this church as a voice for the black community is on the line. There's a certain type of leadership they want from their pastor going all the way back to Bishop Williamson in the 1960s. It was a role I embraced when I accepted the call to come here, and they expect me to live up to it."

Adisa hadn't thought she could feel more embarrassed and stressed, but Reggie's words were proving her wrong.

"What can I do to help?" she asked, calling on the last tiny drop of emotional reserve in her tank to keep from bursting into tears.

"I'm not sure, and this shouldn't be all about me. I'm sure this stung you, too."

"Lawyers have to be thick-skinned," she said, trying to sound strong, "especially if they take on controversial cases. Mr. Grayson thinks the publicity may actually help the case."

"How?"

"Uh, I'd better not say." Adisa paused. "Should we not see each other for a while?"

"This case could drag on for months."

Reggie's simple statement helped restore Adisa's soul. "I didn't mean that long," she replied. "But maybe just talk on the phone for a few weeks. I won't come to the church, either."

Reggie was silent for a moment before he spoke. "I can't remember the last time I told someone not to attend church, but in this case you're right. Do you want me to come by and see your aunt one morning when you're not there and try to straighten things out with her?"

"That's up to you, but I think it would be a good idea so long as it wouldn't create more problems for you with Simone listening in. It would be tough to make her leave while you met with Aunt Josie."

"I want Simone to be part of the conversation since she's the one who upset her. If Simone spreads gossip or says something that's wrong, I'll have to address it as her pastor. That's part of my job, even if I don't like to do it."

"Okay," Adisa said. "I'll tell Aunt Josie that you'll be in touch. Let me know how things go with the church."

"Sure, although I expect you'll be able to read about it in the newspaper."

The call ended, and Adisa trudged back inside the house. She told Aunt Josie to expect a visit from Reggie.

"Hmm," the older woman said. "If he goes to that much trouble to talk to me, I'm certainly willing to listen, but I'm still going to inspect the fruit."

Adisa contacted Dr. Massey to make arrangements for him to test the package of beef jerky.

"I can drive to Campbellton and set up at the local community college," the chemist said. "One of my former students is a teacher there."

"That would be perfect," Adisa replied. "It would make it much easier to deal with chain of custody issues and any unwillingness by the local DA to allow potential evidence to leave the county. And remember, this may not be about the beef jerky but something else in the bag."

After the call ended, Adisa sent an e-mail to Jasper Baldwin informing him of the next steps with regard to Dr. Massey. A few minutes later, the receptionist buzzed Adisa's phone.

"Jasper Baldwin is on the phone and wants to talk to you," she said.

"I'll take it," Adisa replied.

"Ms. Johnson," the DA said when Adisa picked up the receiver. "Per Judge Andrews's instructions, we're putting together our responses to your discovery requests; however, before bringing in an out-of-town expert to examine the package of beef jerky, it's going to be necessary for me to circle up with you and Theo to discuss the issue further."

"The judge approved Dr. Massey, and there's nothing to discuss," Adisa replied firmly. "If we need to involve the judge to force compliance with his order, then —"

"Are you and Theo available to meet with me sometime today?" the DA said. "I have a motion hearing later this morning, but I'm free this afternoon. Trust me, you want this meeting."

So far, "trust" wasn't a word Adisa had associated with the DA.

"I'll talk to Mr. Grayson and let you know," she replied. "I'm not sure about his calendar."

"I'll wait to hear from you. Good-bye."

Puzzled by the DA's conciliatory tone of voice, Adisa lowered the receiver and walked down the hall. Grayson's door was open, and the older lawyer was on the phone.

"Your client can certainly take that position if he doesn't care how it's going to damage his business five or ten years from now," Grayson said to the other party. "However, there comes a point in this type of dispute at which both sides need to do some risk analysis and avoid actions that will hurt them more than they'll help them."

Grayson saw Adisa standing in the doorway and motioned for her to enter. She sat across from his desk as he listened to the lawyer on the other end of the line. Grayson rolled his eyes.

"I hear you," he said after several moments passed. "I promise to read the riot act to my client if you do the same. If only one of us tells our guy the truth, it's not going to work."

Grayson listened some more. "All right. I'll talk with Tommy and you meet with

Butch. Remember, my proposal is for settlement purposes only. If Butch wants to go to war, Tommy is willing to do battle."

Grayson lowered the phone. "That's a case you might enjoy working on," he said. "There are sticky financial questions that need someone with an eye for detail to work out."

"It sounds like it might settle."

"Chances are slim to none," Grayson said with a shake of his head. "The other lawyer's client is convinced he's going to win, when at best he has a fifty-fifty chance."

Grayson adjusted his glasses. "What were the aftershocks in your world from the article in the newspaper?" he asked.

"Quite a few," Adisa answered. "But I'm here about another aspect of Luke's case."

She told Grayson about the phone call from Jasper Baldwin. "What do you think it means?" she asked as she finished.

"Baldwin has spoken with Detective Mitchell and knows something. What else could it be?" Grayson turned toward his computer screen to check his calendar. "I have an open slot at three o'clock. You set it up."

"Should I call Luke? He wants to know everything that happens."

"Not until after the meeting with Baldwin."

Adisa and Grayson left the office a few minutes before 3:00 p.m. for the short walk to the courthouse. As they waited to cross the street, her cell phone vibrated. It was Reggie.

"It's Reggie Reynolds," she said to Grayson. "May I answer it?"

"Not if it's going to make us late."

Adisa returned her phone to her purse. They reached the courthouse and climbed the steps to the DA's office. As they sat in the reception area, Adisa thought about all that had happened since the last time she'd been there to discuss the possibility of going to work for Jasper Baldwin.

"Mr. Baldwin will see you now," the receptionist said.

The DA was sitting behind his desk with his feet propped up on the edge. He dropped his feet to the floor and stood as they entered.

"Have a seat," Baldwin said and then walked behind them to close the door. He resumed his place behind his desk and leaned forward so his elbows rested on the wooden surface.

"I'll cut to the chase. I assume your client still has contacts within the police department who are feeding him information outside the judicial process. Once I find out who's doing it, and believe me, I will find out, the consequences will be swift and final. In the meantime, there's no use dragging your former GBI chemist up here to test the package of beef jerky. As you know, there were bits of black tar heroin in the bag."

Adisa tried to maintain a stoic expression as the news dropped on top of her head like a bombshell.

"How much?" Grayson asked.

"About three grams. There's no connection between the drugs and the shooting, but you have your red flag to wave in front of the jury. You can argue that Deshaun Hamlin was engaged in a criminal enterprise at the time of the shooting. But Officer Nelson didn't know about the heroin, or at least he never told anyone at the police department about it. It would be a travesty for him to go free because someone on a jury thinks the presence of a minuscule amount of drugs in a bag of beef jerky justified the shooting."

"Will you stipulate the presence and amount of heroin in the bag?" Grayson asked.

"Yes."

"We'd still like to keep the option open to have the substance evaluated by an independent expert."

The DA shrugged. "Suit yourself, but it will be a waste of time and money."

"Thanks," Grayson said, rising to his feet. "I appreciate the chance to talk this over informally."

Grayson didn't say anything to Adisa until they were outside the courthouse.

"Well," he said, glancing over his shoulder. "What do you make of this new information?"

"It's better for the DA to stipulate the presence of the drug rather than have our expert discover it," she replied. "By admitting it, he removes any suspicion the public might have that we would tamper with evidence, as unlikely as that would be. People who are upset are more prone to believe conspiracy theories. This takes that off the table."

"Anything else?"

Adisa paused for a moment. "My heart breaks for Deshaun's grandmother," she said.

Grayson glanced sideways at her. "It may surprise you, but that thought crossed my mind, too. Do you think Baldwin is right that it's a red herring and doesn't have any true relevance to the case?"

Adisa didn't immediately respond to the older lawyer's question. They crossed the street at a corner near the law office.

"We have to make a big deal about the drugs," she said. "It's the most likely explanation for Deshaun's bizarre behavior as he approached Luke. If Deshaun was acting crazy for a reason, it makes Luke's response more justifiable."

"And provides another reason why we need to review all of Deshaun's medical records from the hospital," Grayson said, nodding. "His lab results will reveal the presence of any illegal drugs in his system. It's not the bullet removed from his brain we need to study; it's the chemicals present in his blood at the time of the shooting."

"I agree," Adisa sighed. "I'll modify the subpoena and serve it on the medical records custodian. Are you going to contact Jamie Standard at the newspaper and let her know about the heroin?"

Grayson shook his head. "No. Even when we have something good to pass along, I'm not going to establish a precedent of trying our case in the press. It will come out in a couple of days when Baldwin files his responses under the criminal discovery statute."

Adisa returned to her office, pulled up the subpoena for Deshaun's medical records, and made the necessary changes. Printing it off, she drove to the hospital. On the way, she remembered the missed call from Reggie.

"Sorry. I was about to walk into the courthouse when you called," she said when the minister answered.

"That's okay, but I wanted to let you know that I'm definitely in the middle of a fiery controversy here at the church. I'm not so naive to believe everyone likes me, but when a mistake like this happens, the matches and kindling come out. The deacons are interviewing people to gauge their reactions before scheduling a meeting with me."

"That sounds like an open invitation to gossip and slander!"

"It all depends on who's talking and how it's characterized. Some folks label it leadership accountability."

Adisa felt sick to her stomach. "I wish there was something I could do," she said.

"Pray. And I'm still going to take time to talk to your aunt and Simone. Anything going on with you that you can tell me about?"

Even if she could, Adisa didn't want to tell Reggie the latest sad news about Deshaun. But thoughts of the young man prompted a different question.

"Just keeping my head down and working," she replied. "How is Deshaun? Has he said anything else?"

"I'm on my way to the hospital now to meet Sister Armistead in the lobby," Reggie said. "From what I've heard, she still supports me, but I'm about to find out pretty quickly for myself."

THIRTY-THREE

Still on the phone with Reggie, Adisa turned into the hospital parking lot and saw the minister park his car in the area reserved for clergy.

"Don't nick that white Lexus," she said. "Who does that belong to?"

"Where are you?" Reggie asked.

"A couple of rows over, but I'll sit in the car so we won't be seen together."

Adisa watched as Reggie, his phone to his ear, looked in her direction. He waved when he saw her. She waved back. They ended the call. Reggie passed through the sliding glass doors. Adisa waited for a couple of minutes before following him. The records department was at the rear of the first floor. She handed the subpoena to a bored-looking young man whose expression didn't change as he read it.

"When was the patient discharged from the hospital?" he asked.

"He's still here," Adisa replied.

"Then you won't receive a complete set of records," the young man replied.

"I understand, but I want what's available now."

"The copy service comes in at ten o'clock at night. It will be quicker if they burn a disc."

"A disc is fine." Adisa hadn't removed the request for the bullet from the subpoena, and she'd added a demand for actual blood samples.

"What about blood samples taken from the patient?" she asked. "Are they still at the lab?"

"We'll have to check with the pathology department about those," the man replied. "They're usually discarded after a week to ten days unless there's a reason to keep them. If preserved, they're frozen, and we don't allow them to leave the hospital."

"You will if the judge orders you to," Adisa replied evenly. "And what about the bullet removed from the patient's brain during surgery? The subpoena covers that, too."

The young man's eyes opened wider. "I didn't see that," he replied.

"That's why I brought it up. Can you find out if it was saved and who has custody of it?"

"Let me talk to my supervisor," the young man said.

He left Adisa standing alone at the counter for over ten minutes. When he returned, an older black woman was with him. She was holding the subpoena in her right hand.

"Ms. Johnson?" the woman asked.

"Yes."

"And what is your role in this case?"

"I'm one of the lawyers representing the police officer who shot the patient."

The woman eyed Adisa for a moment and then cleared her throat. "All physical property of the patient and anything removed during surgery was handed over to the police department. All we have are medical records."

"And blood samples. Were they discarded or frozen?"

"Given the circumstances of the patient's admission, they may have been retained."

"I hope so," Adisa answered. "How soon can I expect to hear from you? Also, who would be the person to verify that the records are complete to date?"

"Within forty-eight hours, maybe sooner. We'll send you a link to a portal where you can access them. Any of the three supervisors in our department can verify what you receive." The woman opened a drawer beneath the counter and handed a card to Adisa. "But Josh Kilian usually handles court-related inquiries."

"Thanks."

Adisa took the card, but instead of immediately leaving the hospital, she went to the second floor to see the nursing staff who'd taken care of Aunt Josie. It was great to be able to share positive news about her aunt's continued improvement. Returning to the elevator, Adisa very much wanted to check on Deshaun, but after the drama at the courthouse, she knew she couldn't.

Luke was sitting in the parking lot of the shooting range when he received the call from Theo Grayson about the presence of black tar heroin in the package of beef jerky. He leaned his head against the back of the seat and offered up a silent prayer of thanks.

"Can I tell Jane? She's been praying that anything hidden in darkness will be uncovered."

"Only if you're sure she won't repeat it to anyone, and I mean anyone," the lawyer replied.

"I understand, but thanks for telling me immediately. I've been persecuted ever since this happened, and even if no one else believed me, I knew there was something wrong with Hamlin. I felt threatened, and now there's a reason why that makes sense."

"We don't know that he had any drugs in his system."

In the rush of news, Luke had jumped to the conclusion that Hamlin was under the influence of an illegal drug.

"But even if his blood was clean, there's no good reason for someone to carry around a bag containing black tar heroin," Luke replied.

"Correct, and the more we can make the case about what Deshaun was doing wrong, the easier it is to create justification for how you responded."

"Right, right," Luke said. "I'm sure they tested his blood at the hospital."

"Adisa is serving a subpoena to obtain the records, and we'll let you know as soon as we receive the results. We may test the material in the package ourselves."

"Why? Won't that be a waste of money?"

"Anything we do that doesn't provide information we can use in your defense will be considered a waste of money in hindsight. But I'm not completely comfortable relying on what the police department and the DA's office tell me."

As a police officer, Luke knew Grayson's comment would have offended him prior to the shooting on Nixon Street. Now he understood the lawyer's concern.

"Okay. Do what you think is best. How are you going to publicize the presence of drugs on Hamlin at the time of the shooting?"

"We're still working through that. It may be best for the DA's office to break the news."

Luke paused. "Is that a decision you'll make or will Ms. Johnson have a say in it?"

Grayson was silent for a moment. "I'll make the final decision, but the reason I wanted Adisa on the case was to provide her unique perspective, as both a former prosecutor and a black person. Are you having second thoughts about her involvement after seeing what came out in the newspaper about Adisa and Reverend Reynolds?"

"Wouldn't you? Reynolds is one of the ringleaders of the people who want to see me locked up. How do we know Ms. Johnson isn't secretly trying to weaken my defense?"

"If she wanted to do that, why would she bring up the tip she received about the package of beef jerky? If she wanted to hurt you, she would have kept her mouth shut, and we might not have ever found out about it. Adisa is on your team."

"Okay, okay," Luke said. "But I'm still counting on you to keep a close eye on her."

The call ended. Luke stared at the gun on the seat beside him. For the first time in weeks, he had something new in his arsenal — hope.

Back in her office, Adisa gave Grayson an update in person following her trip to the hospital to serve the subpoena.

"The notice for the records may turn up in your computer since the firm name was on the subpoena," she told the older lawyer. "The password to access the information will follow separately."

"Good."

"And I left in the request for the surgically removed bullet and added a demand for blood samples that can be tested independently."

"Excellent," Grayson replied. "We're building momentum. Where do we stand with experts to do the testing?"

"Good for everything except a blood expert, but that should be easy to find. There's a doctor I worked with in Cobb County who would be a good choice."

Grayson checked his watch. "It's not too late to call Baldwin and find out if he has the surgically removed bullet."

Grayson scooted his chair closer to Adisa's desk while she placed the call and identified herself.

"Just a minute, and I'll see if Mr. Baldwin is available," the receptionist said.

"Should I record this phone call?" the DA began as soon as he came on the line.

"Excuse me?" Adisa said.

"So you can't misstate what we discuss at a later time."

"Jasper, I'm here, too," Grayson said before Adisa could respond. "We have a question that may not be included in your discovery material. Do you know who has the bullet removed from Deshaun Hamlin's brain?"

"It was delivered to the police department by Dr. Steiner and is now in an evidence locker there."

"Have you seen it?"

"No, but there's nothing exculpatory about it. It reveals the mechanism of trauma to the victim, and I don't think you can seriously argue it won't be admissible. Dr. Steiner is going to testify that she gave Hamlin less than a twenty-five percent chance of survival. Are you going to try to trot out a doctor who's going to testify a bullet to the brain was a slight flesh wound?"

"No," Grayson said. "But we may ask

someone to take a look at both the surgically removed bullet and the one that hit Deshaun Hamlin in the chest."

"I won't oppose that so long as it takes place in a properly controlled environment."

"Thanks."

"Oh, one other thing," the DA said. "Are you and Ms. Johnson the only people in the room?"

"Yes," Grayson replied, raising his eyebrows.

"I have a proposal for your client to consider. Are you interested in hearing it?"

Adisa's eyes widened. Grayson looked at her. She nodded her head.

"Go ahead," the older lawyer said.

"It looks like Hamlin is going to make it. What he's lost in terms of cognitive and physical ability is unknown, but based on my conversation with Dr. Steiner, it's not likely that Officer Nelson is going to face a murder charge."

Adisa's mouth was suddenly dry. She licked her lips.

"I'm not in a position to make a formal plea offer," Baldwin continued. "But I'm willing to run up a flag of truce and see which way the wind is blowing. This case is about to take a lot of time and resources on both sides, and it would make sense to resolve it. You saw what happened the other day at the courthouse. The more this case is kept in the public eye, the greater the likelihood another act of violence will occur. If we can do something sooner rather than later, it will move the community toward healing instead of vengeance. Should I continue?"

"Yes," Grayson replied. "Go ahead."

"First, there's no room for a lesser included offense. Nelson is delusional if he thinks he was justified in shooting the victim, regardless of what was in a bag of beef jerky. Any deal is going to involve an aggravated assault charge."

Adisa's jaw tightened. The truce flag might not make it off the ground.

"I also believe a plea of no contest or nolo contendere under the First Offender Act would be a reasonable approach. That way, Nelson can avoid admitting guilt to save face, and once he completes his sentence and probation, his record will be wiped clean. If he's convicted, you know the judge is going to give him at least ten years to serve in prison, and he could go all the way up to twenty years behind bars."

"That's not happening," Grayson countered.

"And I won't argue the point," Baldwin

replied smoothly. "But you can't promise him anything less than a decade in the penitentiary if a jury finds him guilty. Am I right? Ms. Johnson knows how these cases were handled in Cobb County."

Adisa didn't say anything. Judge Andrews could certainly do what the DA suggested.

"I'll take silence as an admission," Baldwin said.

"No jail time," Grayson replied.

"That might work for me, but it won't for the community. Nelson has to serve at least a year or there will be a riot. He can be assigned to a new facility where inmates serve as firefighters for rural areas of the state. He doesn't have fireman training, but there are plenty of transferable skills, especially in the emergency medical field, that would enable him to fit right in. Then twelve months later he's back at home with his wife and little girl. After knocking out five years on probation he can walk down the street with no felony conviction on his record."

"Any fine?" Grayson asked.

"No, and you should refund some of the retainer he paid you."

"That wouldn't be a problem," Grayson replied with another glance at Adisa.

"The flag is up the pole," the DA said.

"And I'll leave it there until the end of next week."

"Okay," Grayson said. "Adisa, do you have any questions?"

She shook her head.

"We'll be in touch," Grayson said.

Adisa pressed the button to end the call.

"What do you think?" Grayson asked her.

"That Luke ought to consider the offer, but I don't think he will."

"We have to tell him."

"I know. Should I set up a meeting?"

"No," Grayson replied quickly. "Let me do it."

THIRTY-FOUR

An hour later, Adisa pulled into Aunt Josie's driveway and immediately noticed that Simone's car was gone.

"Aunt Josie!" she called out.

"I'm in the guest bedroom," the older woman responded in a weak voice.

Adisa rushed in to see her. "What are you doing in here?" Adisa asked. "And where is Simone?"

"I've been taking a nap," Aunt Josie replied with a yawn. "When the surrounding scenery changes as little as it does for me, I decided that even if my eyes were closed, it would be nice to fall asleep and wake up someplace other than on the couch or in my bedroom. So I sent Simone out to run an errand for me at the grocery store while I rested. She made me promise not to do anything dangerous while she was gone."

"Okay," Adisa replied with relief.

"And you missed Reggie," Aunt Josie

continued. "He came by to see me."

Adisa sat at the foot of the bed. "How did it go?"

"A man in love will say foolish things," the older woman replied, shaking her head.

"A man in love?"

"Come on, child. I may be old and recovering from a stroke, but I have enough brain cells left to read Reggie like a children's picture book. He talked to me for quite a while. It let me see his heart, and I've decided that's his best feature."

"He's amazing," Adisa responded with a smile. "What did he say that was foolish?"

"That he has everything in its proper place related to you and the shooting. He's underestimating how people are going to react. Sadly, folks look for a reason to tear down those in positions of leadership like you and Reggie. The feelings you have for each other cause the world to change shape and look different than it did before you met. It's not fair to judge Reggie harshly for following his heart instead of his head and sense of duty to the black community. He saw that you needed him the other day at the courthouse and didn't hesitate to jump in and protect you. Now that I've had time to think about it, I'd have been disappointed if he did anything else."

"He made me feel special."

"And I'm happy about it. Did you tell him?"

"I hinted at it," Adisa said and then paused for a moment. "But I need to let him know in plain English. Sometimes I feel like we're communicating at a level deeper than words."

"Hallelujah for that," Aunt Josie said as a big smile creased her face.

"Did he talk to Simone, too?"

"They stepped outside for a few minutes, but I don't know what was said."

"Do you think she'll support him at the church? He's catching a lot of flack."

"I'm not sure. All she mentioned to me was that she was going to keep her mouth shut if the topic of you and Reggie came up. A lot of times that's the best thing we can do. I wrote her a little note and put it inside the envelope with her check."

"What did you say in the note?"

"Can't I have a tiny little bit of secrecy all to myself?"

"Yes, but only if you do your evening physical therapy. I want to see how your manual dexterity in your right hand is progressing."

Adisa turned on her computer at the law

office and scrolled down her in-box. The third item was from Campbellton Memorial Hospital with the subject line "Deshaun Hamlin." As she read the medical records, Adisa pictured in her mind's eye the chaotic scene that lay behind the dry medical verbiage: "nonresponsive, sixteen-year-old, African American male with gunshot wounds to upper-right quadrant of chest and right cranium near the ear canal." Page after page documented the ebbs and flows of Deshaun's fight for life.

She reached the operative records of the surgery to remove the bullet from the teenager's brain. The surgical notes dictated by Dr. Steiner were particularly chilling: "dissection, hemostasis, cannula, cranium drill." Adisa knew the bullet was hidden in vital brain tissue and not as easy to spot and pick up as a shiny penny lying on the sidewalk. Each probe, every microscopic movement by the surgeon, could create problems that would impact the rest of Deshaun's life. Though she knew the outcome, Adisa sighed with relief when the notes reported that "the patient was transported to the ICU in stable condition."

Adisa started skipping words as she looked for the answer to her most important question: What was present in Deshaun's blood at the time of the shooting? In their present form the records weren't in chronological order, and the lab reports came after the operative notes. Adisa slowed when the first of several pages of lab data came into view. She wasn't sure how comprehensive the testing might be, but it became quickly clear that the teenager's blood had received an extensive protocol of testing: alcohol, amphetamines, barbiturates, methadone, cocaine, phencyclidine (PCP), tetrahydrocannabinol (THC), and opiates. After each category the same word appeared — "negative." Only the final and most important group revealed a different result. Next to the category "Opiates," where a drug like heroin would appear, was the word "positive." Adisa sucked in a quick breath. She checked the date and time of the blood test. It was conducted within three hours of Deshaun's admission to the hospital.

Adisa continued through the records to the next round of blood tests. The results were once again positive for opiates. At that point Deshaun would have been on prescribed painkillers that would show up in the opiate category. She backtracked and found the earliest record of a urinalysis. Although not as precise as a blood test, it could sometimes yield a different result.

There was a knock on her doorframe. She glanced up and saw Grayson standing in the opening.

"Just a minute," she said, holding up her hand. "I'm in the middle of something important."

Out of the corner of her eye she could see Grayson enter the room. She opened the next page of the records and found the results of the urinalysis. Adisa leaned back in her chair and glanced over at Grayson.

"Deshaun's blood and urine were positive for opiates when he arrived at the hospital," she said. "He was high at the time of the shooting."

Grayson slowly nodded his head. "I'm surprised and not surprised, if that makes sense. I'm surprised based on the kind of young man he seemed to be and not surprised because of the heroin in the package of beef jerky."

"Should we have Deshaun's initial blood samples retested?"

"Do you have any doubt?"

"Not really. The lab technicians were just doing their job. They don't pick sides."

"Let's bring in Luke and show him what you've found. It will also be a good time to bring up the possibility of a plea bargain."

For a split second, Adisa wanted to suggest holding back the results of the blood test as a way to increase the slim likelihood that Luke would accept the DA's informal proposal to end the case. She kept her mouth shut.

"I'll ask my paralegal to call him," Grayson continued.

Luke hung up the phone in the kitchen.

"Who was that?" Jane called out from their bedroom.

"Mr. Grayson's office. He wants to meet with me this afternoon at two o'clock and give me an update."

Jane appeared with Ashley in her arms. The little girl had a jagged red splotch on her left cheek.

"At least they took you seriously when you said you didn't want to be kept in the dark," Jane said.

"What happened to Ashley's face?" Luke asked. "Did she fall down? I didn't hear her crying."

"You would have heard me crying. She got into my lipstick."

"She's a girl," Luke replied with a smile. "Of course she loves lipstick."

"Then it's your job to teach her it's not a crayon."

■ ■ ■ ■

Luke parked in front of Grayson, Baxter, and Williams. He no longer had to introduce himself to the receptionist.

"You may go on back to the main conference room," the young woman said.

Luke was staring at the Augustus Frampton portrait when he heard movement behind him. It was Adisa.

"Have a seat," the lawyer said. "Mr. Grayson is tied up in a deposition that's run longer than he anticipated."

Luke sat across the table from Adisa, who slid several sheets of paper across the shiny surface.

"These are the results of the initial blood and urine tests performed when Deshaun was admitted to the hospital. They're positive for the presence of opiates."

Luke scanned down the list and looked up. "Is there a question about the validity of the results?" he asked.

"No, not in my mind."

Luke was silent for a moment before he spoke. "The fact that Hamlin was high and in possession of an illegal substance like heroin ought to count for something."

"It's another stone in the wall of the

defense we're building."

Luke could tell the lawyer had something else to say, but she didn't seem eager to continue.

"What else?" he asked.

"During a conversation with Jasper Baldwin yesterday, he brought up the possibility of working out a deal that will end the case. It wasn't a formal proposal, but Mr. Grayson and I believe it could become one if there's any interest on your part."

Luke's jaw muscles tightened.

"And under the ethics rules, I have to communicate any offer even if you choose to turn it down."

Luke bit out his reply. "Go ahead."

Adisa laid out the terms of the plea deal. Luke was well aware of the provisions of the Georgia First Offender Act and had heard about the minimum security facility where inmates served communities without adequate numbers of firefighters. He swung between anger at the suggestion that he admit he did something wrong and fear that making the wrong decision would separate him from his family for a decade or more. All the secret thoughts and fears that had plagued him in the night hours since the shooting rushed to the surface. He knew there was the possibility that he could be found guilty and end up in prison, but hearing the words from Adisa's mouth caused a sense of fierce resentment at his predicament. He struggled to maintain his composure.

"Oh, I should have mentioned that all of this would be based on a nolo contendere plea, not a guilty plea," Adisa said as she wound down. "That means —"

"I'm not admitting guilt, just agreeing to be punished," Luke managed.

"Yes, that's a fair way of describing it."

Luke clasped his hands together in front of him and rested them on the table. He bowed his head for a moment.

"It's a huge decision," Adisa continued. "Any objective analysis of the evidence in the case would result in a conclusion that you are at risk for a guilty verdict that would be devastating to you and your family. I hope you won't have a knee-jerk reaction —"

"A what?!" Luke looked up and raised his voice.

"It's just a figure of speech," Adisa said, her eyes wide. "I didn't mean to imply you wouldn't carefully consider —"

"Yes, you did!" Luke shot back. "You think I'm a deranged, racist cop who can't make a rational decision for myself and my family!"

Adisa licked her lips and slid her chair away from the table. "Luke, I think this conversation is over," she said. "We'll reconvene when Mr. Grayson can join us —"

Luke pointed his finger at Adisa's face. "The next time we reconvene, or whatever you want to call it, you are not going to be in the room. I'm not guilty! Is that clear?"

Adisa nodded nervously as she replied, "Yes. Very clear."

THIRTY-FIVE

Adisa glanced apprehensively over her shoulder as Luke exited through the door that led to the reception area. She made it to the chair behind her desk and collapsed. It took several deep breaths for her to calm down.

Maybe Luke was right. She knew her heart and her mind were divided. Part of her saw no basis for Luke's actions other than a deeply rooted racial bias. Another part was determined to vigorously argue that the officer was innocent until proved guilty beyond a reasonable doubt. Adisa glanced at the computer and saw an e-mail from Theo Grayson:

Ask Nancy Kate to reschedule the meeting with Luke Nelson for tomorrow afternoon.

Adisa had gone into the conference room

without checking her in-box. With one last sigh to calm her nerves, she began to check other e-mails in an effort to restore a sense of stability to her day. The phone on her desk buzzed, causing her to jump. She wasn't settled down yet. She picked up the phone anyway.

"Who is it?" she asked.

"Reggie Reynolds. Do you want to send him to voice mail?"

Adisa hesitated for a moment. "No, I'll take it."

She put the phone on speaker. "I just came out of a four-hour meeting with the deacons at the church," Reggie began. "It started over a late breakfast and stretched into the afternoon. One of the things that came up had to do with threats against you."

"What?" Adisa buried her face in her hands.

"The son of one of the deacons mentioned it to his father last night. The young man runs with a rough crowd and heard people identify you as a target for an attack. I didn't want to scare you, but I wouldn't have felt right if I hadn't let you know right away."

"Sure, thank you," Adisa answered.

Her thoughts immediately went to her close encounter with the group outside the rec center the night of the big rally.

"People talk among themselves, but nothing comes of it," Reggie said. "That doesn't make me feel better about your safety, though."

"I'm more worried about Aunt Josie," Adisa replied, trying to get the focus off herself.

Whoever fired the shots at Luke Nelson's house could do the same at her aunt's place.

"I'm not sure what to do," Adisa said.

"I do," Reggie said in an emphatic tone of voice. "You should withdraw from representing Officer Nelson. Mr. Grayson would issue a press release so it gets out to the public. You can help in the background but won't show your face at the courthouse or do anything that looks like you're still defending the white cop. This isn't about Officer Nelson or Deshaun. It's about you."

Reggie's words brought pent-up tears to the corners of Adisa's eyes. She tried to steady her voice before answering.

"Are you a pastor or a prophet?" she managed.

"What do you mean?"

"I hear what you're saying, and I'll discuss it with Mr. Grayson, but when I accepted a position with the law firm, I had to agree to be part of the team representing Luke. It was a condition of getting the job."

"Then leave. You don't need Mr. Grayson to practice law in Campbellton. With our connections in the black community, you'd have tons of clients in no time. All you'd have to do is open an office."

"Reggie, that's not the type of law I want to practice. You're talking about a business model that hasn't worked for a generation. Attorneys have to specialize to be competent, and I've found a niche in the business law area that I enjoy. Those types of corporate clients in Nash County come to firms like Grayson, Baxter, and Williams, not someone who hangs out a shingle and offers free coffee."

Reggie was silent for a few seconds. "I'm just trying to help," he said.

"I know. Tell me what the deacons decided."

"I'm still the pastor at the church," he said. "All but one of them understood why I stood by you at the courthouse the other day."

"That's a relief. I needed to hear some good news today."

"I hope I didn't come on too strong, but please, think about what I've said," Reggie continued.

Adisa thought about Luke's reaction to an

innocent verbal slipup. "No, I know you care."

"I'm sorry," Jane said. "But it may work out for the best. I guess she wasn't able to separate who you are and what happened from the color of your skin."

"She was so condescending," Luke said and stopped. "I may have overreacted."

"But you had to speak the truth."

"And the plea bargain?" he asked. "Whenever I imagine myself caving in and giving up, it causes my stomach to twist into a huge knot."

"Mine does the same thing."

Luke buried his head in his hands for a moment before looking up. "But I have to talk to Mr. Grayson."

Jane placed her right hand on top of Luke's. "I understand less about the law than you do, and Mr. Grayson knows more than anyone else we can turn to. You should talk to him."

"Yeah," Luke said and nodded.

Jane continued, "If there's a way to end this torture without violating your integrity as a man, I want us to consider it. You know, I know, and someday Ashley will know, that her daddy is a good man who would do anything he could for his family. I believe you're not guilty, but I'm not sure it's possible for you to get a fair trial in this town. And the unknown terrifies me. You being branded as a criminal makes me so mad I can't even think about it, but what I believe or wish won't mean a thing when you face a jury."

Luke sighed.

"Look in my eyes," she said.

Luke met the gaze of the only woman he'd ever loved.

"I am determined with all my heart to support you one hundred percent whatever you do and whatever happens. Do you believe me?"

"Yes, I do. And that means the world to me."

Grayson didn't return to the office by 5:30 p.m., and Adisa wasn't ready to talk to him anyway. She ate a quiet supper with Aunt Josie. The older woman wasn't feeling well, and Adisa kept quiet about the day's events.

"I'm going to sleep early," Aunt Josie said with a yawn.

"Maybe you should sleep in the guest bedroom," Adisa suggested.

The small guest room had only one window with a large oak tree positioned like a rugged shield in front of it.

"No, I took a nap in there this morning, and my own bed is calling my name," Aunt Josie replied. "Why would you care where I sleep?"

"Oh, you mentioned a change of scenery the other day. What would you think about going to spend a week or two with Shanika? You've made so much progress with your therapy. I can take care of things around here."

"I'm not sure I should be around the children. They're rambunctious, and Ronnie Jr. doesn't know his own strength. Shanika called this afternoon and was telling me about all he's getting into at school. He's taller than any other boy in his class."

Aunt Josie perked up talking about Shanika's children. Adisa only half listened as she cleared the table and loaded the dirty dishes into the washer.

"Do you need help taking a shower?" Adisa asked when the older woman finished telling her about the latest antics of the twins.

"No, I didn't do anything to get sweaty today, and Simone can help me in the morning after you go to work."

Pushing a walker, Aunt Josie slowly made her way to her bedroom.

"You're doing great with that!" Adisa

called out after her.

Aunt Josie raised her left hand in the air. "I know where my strength and healing come from," she replied.

As soon as the sun went down, Adisa turned on every outside light for the house. She hoped it signaled vigilance to anyone on the outside. She lay down to a fitful night of sleep interrupted by disturbing dreams.

Grayson's car was in the parking lot when Adisa arrived the following morning. She marched directly to his office. He smiled in greeting when she entered.

"Nancy Kate said Luke stopped by yesterday afternoon. How did the meeting go?"

"Not good," Adisa said.

Grayson's face grew more and more serious as she repeated the conversation. "I should have warned you," he said when she finished.

"About what?" Adisa asked.

"I could tell Luke was getting suspicious of your loyalty after the incident at the courthouse with Reverend Reynolds."

"If I were in his shoes, I could see how it might look." Adisa's shoulders slumped. "And then I tell him not to have a 'knee-jerk reaction' to the DA's plea offer."

"A poor choice of words."

Adisa shook her head. "Terrible. I lay awake for over an hour last night playing that over and over in my mind and wishing I could erase the tape."

"It's done," Grayson replied. "And once a bell is rung, the sound reverberates all over town."

"So you're taking me off the case?"

"We have no choice."

Adisa experienced an odd mixture of embarrassment and relief.

"You can still assist me behind the scenes," Grayson continued. "That will be a big help, but I don't want to go it alone in a high-profile case like this. The deposition yesterday was in Richard Lankford's office. He asked me how things were going and seemed very interested in what I could tell him. Rick is one of the best young trial lawyers in the circuit."

"Do you think he'd take it on pro bono?"

"No, no," Grayson replied. "He's building a law practice, not riding off into the sunset. He would want a sizable fee even if he was second chair at trial."

"Can Luke pay the fee?" Adisa asked as much to herself as Grayson.

The older lawyer leaned forward. "He made a choice yesterday. He'll either come up with the money or seriously consider the plea bargain."

Adisa was able to focus enough to complete her review of the discovery materials provided by the DA's office. There were a lot of documents, but no big surprises. Officer Bruce Alverez's account of the scene on East Nixon Street after the shooting confirmed what they'd heard from Luke. Included were interviews with people who lived in the area, some of whom Adisa knew slightly. Several heard the gunshots and looked outside but didn't see anything relevant. As she worked, Adisa began transitioning into her new, limited role as support person to Grayson.

She prepared a detailed memo for Dr. Briscoe, the expert in police conduct, and sent it to her. Within an hour, Dr. Briscoe promised to review the information by the end of the week and provide preliminary observations and additional questions that might need answering.

Vic Robinson, the ballistics expert, agreed to squeeze in a preliminary examination of the bullets the following day on his way to Greenville, South Carolina, to testify in federal court. Adisa stuck her head in Grayson's office to give him the news.

"Once Dr. Robinson takes a look, he'll

decide the type of testing necessary, from microscopic comparison all the way to instrumental neutron activation analysis," she said. "Do you think it's okay for me to attend that meeting? It will be at the police department."

"You have to do it. I'm unavailable. What about the crime scene reconstructionist?"

"It's set up for two days next week here in Campbellton. I checked your calendar, and Wednesday and Thursday seemed best. I sent Dr. Briscoe a detailed description of what happened based on the police report and the recorded interview with Luke at your first meeting. The more interaction I have with her, the more impressed I am."

"Anything else?" Grayson asked.

"No. Have you contacted Luke?"

"Yes, he's coming in at two o'clock."

The phone on Grayson's desk buzzed, and he picked it up. "Yes, she's here with me," he said, looking at Adisa. "I'll let her know."

Grayson lowered the receiver. "Reverend Reginald Reynolds is in our reception area and wants to see you."

"After what happened the other day at the courthouse, Reggie and I weren't going to see each other for a while," Adisa said. "What do you think?"

"Beyond the rules of attorney-client confidentiality, I claim no right to influence your interaction with Reggie Reynolds," Grayson said. "And Luke forfeited his ability to try to regulate that part of your life yesterday."

Adisa walked down the hall into the reception area, where she found Reggie sitting in a corner.

"What's going on?" Adisa asked in a low voice.

"Let's go someplace private where we can talk," Reggie replied.

"We could use our conference room."

"No." Reggie shook his head. "Not here."

Adisa thought for a moment. "I know a place," she said. "Drive around to the rear of the building. You can leave your car there, and I'll drive."

"Where are we going?" Reggie asked as soon as they were in the car.

"The old cemetery for the Westside Church." Adisa noticed that Reggie was wearing a very nice suit and a tie. "Why are you dressed up?"

"I'm helping Pastor Kolb officiate at a funeral later this afternoon. It's a graveside service at the main cemetery on Oaklawn Street. But what I wanted to talk to you about was Deshaun."

"How is he?"

"Better."

Adisa waited, but it was obvious that Reggie wasn't going to say anything else for now. It took only a couple of minutes to reach the cemetery. She pulled onto the gravel road and parked beneath the limbs of the gnarly sycamore tree. They sat on the streaked marble bench with the Bible verse engraved on the front.

"What's going on?" she asked.

Reggie loosened his tie. "I debated whether to tell you what's happened, but I can't keep this information to myself. As you can imagine, Thelma Armistead has been devastated since the news came out about the heroin. I spent a long time with her in my office yesterday morning listening to her and praying for her. She blamed herself for being blind to a problem and was gripped with fear that even if Deshaun lives, he might not get a chance to make it right with the Lord. I tried to tell her that even when we do our best, young people have the power to make choices, but it sounded hollow to me, and I don't think it helped her. Anyway, she asked me to come to the hospital this morning and pray for De-shaun."

"I bet you helped her more than you realized," Adisa said.

"When we arrived at the hospital, Deshaun was lying in bed unresponsive with his eyes closed. The nurses said he mumbled gibberish in the night but nothing since. His breathing was strong, and the postsurgery MRI scan showed a small decrease in the swelling of his brain. Thelma pulled a chair close to the bed and asked everyone except me to leave the room. She grabbed Deshaun's hand and began to pray." Reggie paused and shook his head. "Adisa, she prayed like I've never heard anyone pray before. And I've heard a lot of prayers from a lot of sincere, godly people. Tears rolled down her cheeks. Some landed on the bedsheet, some on Deshaun's hand. When she said 'Amen,' she asked me to pray, but I had nothing to offer. That's when it happened."

Adisa held her breath.

"Deshaun opened his eyes. He saw his grandmother, and there's no doubt in my mind he recognized her. Sister Armistead saw it, too, and she shouted 'Hallelujah!' so loudly I thought it would bring a flood of people into the room."

Chill bumps appeared on Adisa's arms.

"Deshaun looked at me, but I don't think he knew me. His grandmother leaned over and told him, 'The preacher is here so you can ask the Lord Jesus to forgive your sins.

Do you want to do that?' While I watched, Deshaun blinked his eyes and nodded his head so slightly that it would have been easy to miss it. Thelma put his hand in mine, and I prayed for him. I asked him to squeeze my hand if he agreed with my prayer, and he did."

"Praise the Lord," Adisa said softly. "What a gift. For him and his grandmother."

"That's not all," Reggie said. "When Thelma leaned over and told him that Jesus forgave him for having anything to do with heroin, Deshaun shook his head. She tried to explain, but he became agitated, and I stepped in. Taking his hand in mine again, I asked him to squeeze my hand once if he remembered anything about heroin. He did. Then I had an idea. I asked him to squeeze my hand twice if the heroin didn't belong to him."

Reggie looked directly into Adisa's eyes. "He squeezed my hand twice. There's no doubt about it, Adisa. There's something we don't know about the drugs they found in the package of beef jerky on the night of the shooting."

The news, if true, would significantly damage Luke's defense.

"That would be up to the police," she replied slowly. "They're the ones with the resources to investigate."

"I don't think so. You may be representing the officer, but you care more about Deshaun than anyone dressed in blue."

Adisa felt trapped. "The purpose of any legal investigation is to determine the truth," she said, more to herself than to Reggie.

"Of course, or at least it should be."

Adisa stood and paced back and forth in front of the bench. "The first thing to consider is a link between the drugs and the man from Atlanta who attacked the clerk at the convenience store. He's not been caught. Nobody even knows his name. The boys in the store could only identify him by a nickname. I was going to talk to them at some point, but I've been focused on Deshaun's medical records and organizing the expert testimony we're going to need at trial."

"You've seen his medical records?" Reggie asked.

"Yes, but I can't talk about any details."

"I know. Did that include tests on his blood the night of the shooting?"

Adisa nodded.

"That's enough," Reggie replied. "Sister Armistead told me early on that Deshaun's blood work and urine came back positive for the presence of opiates."

"She did?" Adisa asked in shock. "Then why was she surprised when heroin showed up in the package of beef jerky?"

"Because Deshaun was taking a pain reliever prescribed by a local orthopedist. He'd injured one of his shoulders in a pickup basketball game, and it was hurting so badly Thelma took him to the doctor to make sure it wasn't something that would require surgery. The orthopedist gave him a prescription for a strong painkiller."

"Do you remember the name of the drug?" Adisa asked, her mind reeling.

"No, but Thelma wanted me to know about it in case word got out and I had to stop any nasty gossip about Deshaun being high."

"That is huge," Adisa said, checking her watch. "I need to get back to the office and talk to Mr. Grayson before he meets with Luke."

"Are you going to tell them that I told you about this?"

"Mr. Grayson knew you stopped by to see me. I was in his office when the receptionist told him you had arrived."

"Okay," Reggie replied.

Adisa stood at the rear door and waved as Reggie turned out of the parking lot. Passing him on the way in was a red pickup truck. Behind the wheel was Luke Nelson. He glared at Reggie and then turned his gaze on Adisa.

THIRTY-SIX

Luke glanced to the left and saw the black pastor who'd been at the courthouse. His eyes then shot to Adisa Johnson, who was waving to one of the main leaders of the movement dedicated to sending Luke to prison. Luke gripped the steering wheel so tightly his knuckles turned white. Adisa saw him and turned to quickly enter the office. Luke parked his truck and walked around to the front entrance. One way or another, he was going to have to get things straight with Mr. Grayson. Exactly how, he wasn't sure.

Luke was a few minutes early for the 2:00 p.m. meeting with the lawyer. While he waited, the pressure inside him built up like a volcano about to explode. It was 2:20 p.m. before a receptionist he hadn't seen before looked in his direction and spoke.

"Mr. Grayson will see you in the main conference room. Do you need me to show you where to go?"

"No," Luke said as he walked quickly through the door and down the hallway.

The conference room door was open when he charged inside. Mr. Grayson sat alone at the head of the table.

"Have a seat, Luke," the older lawyer said. "This will be a short meeting. I know you mentioned taking Ms. Johnson off the case, but I want to make sure that's what you want me to do."

"Yes, sir," Luke said emphatically. "And I don't want her to have access to any of my records. I just caught her with the black preacher heading up the campaign against me."

"Adisa's role will be limited to legal research that I'll double-check for accuracy," Grayson replied smoothly.

Luke knew if he pushed too hard he'd be without any lawyer at all. "All right," he said reluctantly. "I've had doubts about her from day one."

"And I'm going to need additional legal support beyond what she can provide," Grayson continued. "Which means associating a lawyer from another firm in town to assist me. That's going to require money. I've talked with Richard Lankford, and he's willing to come aboard."

Luke was familiar with the brown-haired lawyer in his midthirties. Lankford was very smooth and confident.

Luke nodded. "That's great."

"Do you think your mother-in-law will be willing to foot the bill?" Grayson continued.

"How much?"

Grayson quoted a figure that made Luke swallow. "One way or another, we'll have to figure out a way to pay it," he said.

"Come up with the retainer by the middle of next week when the crime scene expert is scheduled to be in town for a couple of days. I want Richard involved in that process."

Luke paused for a moment. "Uh, I guess we should talk about the plea bargain," he said.

"Which Baldwin confirmed as a solid offer ten minutes ago. But it can be withdrawn at any time as the case unfolds."

"What do you mean?"

"It turns out there's a legitimate reason why opiates were found in Deshaun Hamlin's blood. He was taking pain relievers prescribed by his doctor at the time of the shooting. There's no proof he was high on heroin."

"But he still had heroin in the bag of jerky, right?"

"Yes, but this undercuts our argument that he was strung out on illegal drugs and therefore acted irrationally."

"For whatever reason, he didn't act normally," Luke retorted. "Why did he charge me when I told him to put his hands on his head and walk slowly?"

"You're absolutely right. That's a very relevant question. The jury will have to decide whether Deshaun's failure to obey your commands justified shooting him in the head and upper chest."

Luke hesitated. The way Grayson framed the issue, without any emotional baggage attached to the words, brought Luke face-to-face with a wall he wasn't sure he could climb.

"Does the DA know about the prescription meds?"

"He hasn't mentioned it, but I guarantee you he is going to find out eventually."

"How long do I have to decide about the plea bargain?"

"Baldwin said he was going to bring down the flag of truce by the end of next week. He can certainly lower it sooner if we don't respond."

Luke felt totally trapped. His hands began to sweat. "Do you think I should take the deal?" he asked, knowing he didn't want to hear the answer.

Grayson paused for a moment before speaking. "Luke, there have been many times in my career when I didn't hesitate to recommend that a client accept a plea bargain. This isn't one of those times. Reasonable people could hear the facts of your case and either convict you or acquit you. Baldwin's offer is a good one if you want certainty about the future. But it will come with heavy baggage that you will carry for the rest of your life, even if you complete the terms of the first offender program."

"I've got to think this through and talk to Jane."

"Of course, and I'm here if you have any questions. In the meantime, I'm going forward with preparation of your defense, and I want to bring Rick Lankford on board as soon as possible. If we work out a deal, Rick isn't needed."

"Okay," Luke said with a sigh.

"It's confirmed," Grayson said to Adisa as he stood in the doorway of her office. "Not that there was any doubt. You're off the case."

"I want to apologize again for messing up the meeting with Luke. Should I apologize to him for the way I came across?"

"Now isn't the time for apologies. We have work to do. Luke wasn't thrilled when he saw Reggie here a few minutes ago. I'm not going to renege on my commitment to represent Luke pro bono, but there are going to be consequences for him cutting you loose. Send me a detailed memo of what you think needs to happen next in the case. I told Luke you were going to perform research. He didn't like it but agreed."

Adisa spent the rest of the day working on the memo. She went far beyond what Grayson requested and included suggestions and thoughts about aspects of the case all the way through trial. He left the office before she finished, so she put it on his desk beneath a glass paperweight in the shape of the state of Georgia.

On her way home, Adisa drove slowly down East Nixon Street. There were fresh flowers at the place where the shooting occurred. Adisa offered up a prayer for truth to prevail and justice to be done.

Parking in the driveway at Aunt Josie's, she picked up the afternoon newspaper. Front and center was an article about the presence of heroin in the package of beef jerky taken from Deshaun's pocket. The reporter referenced only "anonymous official sources" for verification. Adisa's heart sank for Thelma Armistead. She took the newspaper inside the house, not intending to let Aunt Josie see it. Her aunt and Simone were eating supper.

"How are you feeling?" Adisa asked the older woman.

"Better and better," Aunt Josie replied. "You've got to try this casserole. Simone put in everything I like and topped it off with cheese."

Adisa joined the two women at the kitchen table. "Is this your recipe?" she asked Simone after trying a bite of the casserole.

"I modified it a little bit, but it's something Sister Armistead brings to every covered dish dinner at the church."

Adisa put down her fork and left the table to retrieve the newspaper she'd taken directly to her bedroom. She read the headline and lead paragraph. Simone's eyes widened. Aunt Josie's face became sad.

"All I'm going to say is that you can't believe everything you read in the paper," Adisa said.

"We need to pray for Thelma," Aunt Josie said. "Right now."

The three women bowed their heads.

The following morning while they were drinking coffee, Adisa told Aunt Josie that she was no longer working on Luke's case.

"I can't give you the reason," she said, "but Mr. Grayson isn't going to fire me over it."

"Theo's a good man," Aunt Josie said with a nod. "And I'm thankful the stress and pressure you've been under are gone."

"Don't tell anybody yet. It won't become public knowledge until paperwork is filed at the courthouse."

"Does that mean you don't have to rush off to the office so early?" Aunt Josie asked.

"Yes, I can stay a few extra minutes."

Aunt Josie rubbed the tops of her legs with her hands. "I'd like to take a little walk this morning before Simone gets here."

"Are you sure that's a good idea?"

The older woman pointed up at the ceiling. "He says it is. Do you want to argue with him?"

"No, ma'am." Adisa shook her head. "Where would you like to go?"

"East Nixon Street where Thelma's grandson was shot. I need to add to what I prayed the other day. It's only three blocks away."

Adisa helped Aunt Josie get dressed. She was able to manage everything except tying her shoes.

"You're doing fantastic," Adisa said when they finished.

"How does my hair look?" Aunt Josie asked.

"Less gray and more white," Adisa replied honestly.

"That's just a sign of the glory."

"Do you want to use your walker?"

"Yes, but I'll bring my stick, too. You can carry it for me."

Adisa grabbed the walking stick from its place behind the front door and helped Aunt Josie descend the front steps. They moved slowly but steadily down the driveway, Aunt Josie pushing the walker with Adisa beside her.

"How are you feeling?" Adisa asked when they reached the end of the driveway.

"Don't be asking me that every ten feet."

"I'll be quiet."

"No, I want you to participate."

Not exactly sure what the older woman meant, Adisa stayed by her side as they passed Walter and Mary Broome's house. Aunt Josie began praying.

"Lord, bless Walter and Mary and strengthen them for all the purposes you have for them until they go to be with you. May their children and grandchildren open their hearts to Jesus and know the height and depth and breadth of his love for them."

Adisa watched as her aunt prayed.

"Your turn," Aunt Josie said.

"What?" Adisa asked.

"Pray what the Lord puts in your heart for the Broome family."

"Okay."

Adisa glanced at the house before she spoke. "Uh, I especially pray for their daughter, Leanne, and ask that she will find the healing you have for her after going through her divorce. May her children know that God is a loving Father even though their natural father abandoned them. May he repent and return to his family a changed man."

Adisa stopped. Aunt Josie continued to shuffle forward. She nodded her head.

"Yes, I was thinking about Leanne, too, but you said it way better than I could have."

"That's not true."

"Don't argue with me." Aunt Josie began moving forward a bit faster.

And so it went. They didn't pray as they passed every house, but twelve families received prayer without knowing or asking for it. When they reached the site dedicated to Deshaun, Aunt Josie stared at the fresh flowers, photo, and basketball.

"Hand me that ball," she said to Adisa.

Adisa picked up the basketball and balanced it on the front of the walker. Aunt

Josie placed her hands on the ball and closed her eyes. Her lips moved, but she didn't speak out loud. Even though it was a warm morning, a chill ran down Adisa's arms, and she rubbed them.

"Amen," Aunt Josie said, opening her eyes. "What do you have to add?"

"I'm not sure what you prayed."

A car drove by and the driver honked the horn and waved. It was a neighbor whom they'd prayed for. Aunt Josie touched her forehead in response. Without thinking, Adisa raised the stick in greeting before quickly lowering it.

"Go ahead," Aunt Josie said. "Just pray what's in your heart."

Adisa thought for a moment. Her eyes went to the basketball, which still rested on the front of the walker.

"I pray that Deshaun will be able to dribble a basketball again. Amen."

"That's good," Aunt Josie said. "Now, will you go back to the house and get the car? I don't think I'm up to walking home."

"Are you okay?"

"Yes, but I've reached my limit."

"Do you want me to leave the walking stick?"

"No." Aunt Josie smiled. "It looks better in your hand than it does in mine."

Carrying the stick, Adisa jogged to Aunt Josie's house. When she returned with the car, the older woman was sitting on the curb with her head resting in her hands. She looked up as Adisa slowed and stopped. Adisa helped her stand and get into the car. Aunt Josie leaned her head against the seat and closed her eyes.

"There was a time when I could walk for two hours and feel the same as when I left the house," the older woman said. "Now I go three blocks and it wears me out."

"I'm impressed," Adisa replied. "You've recovered wonderfully."

Aunt Josie opened her eyes and turned her head toward Adisa. "I love you," the older woman said.

"I love you, too," Adisa said as her emotions rushed to the surface.

Aunt Josie reached across and touched Adisa's smooth hand with her wrinkled one. "And when I go to heaven I want you to have my stick."

The feeling that had washed over Adisa at the old cemetery returned. She gripped the steering wheel a little tighter. They turned onto Baxter Street and slowed to enter the driveway of Aunt Josie's house. Thoughts of unworthiness and inadequacy flashed through Adisa's mind. She turned off the motor but didn't move from her place behind the wheel.

"Aunt Josie, I don't want to seem proud," she said, "but I'm not sure I'm cut out for walking all over town with a stick in my hand."

"I wouldn't expect you to." Aunt Josie smiled. "My grandfather wore a straw hat and overalls and held his hands behind his back. I'm the one who added the stick. You'll need to do things your own way. And Campbellton is a lot bigger now. It might be best to drive the streets. Of course, you'd have to pray faster."

Adisa glanced over her shoulder at the stick that lay across the rear seat of her car. "I like the stick. Maybe I could carry it in the car."

Aunt Josie nodded. "That works for me."

Jane wiped away a few final tears and hung up the phone in the kitchen after a long conversation with her mother. Luke, who was sitting at the kitchen table, glanced up at his wife's face, which told the whole story.

"She's not going to budge, is she?" Luke asked. "I could hear it in her voice when I was explaining the situation to her."

"No, she's not." Jane shook her head. "I thought she would see it from our point of view, but she's not going to do anything else to help. No more money. She was crying, too."

"It's not her responsibility to take care of us. That falls on me."

"What are we going to do?" Jane asked, sitting down across from him.

Luke took a deep breath before answering. "Face the truth," he replied. "I love you, and I love the faith you have in me and in God. But I can't get my last conversation with Mr. Grayson out of my mind. What are the chances a jury is going to believe I had the right to shoot Deshaun Hamlin?"

Jane didn't respond.

"There's a chance I'll be acquitted," Luke continued. "But it's a slim one. And the risk of being sent off so that I'm not here for you and don't have a chance to be a father to Ashley —"

Luke stopped. Jane kept her eyes focused on his face.

"Do you want to know what I think?" Jane asked in a slightly trembling voice after a few moments passed.

Luke nodded. Jane reached out with her right hand and gently cupped Luke's cheek. "I think you're a good man. And I'm going to trust you to make the right decision for all of us."

Luke didn't want the burden of choosing to go to trial and risk a decade or more in prison to fall on the woman he loved. But the weight on his soul was beyond comprehension. He leaned into Jane's hand and closed his eyes, trying to will away the harsh reality that stared him in the face.

Images flashed through his mind in rapid succession: he saw himself standing before Judge Andrews, entering a plea of nolo contendere, being escorted from the courtroom under guard, taking a long, lonely prison bus ride to a work camp, and finally, lying on his back on a flimsy bunk bed where he was forced to inhale the breath of despair every minute of every day. Luke's eyes hadn't known tears since he was a boy, but in that moment he was driven back so far and so deep that two large teardrops escaped from the corners of his eyes and ran down his cheeks. He raised his head to wipe them away with the back of his hand and looked at Jane. He had to accept the horror he knew rather than risk an even greater tragedy.

"I'm going to take the plea deal," he said, trying to sound strong when he felt incredibly weak. "It will be bad, but I'll come back home. I promise."

THIRTY-SEVEN

Leaving Aunt Josie with Simone, Adisa spent a productive morning working on files for Mike Williams. Grayson stopped by her office at noon and invited her to lunch.

"Only if you let me pay," Adisa replied. "It's part of my penance."

"Then I select where we go."

They went to the Jackson House and sat in the same booth Adisa occupied when she first read the article in the *AJC* that precipitated her firing at Dixon and White. Adisa mentioned it while they waited for their food.

"I've finally reached a place of internal peace toward the reporter," Adisa said, pointing to her heart. "Not that I want to talk to her, but I believe I could do so without letting the past make me angry."

"I've always had a different take on the article," Grayson replied.

"Really?" Adisa raised her eyebrows.

"It was the article that led me to you," the older lawyer said. "I know that was a painful time for you, but it's been positive for me and you."

"I'm thankful for the job, but upset that I messed up my opportunity to help share the burden of Luke's case."

"Even that may work out for the best. I have a feeling once Luke and Jane consider the plea bargain and what it's going to cost to bring Richard Lankford on board, they might see it's better to negotiate a favorable peace than fight a futile war."

"You don't think you could win in front of a jury?"

"Of course I do," Grayson replied immediately. "If I didn't, then I shouldn't walk into a courtroom. But Robert E. Lee probably believed General Pickett could charge a mile across open land against entrenched positions and capture Cemetery Ridge at Gettysburg."

Adisa laughed. "Mr. Grayson, I'm not sure that's the best example to share with me. I'm glad Pickett failed."

"Me, too," Grayson replied with a serious expression on his face. "My ancestors would likely disagree, but his failure helped bring our nation to the place where you and I could sit together as colleagues in a booth at the Jackson House Restaurant. And we need to help the rest of Campbellton get to where I hope we are."

"I'm with you," Adisa said. "And it's an honor."

"If that's the case, I want you to start calling me Theo."

Adisa hesitated. "Just try it out," the older lawyer said.

Adisa smiled. "Okay, Theo it is."

As they finished the meal, Grayson touched his abdomen with a pained expression on his face. "Something isn't agreeing with my stomach," he said. "Excuse me."

By the time the older lawyer returned to the table, his face was pasty white, and Adisa could see beads of sweat on his forehead.

"I feel worse than I did," he said.

"Should you go to the doctor or the ER?" Adisa asked with concern in her voice. "Is your heart okay?"

"Yes, it's my stomach that's in open rebellion. I just need to make it home and collapse there."

"Check in with me later, please."

"Sure. I hate to ask you to do it, but can you cover one last thing in Luke's case?" The older lawyer raised his hand to cover his mouth.

"The initial meeting at the police department with the forensic expert who's going to examine the bullets?" Adisa asked.

"Yes. All you need to do is make sure everything is set up for future analysis."

"Will do."

Grayson's face became even paler and he quickly left the restaurant. Adisa paid for the meal and left.

After a quick stopover at the office, she drove to the police department. She was a few minutes early and decided to wait in the car. A young white officer and a young black officer came out together talking and smiling. Adisa watched them walk across the parking lot and get in the same police car. The comfortable, natural interaction between the two men was apparent. Adisa suspected the bond forged by their choice of career helped them overcome at least some of their ethnic differences. Resting her right hand on the center console, she looked out the windshield past the police department building and down the street toward the fire station where she suspected white, black, and brown firefighters served together in a fraternity dedicated to saving lives and protecting property.

And Adisa felt a prayer rise up in her spirit.

Barriers between races weaken in the face of a common purpose that unites people in a cause bigger than any individual. So Adisa prayed and asked God to give the people of Nash County ideas, vision, plans, and the willingness to cooperate across racial lines.

Adisa let her sanctified imagination run free. In her mind's eye she saw men, women, and children of all colors: building, feeding, sharing, reading, teaching, playing sports, studying, singing, and praying together. The images were so vibrant she wondered if she was experiencing a vision of what would actually happen in the future or an expectation of what God desired. In any event, she knew her job at that moment was to pray. More ideas came, followed by flashes of activity. Churches should take the lead, and Adisa determined to talk to Reggie about it as soon as possible.

Checking her phone, she realized she was a few minutes late for the meeting with the ballistics expert. She hurriedly went inside the police department and introduced herself to the young woman on duty at the front desk. The woman escorted her to a plainly furnished conference room where Detective Maxwell waited.

"Sorry I'm late," Adisa said.

"Dr. Robinson hasn't arrived yet," the

detective said. "Would you like a cup of coffee?"

"Sure," Adisa replied. "Black, please."

Maxwell returned with coffee in a Styrofoam cup and two clear plastic bags containing small pieces of brass-colored metal. He set the coffee on the table in front of Adisa, who took a sip. It was strong enough to tarnish a silver spoon. There was a knock on the door.

"Come in!" Maxwell barked.

The receptionist opened the door, and a short, balding man in his late fifties or early sixties entered.

"I'm Vic Robinson," the man said.

Adisa and Maxwell introduced themselves.

"Let me see what you have, and I'll conduct a quick visual exam. After that we'll discuss next steps."

The detective placed two clear plastic bags in front of the expert, who sat at the head of the table.

"The one marked 'Bullet A' was recovered at the scene of the shooting," Maxwell said. "It passed through the victim's body. 'Bullet B' was surgically removed from the victim's brain."

From her vantage point at the table, Adisa couldn't tell any difference. Both bags contained misshapen pieces of metal. Robinson took a white cloth from his briefcase and laid it on the table. Then, using a pair of tweezers, he removed the bullet that went through Deshaun's upper chest and landed in the middle of East Nixon Street.

"No doubt about it," the ballistics expert said. "It's a 9 mm parabellum hollow point that failed to expand on impact. Thus, it acted more like a full metal jacket round. That's why it passed through the body."

He opened the other bag, removed the bullet, and placed it on the cloth. The second piece of metal was much more mis-shapen as a result of its impact with Deshaun's skull. Robinson placed a jeweler's magnifier in front of his right eye and held the bullet close to his face with the tweezers. He rotated it several times before returning it to the cloth.

"No question about this round, either," he said. "It's a 22-caliber long rifle."

Adisa's mouth dropped open. She stared at the two bullets, now realizing they looked nothing alike. She glanced at Maxwell, who seemed less surprised than she was.

"Did you know?" she asked the detective.

"Only a reasonably confident suspicion," Maxwell replied drily. "I was going to send the bullets to the GBI crime lab in Atlanta, but when I found out Dr. Robinson was

608

coming today, I decided to sit in and listen to what he had to say."

Adisa stared again at the two small pieces of metal. "That means Officer Nelson didn't fire the shot that hit Deshaun in the head," she said more to herself than anyone else.

"And someone else did," Maxwell concluded.

Robinson placed the second bullet in the bag and handed both bags to Maxwell. Adisa was still reeling in shock from what she'd heard.

"You're one hundred percent sure the bullets came from different guns?" she asked.

"Let me put it to you this way," Robinson replied. "I don't think one out of a hundred people trained in forensic ballistics would disagree with my opinion."

"Is that good enough for you?" Adisa asked Maxwell.

"The purpose of a criminal investigation is the determination of the truth," the detective answered. "That's always been my only concern."

"Do you want me to do anything else?" Robinson asked Adisa. "If you need a written report, there won't be much in it."

"Not necessary," Maxwell said before Adisa could respond. "I'll include your findings as part of my investigation."

"Then I'm done here," Robinson said.

"I'd like to talk to you for a minute after I see Dr. Robinson out," Adisa said to Maxwell.

"I was going to suggest the same thing."

Adisa and Dr. Robinson walked together down the short hallway. "Do you realize the impact your findings will have on our case?" she asked.

"Of course, but I believe Detective Maxwell already knew the truth. I confirmed what would have eventually come out anyway."

When Adisa returned to the conference room, Maxwell was gone. She glanced in both directions down the hallway, but the detective wasn't in sight. A couple of minutes later, he returned with a large box in his arms.

"This is the entire contents of the evidence locker in Officer Nelson's case," he said.

While Adisa watched, the detective emptied the box and laid everything on the table. Included was Luke's gun, which didn't look as lethal now as it would have ten minutes earlier. When the detective reached the slip of paper found in Deshaun's pocket on the night of the shooting, Adisa stopped him.

"Was that found in Deshaun's pocket?"

"Yes."

"Is it from the Westside Quik Mart?"

"Yes." Maxwell unfolded it and handed it to her. "On the evening of the shooting, Hamlin bought a bottle of sports energy drink and a bag of pistachios."

Adisa quickly inspected the flimsy slip of paper.

"But no beef jerky," she said.

"Correct. That came from someplace or somebody else."

"Do you have any ideas or theories?" Adisa asked.

"Not about the jerky, but it looks like Hamlin was caught up in the criminal activity that's brought black tar heroin to town."

Adisa was silent for a moment before she spoke. "What I'm about to tell you may not convince you, but it might change your perspective a little bit."

Maxwell listened while Adisa relayed the information Reggie provided at the cemetery.

"Squeezing a hand to deny something you wouldn't want your grandmother to believe about you doesn't move the meter for me," the detective said when she finished. "But I'll toss it in the basket for the new investigation I'll be opening this afternoon to identify who shot Hamlin in the head."

"What about Luke's case?" she asked. "When are you going to contact the DA?"

"Immediately. I'll report Dr. Robinson's findings, add my own opinion, and tell him Officer Nelson's claim that he heard a gunshot prior to discharging his weapon is plausible. There's no way to determine who fired first — the unknown shooter or Nelson — but in that scenario I'm going to give greater credibility to the officer's version of events."

"And you'll ask the DA to dismiss the charges against Officer Nelson, right?"

"That's his call." Maxwell smiled slightly. "But you're a former prosecutor. What would you do based on the evidence you just heard?"

Adisa left the police station caught up in a mixture of relief and euphoria tempered by the knowledge that nothing was final until Jasper Baldwin formally dismissed the charges against Luke. Adisa's false success in the Larimore case had proved the illusive nature of victory. But in her heart, she knew this was different. There weren't any skeletons in Luke Nelson's closet.

She returned to the office and called Grayson on his cell phone. When he didn't answer she tried his house line. He picked up on the fifth ring.

"Hello," the older lawyer said in a weak voice.

"I wouldn't call unless I had something to tell you that should make you feel better," Adisa began.

"You can try, but I'm lying on my back staring at a ceiling that's refusing to stay still."

"Should you go to the doctor?"

"It's a fever that's making me slightly delusional. Some folks claim that is a lawyer's natural state."

The glimmer of Grayson's wit made Adisa feel better about his condition.

"Well, what I'm about to tell you isn't part of a hallucination that will disappear when your fever breaks."

Adisa told the older lawyer what the ballistics expert discovered and about the follow-up conversation with Detective Maxwell.

"Call Luke," Grayson replied. "Better yet, go to his house and deliver the news."

"Shouldn't you notify him?"

"They don't want their baby exposed to whatever virus has leveled me. And at my age, I may not bounce back from this within twenty-four hours."

"Should I wait until I hear something from Jasper Baldwin's office?"

"No, that will take a few days. He's not going to immediately fold his tent. But once the DA realizes his case against Luke is full of holes big enough for a possum to climb through, he'll shut it down."

"What about the newspaper?"

"Let Jasper get the credit for uncovering the truth."

"Why?" Adisa asked in surprise.

"Are you trying to build a reputation in Campbellton as a hotshot criminal defense attorney?"

"No."

"Neither am I. And if I ever come into your office and tell you we're going to handle a major criminal case pro bono, I want you to call the psych ward at the hospital and tell them to involuntarily commit me."

"I promise."

"Oh, and let me know how it goes after you meet with Luke and Jane. If this is a fever-induced dream, I'm really enjoying it."

"This isn't a dream. It's real."

Adisa hung up the phone. She considered calling ahead to Luke's house but decided not to. If the Nelson family wasn't at home, she would take it as a sign to wait before sharing the good news.

"Oh no!" Jane called out to Luke from the den where she was watching Ashley play on the floor.

Working his way down a list of things to do around the house before he was shipped off to jail, Luke was in the master bathroom fixing a finicky toilet. He jumped up from the floor and ran into the den.

"What is it?"

Jane pointed to the front windows. The blinds were open.

"It's Adisa Johnson," Luke said.

"I'll go outside and talk to her," Jane replied. "You stay here with Ashley."

"No, I should do it."

"Are you sure?"

"Yes."

Jane picked up Ashley. "Luke, please don't do or say anything that is going to cause us more trouble," she said.

"Don't worry. This will be short. There's not much fight left in me."

Luke opened the front door as Adisa was approaching the front steps. "There's no need for you to cause any more trouble for my family," he said calmly. "I have nothing else to say to you."

"But I have something to say to you," Adisa replied. "You didn't fire the shot that struck Deshaun Hamlin in the head."

"What?" Luke managed.

Adisa climbed the steps and stood directly in front of him. "According to our ballistics expert, the bullet they took out of Deshaun's brain was from a 22-caliber long rifle. The one that pierced his upper chest was a 9 mm from your handgun. When you said you heard the sound of a gunshot before you fired, you were telling the truth."

Luke felt his knees wobble. He put his hand on the doorframe to steady himself.

"Would you like to hear more?" Adisa asked.

"Yes, yes. Please, come inside."

It was almost six o'clock when Adisa finally left the Nelson house — with a huge piece of homemade cherry cheesecake to share with Aunt Josie. But much more precious to her was the memory of Luke's apology ringing in her ears. She sat in the den with Luke and Jane while Ashley, oblivious to the magnitude of the moment, tried to place the different shapes into the hollow ball. Jane was on her fourth tissue by the time Adisa reached the halfway point of explaining what had happened at the police station.

"This is what I've prayed since the beginning," Jane said through sniffles. "That the Lord would uncover what happened and expose the deeds of darkness."

"Prayer answered," Adisa said.

"Did Maxwell have any theories about who fired the shot that hit Deshaun in the head?" Luke asked.

It was the first time Adisa had heard Luke refer to the teenager as Deshaun. She couldn't help savoring Luke's recognition of the black teenager's humanness.

"That's the police department's newest case. Detective Maxwell is on it."

"I wish I could help," Luke began and then stopped. "But there's something I can do right now."

He put his hands together and looked directly into Adisa's eyes.

"I owe you an apology," he said. "I've been under a ton of stress and pressure, but that's not an excuse for accusing you of something I couldn't prove. It's the same thing that was done to me, and I should have recognized what was going on. I'm sorry."

"Apology accepted and appreciated," Adisa said.

"There's more," Luke continued. "I overreacted the other day at the law office when you were simply doing the job I'd asked you to do — informing me about the latest developments in the case. Later, I could tell from the expression on Mr. Grayson's face that I was wrong about you, but I listened to the negative voices in my head instead of the attorneys God provided for me. You took a huge risk to stand with me, and I know you probably experienced a ton of negative fallout because of it. The last thing you needed from me was an attack. Not only do I owe you an apology, I also want to thank you for your courage."

"That means a lot," Adisa replied simply.

Jane scooted closer to Luke and hugged him.

Adisa had a smile on her face when she walked through the door of Aunt Josie's house.

"Good timing," Aunt Josie said. "Simone left five minutes ago."

Adisa set the cheesecake on the coffee table in front of Aunt Josie.

"Where did that come from? If it tastes as good as it looks, it will be delicious."

"Jane Nelson gave it to me. It's an extra-large piece so I can share with you."

"What?" Aunt Josie asked, her eyes wide.

"Have you had supper?" Adisa responded.

"No, but Simone put our plates in the oven so we could eat as soon as you came home. She fixed baked chicken with a spicy rub, green beans, and macaroni and cheese."

"I was going to suggest we eat dessert first," Adisa replied, "but that changes my mind. While we eat, I have something to tell you that probably violates the attorney-client confidentiality rules, but if I don't let it out, I'm going to burst wide open."

While Adisa talked, Aunt Josie chewed slowly and kept shaking her head.

"God is at work, child," the older woman said. "You stood your ground for what you believed was right, and he used you to do his will."

THIRTY-EIGHT

One Year Later

Luke slowed his patrol car and stopped to wait for the light to change at Ash and Chestnut Streets. Near the corner was a house that a group of people from six different churches had renovated for an elderly woman who'd lost most of her vision due to diabetes. Eighteen men, six women, and ten teenagers came together on a Saturday and fixed a leaky roof, replaced floorboards in a bathroom that had collapsed due to water damage, and repainted the entire interior of the home. Luke and a black man from Reggie's church spent most of the day working on the roof. Afterward, the two families grabbed a bite to eat at the Jackson House. The other family had a little boy the same age as Ashley. The youngsters took turns eating food from the other's plate.

The dispatcher came on the radio. "Officer Nelson, return immediately to the station for a meeting with Chief Lockhart and Detective Maxwell."

"10–4."

During the five-minute drive, Luke tried to guess the reason for the summons. The previous evening he'd arrested a man accused of domestic violence who ended up with a broken hand after taking a swing at Luke and hitting a doorframe instead.

At the station Luke found Chief Lockhart and Detective Maxwell looking at photographs. The chief glanced up when Luke entered.

"Have a seat, Nelson," the chief said. "We have news that will be of interest to you."

Maxwell handed Luke a photograph. It was a mug shot from the Morris Correctional Institute in Dover, Delaware. Beneath the photo was the man's name: "Kelvin Fitzgerald."

"That's the individual who may have shot Deshaun Hamlin in the head," Maxwell said. "Stanley Jackson, the clerk at the store, identified him from a photo lineup as the robber."

Luke stared at the face that impassively stared back.

"I sent the photo to the Jackson CI and an administrative officer showed it to Gregory Ott," Maxwell continued. "Ott now claims Fitzgerald is the person who shot Hamlin. Once Fitzgerald is extradited, we'll bring in Ott to testify against him."

Greg Ott was serving eighteen months in prison after pleading guilty to possession of black tar heroin with intent to distribute. He'd steadfastly denied knowing the real name of the man who shot Deshaun.

The night of the shooting, Deshaun, unaware of the robbery, stopped by Ott's house for a few minutes, where he discovered black tar heroin in his friend's bedroom. The bag of beef jerky was a way samples of the drug were passed along to prospective customers. While Deshaun was telling Ott that he was crazy to get involved in stuff like that, Fitzgerald returned to the house. Deshaun saw blood on the young man's shirt. Scared, Deshaun grabbed the bag of beef jerky and ran out of the house so he could turn it over to the police.

"Because the rifle used to shoot Hamlin was owned by Ott, the DA may decide to indict both of them," Chief Lockhart said. "The trial would end up being a swearing contest between the two of them as to who shot Deshaun."

"My money is on Fitzgerald," Maxwell said. "He has a criminal record, including an assault on a police officer in Savannah four years ago."

Luke returned the photo to Maxwell. He wasn't interested in speculating about what really happened. The facts he knew were horrific enough.

"Do you think I'll be called to testify?" he asked, already knowing the answer.

"Only to explain what you heard and saw."

Luke steeled himself. At least there would be people in the courtroom to support him, not condemn him. And it might be an opportunity to express regret that he'd fired his weapon, even though he was justified in doing so.

"Go ahead and complete your shift," Lockhart concluded. "Keep this information confidential."

"Yes, sir," Luke replied.

Adisa was sitting at her desk when she received the news about Kelvin Fitzgerald's arrest. One of the law firm's secretaries had a sister-in-law who worked as a file clerk at the police department.

"Sheryl knew we'd want to know because you and Mr. Grayson represented the officer," the secretary said.

"Thanks. Are you going to mention it to Mr. Grayson?"

"He's in a deposition in the conference room."

"I'll let him know when he finishes."

Now a permanent employee, Adisa was working on one of Mike Williams's cases. She downloaded another batch of records related to the acquisition of a local bank by a regional financial firm. It was a huge deal by Campbellton standards, and Adisa relished every aspect of it. However, something seemed amiss in the valuation of the acquiring bank's portfolio for several offshore properties in the Caribbean, and she was determined to get to the bottom of the issue. An hour later there was a knock on her doorframe. It was Theo Grayson.

"Did you hear about the arrest of the possible shooter in Luke's case?" Grayson asked.

"Yes. I was going to tell you."

"It's all over town. The suspect is also the man who robbed the convenience store and attacked Stan Jackson. They're going to extradite him from Delaware. When he lands in the local jail, he's going to need a good lawyer."

"Yes, he will."

"Interested?"

Adisa shook her head. "No."

"I thought that was what you would say,"

Grayson said with a smile as he turned to leave.

"Theo," Adisa said. "Don't forget about Sunday morning."

"Oh, I'll be there, wearing my best suit."

At the end of the day, Adisa paused before starting her car. "Where to, Lord?" she asked.

She waited a few moments. Turning right from the parking area, she drove to the north side of town and made her way toward a new subdivision not far from Luke and Jane Nelson's neighborhood. Lying across the rear seat of the car was Aunt Josie's walking stick. Driving slowly down the newly paved streets, Adisa prayed blessing, safety, and anything else that dropped into her spirit for all who'd eventually live there.

She turned down a short cul-de-sac and lot number 302 caught her eye. Adisa stopped the car and grabbed the walking stick. According to a diagram nailed to a stake, the lot was 1.6 acres. Large residential lots were still possible this far from Atlanta where land was cheaper. Adisa inhaled air that seemed especially fragrant. Not far from the street she saw the reason — a tangle of honeysuckle vines. She pinched off the green tip of a yellow flower and touched the sweet nectar to her tongue.

Adisa couldn't make her way through all the underbrush, but she was able to reach a spot 150 feet from the road that looked like an ideal building site. Along the side of the property she discovered a tiny rivulet of water. Moving closer, she came upon a damp area where water bubbled up from beneath the earth. A couple of massive old trees nourished by the plentiful water at their roots provided shade. Several smooth rocks were scattered about. At some point in the past the spring had been well maintained. With a little work, it could once again become a private oasis.

Adisa leaned on the walking stick and closed her eyes. Yes, it would be a wonderful place to build a house and establish a home.

"I need to bring Reggie here," she whispered in a soft voice.

Sunday morning Adisa awoke early and made an extra-large pot of coffee. Aunt Josie had resumed drinking a morning cup. Sitting together at the kitchen table was a perfect way to start the day.

The older woman had reached a plateau in her recovery from the stroke. She was able to stay at home alone while Adisa worked, but she wasn't able to work in her garden. She shuffled into the kitchen without the need for a walker; however, she often used a cane when venturing outside to church or to go shopping.

Every so often, when Adisa could go with her, Aunt Josie would want to venture over to Westside Cemetery and spend time where her body would soon find its final rest. Every time they went, Aunt Josie always told Adisa the same thing: "Remember, I won't be here when I pass on. I'll be joining that great cloud of witnesses cheering you on."

Adisa poured a cup of coffee for Aunt Josie and added the amount of cream and sugar she knew her aunt preferred.

"How do you feel this morning?" she asked.

"Thankful to see another day but not worried if I don't."

Adisa chuckled. Aunt Josie sat down and took a sip of coffee.

"This is good. Who taught you how to brew coffee, child?"

"You did, and you also taught me just about everything valuable I've learned that has to do with life."

"Don't lie. It doesn't sit right on your pretty face."

Adisa joined her at the table. "What do you want to wear to church today?" Adisa asked.

Aunt Josie wrinkled her nose. "Same thing as you," she answered.

"What would that be?" Adisa asked. "We've not been shopping for matching outfits like Shanika does with the twins."

"You pick out something that Reggie likes and so will I."

"I'm not catering to what he wants all the time," Adisa began.

"I know, I know." Aunt Josie shrugged. "You don't have to prove how independent you can be to me, and it doesn't seem to bother him."

The older woman took another sip of coffee. "Is Theo Grayson going to come?" she asked.

"He said so on Friday."

"He's in for a treat, but I'm not sure he'll see it that way."

"He'll join in. You watch. It's Luke and Jane I'm more worried about. What if some of the women in the Amen Corner start shouting?"

Aunt Josie smiled. "Do you think I still have the lungs to shout?"

"No," Adisa said, getting up from the table. "You sit there quiet like Shanika and

I had to when we were little."

"That was years and years ago. I've learned a lot since then."

They arrived at Zion Hills Church, and Adisa parked in a handicap spot to make it easier for Aunt Josie. They found seats on the front row to the left of the pulpit. Reggie was meeting with the choir and out of sight.

"I like that green dress," Aunt Josie said to Adisa. "Green always says welcome home to me."

"And you always shine in white," Adisa replied. "You look fresh enough to be baptized."

At that moment Ashley Nelson ran up to Adisa and jumped in her lap. Adisa planted a quick kiss on top of the little girl's curly blond head. Following after Ashley were Luke and Jane, who was six months pregnant with a baby boy. Jane slipped into the pew beside Adisa.

"I'm nervous," Jane whispered to Adisa. "And I'm not the one who's going to speak."

"He'll do fine. Did he write it out like I suggested?"

"Yes, and he even let me make a few suggestions."

Ashley touched the diamond on Adisa's left ring finger and began to move it back and forth.

"She's been fascinated with your ring since the first time she saw it," Jane said.

"I catch myself staring at it, too."

"You'd better!"

"Do you think Reggie and I will make it to the altar before baby boy Nelson arrives?" Adisa asked.

Jane touched her swollen abdomen. "It's going to be close."

The choir entered, swaying back and forth as they sang. Reggie followed. As soon as he came into view, he looked directly at Adisa and beamed. Adisa's face lit up with her brightest smile. After the first song ended, she glanced over her shoulder toward the rear of the sanctuary. There was no sign of Theo Grayson.

The Sunday-morning worship service at Zion Hills might have seemed old-fashioned to some or too emotional to others, but Adisa's heart and spirit were broad enough that the joyous celebration found a welcoming place in her soul. She'd learned to adapt to other expressions of love for God, but on this day she was at Zion Hills Baptist and didn't hold back. She swayed when she wanted to sway, lifted her hands when it seemed like the thing to do, and closed her eyes as the songs grew slower and more worshipful.

Jane seemed to enjoy the lively singing and joined in once she caught on to the unfamiliar choruses. Luke's lips didn't seem to be moving, but he clapped his hands in rhythm. The women in the Amen Corner never exploded in "Hallelujahs," and Aunt Josie didn't try to jump-start an outbreak.

After over half an hour the congregation settled into their seats. Out of the corner of her eye, Adisa caught sight of Theo Grayson, wearing a blue seersucker suit and a red bow tie, entering the church. There was room for him to squeeze onto their pew.

"I never sit on the front row in the Presbyterian church," the lawyer whispered as soon as he was settled beside her.

"You're not at the Presbyterian church," Adisa replied. "Did you bring a handkerchief?"

"Why?"

"This close to the front there's a good chance Reggie might spit on you if he gets excited during the sermon."

Grayson smiled and shook his head. Reggie took his place behind the pulpit.

"Greetings to members, visitors, and honored guests," he began. "As you know from your bulletin, this is a special Sunday in the life of Zion Hills."

Reggie continued with the announcements. Adisa could see Thelma Armistead sitting with her friends in the Amen Corner. Deshaun's grandmother was wearing an orange hat.

"And at this time I'd like to ask one of our special guests, Officer Luke Nelson, to join me on the platform," Reggie said.

Adisa's heart began to beat a little faster. She could feel tension in the room and hoped Reggie hadn't made a mistake in inviting Luke to come.

"I've asked Officer Nelson to say a few words this morning, but before he does that, I want to speak to you from my heart," Reggie said. "This isn't the sermon. That will come later and last a lot longer."

There were a few chuckles across the congregation. Reggie placed his hand on Luke's shoulder. Luke was wearing a nice gray suit, a white shirt, and a yellow tie.

"I'm not going to try to summarize race relations in America in a few sentences," Reggie continued. "That would take months by somebody a lot smarter than I am. But I am going to tell you there is only one definitive, all-encompassing answer to what divides us, isolates us, and causes us to mistrust — transformation of the human heart through the power of the gospel of Jesus Christ."

A scattering of "Amens" greeted Reggie's words. Adisa whispered one of them. Reggie began to warm to his message. He began pointing his finger at people all over the sanctuary.

"And transformation takes place within your heart and your heart and your heart, and the heart of every person, black or white or brown, who humbles themselves enough to receive the grace of God. And what is the fruit of that transformation? It's not more people sitting in pews on Sunday morning. It's more people demonstrating what it means to be a child of God in their lives on a moment-by-moment basis. It's more people working toward reconciliation instead of complaining that it doesn't exist. It's more people doing the practical things that reveal a changed heart. It's more people loving God with all their heart and loving their neighbor, regardless of skin color or culture, as they love themselves. This type of love isn't a sentimental feeling — it's the most practical, revolutionary force that's ever existed on planet Earth. As it says in 1 Corinthians 13, this type of love sacrifices for others, isn't easily angered, and" — Reggie paused — "keeps no record of wrongs. If that's the kind of person you want to be, I'd like you to rise to your feet."

Slowly at first, but with gathering momentum, everyone within Adisa's line of sight stood up. Reggie gripped the edge of the pulpit and watched. When the room became quiet again, he leaned closer to the microphone.

"Ecclesiastes states that there's a time for everything under the sun. A time to be born and a time to die, a time to weep and a time to laugh, a time to be silent and a time to speak, a time for war and a time for peace. I'd like to suggest that it's time for something else in our day and in our community." Reggie raised his right hand in the air and his voice thundered. "It's a time to stand! To look past differences the Lord created and come together in the unity of God's Spirit! To stand in agreement that God's will be done on earth as it is in heaven! To stand together on earth as we will one glorious day stand before the throne of God!"

Shouts of "Amen!" echoed off the walls of the sanctuary. Adisa saw Luke voice his assent. Reggie took a deep breath and stepped to the side. Grayson leaned over and whispered to Adisa.

"I'm going to ask my pastor to invite Reggie to speak at our church. We need to hear that, too."

"I'll come, too," Adisa replied. "A second time wouldn't hurt me, either."

Reggie touched Luke on the arm, and the police officer stepped forward, unfolded a piece of paper, and placed it on the pulpit. He cleared his throat. Adisa could tell he was nervous.

"I feel like sitting down because I agree with everything Pastor Reynolds just said, and he said it way better than I could do in a hundred years of trying," Luke said. "I want to be the type of person he described."

A healthy chorus of "Amens" greeted Luke's declaration.

"But there are a couple of things I want and need to do. First, I want to thank Mr. Theo Grayson and Ms. Adisa Johnson for having the courage to help me. I've learned a lot about myself over the past year. Some of it wasn't pretty." Luke glanced down at Adisa. "And I've realized there were things I thought I understood but didn't. But by God's grace, I'm going to do better and be better. Second, there are two people I want to join me on this platform. Will Thelma Armistead and Deshaun Hamlin please come up here?"

For months after Deshaun's release from the hospital, Adisa had trouble fighting back tears whenever she saw the teenager. Each tiny improvement in his mental and physical functioning caused her heart to overflow with thanksgiving and tears to stream from her eyes. She turned in her seat as the young man made his way to the front of the sanctuary. He was deaf in his right ear and wore glasses due to vision problems, but he'd recovered remarkably well. Dr. Steiner's prediction that Deshaun's brain would adapt had proved to be accurate. He didn't have the quick reflexes needed to play varsity basketball, but he could dribble and shoot free throws. And two weeks earlier Sister Armistead had proudly announced to Adisa and Aunt Josie that Deshaun made the honor roll his final semester in high school and was planning to go to college in the fall.

Deshaun stopped and waited for his grandmother, who slipped her arm in his. They climbed the steps together.

"Isn't that beautiful?" Adisa whispered to Grayson.

When he didn't reply, she glanced sideways and saw two tears stream down Theo Grayson's cheeks.

Deshaun and his grandmother reached the top of the steps and stood beside Luke, who was also overcome with emotion. He raised his fist to his lips for a moment.

Shouts of "Amen!" echoed across the room. He turned to Sister Armistead.

"Mrs. Armistead, thank you for forgiving me when everything around you was shouting that you had a reason to hate. When Adisa told me what you said in church and how you cried out for mercy for me and Deshaun, I thought, 'What kind of person can do that?' Over the past year you've been gracious enough to let me spend some time with you and your family and find out."

At that point, Thelma Armistead stepped close to Luke, wrapped her arms around his neck, and hugged him. And she didn't let go.

"Hug," Adisa heard Ashley say from her place on her mother's lap.

Adisa nodded. Yes, that was the ultimate hug. When Sister Armistead finally released her grip of love, she planted a solid kiss on Luke's right cheek. He looked at the congregation and grinned.

"I know envy is a sin," Luke said into the microphone. "But it's impossible for you not to be jealous of what just happened to me."

Laughter rippled across the room. Luke turned to Deshaun. Chills ran down Adisa's spine. Luke stared at the young man for several seconds.

"Deshaun, I've told you that I've wished a thousand times things would have gone differently the night of the shooting. You were the most innocent person on that street. You were the most courageous person on that street. And over the past year, you've shown the greatest strength of character and will that I've ever witnessed in another human being. I'll never forget the Bible verse you quoted to me the first time you were able to talk to me. Do you remember that verse?"

Deshaun nodded.

"Would you quote it for the people here this morning?"

Deshaun stepped to the microphone and in a loud, clear voice said, " 'And we know that in all things God works for the good of those who love him, who have been called according to his purpose.' "

Luke rejoined Deshaun at the microphone. "We've not yet fully seen how that verse is going to be revealed in Deshaun's life, my life, and perhaps your life," Luke said. "But I'm here to tell you I believe we will. And part of that good is what's happening here today. May this not be a moment, but a movement. Thank you."

As Luke left the platform and walked down the steps, the applause began. At first it was scattered, but it grew, and grew, and grew, until everyone in the sanctuary was once again on their feet. Deshaun, too, left the platform, but his grandmother stayed at Reggie's side, which seemed right. Her words of forgiveness and cries for mercy to triumph over judgment had ignited a flame capable of consuming the dead, dry wood of prejudice and hate. She closed her eyes and raised her hands high in the air. Adisa didn't try to fight her tears.

"That was a pretty good service," Grayson said casually to Adisa when the meeting ended. "I'm glad I came."

"Theo —" Adisa began.

The older lawyer smiled through shining eyes. "Okay, it was historic. And I believe it will be a part of the history of Campbellton that future generations will celebrate rather than regret."

Aunt Josie joined them and gave Theo a hug of his own. "Thanks again for taking in my baby and giving her a job," she said.

"I think we both gave her a job," Theo replied, glancing at Adisa. "And the one you passed on to her is much more important."

Adisa, Aunt Josie, and Theo watched as Reggie and Luke stood in the midst of people greeting them with smiles on their faces. Adisa spoke to Theo.

"Do you want to join us for Sunday dinner at the Jackson House? The Nelsons are coming."

"Yes," Theo replied. "A church service like this makes me hungry in more ways than one."

ACKNOWLEDGMENTS

I'm grateful for the multiethnic prayer meeting in the fall of 2015 where the idea for this novel was birthed in my heart. Special thanks for the unfailing support of my wife, Kathy; for the excellent, insightful editorial guidance from Becky Monds and Daisy Hutton at HarperCollins Christian Publishing; and for the sharp eye of Deborah Wiseman, who catches and corrects my mistakes. Thanks to my son, Jacob Whitlow, for steering the novel into deeper waters; and to Steve Sellers for his technical, practical insight.

DISCUSSION QUESTIONS

1. What did Dr. Cartwright mean when she talked about the need to move from integration to reconciliation?
2. Why did Dr. Cartwright question Luke's moral authority to speak to racial issues? Was she right in doing so or too harsh?
3. How did Adisa, Reggie, and Luke grow in their understanding and response to racial issues and challenges? How do they need to continue to grow?
4. What was your internal response, if any, to Rafe, Aunt Josie, and Adisa as intercessors for their community?
5. What stood out about the final church scene?
6. What additional influences/pressures/ challenges would people in Adisa's and Luke's positions have in a situation like the one in the book? How about Theo Grayson and Aunt Josie?
7. What was your reaction to Thelma Armi-

stead's declaration of unconditional forgiveness and cry for mercy in chapter 20? What tragedy in America's recent past resulted in this type of forgiveness?

ABOUT THE AUTHOR

Robert Whitlow is the bestselling author of legal novels set in the South and winner of the Christy Award for Contemporary Fiction. He received his J.D. with honors from the University of Georgia School of Law where he served on the staff of the *Georgia Law Review.*

RobertWhitlow.com
Twitter: @WhitlowWriter
Facebook: RobertWhitlowBooks

The employees of Thorndike Press hope you have enjoyed this Large Print book. All our Thorndike, Wheeler, and Kennebec Large Print titles are designed for easy reading, and all our books are made to last. Other Thorndike Press Large Print books are available at your library, through selected bookstores, or directly from us.

For information about titles, please call:
  (800) 223-1244

or visit our website at:
  gale.com/thorndike

To share your comments, please write:
  Publisher
  Thorndike Press
  10 Water St., Suite 310
  Waterville, ME 04901